Dav

THE ORACLE DESIGN

This book is a work of fiction. Names and characters are the product of the author's imagination and any resemblance to actual persons, living or dead, is purely coincidental.

Copyright © 2012 Dave Barsby
Second edition published 2017
All rights reserved

follow @DaveBarsbyAuthor on Facebook and
Dave Barsby on Amazon Author Central

ISBN 978-1-549-73392-5

*For my parents, who have always believed in me,
and to Russell, Tim, Raf, Allan, Laura and Meg for your
feedback.*

ONE

*The following combines situation reports from field agent
Jack Stone and interviews with suspect C-27B/6*

"How's your arm?" I asked. I glanced across at Hera. She was picking chunks of mud from her sling. Our grime-strewn camouflage clothing jarred with the décor of the bright, clean outer office.

"It hurts," she confessed. She leaned towards me and whispered: "I got shot."

"I'm aware of that," I answered. "I was the one who shot you."

I looked around the office. Cream-colored walls. Dark wood furniture. There was the faint regular tick of a clock on the wall. It read 23:47, and below it the date 03/26/2056. The sweet aroma of fresh begonias on the secretary's desk mingled with the stench of blood, sweat and dirt on our musty, barely-dry clothes. My limbs ached from the day's exertion and my stomach was bruised and sore. The Duke had landed a lucky sucker punch during our scuffle.

Hera and I were seated in the outer office of General Armstrong Miller, head of the top-secret North American Security Response Unit. NASRU was an organization so covert even the President didn't know we existed. We had the best operatives in the country. We had the best technology in the world. We were above the law. We saved the lives of thousands of citizens on a daily basis without them ever knowing. We were the super-spies of the 21st Century.

I was a Lieutenant in the organization. Technically desk-bound but often hands-on with assignments. Hera was a field agent. Like all field agents, she had been assigned a codename from Greek mythology.

We were waiting to be debriefed on our most recent assignment. It was the first time Hera had worked for me. At 24, she was beautiful, strong and intelligent, but still very much a rookie. This day she had performed well.

We had been waiting in the outer office for half an hour. The day had taken its physical toll on both of us. We had infiltrated and destroyed a chemical weapons distribution facility in the Everglades and fought leader The Duke on a speeding boat. Then we had been called to an immediate debrief in Washington D.C. We didn't even have time to change clothing.

Hera looked groggy. She should have been in a medical facility. She'd only been given a quick field stitching of her wound.

A signal from the General's office buzzed on the secretary's computer, quickly followed by a gruff voice telling her "I'm ready." She looked up.

"Lieutenant Jack Stone," she said. "Agent Hera. The General will see you now."

Hera looked at me. Her large blue-green eyes were wide. "Do you think he'll be angry The Duke got away?" she asked.

I silently shook my head. If he was angry it would be unjustified and I was prepared to stand my ground with him.

I opened the door to General Miller's office, allowed Hera to enter first.

The General rubbed his greying moustache thoughtfully as he closed a file on his desktop screen. His dark green uniform shone with a litter of medals on his left breast. His polished mahogany desk was sparse. It contained the two most beloved things in his life – an ornately framed vidimage of Mrs. Miller and a Double Corona sized Cohiba cigar on a stand.

He looked up at us as I pushed the office door shut.

"Sit down," he said. He gestured to two chairs facing his desk. I sat in mine stiffly. Hera wearily slumped.

"So..." he began. The General leaned forward, elbows on the desk. "What happened?"

"Using a Mk-12 Night Attack dinghy," I began, "Agent Hera and myself approached the facility at 20:26 hours from the West–"

"Jack," the General interrupted. "Let's forgo the official briefing for now. It's late. Just...tell me what happened. To The Duke."

"Yes, Sir," I responded. "After I had located The Duke, I rammed him out of a second-floor window. My plan was to physically distance him from his men, force him into the water and from there subdue him. By a stroke of luck, Hera had moored the dinghy under that very window, so we landed on the boat and were able to speed off straight away.

We had long cleared the area before the missiles destroyed the facility."

"Yes," the General said. "I've had the report from the clean-up team. Nothing left, they say. The chemical weapons were vaporized. It was a good call to use thermite warheads, Stone."

"Thank you, Sir."

"So, that's the primary target taken care of. The warehouse. What about the secondary target? The man?"

"The Duke was very strong, Sir. He put up quite a fight."

"This was on a speeding boat?" Miller asked.

"Yes, Sir," Hera answered. "At forty knots. Quite choppy."

"At one point," I continued, "The Duke was strangling Hera as she tried to steer the boat. In order to preserve both their lives I shot him in the leg. This caused The Duke to pitch over the side of the dinghy and into the water."

"And her wound?" the General asked, pointing one finger at Hera's shoulder. "Where does that come into it?"

"The bullet had to go through her to get to him, Sir."

The General nodded. "I see," he said.

"We searched the area," I told him. "But we couldn't locate him."

"He might have been eaten by alligators," Hera said. I glanced at her, annoyed. She had a thing about alligators. Now was not the time or place.

"He's still out there, Sir," I said. "Wounded, but alive. He's just the middle man. But he knows who the bomb manufacturers are. He knows who the buyers are. We need to find him."

The General nodded. "We will." He sighed and leaned back in his expensive office chair. Silence filled the room while he contemplated.

"I want you to head back to New York, Stone," he finally said.

"Sir?" I questioned. Why would I hunt for The Duke in New York? "He's still in the Everglades. I should be there–"

"Go home, Jack," the General interrupted. "Get some rest. Tomorrow, you start on a new assignment."

"A new assignment? This is still an ongoing case. I have new leads to follow."

"Which are?"

"There were letters on the barrels the bombs were transported in. Some had B.M. Others D.S. More with S.K."

The General frowned at this, deep in thought. "What are you thinking, Stone?"

"Initials. Names. Places of origin, destinations or names of buyers. This could blow the case wide open."

"Good," he answered. "I will pass the details on to your replacement."

I breathed in deeply, ensuring my anger remained hidden. I had spent six months on this. I was closer than ever before to significantly reducing the number of terrorist attacks in this country. And as a reward, I was off the case. "I have to protest, Sir. This is my case. Why am I being replaced?"

"To concentrate on your new assignment, Lieutenant. You'll be leading a team back home. Someone is already over at your New York office changing the lettering on your door. You're being promoted from Assistant Regional Manager to Deputy Regional Manager. No pay rise."

"Thank you, Sir," I said. "But capturing The Duke is more important than a promotion." Besides, it was a promotion in name only. No extra benefits, no extra responsibilities within the organization. I was going to be solely in charge of a team for the first time, but that didn't make much difference either. I'd shared command on joint operations before. Being solely in charge just meant I didn't need to argue with anyone else over tactics.

Miller turned to Hera. "Thank you," he said. "That will be all. Well done, good work. Go get your arm looked at."

"Yes, Sir," Hera answered wearily. She was very tired now. The pain, the blood loss, the physical exertion. She'd be lucky to make it to the medical facility without assistance. "Thank you, Sir."

I stood to help escort her as she opened the office door.

"Jack," Miller said quietly. "Stay here a moment, will you?"

I sat back down and waited until the office door closed behind Hera. "Sir," I began. "I've put a lot of time into this case. You can't just take it away from me when I'm so close. I must protest–"

"I know," Miller answered, cutting me short. "I understand. But the decision has been made. We have other people who are capable enough of finding The Duke now. This assignment needs my top man."

He opened a desk drawer and removed a beige folder from it. He slid it across the desk to me.

"Here's your new case," he said.

I stared at it blankly. Assignment orders usually arrived via secure, encrypted email. I hadn't been handed a folder before.

I picked the folder up.

"I want you to find him for me," the General said.

"Find him?" I asked. "And...?" I prompted.

"Just find him," I was told.

I suddenly got the feeling this was a demotion in disguise. I had prevented madmen from nuking cities. I had engaged in black ops in foreign warzones. I had taken out some of the most hardened mercenaries on the planet. And now my talents were to be put to use on a simple missing persons case.

"Excuse me, Sir," I said after a moment of stunned silence. I waved the thin folder containing my new assignment. "Why me?"

"You are our best man, Stone," General Miller told me. "Not as experienced as some, granted. But you can think outside the box. Your annual review results are second-to-none. You–"

"Sorry to interrupt, Sir. It's just... This is a missing person's case. Wouldn't this be better off being handled by the FBI, a GovPol All Points Bulletin, photos on milk cartons...?"

"Don't be flippant, Jack," the General responded. He plucked the unlit cigar from its stand, rolled it in his fingers and sniffed its rich aroma. "You don't realize the importance of this case. But you will. In time."

"I would prefer a bit of clarification *now*, Sir, if it's all the same to you."

The General glanced at his watch with impatience. He didn't need to tell me it was late. Since the sun set I had used stealth to infiltrate a heavily-armed area, shot twenty seven men, blown up a three-storey building, traveled twenty three miles in a dinghy, eight hundred and seventy two in a helicopter and waited forty five minutes in an outer office before this moment.

"This man is very smart," the General informed me. "Very dangerous. I need you on this. Data on the case is being collated in New York and will be delivered to your office tomorrow afternoon. In the meantime I suggest you familiarize yourself with the details you have in your hand."

I glanced at the cover of the beige folder, but all it displayed was the date March 26th 2056. I flicked the folder open and checked the details inside. A single sheet of white paper contained one name (Zeus Jackson), two aliases (Apollo Carver and Jose Manula) and an age (34). There were no other details. No photograph. No address. At the back of my mind I was aware that this felt like a practical joke, but I was also aware that April Fool's Day was still a week away.

"I have familiarized myself with the details, General."

The General looked up from his cigar. He sighed disparagingly. "Why do I feel you're not fully committed to this case, Lieutenant?" he asked.

"Three names. One age. This doesn't tell me who he is, why we need to locate him. You want my commitment, Sir? Then tell me why."

The General placed his cigar to one side and leaned forward, a stern look on his face. "Stone, this man poses the single greatest threat to human civilization since recorded history began."

"Why? Why is this man such a threat? Why is there so little information? And why is it printed on *paper*?"

The General leaned back. "Good, Jack," he told me. "Good. I was hoping you'd ask questions like that. A man who goes away and does what he's told without question is exactly the reason why this Jackson fellow has eluded us for three years." He studied me, then sighed. "Very well. I will explain who he is."

"Thank you, Sir," I said.

"Where to begin?" the General muttered to himself. He had a sudden thought and plucked his cigar from the desk. "Here at NASRU we answer to no one, we are accountable to no one. Do you know what that means, Lieutenant?"

"That we are the last line of defense, Sir. We have autonomy. We have the authority to get the job done by any means necessary."

"It means I can defy this ridiculous ban and light this cigar if I want, and no one can do anything about it. We are untouchable."

"Yes, Sir."

"Yet we aren't, Lieutenant. No one is untouchable. No official authority can touch me, yet if I smoke this cigar it will stain my breath and when I go home tonight Mrs. Miller will play merry hell with me. Likewise, despite appearances, this organization is not untouchable. One man out there knows about us. That one man can hurt us."

"Zeus Jackson," I responded.

"You ask why there is so little information? What you hold in your hand is Security Level Alpha. Only a dozen or so people know of the other information you will be privy to.

"As for why it is printed on paper...each page is electronically tagged and will self-destruct if removed from this building. The ink cannot be scanned, photocopied, faxed or photographed. It provides extra security. Electronic devices, you see, can be hacked by remote link, infrared, Bluetooth or wireless ISPs. Our security is very high,

Lieutenant. We have exemplary firewalls in place. But all it would take is one slip-up and the information could be hacked and extracted. Especially by Zeus Jackson."

"Is that why he's such a threat?" I asked, absently wondering what security measures were in place for me jotting down the details on another piece of paper. "He's a professional hacker?"

The General snorted. "He is everything, yet he does not officially exist. If you want to know what a god is like..."

"Meet Zeus," I finished. The General looked disparagingly at me.

"Maybe his name is why he was chosen," the General said. "Maybe when they decided to turn a man into a god, the name Zeus leapt out at them. Whatever the criteria was, it is unimportant now.

"Zeus was the test subject for a radical new experiment involving genetic manipulation and mind enhancement. It succeeded beyond anyone's wildest dreams. His IQ count was off the scale, several hundred at least. His powers of logical reasoning were unimaginable. His enhanced brain could cope with an influx of data from his five senses far beyond any other human."

"As in a blind person having better hearing," I pointed out.

"Exactly. It's because the brain no longer has to set aside part of its processing power for interpreting images. Now it only deals with four senses at once, instead of five. As a result, those four senses are 'enhanced'. The brain can process more information so it doesn't filter out as much data. Jackson's rewired brain can exploit all five senses to their maximum capacity at the same time."

"So you created a genius," I said. "I'm guessing he didn't much like what we did to him."

"We were holding him in a secure facility," the General clarified. "So secure it would make a bank vault seem like a padlock. But security means nothing to someone with such immense powers of logic and cognitive abilities. Our alarm systems, security codes, encryption programs... He escaped his holding pen, the labs and the facility, and he did it with such ease it took him twelve minutes from leaving his room to leaving the grounds. And in those twelve minutes, he killed seven scientists and broke through the highest security levels on the lab's systems, wiping all the data from the drives.

"The threat he poses is entirely based around his highly-developed intelligence. He can do things you cannot imagine. Chances are he could bring this country to its knees. We need to find him. We need to contain him. We need to learn from him."

"You want me to bring him back so you can see what's different in his head," I said. "Does he officially represent a clear and present danger, Sir?"

"He does. We've been after him for three years now. Two agents have come close – Bolan and Keiler. They disappeared completely, as did all their research. We've never recovered any bodies."

"I presume, then, that I can use any means necessary to apprehend him."

The General nodded. "You can, but remember: we want to examine him."

"So we need him captured alive."

The General puffed out a gust of air. He fingered his cigar again. "Electrical stimuli, a CAT scanner and the right software can retrieve the information we require."

"Which means?"

The General looked at me briefly before returning his attention to the cigar. "We need his brain intact, Lieutenant. The state of the rest of him is at your discretion."

The following morning, after a quick flight back to New York and an uncomfortable night's sleep, I headed to my office.

It was a small, glass-paneled corner room overlooking East Manhattan. Framing it was an outer office where my operations team would be basing themselves later that afternoon. It looked forlorn and lonely. Five bare white desks marked only by unused data ports. Each one accompanied by a black swivel chair still in plastic wrapping. It had been like this since I received my original promotion and stopped being a field agent. I'd either work alone in my office or be seconded to another part of the country. I'd never had a team in my outer office because I'd never needed one. It would be strange to see this area populated.

I opened the door to my inner office. I paused a moment and looked closely at the lettering emblazoned on the door's glass panel. It read "Lt. Jack Stone" and below it "Deputy Regional Manger, NY". They'd already altered my job title but for some reason they'd felt the need to describe my new position as an indoor trough rather than a man in control of something. I couldn't see any way of squeezing the second 'a' into 'Manger' without them starting all over again. I'd file a complaint with maintenance later.

My office was bare. Just the way I liked it. Few distractions from the job. A small vidimage of Natalya sat near the corner of the monitor. She was playfully trying to wrestle the camera from me. The infrared keyboard, a motion-sensitive hologram, beamed onto the desk. An unnecessary but aesthetically-pleasing yucca plant grew wildly in one corner. Three small, padded chairs resided on one side of the desk, a large leather recliner on the other.

I tossed the folder onto the desk and enjoyed the slap it made in the silence. I slipped into the recliner and groaned with pleasure as the soft fabric molded to the contours of my bruised body.

I glanced at the photograph of Nat again. I forgot to ask what her plans for the day were that morning.

I took my cell phone out of my pocket and pressed the voice activation button on the side.

"Open screen, call Nat," I said. A small tube rose from the top of the phone, swiveled 90 degrees and unfurled the Organic LED widescreen display. The phone rang five times before it was answered.

"Jack," Nat answered in her sexy Russian accent. The screen was blurry. She was in motion. Out of breath. I caught glimpses of lips, one blue eye and tousled, dirty-blonde hair swaying behind her in a ponytail.

"What you up to today?" I asked.

The image clarified as the motion ceased. She was beautiful. I knew that, as she was my partner, I was biased. But I'd seen the way she turned heads.

"Jogging," Nat told me, catching her breath.

"I mean later."

"Nothing much, but I'm on call. Why? Did you want to meet for lunch?"

"No," I smiled and shook my head. "Can't. Got a new assignment."

"Top secret as always I presume."

I shrugged apologetically. "Of course."

"Going to take up all your time?"

"I don't know."

Nat tutted. "Great. When was the last time we saw each other, Jack?"

I looked confused at the screen. "Breakfast."

"No. That was you coming into the kitchen, taking an apple and saying 'bye honey'. That doesn't count."

"Well, if you're not called in, maybe I'll see you this evening. This new assignment isn't really going to heat up until tomorrow. I might be back by six."

Nat sighed and nodded. "I won't hold my breath. I'd better get back to my run. It's no good if I keep starting and stopping."

I nodded at the screen. "Love you," I said, but I got cut off halfway through. No matter, I thought. I could reiterate it back home.

I poked at my desk where the projection of the keyboard showed and flicked my computer onto the news channel. It brought up the latest headlines.

There had been an explosion in the center of Brooklyn. A car bomb outside a café frequented by off-duty Government Police officers. The explosive was low-grade and damage was minimal, but several were fatally injured. Due to this and the other recent terrorist attacks on mainland America that had been perpetrated by home-grown terrorists, the

President had been forced to divert funds from inner city regeneration to military and intelligence networks. The President had also announced that, due to the climate of fear, elections were postponed again for safety reasons, invoking the Emergency Rule. A poll conducted by the station showed a 92% positive reaction from the public.

Government funding for education had been lowered in accordance with the rising school grades. As the standard of education rose, the need to invest money in it fell. Instead the funds were diverted to the Mars terraforming project which was already $300bn over budget despite being just a third of the way through its 40-year program.

The stalemate continued in Havana. With the rest of Cuba now under the control of US troops, its capital city continued to hold off the brunt of the American military behind its fortified walls. General Myrmid assured us the bombardment of the city would continue, even though we all knew they couldn't slip a single shell, missile or bomb through Havana's defense grid.

In world news, the English King had announced the birth of a new son. His first-born was still on the run. Syrian refugees continued to pour into neighboring Turkey after Iran's pre-emptive strike. And fighting had renewed between China and Korea despite the cease fire being just a week old.

I flicked my computer to desktop mode. I needed to start making notes on Jackson. He was vastly intelligent. Enhanced senses. Murderous. Difficult to locate. Why? With all the technology at our disposal, we should have been able to locate him within seconds. Three years was a long time on the run for anyone. For someone up against NASRU it was unprecedented. I knew his new intelligence was the key, the reason why he had avoided us for so long. What I needed to know was how.

TWO

Andi Clayton had been at work for just under an hour. She was typing up the previous night's report on the Martian terraforming crisis when she received a phone call.

The office of the New York Times was quiet. A handful of reporters were at their desks, typing up their own copy for the afternoon edition. Everyone else had been called away to cover breaking stories. The only breaking story Andi was aware of was the terrorist bombing in Brooklyn. As terrorist attacks were commonplace those days she couldn't see why that would require the attention of so many journalists.

When the call came she felt relaxed and a little sleepy. She activated the call, but the vidscreen remained blank. Andi thought little of this. Many New York residents still used archaic audio-only telephones. It was a resurging fashion trend.

"New York Times, Andi Clayton," she uttered in a bored tone. She briefly twirled a lock of long, dark hair around her finger. There was a moment of silence from the other end. She could hear constant traffic in the background.

"Good day, Miss Clayton," a male voice replied. "I have a story for you."

"I'll transfer you to the news desk," she said, maintaining her apathetic tone. Her hand reached for the transfer button, but paused. It sounded like this man was calling from a payphone. If that was so, why was the screen black?

"No, Miss Clayton, I have a story for *you*. And to answer your next question, the reason why the screen is blank will become clear later."

"O...kay," she responded, already starting to note this person down as a crackpot time-waster. However, she slid the computer's pointer over the 'new page' tab in preparation. "What is your story, Mr...?"

"No names, not over an open line. The story...well, you're already thinking this is a hoax call from some conspiracy theory nut job, so I won't go into details."

"You reading my mind, is that it? Aliens gave you telepathic abilities?"

"Heh," the man responded. "Not quite. Suffice to say it involves illegal experiments, terrorism and Government secrets. I realize there is little I can do right now to convince you of the importance, and truth, of this story. But you're already intrigued, and after I show you why the screen is blank...well, you'll be hooked."

"Well, thank you very much," Andi said sternly, "but I don't have time for fun and games. Goodbye."

She moved to cut off the call, but her hand wavered. She was becoming intrigued by this cryptic conversation.

Silence greeted her. The tapping of fingers working the infrared keyboards drifted over the partitions of the office. The drone of cars, chatter of pedestrians and honk of irate taxi horns filtered through the phone's speaker. No plea from the man on the other end. No attempt to stop her hanging up.

"Hello?" she said after a pregnant pause that gave birth to several seconds.

"Hello," the man responded casually.

"What...?" she began, surprised at his blasé approach.

"Why didn't I say anything when you were about to cut me off?" he repeated her unspoken question. "Because I knew I already had your interest. Because I knew you would reach for that button but intrigue would prevent you following through with it. How do I know this? Two reasons, Miss Clayton. One is that it has been a while since you've sunk your teeth into a really meaty story, and you can't pass up on the idea that this may just be one. After all, you have a reputation for being ruthlessly ambitious, and your dry spell has to come to an end some time."

"The other reason?" Andi asked.

"Again, that can wait until later. However, you're still far from convinced, Miss Clayton. This conversation may be intriguing. But there is nothing here that may inspire you to follow anything up, to want to speak to me again."

"Look, this is just getting silly now. You're spouting lots of cryptic nonsense. I–"

"Never mind, Miss Clayton," he interrupted.

She toyed with the idea of hanging up again.

"Before you press that button and cut me off," he continued, "I would like you to take a snapshot. Your phone does have photographic abilities I presume?"

"Of course. Snapshot of what? It's just a blank screen."

"If you want to meet me again, I will be at the South pool of the 9/11 memorial at 2pm tomorrow."

"How will I know you?" she asked.

"I will know you," he responded. "Ready for the snapshot? You will have two seconds."

"Erm…yes," she responded. "Two seconds before what?"

The screen brightened. A sheet of white card had been placed over the phone's visual iris to blank it out, but the card was now being moved back. It was retracted until it filled the screen. Something was written on the card – words too small to read. Andi stabbed the snapshot button and the image was stored in the phone's memory bank. The line went dead.

It was the most bizarre phone call Andi had ever experienced, and she'd had quite a few crackpots calling her over the years. Was this someone with a dark secret, or just another crank caller? Current thought favored the latter, but there was still room for the former to win out.

Andi transferred the snapshot to her computer screen and zoomed in on the image, hoping to make out the words written on the card. As she tucked a stray piece of hair behind her ear, her large green eyes studied the image.

At 400% zoom, they became clear. They displayed something that would have been impossible for the man to write while she was having the phone conversation with him. Yet it would have been truly impossible to have been written beforehand. Down to the last word, stutter, clearing of the throat and pregnant pause, the card displayed an exact transcript of the conversation she'd just had.

I was still awaiting the appearance of my research files. They were the key, I felt, to unlocking the secret of Jackson's continued evasion.

My cell phone sprang into action.

The little LCD screen on the front showed no caller ID. I activated the video mode and answered the call. The sound of a busy street came through, but the screen was blank.

"Lieutenant Stone," a male voice stated.

"Who is this?" I asked.

"Congratulations on your new assignment. How's the search for me going? Any luck yet?"

I quickly slid my feet off the desk, sat up straight and stared at the blank screen. "Zeus Jackson," I stated.

"I haven't been called that in a long time," the other man answered. I opened a desk drawer and searched for the cable that connected my cell phone to the desktop.

"What should I call you then?" I asked, stalling until I could locate the cable and run a trace.

"Don't bother," the man answered.

I found the cable and began untwining it. "Don't bother what? Calling you anything?"

"Don't bother trying to trace this call, Lieutenant. You think I'm stupid? I've rerouted it through twelve networks and several hundred servers. It would take you nearly ten minutes, and I won't be on that long."

I threw the cable on the desk in frustration. I should have expected that.

"So, I guess you've been on the case for a few hours now," the man said. "Have they told you anything about me yet?"

"Yes," I responded, relaxing into my chair. "They've told me."

He snorted. "I doubt it."

"How did you know I've been given the case?" I asked.

25

"I guess that just proves how little they've told you about me. Never mind, Lieutenant, I'm sure the General will fill you in eventually."

"Why don't *you* fill me in?"

"I haven't called for a *chit-chat*, Lieutenant," he spat. "The bomb this morning. Brooklyn café. Why wasn't anything done about it?"

"What could we have done?"

He sighed. "So they haven't even told you that. Why do you think all these terrorist attacks over the last couple of years have yielded hardly any fatalities?"

I considered this for a moment. "Incompetence?"

"Try again. I know you can do it, Stone."

"You're the tip-off," I stated.

"Very good, Lieutenant. There's promise in you yet. I acquire the information of time and location prior to these attacks. I call it in. You lot evacuate the area as best you can. This is how it's always been. Except this time you idiots did nothing and twelve people died."

"How do you come across this information?" I asked.

"That's another one to ask the General later. Right now, I have some more information for you."

"If it's regarding your whereabouts, I'm all ears," I said.

"They're stepping up their campaign, Lieutenant. They can sense the civil unrest, feel the backlash starting to undermine the present administration. They feel the time is right for one final push against the Government. Their attacks will be more frequent and more powerful. And just to prove this, they've planned another attack today."

"I repeat, how do you come across this information? I can't take action based on your word alone."

"Then on your head be it. But in fourteen minutes, an explosive device is going to detonate outside the FBI Academy in Quantico, Virginia, reducing it to rubble. I suggest an evacuation."

I shook my head at the blank screen in incredulity. "In fourteen minutes? We can't-"

"Then try your best," he interrupted.

The line went dead before I could begin a response. I stared at the dark screen for a moment, then activated the voice-control and said "Close screen." The screen rolled back into place and I pocketed the cell phone.

I activated the communications system on my desktop and patched through to General Miller in Washington.

"Miller here," he said gruffly as he leaned back in another plush office chair.

"Sir, I've just had a call from Zeus Jackson," I told him. "He already knew who I was. Has he breached our security?"

"What did he say?" Miller asked. He didn't offer any answers to my questions.

"That the Quantico Academy will be targeted in fourteen minutes," I told him.

Miller placed one hand to his mouth. He rubbed his chin thoughtfully. "Thank you, Lieutenant," he eventually said. "I'll make the evacuation call myself."

"Sir, I don't like that he knows more about me than I do about him. There's something you're not telling me."

Miller studied my image on his desktop screen for a few moments. "I don't know what you mean, Lieutenant."

"Sir! I'm not a fool. I need to know."

The General reluctantly nodded. "Okay, Stone. Prove to me you're worthy of this assignment. Look at what you know so far. Work it out. Then give me a call back." Without offering any more information, he leaned forward and cut off the call.

It was thirteen minutes since I received the phone call. Panic surrounded the FBI Academy in Quantico. Everyone had moved fast to evacuate the area. Maybe too fast.

They hadn't had time to check personnel IDs and verify that everyone on-site was authorized to be there. They hadn't had time to back up the data they'd been working on in the morning. They hadn't had time to check that all the rooms were evacuated, search for the explosive, or clear all the vehicles from the area. Hundreds of trainees had gathered outside the main gates. Trainers and upper-level staff were ushering the last vestiges of personnel down the main driveway.

A customized black Sedan had been parked outside the main building for the last two days. Surrounded by similar vehicles, it had remained unnoticed and unchecked.

Nitric acid seeped out of the Sedan's radiator through a custom-built tube. It flowed down the tube and into the vehicles tires. The tires were packed with plastique explosives. The mixture of the acid and plastique caused an intense chemical reaction, activating the bomb.

The resulting explosion disintegrated the vehicle and several surrounding it. The blast wave shattered glass in a four mile radius. The front third of the building was reduced to a heap of masonry and twisted metal. A cloud of dust and smoke blossomed from the wreckage. The silence from the crowd at the front gate was palpable.

Thanks to the rushed evacuation, no injuries were reported. Irreplaceable possessions and confidential data had been lost, left behind in the panic. But everyone was alive.

The attack sent shockwaves of its own through the espionage and law enforcement communities. The terrorists had shown they could hit us where it hurt. They'd managed to sneak a high-grade explosive device through the FBI's strict security protocols. Anyone could be next.

THREE

I had checked and re-checked the data I had at hand about Zeus Jackson. His intelligence and senses had been enhanced. He had avoided capture for three years. He knew I was on his case before anyone else did. How would he know I'd been handed this assignment? Hacking into NASRU systems was out of the question, so maybe he had somehow planted bugs or a mole within our organization. But even if that were the case, if he had someone on the inside working for him, it would be impossible to cover his whereabouts for three whole years. And what effect would this mental enhancement have on his ability to think? He could see better, hear more clearly. He could detect subtleties that would bypass a normal human. Then he could analyze those subtleties and use the information gleaned from them to his advantage. He was more than just a genius. He could read people.

I called the General.

"Have you made any progress, Lieutenant?" Miller asked me.

"I have a theory," I responded. "He's a mentalist. Joseph Dunniger in the 1950s, The Amazing Kreskin in the 1970s, Derren Brown in the 2000s, Claudio Marina in the 2030s. Now Zeus Jackson in the 2050s.

"He can effectively read your mind and influence your actions," I continued. "Through observation he can create personality profiles, lip-read, detect body language. He can tell what kind of person you are and know your most likely actions. In a way, he can tell what you're going to do."

"That's very good, Lieutenant. But if anything you haven't extrapolated this far enough. Using a sound logical basis he can predict all right. But not just with individuals. He can do it with crowds."

"He can create personality profiles and predict movements with whole crowds? At just a glance?"

"He can."

I took a moment to consider this, then leaned back in my chair. The implications had left me in shock. "So, translated," I said, "if he can do all that, Jackson can basically see into the future."

"That's the gist of it."

I blew out a sigh of amazement. "I'm supposed to catch a man who always knows when I'm coming. Who knows where traps are set. Who knows how I'll operate. Who will know, predict and avoid every conventional method of capture that we have."

"And that," the General stated, "is why I have chosen you, Lieutenant. We've tried the conventional method for three years without success. The two agents who came close, the two who discovered the new identities you have in front of you, they were able to bypass conventional thinking and track him down. But in the end, they weren't smart enough, because Jackson was waiting for them. We need you on this, Stone, because you think outside the box, because you don't always follow the rules. Because you're unpredictable."

"Even to a man like Jackson?"

The General shrugged. "I guess we'll find out."

"If he can do all this, Sir, then what's to stop him from influencing and controlling everything?"

The General nodded again. "And that is why he's the most dangerous man on the planet."

I glanced through the window in my office. The outer office door had opened and equipment was being wheeled in.

"My operations team is here, Sir."

"I don't need to tell you, Lieutenant, they don't have clearance for this information."

"Of course not, Sir. I am aware of the security level on this assignment."

"You'd better go and oversee their move, Stone. I know you have plenty more questions. They can be covered at a later date. For now, you have enough to go on. Now you know what you're up against."

The General ended the call. I rested back in my seat for a moment. The information needed to sink in. I had to capture a man who knew my every move.

First I needed to know where he was. That at least would involve the application of technology, something which we had plenty of. Working out how to capture him would be another thing entirely. That would involve being unpredictable, thinking outside the box. But if I thought outside the box, would he predict I'd do that and compensate?

I moved into the outer office to deal with my operations team. There were four of them: data analysts and technical experts. I browsed the bustle of activity. No one I recognized from previous assignments but they looked like an efficient bunch. If they could perform their tasks as expertly as they set up equipment, I would have no objection to them.

I moved over to Surveillance, who had connected and booted up his computer, complete with the VICs operating system, in record time.

"Status?" I asked.

Surveillance, an ex-pat Englishman whose name was Sam, was slumped in his chair. He leaned forward and pushed his VR-enabled prescription glasses higher up the bridge of his nose.

"All set, Sir," he replied. "Got anything for me to do yet?"

"What kind of access do you have?" I asked, leaning on the side of his desk.

"All areas," Sam answered smugly. "We have the Cyclops satellite system at our disposal, the electricity grid, flight manifests for airports worldwide, CCTV, drones, census, hotel registers, bank accounts…you name it."

"I'm impressed," I said. It wasn't often anyone was given access to the best spy satellite system in the business. The General was pulling out all the stops for us. "I haven't seen Cyclops since the briefing when it first started up. How accurate is it these days?"

"Hold out your left hand please," Sam told me. I stretched my arm at a right angle to my body, flexing my fingers.

Sam input the encrypted password onto the computer. He used his hands to manipulate the Virtual Imagery Controls only he could see in front of him and entered a few basic codes. A detailed map of the Earth was displayed on an 8-ft OLED screen that hung on the wall in front of us. The map zoomed in via the USA, via New York and via Manhattan straight to the office I stood in. Slightly off to one side, in the rough area that Sam's desk occupied, a winking red dot appeared.

"Hand down," Sam told me. I did as he said and the red dot shifted a couple of pixels to the right on the screen.

"Very impressive," I said. "The RFID?"

"Yes, Sir," Sam answered, switching off the image. "The Cyclops can pinpoint someone's Radio Frequency Identification chip down to an accuracy of about four inches. Worldwide coverage too if Cyclops pings the signal off telecoms sats. Implanted citizens or a foreigner with a card, the RFID is the one thing they can't mask via conventional means, and the one thing people can't live without in this country because it acts as passport, credit card, door key, etcetera, etcetera…"

I rubbed my right hand over my left, feeling the small electronic chip imbedded in the soft flesh. It made me uneasy, knowing that my life was dependent on this sliver of silicone. It meant I could easily be targeted by a satellite system orbiting two hundred miles above my head. Down to four inches. Didn't leave much room for error.

"Cyclops can detect heat signatures too," Sam said. "Infrared, thermal. We can display the image as a wire frame, road map, real-time video, 3-D projection…"

"I don't suppose by any chance it can see into the past," I muttered. "Or maybe the future…"

"Well, we have archived files," Sam responded. "Nowhere near as detailed."

"What kind of detail?"

"Wire frame display with RFID locators pinging every time a transaction is made, or flight taken, etcetera. If you want standard video, we can go back roughly six hours without any degradation of image quality because the satellite constantly backs up all the information it gathers. Even so, it only has so many terabytes of storage space."

"And with the RFID? How far back can you go?"

"Actual tracking on the wire frame map can go back five days. As for the transaction pings, the system first booted up four years ago, so..." He paused for effect.

"That far," I answered for him. "Four years. Okay."

I stood. I moved to a more central position in the office. The operations team seemed to be set now. I clapped my hands loudly.

"Right, people, thank you for coming in on a Sunday. Here's what we're going to do first. We have three names for our quarry – one birth name, two aliases. Zeus Jackson, Apollo Carver and Jose Manula. All three names will be based primarily in America. That's all we have to go on for now. We like to make you work for your paycheck here.

"Surveillance will trace the RFID usage of these names over the past four years. Analysis team, I want you to go through all the data retrieved, look for a pattern. There will be multiple personalities for each name. We need to eliminate these until we have the man we're looking for. He can't be in two places at once, so if we have a Zeus Jackson *and* an Apollo Carver in different locations in the same time period, at least one of them can be eliminated. When you've narrowed down the search, cross-reference with any stored CCTV images you can find, see if the same man crops up.

Collation, I want progress reports every half hour. And order some Chinese. I'm starving."

"Anything in particular, Sir?" Collation asked.

"Surprise me," I answered.

I took one step towards my office. The operations team knew I had completed my briefing. Like greyhounds out of the gates, the Analysis team dashed into a flurry of activity. Sam was already logged on and calling up data. The Collation officer, a glorified personal secretary called Brent, rang through an order to the takeaway. I closed my office door and sat down in my plush chair. While I waited for the results to pour in, I could consider the best way to subdue Jackson once we located him.

When the archived materials on Zeus Jackson arrived from downstairs two hours later, I was hugely disappointed. It was a similar feeling to the one I had when the bland and unadventurous takeaway order arrived. I would need to speak to Collation about his uninspired choices later, once I'd scanned through the information we had on our quarry.

"Is this it?" I asked, weighing up the single, light cardboard box. I opened the lid and found a pair of bulky folders inside.

"That's all we have," the delivery man from Archive informed me. He turned and exited my office, leaving the door forlornly open. I crossed to the door and closed it with a prod of my foot, then returned my attention to the box. The folders were thick, maybe 300 loosely-filed pages in total.

I opened one and flicked through the contents. It was thorough. All useful for developing a study of the man's personality. But it may not be useful to me, as the experiment he undertook could have altered his personality as well as his intelligence. I could tell that sifting through this data was going to be a long haul, and would yield few results. I couldn't even pass the job over to Analysis because they didn't have the security clearance. This was going to be an all-nighter.

I switched off the infrared keyboard and spread the folders across the desk. Before I began with the analysis, I had one more task to do – the most difficult task of all. I was going to have to cancel on Nat again.

I removed my cell phone from my jacket pocket, voice-activated the screen and said: "Call Nat."

The screen flicked into life. I greeted Nat with a warm smile, but it was not returned. I got the feeling she had been expecting this call.

"Hello, Jack," she said with apathy.

"Hi," I began. "So, you weren't called in, then?"

"I know what you're going to say, Jack, so just say it." She ran her fingers through her long hair and slouched into the leather settee. The landline's screen automatically panned down to focus on her face.

"Yeah," I said, "I'm going to have to work late again. Sorry, honey."

"I thought you said this new assignment, whatever the hell it is, wouldn't start until tomorrow. Promises, Jack. More broken promises." She sighed before continuing. "So…what time can I expect you? Will you, you know, actually make it back in time for dinner?"

"I don't think I'll be home tonight," I said.

A look of anger and disdain crossed her beautiful face, and she nuzzled her chin into her thick turtle-neck jumper.

"I'm sorry, I'll make it up to you," I said with hope.

Nat rested one elbow on the back of the settee, bunching up her hair with her hand. "That's what you always say, Jack. I've been keeping a tally of how much you owe me. According to my latest calculations, tonight included, I am owed…" She began counting the points off on her fingers. "A 2042 Corvette in mint condition. A bells-and-whistles wedding. A honeymoon – preferably three months in Tahiti. A money-no-object shopping spree in Bloomingdale's. And a modestly-sized mansion in the Hamptons. With a pool."

"I…" I began, a little taken aback at the mention of the W-word, a subject which I thought we had decided not to discuss for another three years. "Maybe I can stretch to a pond in the back garden?" I shrugged.

Nat sighed, exasperated. "Вы тупоумная сволочь! Just do what you've got to do, Jack. I'll see you when you've finished." She leaned forward and the screen went blank.

I tutted with annoyance. I folded the OLED screen back into place and pocketed the cell phone. She was angry with me. She often was in recent days. I knew I prioritized work over her. But in this job that was the way it had to be. She knew that, from the first time we met. She knew that work would have to come first. She used to accept it. She used to be okay. But lately she had changed. Lately she had become more demanding of my time. And time was a rare commodity for me.

I quickly opened my email and told her I'd take her to dinner at her favorite restaurant the night after next. I hoped that would make things right.

I frowned at the folders. I flicked them open and began reading.

Zeus Jackson, born June 27th, 2021 at the Henry Ford Hospital in Detroit, Michigan. Mother: Evelyn. Father: unknown. A middle child with two sisters: older Sacha and younger Mirabelle.

Underperformed at school. Grades low. Often in trouble for bullying. Suspended three times but never expelled. Sported a hairstyle that probably left him scarred for life.

Barely scraped through high school. Joined the army soon after. Excelled in training. One tour of duty in Saudi Arabia. 27 confirmed kills. Won the Purple Heart and the Bronze Star. Promoted to Corporal. Granted special leave before his second tour when his mother and both sisters died in a house fire over the Thanksgiving weekend.

Trained with Navy SEALs in an inter-services exchange program. Considered too hot-headed and uncontrollable, so training cut short after seven weeks.

Second tour in Saudi Arabia, another 17 confirmed kills. Won another Purple Heart and the Silver Star. Quickly rose through the ranks to Sergeant. Toyed with the idea of setting up a hardware store upon completion of his military contract but stop-lossed into a third tour of duty in Panama. Two confirmed kills, no medals awarded.

2052, selected by NASRU for a supersoldier program. Assignment accepted.

It painted an interesting picture of the man. He obviously had some father issues when he was young and became an underachieving bully at school. Probably felt the world was against him. He found his true vocation as a grunt and performed well enough to be commended and promoted.

But it didn't seem he was special forces material. Maybe he still had a few issues with authority and didn't gel with the extra discipline required from Navy SEALs.

Then came the moment that drove him over the edge, something that really should have been highlighted when NASRU was making its selection. Ready to retire, settle down and start his own business, he was stop-lossed. He was told this on the day he was to be discharged. A clause in his military contract stated he could have his contract forcibly extended if the country was at war and needed more military personnel. He had little choice but to accept it. It was either that, a court martial and prison sentence or go AWOL, flee the country and never return.

His military record in Panama showed his distrust of the system. Only two kills. No medals. There was no patriotism left, no enthusiasm. He coasted.

Why was he selected after that? I understood that he was chosen because he had no family ties. I got the idea that it would be easier and more quantifiable to boost the IQ of someone whose intelligence was low. But he was starting to rebel. And when he had the intelligence to be able to do something about it, he rebelled against us.

My assistants arrived the next morning. They timed it to coincide with the completion of the task I gave the operations team.

My eyes were bleary, having examined all the data that Archive sent to me overnight. I had managed to grab sleep in fits and starts – being professional, Brent woke me every half hour to deliver progress reports. They were always 'nothing new to report'.

When the assistants walked in through the door, I was filled with a sense of dismay. These were by-the-book, fresh-from-training operatives as far as I could tell. Two men and one woman. They were all attired in black suits, wearing sunglasses and scanning the room.

I waved them into my office. They filed in silently and stood to attention just inside the doorway. I briefly shook my head with annoyance and forced them to sit in the available chairs. They handed me small electronic ID badges, but I waved them away. I'd preferred to have an interactive conversation with these people than read their specs on a screen.

"First things first," I said. "Take off the sunglasses."

"Sir?" the middle one said. He was a wiry, sinewy man.

"Take them off. We're not the Men in Black."

"I thought we were, Sir," the same man answered, removing his glasses to reveal intelligent, steely blue eyes. The woman on my left was slim, with brown hair and daubed in make-up. The other man sat on the right. Thick-set with a shaved head, he was clearly the hired muscle of the group. They also removed their sunglasses and thrust them into their breast pockets.

The woman let her shoulder-length hair spill forward, before brushing it back with black-gloved hands. She looked at me with a sultry smile. I frowned back at her. Why was she giving me a come-on? Surely she knew that in NASRU, where you have to be at the peak of your mental prowess, office relationships were punishable by dismissal. Even imprisonment if found to have been compromised on an emotional level.

I stared at her until her smile dissipated. I couldn't tell if she was interested in me particularly. Maybe she was trying to provoke a similar response to boost her own confidence. Vanity. Narcissism. I'd need to keep those traits of hers in check.

The stocky, strong-jawed man sitting on the right blinked a few times to adjust his eyes to the light. His stony, blank expression gave little away. I got the feeling he wasn't going to be the talker of the trio.

"Well," I said, responding to the thin man's earlier statement, "we are and we aren't. What we *are* is secret. Unknown to the public. Undercover. With your suits and glasses you're as subtle as a party balloon at a funeral. Wear sunglasses when you're outside and it's sunny. Wear black suits in court. Normal people do not dress like that, so sort it out next time."

"I apologize, Sir," the same wiry man continued, "but in the academy we were given very specific training – discipline, dress code…"

"I realize that. I went through the academy as well. But here in the real world, things are different. No need to keep calling me Sir or Lieutenant. Certainly not in public. My surname will suffice. As long as you're professional when the job requires, that's good enough for me. Just…be more casual."

"In that case, Stone," he said. "It was quite funny on the way up here. Some workmen moving a large marble statue. Think it's one of those Venus De Milo ones with the missing arms. Wouldn't fit in the elevator so they're having to move it up the stairwell one step at a time. Going to take them weeks."

"That's taking casual too far. We're not familiar with each other enough to be having a gossip over a cup of coffee yet, okay?" I sighed and leaned back in my chair. These three were going to be my bane. I must have done something truly despicable in a past life.

"I apologize, Sir," the same man continued after an awkward silence. "Can I just say what an honor it is to be serving under you, and–"

"How about you tell me a bit about yourselves?" I suggested, interrupting. "Then I'll brief you on the assignment."

Collectively, my assistants' code word was Erinyes, which if I recalled correctly from my studies was also known as The Furies. Befitting their collective code word, each operative had been given the code name of the three Furies from age-old mythology. The wiry, intelligent fellow was coded Alecto, the stocky man was Megaera and the woman was code named Tisiphone. To avoid mistakes, I condensed their code names into bite-size form. Al and Tisi seemed more than happy with this arrangement, though the burly Meg put up half-hearted objections.

All three seemed very competent. Top of their classes at the academy and two years in the field. Meg had a particularly good knowledge of weaponry, Tisi specialized in psychology and social studies, while Al excelled in every subject. I had decided, unfairly considering I'd only just met them all, that if we split into two teams I wanted Al on mine.

I briefed Al, Meg and Tisi on the background details of Zeus Jackson. I left out the part where he could see into the future. They had the security clearance but they weren't ready for that kind of information yet. It would just confuse things, and I wanted them tackling this problem from the ground up.

A rap on the glass door alerted me to the presence of the Collation operative. I beckoned him in.

"We've finished the analysis, Sir," he said, passing me a hand-held. "It's...strange," he finished.

"In what way?" I asked, activating the screen.

"Best to see for yourself, Sir," he responded, then backed cautiously out of the room. Beyond, the other three members of the operations team stared anxiously at me from behind their desks.

I scanned the details on file, then began to read portions of the data out loud.

"Zeus Jackson," I said for the benefit of the Erinyes. "Last recorded location, entering the NASRU research facility in Idaho three years seven months ago. Experiment complete, he's transferred to holding pens in Washington D.C. Fair enough, that much we already know. Three years two months ago, a fortnight after Jackson escapes from the pens, we get the first recorded entry for an Apollo Carver in Detroit. Maybe visiting family graves. Traveling a lot, both in and out of the US, but mainly inside. Last recorded location, one year nine months ago in Texas. The following week, Jose Manula appears in Sacramento. Disappears six months ago in Texas."

I looked up at the Erinyes. Tisi and Meg seemed vaguely puzzled, Al was deep in thought.

"What does that indicate?" I asked. I'd already formulated my answer but I wanted to see how well these Erinyes could think on their feet.

"If this is all the same person," Al began, "then he has somehow found a way to disable, replace or recode his RFID chip."

I nodded. "He's done what is widely considered to be impossible. The RFIDs can't be hacked, can't be illegally scanned, can't be recoded without bypassing a constantly morphing 512-bit fractal encryption. They *can* be removed and replaced under massive pain. But RFIDs are implanted at birth and if any had been stolen from the chipping facility, or collected from implant hospitals as replacements it would have been flagged up long before now."

"There's only one possibility, then," Al said. "This isn't the same person."

"Or," I pointed out, "he's good enough to hack the fractal encryption."

Al snorted in derision.

"Sir," Tisi piped up. "That's impossible. You've just said so yourself."

"Maybe not for him," I responded. "His IQ's off the chart. He's a line that's crept off the graph and is steadily heading up the wall. Who knows what he can do?" I scanned the rest of the data I had been given. "One more thing," I said. I handed the screen over. "Take a look at these CCTV images."

The Erinyes quickly scanned the videos. "Different person," Meg answered, satisfied this was all a wild goose chase.

"Yet…" Al began, "…similar structure."

"Exactly," I said. "Zeus Jackson was a dark-skinned African-American, bulky, strong, tight dark curls, wide nose. Apollo Carver was lighter-skinned, slimmer but still toned, long dreadlocks, a thinner, more angular nose. Jose Manula was a Latino, slim, cropped bleached hair, tattoos, small rounded nose. But look at the height, the body structure, the gait and body language. All very similar."

"He's been changing appearance?" Meg asked, disbelieving.

"Extensive cosmetic surgery," I pointed out. "Back-street, illegal, otherwise it would have flagged up with such a change in appearance. We're not just talking a wig and false moustache here. He changed hair style and color, body and muscle weight, skin pigmentation. He's altered lip size, eye color, nose structure, had his ears pinned back or pushed forward. But it's still him. It's still the same bone structure, the same body language."

"Say that's the case," Tisi said. "How do we find him? We don't know his name, any RFID details or even what he looks like."

"That is true. For all we know, he could now be Kiki Mikado, Japanese female striptease artiste. But, there is one person aside from Zeus himself who knows what he looks like now. The cosmetic surgeon."

"But," Al pointed out, "we don't have a database of illegal back-street cosmetic surgeons to investigate." He paused. "Do we?"

"No," I answered. "That would just be silly. But Zeus hasn't quite covered his tracks well enough. Before he gets each new identity, his last port of call is the same small town in Texas. That's where our illegal, back-street cosmetic surgeon is."

FOUR

It was 2.07pm and Andi Clayton was already late for her meeting with her mystery caller. It didn't bother her. She was intrigued, but her current thought still favored 'crackpot'.

The clack of her heels was drowned out by the drone of nearby traffic. Andi entered the 9/11 memorial plaza at the North end, the trees masking all but the peaks of the cityscape around her. One World Trade Center rose behind her. It was a twisted, abandoned shell of a skyscraper, troubling wisps of gooey cloud with its huge antenna.

Andi set off down a wide path of stone. She spied the two dips in the soft grass that mark the sunken depths of the Reflecting Absence memorial pools.

She trotted down the dark North Pool ramp into the quiet depths. It was a vast square of water cut into the ground, outlining where a tower of the World Trade Center once stood. It was fed on all four sides by thin slices of waterfall cascading from ground level. Etched along all four walls of the memorial were the names of 2,628 people whose lives ended on September 11th, 2001.

There were few people here, in the sunken depths. Andi skirted the edges of the pool and entered the thin tunnel that linked it to the South Pool. Half-way along she passed a large alcove and dais where homages were paid. Only a dozen or so candles burned. Once, there were a thousand ablaze. But 54 years was a long time and the dead here were laid to rest a long time ago.

Leaving the tunnel, Andi entered the South Pool. A couple of strangers flitted past her in the gloom. Tension was rising in her. This moody, subterranean tomb to the masses was far too quiet to reassure her.

Andi spied the man at the far end, nestled into a corner. He was disheveled, an untidy mess of hair and a few days of stubble perfectly matching his worn pumps. His trench coat was wrapped around him as he sat lazily on a bench coated in a fine mist of spray from the waterfall. She thrust one hand into a pocket of her beige overcoat.

"You're late," the man said harshly in a roughly-hewn voice as Andi approached. He didn't look up. "I knew you would be anyway. That's why I only just got here myself."

"Well," Andi began. He was playing mind games. He was pretending he knew everything about her. The hand in her pocket instinctively tightened its grip around a small black oblong of metal.

"You won't be needing that," the man said, nodding towards her coat pocket.

"What?" Andi asked.

"The taser. Keep hold of it by all means if it makes you feel safer. But you won't need it."

She studied the man. He didn't seem threatening as yet. Occasionally he projected a breezy smile, and the intonation of his voice was noncommittal. He looked like he was a homeless bum, and was being far too secretive and enigmatic to instill confidence. But there was something about him…charisma, intrigue…something quite hypnotic and attractive.

The man cleared his throat and attempted to smooth back his hair, uncomfortable with the scrutiny.

"Sit, Miss Clayton."

She perched on the edge of a bench to a right angle, smoothed down her knee-length cream skirt, unbuttoned her matching suit jacket and placed her handbag carefully in her lap.

"So," Andi began. "Do I get a name this time?"

"Daniel," the man answered.

"Daniel what?"

"Just Daniel." The man leaned forward, his strong, blue eyes studying her for a moment. "Ask away."

"About what?" Andi demanded with a withering tone. "I have no clue as to why you asked me here."

"But you came anyway. Why was that?"

"The phone call. The written conversation. How did you do that?"

"Ah," the man answered satisfied. "Now you're asking the right questions. Now you're showing that glimmer of intelligence I expect of you. Tell me, Miss Clayton, how do *you* think I did it?"

"Why don't you tell me instead?" she demanded.

Daniel sighed. "You're just not entering into the spirit of things, are you? Maybe this was a mistake. Maybe…" He leaned forward again, studied her for a moment, then rested back. "Okay, I will tell you what you thought.

"You've already dismissed the idea that it was a large OLED board, with a voice-activated word processing chip.

You know that the board is nothing more than white card and the writing was made by a black marker pen.

"You've also discarded the theory that it was some form of magic because, well, you simply don't believe in it. Most people know that so-called magic is based on hypnosis, suggestion and sleight of hand. This was not 'magic'. It was something that defied belief, but also something deeply rooted in scientific reality."

"Which is?" Andi asked. He was correct – that was exactly what she thought.

"You ever heard of Deep Throat?" Daniel asked. "*Not* related to porn," he added. "Though we could discuss that…if you want."

"Watergate," Andi responded. "Around eighty years ago. What does that have to do with this?"

"Deep Throat didn't tell Bob Woodward and Carl Bernstein everything they needed to know in one go. He slipped them clues, bits of information to lead them on the right track. Likewise, I will not reveal all to you straight away. Don't want it to be too easy. You've got to work at this."

"But Deep Throat was advising them of a Government cover-up involving others. You are telling me about yourself."

"And did you think that maybe by telling you about myself, I will reveal a lot about our Government they don't want made public? There isn't just a rotten apple in the White House, Miss Clayton. The whole barrel's turned to mush."

"Ah," Andi nodded. "You mentioned conspiracy theories."

"I did," Daniel answered smugly.

"The President has been in office seven years now, and only you have managed to uncover something? I can't see it.

Surely by now we'd have had some indication that something was amiss."

"You've had many indications, Miss Clayton. A great many. But this country has been crafted, molded to see only what the Government wants them to see and nothing else. Clues are all around you, but you are blinded to them."

"Such as?"

He sighed. "I guess I'll have to spell some of this out to you. Such as, as you've just said yourself, the President has been in office seven years now and he is still in his first term, invoking non-stop Emergency Rule."

Andi shrugged. "We live in a climate of fear, Mr...Daniel. How can you open polling stations when you know they would be a prime target for the terrorists?"

"And how much do you know about these terrorists?" he asked. "Maybe they don't want to destroy America. Maybe they want to restore its freedom and democracy, things that have slowly and subtly been taken away from the people."

"That's rubbish," Andi answered, getting angry. "I've never heard anything so ludicrous."

Daniel sighed again. "Open your eyes, Miss Clayton. I thought you'd be better than this. Maybe I'm wrong. Maybe you *are* just a hack."

"I'm not sure I like your current attitude," Andi responded.

"So? I thought you came here because of a story, not my personality."

Andi shook her head in condescension. "So, you're advocating terrorism. Why?"

Daniel merely shrugged.

"One more thing before I go," he said. "I want you to do something for me. You have a Government Advisor at the paper? Of course you do. They're everywhere. I presume you'll be required to write an article about the Quantico bombing at some point."

"It's likely."

"Add the following line into your story somewhere: "The terrorists' motives were unknown and we can only wonder what their grievances may be." I guarantee your Government Advisor will excise the line, and you'll be called in for a chat with your editor."

"And what would that prove?"

"Ah, yes, I forgot. The Government Advisor is there purely to prevent falsehoods from entering the news. There to protect the public from malicious lies directed against their fair country." He snorts with this. "The sentence I just asked you to write contains no falsehoods. No lies. Therefore why should it be excised, yes? Check the Constitution sometime. There's something about freedom of speech in there."

He placed a small card on the bench next to her, tapped it once.

"That's where and when we'll meet next," he said. He stood and began to move towards the exit.

"What if I don't want to meet you again?" Andi asked.

He turned back, snorted with derision again. "You will."

"Wait!" she called as he took a few more steps away. "Daniel!"

He stopped again, turned with a wry smile on his face.

"I haven't finished," Andi told him, standing herself. She felt the moist back of her overcoat slap against her bare legs.

"I know," Daniel answered. "So, go ahead. Ask that one question that is niggling the back of your mind and I will answer it truthfully."

"What...how did you write down our phone conversation on that board?"

"The same way I know all about the terrorists. Even where they'll strike next."

"How?"

He grinned, and Andi could feel his own self pride emanate from him. "I can see the future," he answered, then turned on his heel and walked away.

FIVE

I was in a bad mood by the time I had landed in Texas. The plane ride was uncomfortable and the check-in desk tried, unsuccessfully, to force me to put my sidearm in the baggage hold. Now the drive through dusty scenery, interspersed with sporadic patches of grass, did little to heighten my peace of mind.

Al had picked me up from the airport in a Cougar. It was running on solar power while we were away from the cities' charging grids. Tisi and Meg had gone on ahead to secure the cosmetic surgeon. I took my time to think during the journey, interrupted occasionally by Al.

"Oh, by the way," he told me. We drove through a small, busy town bordering the desert wastes. "Have you heard the news?"

"No," I responded. It was at times like these – awkward flight to Texas, long winding drive through America's dustbowl – that I wished someone would hurry up and invent a teleportation device. They'd been partially successful in teleporting an apple pip thus far. But that didn't instill me with confidence for the near future.

"It was announced about four hours ago," Al continued. "General Myrmid has died in Cuba."

"How?" I asked, running through the motions of conversation. I just wanted to get this trip over with. I wanted to head back to the towering, gleaming civilization of New York. Besides, the Cuban war had never sat easily with my conscience.

"Stepped on a land mine," Al continued.

"What an asshole," I responded. America's most highly-decorated officer, in charge of an entire invasion campaign, and he steps on a mine. I had no sympathy at all.

"We've asked Havana for a temporary ceasefire to grieve and they've agreed," Al finished.

"Good," I said. "Maybe someone will come to their senses and end the war."

"Well, it's Cuba's fault for kidnapping that Senator woman in the first place."

I looked disparagingly at Al. "Don't even get me started on that," I told him. "You're smart enough to know the CIA was involved in that. The President just wanted another war. I think he got bored."

I stared out the side of the vehicle, letting its soft electrical hum calm my mind. The small town had now filtered away to sporadic outcroppings of wooden shacks with the occasional dirty concrete structure looming over the road. In the distance, forests of artificial trees sprouted from the barren ground like giant white flyswats, sucking in and storing some of the excess carbon dioxide of global warming.

"What's the situation with the doctor?" I asked.

"Denying all as expected," Al answered. "The others went on ahead. They've secured him to his own operating chair.

The dentist's chair, that is. They haven't uncovered his other operating venue yet."

I snorted in derision. "A dentist with a secret life as a cosmetic surgeon. Wonder where he learnt his skills."

"There's no record of him attending classes beyond dental school. Maybe the internet?"

I shook my head. "No, if Zeus Jackson thought he was good enough, it couldn't be a home-schooled hack-and-slash job."

"Well, it's not really our concern, is it Sir? We just need information from him regarding a client, not where he honed his skills."

"True. And I thought I told you all not to call me Sir."

"Sorry, Stone," Al responded. He nodded ahead of him "Here it is."

He pulled into a short drive-way leading to a reasonably-sized two-storey building. It was wood-paneled on the front and white-painted concrete down the sides.

I opened the door before the car had stopped moving and stepped out. "Which room?" I asked.

"Second on the left," Al responded from the car. "Past the reception."

The reception and hallway were dark, filtered with weekend dust. A pool of harsh light seeped through the open doorway to the left. I strode through it. Behind me, Al had removed a large black case from the trunk of the car. He was struggling to direct it through the spring-hinged screen door into the reception area.

I entered the room. Tisi was yawning widely as she perched on a stool. Meg was seated on the floor with his back to a cupboard, picking flecks of dirt from his fingernails. In the center of the room, surrounded by dentist paraphernalia, was the operating chair upon which the doctor had been tightly bound. He was secured to the chair with thick straps of leather, belts, surgical gloves and anything else that could be found to bind him. I admired the Erinyes' choice. They could have used their handcuffs but they would have afforded him too much freedom of movement. Bound like this he could hardly move his limbs so the loss of control would feel more apparent. He seemed rather sedate, having been inert for a couple of hours now. He perked up when he felt my presence in the room.

"Hello, Doctor," I said. I walked over to him so we could view each other in the eye.

"Wh...what is this?" he asked. "What's going on? Why won't anyone tell me anything?"

I glanced across to Tisi. She had now been joined by Meg, dusting down his suit. I considered berating all three Erinyes for still wearing their black suits, until I realized it actually conveyed a sense of menace upon the doctor.

"We thought it prudent to only ask *what* we want to know without explaining *why*," Tisi told me.

"Well, there you go, Doctor," I said. "We find it prudent not to tell you. Now, have you been telling *us* anything?"

"I...they keep asking me questions. I don't know what they're on about. Who are you people anyway?"

"We're the people asking the questions, Doctor. I thought you'd realized that by now. We want to know..." I snapped my fingers once and Tisi handed me an ePad. I showed the digital images it displayed to the doctor. "...About this man," I continued. I pointed at each image in turn. "This is Zeus Jackson, this is Apollo Carver, and this is Jose Manula.

All three are the same person, and he looks different because you performed cosmetic surgery on him. And you've done it again. I'd like to know what he now looks like and what name he goes under."

"But…I'm just a dentist. Just a local dentist."

"Of course you are," I said, lightly patting the ageing, portly man on his shoulder. "Of course. Where's the operating theater?" I glanced around the room. It was musty. It had been out of use for a couple of weeks. A sink and large window adorned one wall, cupboards littered with utensils on another. A third contained an x-ray machine and an empty, disused fish tank. The fourth was a long, dark bookcase stuffed full of hardback tomes.

"Op…operating theater?" the doctor stammered. "But *this* is where I…"

"No, no, no. The surgery theater. The one where you add hair plugs, fatten lips, alter skin pigmentation and the like."

"I…I told you…"

I placed one hand firmly over the doctor's mouth. Fearing that I was going to suffocate him, the doctor struggled with his tight bonds. His thrashing amounted to little more than a squirm. He stopped wriggling when he realized he could still breathe through his nostrils. I removed my hand and the doctor obediently kept quiet.

"It's behind the bookcase," I said. "Judging by the outside shape of the building there should be another large room over there."

"Shall I break it down?" Meg asked.

"No, no," I answered. "Let's not be so crude. I'm sure there's an easy way of opening it. Judging by the books on the case, I'd say one of them opens it."

"We've already checked everything," Tisi interjected. "None of the books have levers attached to them."

"Ah," I casually dismissed her and started inspecting the books. Medical tomes abounded, but the upper two rows were filled with classics of fiction. "You're thinking too traditionally. A book that you pull forward and it tugs a lever! What we're looking for," I continued absently, "is a remote trigger secreted inside the front or back cover. But which book, I wonder? Dante's The Divine Comedy? No, he has no sense of irony. Swift's Gulliver's Travels? Too full of Yahoos. Ah, here it is."

I plucked a burgundy hardback from the shelf and displayed it to the doctor with a knowing smile on my face. "Kafka's Metamorphosis." I opened the book and briefly checked the front, then the back cover. There was a slight indentation in the inside back cover. I jabbed it and a small stud clicked down. The bookcase split down the middle with a crack, and I wheeled one of the disguised doors open.

The room beyond was much larger, but of a similar set-up. Medical equipment littered trays and tables, a large flat surface in the center. It was all wrapped in protective plastic sheeting that in turn had a slight coating of dust. Several steel filing cabinets rested against one wall and bright circular lights were set deep into the ceiling.

I turned back to the Erinyes. "Let's do this."

Leaving the doctor tied to the chair, the Erinyes and myself moved into the newly-located surgery room. We began scouring for information.

Tisi engaged herself with a general search. The rest of us headed for the more logical spot: the filing cabinets. I opened one drawer and I was greeted by a mass of paper folders, arranged seemingly haphazardly. I plucked a file from the cabinet and flicked through it. The records were thorough in a medical context, but there were very few personal details recorded. No 'before' photographs. No names or addresses. The doctor had retained the secrecy of his clients well. It would be a huge task to locate the new visage of our wanted man within this vast collection.

"My, we have been busy," I called through to the doctor. "And congratulations on having the forethought to use paper records so your database can't be hacked into. But this doesn't really help *us*."

I headed back into the dentistry room. "Where is the file for Jose Manula? That's the one we want. Where is the file that shows us an image of what he looks like now, Doctor?"

The doctor stared at me stubbornly. He was not one to crack so easily. Al, Tisi and Meg returned to the smaller room, shrugging apologetically. It could take weeks for character-mapping software to cross-reference all the 'after' shots with the bone structure and facial dimensions of Jose Manula before we got a match. We needed the doctor to talk.

"That is all we need, Doctor," I told him. "One image, one name. Where does he go to get new identity papers? What does he call himself now? Is he black, white, Hispanic, Asian? Male, female? Old, young?"

The doctor was quiet. His judging stare remained in place. I sighed and rested my crossed arms on his chest so I was staring into his eyes.

"You're not dealing with the criminal underworld here, Doctor. We're not mere thugs who'll threaten to beat you up if you don't tell them what they want to know. We're far more sophisticated than that."

Again, the doctor refused to speak. I levered myself up off his chest and grabbed a sharp, pointed tool from a worktop. The doctor's eyes opened wide and I saw him try to prevent a gulp of fear. "Too crude," I said, studying the instrument. I dropped it on the worktop and turned my attention back to the doctor. "Too crude by far," I told him. "Let me show you this instead."

I clicked my fingers once. Meg lifted up the large black case. He set it down on the small metal table to the left of the operating chair. He began to fiddle with the combination lock. I left him to it.

"I presume you know all about the VR headsets you can buy these days. Clumsy things over your eyes, allow you to fully immerse your visual cortex in another world. Popular with net-heads, I believe. They spend hours at a time plugged into the latest online community. Being who they've always wanted to be. Doing what they've always wanted to do. Interacting with people half-way across the world in an environment that is graphically almost as rich and detailed as reality. Amazing, really."

Meg defeated the stubborn combination lock and flicked the lid open. The doctor strained at his bonds to discover the contents. He was ashen with worry.

"This," I told him, "is the next step in that technology." A large shiny black box was removed from the case and handed to Al. Next came some thin filaments, circles of sticky white plastic encasing one end of each fine wire. Lastly, Meg withdrew a sleek, fashionable VR eyeband and placed the case on the floor. With the box now replacing the case like a fresh-born child from its padded womb, Al and Meg began to untangle the spidered web of wires.

"What the...?" the doctor whispered in fear.

"This is called a Melp, short for Melpomene, which as I am sure you know, good doctor..." I patted him reassuringly on the shoulder as he continued to strain at the head strap, "...was the Greek muse of tragedy." I paused for effect, but the doctor was paying little attention to me. He was preferring to let his own mind spell out the purpose of the device. "Tragedy, doctor." I said, leaning in closer. This brought the doctor's attention back to me, his eyes wild and bulging.

"I personally think it should have been called the Pandora's Box, if they were insistent on the Greek mythology route. Pouring out disease and sorrow, leaving hope firmly encased inside, locked away. But..."

I paced the room in silent contemplation. What I said next needed to be exact. It needed to seem chatty and unprofessional as though I were a friend giving advice. But in addition I needed to instill such fear in the doctor he'd be crying for mummy within five minutes. Imagine the difference in terror levels between someone shouting 'shut up!' and someone calmly whispering in your ear 'if you don't shut up I will tear out your tongue'. One was a quick rush of adrenaline, the other was deeper and longer lasting. I was going for the latter.

The Melp was set up now. Meg awaited the go-ahead to attach electrodes. Al was standing to one side with the VR eyeband.

"In addition to the traditional VR band," I started, waving a hand in the direction of the Melp, "electrical stimulators are placed on your temples and an electric subduer at the base of your neck. The subduer intercepts those little electrical stimuli your brain fires down the central spinal cortex telling your arms and legs to move. It translates them into movement in the virtual environment. In contrast, the stimulators are able to translate the sound, smell, taste and feel of this computer generated world into pulses the brain understands. Together with the band projecting directly into your retinas, it allows you to become immersed in a realistic virtual world designed to your specifications, with all five senses fully accommodated."

I leaned in close again and whispered. "Problem is, doctor, this isn't going to be a world you'd want to be in." I paused again as he twisted his head towards me. He wondered if now was a good time to speak. I decided not and interrupted his still-born words. "I heard about a woman once who was withholding information vital to the security of our great nation. She was plugged into the Melp for nearly three days. Held out brilliantly, I must say. In the end, she only gave us one tiny morsel of information – a contact name. Fortunately, the contact proved easier to persuade and everything turned out just rosy in the end. But imagine..." I leaned closer. "Sixty eight hours she was under. Sixty eight hours straight, set on a loop of imagining, of feeling...proper physical *feeling*...that she was being pursued, raped and tortured. Again and again and again. No rest, no respite, no toilet breaks or nap times."

I stood and began pacing again, my hands clasped firmly behind my back. My three deputies awaited motionless for their next instructions.

The doctor, mouth dry and rasping, attempted to speak. He only got far enough to grunt and wheeze.

I continued. "However, we will not be putting you through that, doctor. While I'm sure you'd recoil at the concept of being raped, there is something about being sexually brutalized that is particularly invasive, physically *and* emotionally, to a woman. It just doesn't work the same with a man. So, we'll skip the pursuit and the rape, and head straight for the extreme physical violence." I paused to allow the doctor to wheeze once more in protestation.

"I've never been a fan of technology, I have to admit," I said as I patted the scuffed mules on the doctor's bound feet. "But this gives us plausible deniability, you see. No marks. The old days of physical torture are pretty much gone, doctor. No longer will there be electrodes on genitals, a blowtorch on the soles of feet, an electric sander on shoulder blades. Why do that physically when we can force you to imagine and feel as though it is being done to you? Then, afterwards, we can stick our hands up and say "Hey, look, no marks. I'm sorry he's spent the last two months in an asylum because he can't stop screaming, but we didn't touch him." It's the advent of technology, doctor. Removes the human touch. Quite sad, really. But, needs must."

I signaled to Meg and Al. They moved forward with a slow, purposeful gait. The doctor shifted his bound head again, staring feverishly at them. "N...nnn....no!" he finally managed, hoarse and breathless.

"I'll tell you what, doctor," I said breezily. "As it's you, we'll start you on an easy program. One where nothing actually gets cut off."

The Melp was a fictional device. We did have the technology, but it was very crude and in early stages of development. The Melp we actually used combined particular software programs with a simple VR eyeband and let the victim's own imagination do the rest. The effect only worked for a few minutes, but for those few minutes the brain was able to convince itself that the pain it believed was occurring actually existed. It was simply mind over matter. As such, this method of interrogation had never been used on professionals. It simply wouldn't work. But non-professionals and members of the public could be easily duped and the Melp concept had a 100% success rate. Leading someone to believe they were about to endure immense physical pain with no break, no reprise: it was far more effective than actually inflicting the pain.

As such, with the doctor's feverish mind working overtime, he started to spill before we'd even placed the VR over his eyes.

Meg loaded the Melp suitcase into the back of his midnight-hued vehicle.

"Stone," he called. "That's everything."

"You sure?" I asked. I squinted at him in the sunlight, wishing I'd brought my sunglasses. "Fingerprints, footprints, clothing fibers…"

"We can't account for every cell of skin we've shed, but they'd be very lucky to trace anything back to us."

I nodded. I took one last look at the doctor's surgery, shielding my eyes from the sun with one hand. The roof shimmered in the heat. "Make the call to the FBI," I told him. "Then meet us at the convenience store three klicks south."

Involving the FBI was frustrating but necessary. I would have preferred to keep this entire operation under wraps and I was in no doubt that some of the paperwork in the cabinets would come in useful to NASRU in the future. But retaining that information for ourselves would cause several more problems. Would we dispose of the doctor, kill him in cold blood? Or maybe take him back with us and lock him up in our own facility? Either way, his disappearance would generate questions we'd be unwilling to answer. This way, by leaving the doctor a babbling mess and trashing his office, we had created the illusion of a bungled break-in. Something they'd half-heartedly investigate for a few days then drop. In addition, we now had the essential paperwork we needed for our investigation. The FBI would discover and secure the rest. They'd scan it all into their database. And we'd quietly, secretly access their database as and when we felt like it. It would save a lot of hassle, but it would also give the FBI access to data they simply weren't qualified to properly handle. It was an acceptable compromise.

Meg slipped on some black gloves and pulled out a kerchief. He'd use the doctor's own reception phone to call the FBI, say the word "Help" then leave the call still connected. The kerchief was to both disguise his voice and ensure he didn't leave DNA traces of spittle around the mouthpiece.

The FBI should be able to trace the call in under a minute. Add another minute for them to realize the call needed tracing in the first place. Then they needed to get here. The nearest stationed agents were over an hour's drive away. FBI agents weren't the kind of people to want anyone else getting there before them, so we could be guaranteed the local GovPol wouldn't be directed here in the meantime.

That gave us nearly one and a half hours to figure out our next move and clear the area. We'd be gone long before then.

I threw my suit jacket in the rear of my car. The tie followed. I motioned to Al to do the same. A smart suit would look conspicuous in this environment, so I wanted to look casual as we headed back into town.

Al drove the car again, and we pulled up outside the convenience store. It was a large, air-conditioned mart with a wide concrete forecourt. Half a dozen vehicles occupied spaces. Across the road was a diner sandwiched in between a fading boutique and an equally crumbling real estate firm.

"This place is dead," I said as Al and I stepped out of the car. "This isn't where we need to be."

We walked across the forecourt to the convenience store. It was cool and refreshing inside.

"What do we need?" Al asked.

"General supplies and a map of the area. Local, county and state if you can."

"My eMag's in my jacket pocket," he responded guiltily.

"Mine too," I admitted. "Go fetch yours and I'll get the supplies." I walked further into the store.

Al headed back to the car.

We had detailed medical breakdowns of what the doctor did to our quarry and a nice new 'after' photo. The man we were hunting was white now. Strong jaw line. Blue eyes. Dark, wet hay-colored hair that threatened to be both blonde and brown but never quite achieved either. But what we still didn't have was a name or a location.

I collected four bottles of water. They were expensive but the bottles were made of a biodegradable plastic that kept the water fresh and cool for hours. Considering the heat inside a locked car in that climate, it was worth the extra expense.

Al returned with his eMag and I joined him at the newspaper port. He had an old eMag tablet, a rectangular box six inches wide, two deep and two high. It looked like it used a letter-size OLED.

Al plugged the eMag into the data port on top of the news kiosk and the kiosk's screen winked into life. It was a drag-and-drop system, probably as old as Al's eMag. The lower two columns displayed options, and the top column remained free for the user to drag the touch-screen icons over. I scrolled down, through the national and local newspapers, the populist and specialty magazines.

"This is ridiculous," I muttered. "No search engine."

Finally I had located the maps section of the kiosk's database. I dragged and dropped maps for the town, the county and the state. After a paused I decided to get the maps for the surrounding counties as well.

"I will get reimbursed for this, won't I?" Al asked. He waved his RFID chip at the scanner while I held down the 'purchase' button. "We could have just used our cell phones for free."

"This image is bigger," I answered. I took his eMag from the port and handed it to him. "We can all gather around it."

I paid for the water, then headed outside.

"What about food?" Al asked me. Further down the road, Meg and Tisi's Cougar shimmered on the crest of a hill. They'd be with us in thirty seconds.

"Overpriced junk in there," I said, handing him a bottle. "Let's try the diner instead. We should be able to discuss details without interruption."

We walked across to our car and deposited two bottles inside. Meg pulled his car up next to ours.

"Diner," I told him and Tisi as they stepped out. "And ditch the jackets." I threw a bottle of water to each of them. They nodded in silent thanks and shed their coats.

Looking like bankers on a road trip, the four of us headed for the diner. We waited for a pick-up to idle by before crossing the road.

The diner contained more staff than patrons. Two waitresses and a cook competed for the attentions of a young couple on a road trip themselves.

We all slid into a booth. I twisted the sprocket-mounted touch screen menu over and selected a black coffee. I twisted it towards Al. He stabbed the same button.

"I'm not hungry either," he said.

Tisi looked at Meg then shrugged. "Just…the same. Four coffees." Al pressed the button twice more then hit 'order'.

Out the corner of my eye I saw one of the waitresses move over to her order screen behind the counter, checking on what we'd requested. I turned my attention back to Al.

"Map," I told him.

Al placed his eMag on the table, unfurled the OLED and activated the screen. He scanned through the list of newspapers and magazines he'd bought recently, then selected the town map. It was displayed large and clear on his screen.

"Here's the situation," I began. "We know what our quarry looks like now. Or at least what he looked like six months ago. Chances are he still looks the same. We also know that he stopped becoming Jose Manula at the point he revealed this new look. That means he got a new identity, and pretty damn quickly. He can't have left the state without new ID. He can't have traveled along most of the roads *within* the state without new ID. We can therefore assume that a professional forger lives somewhere nearby. Not in this town. A plastic surgeon is one thing, but ID forgers need access to equipment and chemicals that would be too conspicuous in this community. Besides, profiling usually suggests that ID forgers like something a bit more urban and gritty. Somewhere with a scene.

"So we're going to check over these maps and extrapolate all possible locations for this forger. Both the kind of environment we'd expect them to be living in, and the places our quarry could have actually reached without being able to buy food or drink, and without having new cards, fingertips, retinas and RFID configurations."

"Retinas?" Meg asked, confused.

"Changing eye color is one thing," I told him. "The plastic surgeon did that. But the retina retains its own unique pattern. Someone else did that bit for him."

"So we'll map all the routes that have tolls or checkpoints," Al confirmed. "Work out which cities or large towns are accessible within a maximum of two days. Then…"

"Then we give our team back home a call. They can go through GovPol and FBI reports on known or suspected ID forgers in those locales. After that it is just a case of analyze, stake-out and eliminate until we have our forger."

The waitress trotted over, chewing gum like a true Southern Belle, and clumsily deposited four black coffees on our table.

I took one quick sip of my coffee. It was bad. Low-grade ground beans and a pot that hadn't been washed in a week. I placed the white mug to one side and studied the map. Everyone else was calmly stirring their coffees with a teaspoon.

"The forger is around here somewhere," I told them. "Let's figure out where, then let's get staking-out. I want them in my custody tonight."

SIX

It had taken two more cups of pretty terrible coffee in the diner to narrow down possible locations before we left for Austin, and a further three hours of analysis from my team back in New York to pinpoint the only ID forger in the vicinity with a realistic chance of having aided our quarry.

We moved quickly and set up a stake-out as the sun shrank behind urban high-rise buildings in Austin's old business district.

Al and I were waiting in the car. We'd just finished listening to the news. The serial-killing English Prince had finally been cornered, captured and sedated. There were rumors of an exchange of PoWs during the Havana ceasefire. The Mars terraforming operation was now expected to conclude fourteen years later than planned.

Rain drove in flurries through the dark of the evening. It peppered the urban street with fresh globules and drummed its fingers on the vehicle's roof. The tall, dark, rust-colored building opposite seemed formidable. The dull, muted pounding of bass music from within was competing with the pitter-patter of the rain.

"What do you think?" Al asked, casually fiddling with his wedding band.

"19th-Century townhouse style," I said. "Going to be tricky to storm. Lots of nooks and crannies."

"So you reckon there's…you know…people inside?"

"Feels like it," I told him. "We'll wait to see what Meg and Tisi have to say, but it might be best to send in the local PD first. Let them deal with the brunt of the firefight."

"GovPol cannon fodder," Al suggested.

"Something like that."

I checked my watch – 10.46pm. A car swept past. It scythed through the film of rain covering the road and its headlights displayed bright sparkles of water droplets in the air. Briefly disturbed, the draining water settled in its wake. It was disturbed once more by the pounding of two sets of feet.

Meg dashed into the driving seat of the dark, somber car in front. Tisi approached my passenger-side door. She looked miserable and sodden. One hand was held up high, trying to shield her hair from the downpour. The other hand clutched thermal imaging goggles.

I wound my window down. Tisi tried to blow rivulets of water and soggy splats of hair from her face.

"Target confirmed," she told me. "There's a fire escape round the back, a side entrance and the main door. Eighteen thermal readings having a party on the second floor. Visual confirmation indicates they're all heavily armed, and all heavily sampling drugs. The music should mask our point of entry, but once we get in there a firefight is inevitable."

"Thank you," I responded. "Wait in the car for further instructions."

I closed the window and Tisi trotted back to the other vehicle. She flapped moisture off the front of her jacket before getting into the warm, dry car.

"Eighteen people," Al repeated. "Heavily armed, drug-fuelled..."

"GovPol," I told him. We were good, but eighteen was too many to handle even for us. I picked up my cell phone. I requested Speed Dial #1.

"Brent," I said as soon as the line was picked up at the other end. "Patch me through to the nearest GovPol Station and give me a new FBI clearance."

"Will do," my Collation Operative answered with a grumpy sigh, evidently wishing he was home in bed. "Lieutenant Nicholson is the main point of contact there. FBI clearance... Agent Tom Harriman, code is Beta eight six three five two."

The line switched to the local GovPol station and I was put through to Lt. Nicholson.

"Nicholson," he said, already bored with whatever conversation he was about to endure.

"This is FBI Agent Harriman, Lieutenant."

"Authorization?" he asked.

"Beta eight six three five two," I told him. He glanced to one side. I could hear the sound of keys tapping as he accessed the intelligence database to confirm my code.

"What can I do for you, Agent Harriman?"

"I need your men to suit up immediately for a drugs raid, Lieutenant. It may be too late by the time we get there, so we need you to move as quickly as possible."

"Yes, Sir," he responded, then moved away from the phone. "Grahams!" he shouted. "Suit up! We're going fishing!" His crumpled, weary face came back to the screen. "Address?"

"142 Colorado Street. We're expecting eighteen suspects, heavily armed, highly resistant."

"Got it." He nodded. "You wish to detain all suspects?"

"Just one. An ID forger. Female, Caucasian, late twenties, five foot six, short spiky blonde hair, name of Ophelia Brigante. Detain her for us, the rest do with as you want. Oh, and Lieutenant? Try not to destroy too much of the place."

"No, Sir, we w–"

I cut him off and slid my cell phone back into my pocket. Now we just had to wait for the GovPol cavalry to arrive. They'd storm the building. They'd shoot and be shot at. They'd kill and be killed. We'd be on-hand to oversee the operation, but even with our training the four of us were heavily outnumbered. Let the frontline take the brunt of the casualties, then the specialists can secure the target. It didn't seem fair, but it was basic military tactics. And I was in no doubt that this would turn into a warzone.

It took the GovPol SWAT team eleven minutes to reach us. We heard them coming two minutes before that.

"What...?" Al began, hearing the distant call of sirens. "Oh dear God!"

"Those idiots," I muttered and activated the comms linking our car with Meg and Tisi's. "They're coming in with sirens wailing," I told them, "so expect the enemy to be waiting and ready to shoot anything that moves."

"Subtlety's never been in their dictionary," Tisi responded.

"What's the chance of you sneaking up the fire escape and capturing Brigante before the fun starts?"

"Roughly zero," she answered. "Even if I had a chance, there's not enough time now. Someone will hear the sirens over the music and they'll be on their guard within a minute."

I blew out a sigh of frustration. "Just hang tight then. And when the firefight starts, if you accidentally shoot any GovPol officers, I'll recommend you for a medal."

"Thank you, Sir," Tisi answered.

"That was a joke," I responded warily.

"Thank you for clearing that up, Sir," she answered. "I'll do it just for the fun of it, Sir. Medal or no."

The police arrived, screeching and swinging their vehicles about in spectacular fashion. There were two armored vans each carrying six SWAT members and four more cars contained two officers each. At the back there was an unmarked vehicle containing three plain-clothes senior rankers staying comfortably out of the way. Even if the plain-clothes officers got down and dirty they were barely out-numbering the opposition.

The thudding bass of the party had stopped. A handful of black-paned windows on the second floor had been opened and the lights within extinguished.

The criminals used the tried and tested method of divide and conquer to start proceedings off. They allowed the SWAT team to storm the front door and pile in shouting nonsensically. Then they attacked.

At first there were a few pitter-patters of bullets on the road, barely distinguishable from the hammering rain. Then muzzle burps from semi-automatics and a single machine gun started cracking open the roofs of the cars. They splintered the flashing lights and spider-webbed the windshields. Officers crouched behind their punctured cars. Their pistols and shotguns retorted back up to the darkened second floor windows.

A few flashes from within the building highlighted windows on the first floor. The SWAT team had encountered its first pocket of resistance on the stairwell. Two officers on the ground had slid out of the line of fire and slipped round the rear of the building, hoping for an easy kill. The remaining six were being pinned down mercilessly, but as yet there were no injuries.

Two more machine guns quickly joined the melee from the second floor and one pistol-packer had opened fire from the third floor. I spied a semi-automatic spin to the ground from the second floor, the shooter having been either clumsy or wounded. More lights flashed from the first floor. The firefight within was now clearly audible amid the chaotic shouting and drumming rain. The three plain-clothes officers joined in the fight. Their car, acting as cover, immediately became a target for two shooters.

"They're making a right mess of this," I muttered. I scratched my chin in thought. This was not going as planned. If we were not careful we may lose our only lead. "Out of the car," I told everyone. "We can't trust these grunts. Let's get involved."

We exited our cars just as the firefight got really exciting. I felt heat and a strong shove in the back that knocked me forward two steps. Then the thunder crack of an explosion assaulted my ears. The unmarked GovPol car behind me was a twisted wreck licked by flames. Its previous occupants were lying dazed, bruised and bloodied on the floor. After being briefly batted aside by the blast wave, the heavy, cold downpour of rain returned.

"They've got RPGs!" Al told me, clearly impressed.

The dynamic of the situation had changed now. Armed with rocket-propelled grenades, the criminals could clear this street in two minutes.

The SWAT team had reached the second floor now. They punctured blackened windows with their shots and allowed slim shafts of light to escape through the holes. The criminals would be struggling to fight on two fronts within the second floor. Roils of smoke were seeping through a broken pane of glass, but I was not sure if it was the start of a fire or the SWAT team using smoke bombs. Either way, it added a further element of danger that Ophelia Brigante may be taken down in the confused cross-fire.

I spied movement out the corner of my eye. A person, gender unidentified and swathed in black, had just slipped quietly out of the side alley. They were nervously considering whether they could flee down the street to safety before an officer spotted them.

"We've got a runner," I shouted. "Side entrance."

The runner checked once more that no officers were in pursuit. Amid the confusion of the RPG blast, they had decided it was an ideal opportunity to make a break for it.

"Tisi!" I shouted through the sheets of water drowning my voice. "The runner's yours!" I pointed towards our fleeing criminal in case she failed to hear me. Tisi withdrew her standard-issue pistol and took aim. The runner flipped mid-jog and snapped off a few rounds first. Two bullets careened harmlessly off the car's bullet-proof windshield and a third drove itself into the car door.

The runner's movements betrayed their gender as male. That meant he wasn't our primary target here. But he was a criminal, he had opened fire on us, he was a threat and he was about to get away. Not on my watch.

"Take him out!" I called to Tisi again. Three shots rang out from Tisi's gun but the runner had made good progress and she couldn't get a decent lock on her target. I didn't want to leave any loose threads.

"Grab him!" I told her.

"Alive?" she shouted back.

I shrugged noncommittally and shouted: "Okay." Tisi holstered her sidearm and sprinted down the street in pursuit.

Another broiling fireball flashed to the cloudy sky. The rear of another GovPol car lay in tattered, smoking ruins. A thin, barely visible and rapidly-dissipating trail of smoky vapor traced a line from the explosion back to its creators. There was a handler and a loader perched atop the building's roof, hiding behind a stone balustrade as they reloaded their weapon. Rapid bursts of gunfire continued to echo from the second floor. It sounded like a stalemate that could only be concluded when one team ran out of ammunition. Too many elements were going on at once.

"Al, with me," I shouted. "We're going in. Meg, break the MPF out of my trunk and see if you can take out the RPG on the roof. Then follow us inside."

Meg lifted a fat, stub-nosed gun from the trunk of my car. He pressed a button on the side of the weapon. The barrel extended to become a silencer, the butt did likewise to become a shoulder rest and a sniper scope appeared from inside the carrying handle. Now armed with a sleek, powerful rifle, Meg steadied himself on the trunk of the car and carefully fired one shot.

He took out the primary weapon-firer on the roof. The man's dead weight dragged his friend over the balustrade and they plunged six stories. They landed on the bubbling wreck of a GovPol car they themselves had destroyed. Poetic justice of sorts, burning on the pyre they made.

Al and I skirted the more immediate zone of fire and approached the building's entrance using its own walls as cover. Showing just how incompetent they were, none of the officers on ground-level had spotted us. We both drew our weapons as a precaution. We slipped inside.

The interior lobby was dark and creaky. Worn wooden steps led up to the first floor. There was no sign of life here. The lobby was barren and dilapidated. Al and I ascended to the first floor of the townhouse and spied three bodies down a narrow corridor. A lone SWAT member rested against a wall with his gun at his side. Sloppy. Very sloppy.

"Who's in charge here?" I asked him. The sound of gunfire echoing down from the next floor started dissipating.

The officer stood to attention, looking confused. He didn't ask me for any identification. "Miles, Sir. They're holed up on the next floor."

The second floor was busier. Wisps of smoke caressed the ceiling and walls were crazy-paved with the impact of numerous firearm rounds. There was more gunfire from further down the corridor to the left.

A strongly-built man in a flak jacket stood at the turn, talking into an ear mic. "Rush them and take them out," he insisted.

I heard the response he received. "They've got us pinned, Sarge," a female voice shouted.

The man sighed and laid his head against the wall. I was not impressed. It looked like he was in charge, but he was not in control of the situation. He should have been up there in the thick of the action. I decided to show him how it should be done.

I strode up to him as Meg joined us from the stairwell. "You Miles?" I asked.

"Yeah," he answered casually. "Who are you? You look like Secret Service."

I wafted a curl of smoke away from my face. "Where's Ophelia Brigante?"

"You the bloke who called this in?" Miles asked me.

"Listen officer..." I began.

"Sergeant," he corrected me.

"Sergeant, Lieutenant, Captain, I really don't care. We're dealing with a national security issue here and any officer of the law who doesn't give me their full cooperation will find themselves out of a job in literally thirty seconds. Where's Ophelia Brigante?"

"Left hand corridor," Miles told me. "Take another left. Door at the end. But...there's a problem."

"Details?" I asked.

"They've taken out two of my men and regrouped in the final corridor by the doorway."

I pushed past him and headed up the first corridor. Four SWAT members were taking cover behind the wall. One more lay in the corridor entrance, cut down when he tried to rush the enemy.

"Stat rep!" I shouted to one of the SWAT. A blonde female turned to me, probably the woman I heard on the radio.

"Sir?" she asked.

"Status report. What's going on in there?"

"Four perps in the room, Sir. They've got machine guns and are imbedded behind cover. Another three are controlling the corridor outside."

"Brigante one of them?"

"Ah, no Sir," the officer said guiltily. "She's on the floor in the room."

"Dead?"

"Not sure."

I sighed heavily. Maybe leaving this operation to the GovPol cannon fodder wasn't such a smart move after all. I could only trust myself to get things done right.

"Three in the corridor," I repeated. I nodded and pushed the SWAT back. I could immediately see where they went wrong. They'd edged up to the corridor wall, then stepped out. That presented an easy target to the enemy before they got their own bearings.

I removed my sidearm and held it in front of me, aimed and primed for use. By standing up against the opposite wall, I could use the angle of the corner to conceal me from half the corridor while I took care of the other half. Even up the odds a little.

One perp came into view as I edged across. He was waiting for action, but he needed to alter his aim to target me. I did not have that problem, and one head shot later there were just two to deal with. Continuing on my angled trajectory, it was easy to dispose of the other two in the corridor. The final perp's gun discharged into the wall as they slid to the floor.

I motioned the SWAT forward. Another SWAT body lay in the entrance to a room on the left. They'd been ambushed then pushed back.

The SWAT rushed down the corridor, taking up positions on either side of the doorway.

"Move," I said quietly.

The SWAT slid out of the way and I edged up to the door frame. I quickly stuck half my head into the open and took the briefest of glances into the room with my right eye. Several machine guns responded to my presence but I was already back behind cover.

The room was a wide, open space that took up half the floor. Wood-effect flooring, bare plaster walls. It was littered with burnished leather couches, classic movie posters and glass tables with half-emptied bottles of alcohol and the remnants of hastily brushed-aside white powder on them. There was a stage at the far end with a built-in DJ booth. Several 82" OLED widescreen TVs cycled through the sick, perverted images of hentai manga and the nastier anime films. Three bodies lay prone on the floor, one of them a SWAT member in the entrance. One of the other bodies on the floor was female, Caucasian, late twenties, five foot six, slim build, short spiky blonde hair, large hole in the chest. One of the armed assailants was cornered behind a couch to the right. I didn't have time to locate the other three, but there was only so much cover they could be using.

"Storm the place," I told the SWAT.

"They've got us covered, Sir. We can't. Jenson tried…" Her voice trailed off. I guessed the SWAT body in the entrance was a close friend.

"I'll provide covering fire. You four get ready to move and shoot anything that could hide a human."

I beckoned to Meg. He handed over the MPF. It was now back in its chunky, snub-nosed state.

"Ready?" I asked the SWAT. I aimed the MPF at the wall. It was a custom-built, NASRU exclusive. Far more powerful than the M4 guns the SWAT used.

I fired a random spray of bullets through the wall into the large room beyond. It didn't matter if I hit anything. I just needed the enemy to take cover long enough for the SWAT to establish a presence in the room.

They rushed the room and immediately opened fire on couches, tables and the DJ booth. One final bullet casing clattered to the floor then silence enveloped the area. I waited for the SWAT to confirm four kills then I moved into the room. I handed Meg the MPF and knelt next to Ophelia Brigante.

She was still alive. Barely conscious but hanging in there.

"She dead?" Al asked.

"Not yet," I told him. "Only a matter of time if she doesn't get immediate surgery."

"Please…" A whisper floated from her bloodied mouth. "Hospital." In her current state she was nothing more than a frightened little girl lost in a world of vice. Her eyes were wide. Full of pain and terror.

I removed a photograph from my inside jacket pocket. It was soggy with the rain, but the image itself was perfectly clear. It was a picture of a man in his mid-thirties. Caucasian. Deep blue eyes. Strong jaw line.

"You want the hospital? You gave this man a new identity. What's his new name?"

Ophelia blinked at the photo, finding it difficult to concentrate on it. The pain and blood loss was getting to her and her mind was starting to slip into unconsciousness.

"Ssss..." she started. Her breath faltered and her eyelids fluttered. She was rapidly falling unconscious. I needed to keep her awake. There was only one viable option. I removed my sidearm and pressed the muzzle against the deep gash in her chest. She barely had the strength to groan, but the sudden rush of new pain dragged her mind back from the abyss.

"Name!" I demanded.

"S...Strin..." she managed. She slumped, unconscious. Prodding her in the chest again wouldn't do any good. I checked the pulse on her neck. It was fading rapidly. She wouldn't make it. In less than a minute she'd be dead.

I stood, holstered my gun and pocketed the photograph.

"Strin," I said. I shrugged. First name or surname? Either way, it would be a very odd name for someone trying to keep hidden. There must've been more to it. Right now, the word 'Strin' was pretty useless.

I looked around the ruined remnants of Ophelia Brigante's apartment. Bullet holes, blood, bodies, cocaine, alcohol, smoke. This was a party venue. A place to hang out. I could see a bedroom with en suite on the opposite side of the hallway, presumably a small kitchen further down. Something was missing.

"Where's her lab?" I called out to anyone who would listen. I received noncommittal shrugs. "Where is Brigante's lab?" I repeated.

"We've cleared all the floors now," Sergeant Miles told me, having finally decided it was safe for him to join us. "There's nothing."

"Do we have any survivors? People we could ask, maybe?"

"Our orders were to take them out, Sir." Miles shrugged. "We were told to secure one person and damn the rest."

"Yes, Sergeant, and this body is that person. You've secured her a place in the morgue. Now you and your men will have to rip this entire building apart until you find the lab."

Miles moved to say something but I interrupted.

"I don't care how long it takes," I told him. "I want that lab."

"Yes, Sir," he answered, resigned and sullen.

This would take a long time, I realized. There was six floors to explore. A roof and a basement too. Even then we couldn't be guaranteed Brigante's lab was in the same location as her living quarters.

A ray of hope entered the room. Tisi arrived. She was soaking wet after a long chase. But she dragged with her a very alive and cuffed prisoner.

"Well done," I told her. I turned to the captured man. He was looking around the room with horror. He was so scared only an immense amount of bladder control had prevented him from wetting himself.

"Name?" I asked.

"S...Stapitski," he answered with fear.

"First name?"

"Ivan."

"Good." I took hold of him by the lapels of his jacket. "Ivan Stapitski, as you are the only person left alive here, you and I need a chat."

"I...I don't know nothing, man. Miles! Come on, man!"

I glanced across at Sergeant Miles.

"It's okay," he told me. "You can let him go. He's my informant."

I shrugged. "But he's not mine." I pushed Ivan up against a wall. "Where is Ophelia Brigante's lab, Ivan? Her ID forging lab?"

"I...I don't know. I don't know nothing. Honest."

"Of course you do, Ivan. Informants rarely tell their contacts more than ten percent of what they actually know. You've been hanging around here, haven't you?"

Ivan remained quiet. He needed a bit more persuading. Pinning him to the wall with my left arm, I withdrew my sidearm.

"What?!" he whispered. "Come on! Jesus!"

"Here's what we'll do, Ivan. I will ask you the question again. If you don't tell me, I will shoot you. Somewhere non-fatal. A limb. I will ask the question *again*. No response, another limb. You get the idea. So, we will start here..."

I jammed my gun into Ivan's lower left arm and cocked back the firing pin.

"Where is the lab?"

Ivan gasped twice. He wet himself. "Trapdoor," he answered hoarsely. "Under the stage."

I holstered my gun and released Ivan. I moved to the back of the large, open room and started prodding the stage front with my shoe. One section gave way slightly. I kicked it harder and a 3-ft portion of the stage front collapsed backwards. Drawing my weapon, I quickly peered inside. A crawlspace ended in a low-lit square room cluttered with junk.

"Hidden room," I called back to my Erinyes. "To the left. It's safe."

I pocketed my sidearm again and crawled under the stage. The crawlspace was littered with fragments of wood. Shafts of light filtered through bullet holes in the stage.

I stood up when I reached the hidden room. It was lit with one low-strength red bulb. It doubled up as a storage area and a photographic dark room. I checked all the equipment. The fingerprint burner and laser eye scanner were both portable. It was unlikely she would have brought her clients into this space. I suspected she brought her equipment out and set it up on the stage before the client arrived. The dark room was set up at the rear. Trays for developing, a washing line to hang the images on, a store of chemicals to the right. A table to the left was set up for replicating ID cards for those clients who had still not embraced the technology of RFID implants. I couldn't see anything that could actually alter the RFIDs, though. That element of our quarry's new identity remained a mystery.

Two large steel filing cabinets rested next to the table. It looked as though Brigante took lessons from the plastic surgeon. She'd kept records, and kept them in paper form.

I opened one cabinet. Fortunately, Brigante didn't take lessons about filing as well. Everything was stored in alphabetical order. I selected the correct cabinet for 'S' and flicked through to 'Strin'. There were three files. Strine, Henrietta. Stringer, Daniel. Strintock, Mervyn.

I could ignore the first file: our quarry was not female. I removed the other two and quickly flicked through them. Stringer, Daniel: perfect match. We had our man.

I quickly called General Miller. I thought he'd be excited by our progress.

"Stone," he said when he answered. "Have you got him?"

"We know who he is, Sir," I answered.

"What?!"

"Who he is, Sir. His new identity. It's only a matter of time now."

The General blinked in surprise. "Is that all? You have a long way to go yet, Stone."

"But now we know who he is, Sir, we can track him down. Once we have a fix, we can work out the finer points of bringing him in."

"Okay, I want a debriefing. We can talk about these 'finer points' as well. See me at eleven tomorrow. My office."

The General cut off the call. There went my good mood. Now I had to fly from Texas to New York so I could upload the data we'd collated today and file reports. That was going to be another all-nighter at the office. Then tomorrow I would have to fly from New York to Washington to see the General.

I crawled back out from under the stage with the file in my hand. I passed it over to Al and removed my cell phone again. I hit Speed Dial #2 and got through to Sam, the Surveillance Operative.

"Stringer, Daniel. Same process as before, so check him for CCTV, RFID, all the usual. Probably first show up in Texas after Jose Manula went off the map. Get back to me as soon as." I didn't wait for a response. I cut off the call and used

Speed Dial #1. "Brent. We're heading back. Contact the jet and tell them to power up."

"Yes, Sir," Brent managed before I cut him off as well. I glanced about the room.

"You can pack up and go home now," I told Miles. "We have what we came for."

"Which is?"

"What we came for," I repeated. "Oh, and get the FBI in here. They'll be interested in the lab."

"The...?" Miles began as I and my Erinyes walked into the corridor. "I thought you *were* the FBI," he shouted after us. "Who the hell are you guys?"

Who were we? I thought. We were the guys who could do whatever it took. We were the guys who were going to hunt down and capture the most wanted man on the planet. We were the guys who didn't have to answer a single Goddamn question from someone like Miles. We could come in, we could cause havoc, we could leave it for him to clear up the mess. We were NASRU, and we'd got a flight to catch.

SEVEN

I finished my fifth cup of coffee. It had been light outside for hours now. The morning rush of traffic had already abated. My operations staff had called it a night, gone home, slept and returned refreshed. I was still putting the final touches to a series of reports it had taken me all night to complete. This was the part of my promotion that I hated – the paperwork.

Alecto knocked on my inner office door. He walked through when I beckoned. He threw a fresh light blue shirt at me.

"Thanks," I said. "Yours?"

He nodded. "Been here all night?" he asked.

"Reports don't write themselves." I removed my jacket and started unbuttoning my day-old shirt.

"That's one area of research they really should look into, then. Same with hangover-free alcohol."

I slipped the new shirt on. The color went well with my suit. "How do I look?"

"It would be wrong to insult a superior," Al answered. It was the answer I was expecting.

I sat back in my chair and began rechecking the last paragraph of my report.

"Shall I join Meg and Tisi?" Al asked. He was not sure what was expected of him right now.

I shook my head. "They're helping the team track the 'Stringer' name on Cyclops. Don't want to overcrowd them. I've got to meet Miller at eleven, so while I'm gone you keep everyone in check."

"Sure you want to put me in charge?" He leaned forward and whispered. "Stone, I'm a control freak."

I looked at him for a moment. "You'll do fine. But my office is out of bounds."

My intercom buzzed. The lobby wanted to patch through to me. I activated the speaker-only button.

"Lieutenant Jack Stone," I said.

"Sir," the lobby guard said through the speaker. "This is the lobby. There is a Miss Natalya Czernokovsky here to see you. Shall I send her up?"

"What?" I said in surprise.

"Sir?" the guard asked for clarification.

I remained, for the moment, in stunned silence. This was something quite unexpected.

"Tell her I'm busy," I decided in the end.

"She told me you'd say that, Sir. She told me to insist you see her. Shall I have her escorted out of the building?"

I sighed. "No. Don't do that. I'll come down to deal with her myself."

I broke the connection. Al looked quizzically at me.

"Girlfriend problems?" he asked.

"It's not a problem," I told him.

"If my wife came to see me at work, I'd think it was a problem."

I checked my watch. I needed to set off to the airport soon. "Your personal life is none of my concern," I told Al as I stood. "And mine should be none of yours."

I strode through the outer office and took the elevator to the lobby.

Nat was standing in the open space, silhouetted against the glass-paneled front in a summery dress and short jacket. Two guards occupied the far end of the lobby but there was no other human traffic.

Feeling a little angry I walk up to her. Nat already had her arms crossed in a defensive stance.

"Nat," I said. "What is it? I'm a little busy here."

She snorted. "Busy," she repeated and nodded her head. "I waited for you last night. Waited for you to take me to my favorite restaurant. Remember?"

"Shit," I said. I'd completely forgotten. The plastic surgeon. The ID forger. Dinner with Nat never once crossed my mind. I'd only made the reservations the day before.

"Then," she continued, "stupidly I thought maybe you were going to meet me there. So I got all dressed up and took a cab to the restaurant. I sat at a table by myself for *an hour*, trying to convince the waiter that *someone* was going to turn up."

"Seriously, it has been a very busy and trying time for me recently."

"It always is, Jack."

"And you knew that right from the start." I sighed. "I'm sorry, okay? I've got a plane to catch."

"Where to?" she asked. She knew I couldn't tell her. She was just trying to provoke a more argumentative state. I was not going to fall for the bait in the lobby of my own office building, so I remained silent.

"I have to go," I eventually told her. "We can discuss this later."

"Later?! It's always 'later' with you, Jack. Problem is, there never is a 'later' because by then there's something else to keep you busy. This isn't a relationship. It's a series of one-night stands."

I slapped my hands against my thighs in exasperation. "You knew. You knew it would be like this. And you were fine with it. Why now, all of a sudden? Why are you suddenly demanding more and more? What do you want from me?"

"You, Jack," she answered quietly. "I just want you. To be with you. I know it is selfish, but this isn't enough any more. Я выхожу вы."

"Don't start with the Russian! Trying to hide behind the language barrier!"

Nat shook her head. She looked as though she may be about to cry. She turned from me and walked out of the building. I didn't chase after her, I didn't call out. I let her go. I couldn't save the world and my relationship at the same time. I still had time to set Nat straight, to show her that I cared. I did not have time to keep General Miller waiting. My job had to come first. She knew that.

I headed back up to my office to collect my cell phone and weapon. Al studied me as I entered my office.

"How did it go?" he asked.

I ignored his question. I angrily thrust my sidearm into its holster. "What time's my fucking flight?" I asked.

"Erm...thirty five minutes," he answered. "Went *that* well, then."

I grabbed my cell phone. "Come on," I told Al. "You're taking me to the airport."

"I am?" he asked, following me out of the office.

I stopped, turned and pointed a finger at him. "And we're driving in silence."

"Yes, Sir."

The plane was delayed as it entered Washington D.C. airspace. It had something to do with another craft that had a malfunctioning beacon. We had to wait in a holding pattern. We circled the outskirts until the city's defense grid could confirm the craft was friendly and posed no threat.

I headed up to Miller's office. Thanks to the plane delay I was an hour late. Miller, with a natural gift, immediately blamed me.

"The plane was delayed," I offered.

"Well, I'm a very busy man, don't you realize that?" the General responded.

"Yes, Sir, but I don't think the pilot was fully aware of it," I answered back. I was a little annoyed that he really did seem to blame me for this.

Miller fixed me with an uncomfortable stare. "Sit," he finally said with great reluctance.

I did so. It was like I'd just been called up in front of the principal.

"Lock the door," he told me.

Annoyance crept back into my psyche. He'd just told me to sit then immediately stand up again. I stepped over, locked his office door, then returned to my seat.

"I've read your report, Stone. You've made excellent progress so far. But it isn't enough. I need tangible results."

"We have a name, Sir. I would say that was tangible."

"And a location?" he asked, leaning forward.

"Excuse me, Sir, but how long did it take for the other two agents to get Jackson's new pseudonym?"

"A few months," Miller admitted. He knew I had done good. He was trying to pressure me, to make me work harder. It wasn't going to happen – I always worked at 100%.

"Then perhaps in the interest of speeding things up, Sir, you can tell me exactly how we came to make a clairvoyant who hates us."

The General quietly nodded. He was my mentor through training. He knew how stubborn I could become, how little I regarded rules and authority when I really needed to know something. He knew he had to tell me.

"What I am about to tell you, Stone, is so classified that by rights I should shoot you as soon as you walk out of this office."

"I understand, Sir," I answered. "But I think I need to know this."

"This whole clairvoyance thing…it was just an accidental side-effect from what we can tell. Project Omicron was designed to create a super soldier. We're not talking strength and robotic implants, but someone whose main weapon is intelligence. When we completed our experiment on Zeus Jackson, we discovered this extra ability, an off-shoot from his mental enhancements. We dubbed it The Oracle Design. We then set up a database of tasks."

"What do you mean by a database of tasks?" I asked. "A list of ways in which we could exploit this?"

"Exactly. If he really could predict the future, we thought it prudent to evaluate the possible ramifications and applications for it. Maybe, he could predict the movements of the enemy, from a single soldier to a battalion, or the enemy's army as a whole. There were other uses, but this was the major factor. This and the ability to forewarn us of imminent terrorist attacks: something that, despite us hunting him down, he is still more than happy to do for us."

I glanced around the office in thought for a moment. "So he's a significant threat to us. If the enemy gets hold of him, he can use his predictions against us on the battlefield."

"It isn't just on the battlefield that he poses a threat, Stone. There are many more ways and many more people who can exploit this."

The General leaned forward and rested his arms on the desk. "You want me to start small? If he's working for the Cosa Nostra he can warn them of raids by GovPol and FBI. Or hunt down undercover agents. Or tell them who is about to assassinate whom and where traps are set. On the other end of the scale…we've had a computer run a simulation of the stock market based on what would happen if you bought and sold shares at exactly the right moment in exactly the right stock. Daniel Stringer could start playing the stock market with just $50 and in two months the country would be in a financial meltdown thanks to the worst stock market crash in history. It would make a mockery of the financial disasters of 1929 and 2008. That is the kind of damage he can do, Stone. Can we really take the chance that he won't? He wasn't smart before the experiment, so in his naivety he could easily be corrupted by someone."

I sighed and rubbed my forehead. "So, he predicts the future by thinking logically, extrapolating the most obvious outcome based on a series of events he has witnessed."

"You have an idea for capturing him?" Miller asked.

"Nothing concrete as yet. But logic must be the key. Acting illogically is what we need. We need to make events more random, more unpredictable. And the most illogical and unpredictable thing of all is human emotion. That is what we need to exploit – his emotions. Somehow we need to get him so emotional he'll slip up."

"Very good, but how do we do that? He no longer has family to use as leverage."

I shook my head. "No, Sir. Loved ones as leverage is too predictable. Too logical. He would see it coming. I'm not sure how yet, but we need to attack him mentally, not physically. Undermine his confidence. Add an element of the unknown."

The General rubbed his chin for a moment. "I like it. The tactics are for you to work out. That's why I chose you for this assignment. I have confidence that you will prevail, Lieutenant. Good luck."

"Yes, Sir," I said, grasping the hint that this meeting was now over. "Thank you, Sir."

I stood and unlocked the office door.

"Oh, and Jack?" the General called. "Try and get some sleep on the flight back. You look terrible."

"Yes, Sir."

I left Miller's office, headed downstairs and out into Washington. I walked across the grounds of the NASRU HQ. I needed to fly back to New York and debrief my team. It was time I told them the truth.

Andi Clayton checked the sliver of card in her hand. It was the one Daniel had given her on their last meeting. It contained details of the next rendezvous, another afternoon meeting. This time it was within the BattleKarts arena on Coney Island, and she was already running late.

She was feeling a little flushed, the last vestiges of anger dissipating from her. She'd just come from a frustrating meeting with her editor. Following Daniel's instructions, she had inserted the line "The terrorists' motives were unknown and we can only wonder what their grievances may be" into an article. The line was immediately excised from the article and she was called in for a chat by the editor. The Government Advisor had stood silently beside him with an ePad. Andi was told that this kind of irresponsible journalism gave voice to the terrorists' cause. When she countered that no one knew what their cause was, she was told it was death, mayhem and the destruction of America, and that nobody wanted that, now did they? It had proven Daniel right: the media was censored. That realization had put her in a bad mood that was only just beginning to wane despite 45 minutes of calming window shopping.

Professional matches were taking place within the BattleKarts arena so she had to pay a small entrance fee. She slipped inside and made an immediate beeline for the restrooms – her professional work suit would be too conspicuous in a place like this, so she'd stuffed a black band Tee, Daisy Dukes and fishnets in her bag. Her heeled ankle boots didn't quite scream rock chick but they would have to do. Quickly changed, she ascended the steps of the concrete viewing platform. She scanned the crowds and spotted

Daniel. He was relaxing on the steps and taking in the sun. He didn't look at her as she approached. He held his head up to the sun. Bright, blinding rays glinted off his sunglasses. He was wearing faded denims, a grey Tee-shirt and a black suit jacket. He seemed flushed, more like he'd been exercising than lazing at the races.

"Late again," he chided. "Quite a habit."

"But you knew I'd be late anyway," Andi responded. She casually dropped her bag on a step and sat next to it.

"Foxy look," Daniel commented. "Like the boots. Rock on."

Andi absently scratched one fishnet-clad calf. It wasn't the kind of opening comment she was expecting.

Daniel looked forward, out over the arena. The next battle was about to start. Go-karts were dotted along the length of the dystopian-themed racetrack. The large, open kill arena raised in the center of the track was empty. Laser guns were primed, the sensors on the go-karts and racing helmets were activated and the special weapon sensors on the floor of the track winked on and off.

"Bubblegum Killer's going to win this one," Daniel said. "She's not the odds-on favorite, but she has the confidence."

Andi scanned the starting grid and spotted Bubblegum Killer. She was the one in pink. She had already removed her secondary laser gun from its holster.

"So immature," Andi muttered. She'd never been a fan of BattleKarts. The mere concept of racing and shooting at the same time appalled her: 'the need for speed, the thrill of the kill' as the BattleKarts tagline went.

An announcer barked out something distorted and unintelligible over the PA system.

"So, if you can see into the future," Andi asked, "I presume you know who's going to win, do you?"

"Yeah," Daniel answered. "Bubblegum Killer. I just told you."

"And you know what's going to happen?"

"I do."

"Then what's the point of watching the race?"

He looked at her. "What's the point of anything?" he asked. "This conversation, for example. I know exactly how it will pan out, what will be said. Kind of makes having the conversation in the first place a moot point. But here I am anyway, talking to you."

"Doesn't that get a little boring then?"

"You have no idea." He looked out over the arena. The light turned green and the go-karts leapt into action.

"So do you know what I'm thinking?" Andi asked.

"No, only what you'll say."

"So explain it to me then. You can actually see into the future?"

"Well," Daniel answered. "Not really *see*, no. Predict."

"Isn't that the same?"

"No. I know what is going to happen, but I can't actually...you know..." He gestured with his hands. "Actually physically *see* it."

"How?" she breathed.

"Ah, the big reveal. Here's where you get your story. Well...the one about me, anyway.

"It all harks back to The Evil Government," he began. "Secret... clandestine... conspiratorial... experimentation." He stopped. "Hmmm, could have been worded better. I guess seeing the future doesn't help with my vocabulary.

"They wanted a super soldier, as evil military types do. Someone with mental abilities far beyond the enemy. I presume you know the theory that we only use ten percent of our brain functions. Utter rubbish, actually. Dispelled a long time ago. Only idiots still think it's true. You?"

Andi realized it was a loaded question and elected to remain quiet.

"Well, okay," Daniel continued. "The military are, of course, idiots, and they believed this nonsense. So they thought, if we're only using ten percent of the brain now, how about utilizing some of the rest of it? Reconnect broken or disused neural pathways, redirect certain functions. It's a bit like rewiring the hardware of a computer – a wire here, a bit of solder there and suddenly you've doubled the memory capacity. Do you see?"

"Yes, but through a haze of fog," Andi answered.

"I know," he replied. "I know you don't fully understand or see the relevance. I also know you were going to give that response. God, having conversations is so wearisome."

"Where do they do these experiments?" Andi asked.

"That doesn't matter, and they don't do them any more. I saw to that. What matters are the unexpected side-effects this experiment had. You know, you're really rather attractive. Beautiful eyes."

"I…erm…thank you," Andi stammered. She felt flushed with embarrassment, a flush that quickly turned to anger as she realized he knew exactly what he was doing.

"You knew exactly when to say that, didn't you?" she demanded.

"Yes, you're right," he told her. "I knew when the perfect time was to say that to you. That's the one good thing about this curse – it makes asking women out for dates ridiculously easy."

"Can we get back to the experiment?" Andi asked.

"Fine. If we must. So, the experiment. Unforeseen side-effects. Well, one unforeseen side-effect. Everything else went as planned. They enhanced my IQ and my mental capacity.

"Now, take the eyes, for example. They work far better than we realize. The problem is not with the eyes themselves, but with the brain's ability to process images. It just doesn't have the speed or capacity to take in *everything* the eye sees, so details are lost along the way, mainly periphery vision and distant objects. With my enhancements this is not a problem. Also, my brain can process those images better, glean information from them far faster than any other human on the planet.

"Combined with my enhanced IQ, this means I can read, for example, body language in such detail I can know all I need to know about a person with a glance. If I look at a crowded street, I can lip-read what people are saying, detect their body language, facial expressions, the clothes they are wearing etcetera etcetera. Then I predict, using a sound logical basis, what they are going to do next and how they will react to each other's presence or that of nearby objects.

"And there we go. That is how I can see into the future."

"Well," Andi breathed. "That sounds mighty impressive."

"Thank you," Daniel answered, insincerely. "But, everyone has the ability. They just don't as yet have the…" he tapped his forehead, "…power."

"And you're infallible? You can always predict the future?"

"I use logical analysis to make my predictions and emotions are by their very nature illogical, so occasionally with extreme emotions I can slip up. But, by and large, yes I'm infallible. Bit like the Pope…"

"Extreme emotions," Andi said, mainly to herself.

"Love, anger…you know what emotions are, don't you?"

She looked at him disparagingly. "I may be in shellshock from the bomb you've just dropped on me, but there's no need for comments like that."

He merely shrugged, then nodded at the arena. Bubblegum Killer had won her race. Andi felt dazed when she realized. Daniel could actually be telling the truth about this.

"She won," Andi said.

Daniel merely nodded and grinned.

"They did this to you?" she asked. "The Government?"

"Yes…" He paused.

"How many others are there like you?"

"I'm the only one. Entirely unique. Special. When I escaped my facility, I made sure I erased all their data on me and the experiments first. I'm now the only one who knows how to replicate it."

Andi thought about this. "Are they after you?" she asked.

"Very much so," he nodded. "Hence you only getting my first name. If they catch me, it won't be to use my abilities. It will be to open me up to discover *how* so they can replicate it. I don't much fancy being lobotomized. I've grown too accustomed to being mentally superior to everyone on the planet to go back to how I was."

"How long have you been on the run, then?"

Daniel shrugged. "Three years, give or take."

"Three years?! That long?"

"They're finding it slightly tricky to locate me. I always know when they're coming."

"Hah," Andi laughed softly, in a daze. "Yeah."

"Unfortunately, Miss Clayton…may I call you Andi?" She nodded and he continued. "Unfortunately Andi, now you know too much. This Government of ours will happily kill you to keep you silent."

"What?!" she exclaimed.

"But they'll never know about you as long as you don't actually go to the authorities and tell them about me." He smiled. "It's a kind of insurance. You keep quiet about me, you stay alive."

"Then why are you telling me all this? I thought you were telling me because you wanted me to write an article."

"I do," he nodded. "Just not yet. A great upheaval is coming. The huddled masses are stirring. They're beginning to realize which side has their best interests at heart. And it isn't the Government. My story is not required to spur the people into action. It would just be a pebble in a growing avalanche right now. I tell you the story. But you do not act on it yet. When the revolution comes, you can tell everyone about me. And believe me, they'll want to know."

"You almost sound as though you're a God."

"Well," he shrugged. "I guess I am the closest anyone has come to being a God. Although, again, there's the Pope, but technically she can't do what I can…

"Anyway," he concluded. "I believe it is time for this conversation to come to an end."

"Will we meet again?"

"Of course," he responded. "We've only just started. Next time let's make it something a little more civilized. Dinner.

My place. We can discuss this more over some nasi goreng and an expensive bottle of wine. You bring the wine.

"Meantime, see if you can find out where all those missing billions of Mars terraforming money have gone. See how long it takes before the Government Advisor shuts you down." He nodded. "I'll…" He made a phone symbol with his hand. "Take care."

"Erm…" Andi answered.

"That's your cue to leave. I've got other things to do. Await my call. Then wear something elegant and sexy. This rock chick thing doesn't suit you. And don't forget the wine."

Andi got up to leave. She took a few steps then turned back. She'd just realized he'd told her to dress sexy and bring expensive wine to an interview. "I…I'm not sure…about the…"

"But you will," he pre-empted her.

"I will?" she asked.

"I know you will," he answered with a wry grin on his face. Of course he knew, Andi thought as she left. He knew everything.

EIGHT

I headed straight to the office from the airport. It was already early evening. I was hoping my team had unearthed some evidence by now.

The elevators were undergoing repairs, so I bounded up several flights of stairs. I passed a curious sight en route, one which I recalled Al mentioning: a large marble statue lay in the second-floor stairwell, having been left there overnight by a team of workmen struggling day-by-day to inch it up to its destination. Their silly plight lightened my mood.

I had already sent the Erinyes home. We'd had a few late nights and if the net was closing in on Stringer I wanted my people fresh and alert to tackle him. I would fill them in on our insurmountable task when they were revitalized.

The offices were largely deserted, with only Sam the surveillance guy still at his post.

"Others have just left," the Brit told me. "They went home, left me to finish collecting the results. Broke the damn lift on the way down too. Idiots."

"Okay," I said. I dumped my coat on a desk and sat on a spare swivel chair. "What results do you have?"

"Not much. Here."

He activated an OLED screen mounted on the far wall. It displayed a green wire frame map of the entire country.

"Stringer, Dan or Daniel. One thousand two hundred and eighty three results."

"That many?" I asked, surprised. "I guess we should just be thankful he didn't choose John Smith as his latest pseudonym."

"Here are the pings."

The wire frame map became covered with millions of small red dots. Most of them were grouped around large cities. Some punctured the relative blankness of rural, mountain and desert locations.

"Reduce the pings to those that have occurred since Jose Manula went off the grid," Sam continued, "and we have…"

The map changed again. Most of the dots vanished but it still left a chaotic mass of red splodges.

"Wait, wait," I said. "Is all this necessary? Can't you just locate a Daniel Stringer who hasn't appeared before Manula went off the grid? Save time going though everyone?"

"As the Spanish Armada said when they tried to sail to Cambridge: Norfolk in way."

"What?"

"Sorry," Sam apologized. "Don't think that joke works unless you know a bit about English geography. Basically, we've tried that. No results. Seems our friend has a new identity that already existed. Or he's somehow managed to create a back-story of RFID pings. Which I consider highly unlikely."

I sighed. "Okay, let's continue with the long haul."

"Right. To reiterate: here are all the pings since Manula went off the grid. Now we map out their travel habits…"

The wire frame map methodically joined the dots for each Daniel Stringer, showing movements over the past six months. It only served to clutter the map even more, with the cities becoming completely lost behind a sea of crimson. More red lines shot across the country and occasionally flew off the map altogether as the owner headed abroad.

"And what does this show?" I asked.

"A complete mess," Sam helpfully pointed out. "Totally useless like this. But, now we have the travel habits mapped out, we can look at each individual person and see if there's anything suspicious about their movements."

"And?"

"I think we might have located a drugs entrepreneur, actually. Often visits Colombia on very short, quick business trips. Anyway, that's not who we're after, and it's not the most interesting thing here. So let me remove the other Stringers..."

The computer rapidly removed the red dots and lines from the wire frame map, and gradually the clutter lessened.

"Anything jump out at you yet?" Sam asked me.

I shrugged. "Not really. Where am I looking?"

"Let me speed it up for you."

Finally the map was virtually clear of red. Twelve dots remained in almost a straight line from Kentucky to Texas.

"There," Sam said proudly.

"What the hell?" I said. "Why aren't they joined up with lines now?"

"Because these are all different RFID signatures, not the same person traveling around. Suspicious, right?"

"Suspicious?" I said. "That's an understatement. Each one of these 'people' has only had their RFID pinged one day in the last six months?! When was the last time you heard of someone buying groceries, checking their bank account, recharging their car, going to a bar etcetera just once in six months? Half a year's worth of groceries in one trip, then being a hermit?!"

"It just...doesn't add up, does it?" Sam answered.

"He's changing it," I breathed. "He's re-encoding the RFID signature every time he uses it."

"Yeah," Sam said. "That's the only possibility I could come up with. He's changing his damn RFID signature every few days. How can someone do that? To completely alter the identity of an RFID seems impossible, but to alter the carrier frequency?! Who *is* this guy?"

I shook my head in disbelief and turned back to Sam. "Unbelievable," I whispered.

"Think *that's* unbelievable? Wait for this one! The last ping was four months ago. He's disappeared. Completely. He has to...*has to* use his RFID in today's society. But it hasn't shown up in four months. Only two explanations for that. One, he's got another new identity. Two, he's dead."

"No," I said. "Why would he use a completely new surgeon and ID forger four whole months before our net is closing in on him? No, that can't be it. As for being dead, believe me when I say it would be very difficult to kill this man. Maybe he can mask the RFID completely."

"Use some kind of special fractal virus that disrupts any systems from recording it?" Sam shrugged. "I guess it's possible. In theory. But the best supercomputers couldn't do that."

"Even so, that's what he's done. He's actually managed to step off the grid, bypass an infallible system. He's made it completely impossible to track him down."

Sam shook his head in frustration. "If that's the case, the only thing we have to go on is his last recorded location. But that was four months ago and he was moving every few days anyway. How can we track him?"

I looked at the map again, and something in my brain clicked. "Moving, yes. But in a fairly straight line. He had a fixed destination, and there's a good chance he still resides in his destination. The first ping was in Texas, right?"

"Yeah," Sam answered.

"And he's been moving North East through Arkansas, Tennessee and Kentucky. Follow the imaginary line to its logical conclusion, Sam."

Sam did so, then looked surprised. "Oh dear God," he exclaimed.

I turned to Sam, grinned and nodded my head slowly. I had a good feeling in my gut. The net was indeed closing.

"It's New York. He's here."

I got home to a dark, quiet house. The living room light kicked in when it sensed my presence. The bedroom light was manually operated, but it offered no more illumination on the status of Nat. Before spying the envelope resting on my pillow, I had already noticed that her vanity chest was devoid of the usual clutter. My stomach grumbled, warning my mind that something bad was going on. I opened the envelope, still not ready to accept the expected message within.

She had left.

Gone.

Just like that.

It couldn't be true, I decided. It must be a joke. We'd had our problems before, but we'd always overcome them. She should by now be used to my absence, the cancelled dinner dates, the nights alone. She'd never done anything like this before. Not even threatened it. She couldn't have gone. She couldn't have left me. Not without talking about it.

I'd convinced myself she was just trying to shake me up, and she'd be in soon after a night partying with her girlfriends. Then I remembered she didn't have any girlfriends – since leaving home and coming to New York I was all she'd had.

I activated my cell phone and called her, just in case she'd been called in for a shift at the hospital. I was told in no uncertain terms that her number had been disconnected. I tried her sister, but she claimed to know nothing. Her mother used a different tactic and claimed not to know English. It still didn't stop them both from berating me for not treating Nat the way she deserved. I tried to explain that it wasn't my fault, that she had changed, not me. But I was fighting a losing battle against biased family members. I switched off the cell phone and flopped back onto the bed.

It was going to be another sleepless night for me.

I was feeling drained the following morning. My mind had not rested at all, even though my body refused to move from the bed for several hours. I had tried to map out my game plan for the next few days with regard to Daniel Stringer's capture, but my thoughts kept sliding back to my problems with Nat.

As I headed to work I knew I must dispel thoughts of Nat to the darkest recesses of my mind and concentrate wholly on the task I had been assigned.

I must have looked terrible as I entered my office. The vaguely surprised stares from the professionals on my floor indicated something about my demeanor that was unsavory. The trot up the stairs didn't help. The elevator was still undergoing repairs. What the hell did my people do to it?

"Where are we?" I asked my staff as soon as I arrived. Everyone seemed frozen in time. Surveillance, Analysis and Collation sat bored at their desks. In my inner sanctum, visible through the glass door, the Erinyes stared into middle distance.

"Where…what?" Brent the Collation Officer started as though woken from a particularly confusing dream.

"Where are we?" I repeated.

"With what?"

"With the…" I paused. My brain certainly was addled. I was getting frustrated with my team for not completing their tasks without realizing I hadn't actually assigned them any tasks in the first place.

"You okay, Sir?" Brent asked.

"No," I responded. "Give me a couple of minutes."

I headed into my office. The Erinyes stood as I entered. It pleased me a little to note they had finally removed their stark black suit / white shirt combos. Suits were still the order of the day, as they should be. But now we had color and pattern. It dispelled the notion that they were Secret Service in favor of perhaps being employees in the financial sector.

"Rough night?" Al asked me as I slumped in my seat. I stared at him for a moment.

"Right, we have work to do," I told the three of them. Now was not the time to enter into a personal conversation, and this was certainly not the environment for it. "Have you been briefed on the latest about our man?"

"Somewhat, Sir," Tisi responded. "We know he's managed to disguise his RFID from tracking, and we know he's probably in New York among roughly seven million other Caucasian men."

"Right. So we're doing the needle search in a field full of haystacks thing. Any ideas?"

"About how to track him? No."

I sighed. I didn't want to spell out the answers to them all the time. These people needed to think for themselves. "Come on, people. Think it through. Are we just going to keep shoving our hands into the haystacks and hope the needle will get impaled on a finger?"

I looked across to Meg, but he simply shrugged. Al was my best hope. He was as sharp as a tack. He was as sharp as a needle buried amongst the hay. But the man we were searching for was so sharp his point had been refined down to a tip just a few atoms wide.

"How much do we know about the man himself?" Al asked.

"You mean likes and dislikes?" I asked back.

"Yeah. Maybe we can build up a profile of where he is most likely to be found. Does he go to bars, restaurants, theater, sports events? For a start, if he's still in New York I'd expect him to try his best to remain inconspicuous. So I think we can rule out him residing in the more up-market areas of the city."

"Okay, good," I said. "At least you're thinking. If you'd like to run your eyes over his personal data and create a profile, be my guest. Problem is, I can't really see the point."

"Meaning?"

"We don't know if his personality has changed since the experimentation, Al. He could be completely different now. It is quite likely he is. Besides, how much is it going to help really? We determine he likes quiet bars, for example. How many are there in New York City, and how many of us are there to keep watch on them? It's just not practical. Certainly not in the short term."

"Then we need some other way of tracking him down," Tisi told me.

"Right," I said. I felt like I was teaching school kids here. They were trying my patience. "Don't make me spell it all out for you. Come on, someone give me an answer."

None were forthcoming.

"He's a terrorism informant," I told the Erinyes. "We can go in via that route. I know it's not much but it's the best game plan we have. We can use the FBI, CIA, NSA and Homeland Security's tracking systems to keep tabs on terrorist cells and see if anything flags up. We don't know how he comes by his information yet and we may be left blowing in the wind. But it is our best shot at the moment. Agreed?"

"Yes, Sir," all three Erinyes answered.

"We'll get Surveillance to monitor the activity of known and suspected terrorist cells and put markers on all affiliated websites. We can sift through reports from agents in the field to see if we come up with anything that way. He may be in contact with someone we're monitoring. Aside from that, our only option would be running the image scanner with filed CCTV and drone footage, but that could take a very long time before we get a result. So, for now, we don't search for Stringer. We search for people he may know."

"There is one other consideration, Sir," Tisi told me. "He may not be in New York anymore."

"True," I told her, "but this is all we have to go on. In situations like this gut feelings are invaluable. My gurgling gut is telling me New York is where all this will play out."

"Right," Al said. "We'll start…"

I cut him off. "Wait," I said. "There's something else you need to know."

"About Stringer?"

"He's going to be more tricky than we originally thought to catch."

"*More* tricky?" Al exclaimed. "Stone, it's looking impossible as it is."

"Then factor in this little nugget as well. He can predict the future."

"Excuse me?"

"What do you mean?" Meg chipped in.

"Exactly what I've just said. When we *do* track him down, when we go after him… He'll know we're coming."

"Is this a demotion?" Al asked, mirroring my own initial thoughts about this assignment. "They've given us an impossible assignment. Are they expecting us to fail?"

"We just have to outwit him, Al. That's all."

"That's all?!" he exclaimed. "Isn't Stringer supposed to be, like, the smartest man on the planet or something?"

"A physics professor at M.I.T is far more intelligent than me," I pointed out. "But I've got more street smarts. He knows about quantum mechanics while I know tactics and weaponry. Stringer doesn't know everything. He can't. When it comes to it, we'll figure out his weakness and use it against him. *When* it comes to it. For now, we need to concentrate on finding him. So get working."

Andi Clayton was completely unaware of the complex manhunt currently being conducted for her mysterious and annoying contact. She felt deep in her gut that she was about to enter something that would forever change her life and the lives of those around her. The feeling multiplied with trepidation, snowballing into a low rumbling fear. She realized that there was still time: time to leave, to back out, to say no to whatever was about to envelop her. But if she left now, if she backed away from Daniel and his words, she could be exorcising herself from the biggest events to hit the country since the Civil War.

Her interest was certainly piqued enough to risk everything for the promise of one glorious story. It had been too long since the country had been given the chance to gnaw on a really juicy piece of news. If what Daniel said was true, she could be the chef.

Determined, with the bit between her teeth, Andi headed into work.

She had decided to research the missing billions of Mars terraforming money, to confirm Daniel's accusations. But she was unsure where to start. She tried the archives. All the data was bland, uniform and watered-down. It seemed that the newspaper had for a long while been blasé about this crisis. In fact, the words 'crisis', 'lost' and 'debt' never featured in any articles, never mind such phrases as 'misappropriation of funds'. The articles all extolled the virtues of the project. They made it clear that costs were bound to rise with such a venture. No amount of money could be too much for creating another habitable world for the good, loyal citizens of the United States of America.

She could see their point. A new world to populate, new resources to cultivate, new horizons for the incessant population explosion to explore and call their own. Even though space-faring technology still called for a crippling lift-off and a full year of zero-G traveling, it would be worth it. In these intervening decades, carbon dioxide would be pumped into the atmosphere by colossal generators. An artificial greenhouse effect would warm the Red Planet. The polar ice caps would melt and trapped oxygen would be released. Maybe during that time NASA would finally deliver their oft-promised fusion drives and perfect the slingshot launch into Earth's orbit. Maybe they would create a viable transportation system for the billions of human beings who desperately wished to travel away from their home planet.

But wishing for something was not what Andi's investigation was about. The concept of terraforming Mars was the most exciting news in the last century. The implementation of it was the biggest story in the last two decades. So why, when such a big deal was made of this venture, were the newsstands now gazing toward their collective navels? How could the analysts have been so wrong with their financial calculations? What snags and problems were causing such massive delays? Why was no one being told?

Her next area of research was equally disappointing. In a bold move, Andi attempted to contact the Director of the Mars Commission. She was bounced around the vast stratum of the Commission machine. She was passed down and down the chain of command until she reached the final link, who knew little and was willing to impart less. A brief, heated conversation ensued, followed by an unceremonious disconnection on the behalf of one of the Mars Commission's Data Consolidation Engineers (which she knew was another way of saying 'filing clerk').

Feeling despondent and with few resources left beyond badgering, stalking and burglary, Andi logged on to the internet. This was a last, desperate attempt, she realized. The overcrowded internet was crammed with useless and often downright incorrect information, as well as the obligatory offensive porn sites that latched onto any keywords. She was expecting 70% of the sites to be inaccurate, 15% to have little to do with Mars anyway, and a further 10% showing distasteful images of sexual romps between alleged aliens. This would leave a mere 5% of sites that could be of use, though most would be of the bland standard of the newspaper's archives.

Andi managed ten minutes of exploration. She uncovered very little detail than she already knew. What she did uncover was too scientific for her. Then her computer screen winked off. Confused, she frowned at the screen and glanced around the office. No one else had suffered a power cut. The terminal began to reboot. Andi rolled her wheeled chair out of her cubicle and glanced along the walkway. There was activity, but nothing out of the ordinary. There was one exception though: the Government Advisor was on the prowl and he was heading directly for her.

She rolled her chair back to her desk. She slipped her bare feet into her heels then rested her head in her hands. It looked like Daniel was right. Trouble was striding up to her in his polished, immaculate shoes, ready to unleash the full power of a bureaucratic nanny state.

The Advisor, like a bland, anonymous robot with the power to reboot a life, stopped at her cubicle. He studied her for a moment. She glanced briefly at him, as much acknowledgement as she was willing to afford him.

"Miss Clayton," he said in a drawn monotone. "I would like a word with you."

"What's wrong?" Andi responded casually.

"Nothing is wrong," the Advisor assured her unconvincingly. "I would just like a word."

Reluctantly, she spun her chair around to face him, crossed her legs and flicked a stubborn piece of fluff off her pants. Though his face remained stonily blank, the Advisor took this as his cue. Looking around mechanically, he retrieved a spare chair from the opposite cubicle and slipped in next to her.

"What are you working on these days, Miss Clayton?" the Advisor asked.

She considered the cheekiest response she could think up, but abandoned it in favor of something closer to the truth. "I'm following up the latest news from England, researching Mars and probing a potential source regarding an as-yet undisclosed story."

"Hmmm," the Advisor said, giving very little thought to what she'd said and doing it purely for dramatic impact. "Very good. Although...what's the story about Mars?"

"Over budget, over schedule."

"These things happen. Where's the story?"

"Well..." she paused. "Why is it so over budget and so behind schedule? There must be some reason."

"Isn't it just that large-scale projects tend to become bigger than originally anticipated?"

"Really?" Andi asked. "You believe that? *Three hundred billion* over budget?"

The Advisor sighed, the first human thing he'd done thus far. "What exactly are you looking for, Miss Clayton?"

"Just..." she began, trying to word her answer correctly. "A story, I guess. The truth."

"And therein lies the problem, Miss Clayton. The truth is what you're after, but all you'll find on the internet are rumors and lies."

"The Commission won't talk to me..." Andi complained

"They *are* busy, you know. The simple truth is that the budget and timeframe may have overrun compared to the initial study. But it is still within acceptable, and indeed expected, limits. There are no particular, concrete reasons for this. It is just a side-effect of such a massive project. Quite simply, there's no story here."

"I think if I dig-" she began.

"Miss Clayton," he interrupted, then emphasized each word. "There. Is. *No*. Story. Here."

Andi considered this for a moment. A casual chat was now turning more sinister. Better not push him too far, she thought. The *real* story was Daniel and she didn't want any of that leaking out just yet. "Right," she said quietly.

"So," the Advisor slapped his thighs. "Back to work, then. Concentrate on the England story. After all, this is a highly respected newspaper and here we stick purely to the truth, not conjecture or unfounded rumor. There is no Mars story. But the mad Prince? That's gold dust. Potential Pulitzer-winning stuff. So I'd get cracking on it, and you can really...*secure* your place here."

Andi nodded slowly. She had already decided to ignore this threat-tinged advice and pay more attention to Daniel's government conspiracies in future.

"Great talk," the Advisor told her, standing. He carefully wheeled the spare chair back to its desk and left her be. Daydreaming, Andi began to wonder what Daniel was up to now, and what he knew that she didn't.

NINE

It was one hour since we'd decided on a plan of action. My staff were still collecting documentation on potential dissidents from various governmental departments.

My cell phone blared into action.

"Stone," I answered.

"Hello, Lieutenant," the blanked-out other end of the line offered back. I recognized the voice from the previous conversation.

"Mr. Jackson," I said back. There was the sound of tutting from the other end, mixed in with background traffic. With hindsight, the traffic sounds were quite obviously New York-based. Most of the vehicle engines were concurrent with one taxi-providing company. They were mixed in with shouts, horns and a bassy echo belying the presence of high-rise buildings. But while presenting itself as clearly from a Manhattan phone booth, it still didn't narrow the area down that much.

"Jackson?" he said. "Come on! Surely you've discovered my current name by now."

I sighed. "Daniel Stringer," I said with finality. "I suppose there must be a pun about stringing people along in there somewhere."

"Not really," Stringer answered, refusing to lighten up. "Still having difficulty locating me though, aren't you. A name doesn't mean much without a location."

"The net is closing," I told him, hoping to undermine his self-confidence. "You've left enough footprints."

"It is still a rather large net, Stone. And I bet you're desperate to know how my RFID doesn't ping on your system. A conversation for a later date maybe."

"When exactly?" I asked, trying to rile him. "Does your crystal ball tell you the exact day and time when we'll have that conversation?"

Stringer laughed. "I see you are pretending that my ability is just some silly bit of science fiction, and that I'm deluded."

"You're many things, Stringer. Deluded is just one of them."

"Come on, Stone. Admit it. You know it's true. You know what I can do. You know you'll never catch me and you're doomed to failure."

"Is this why you've called me? To tease? To verbally spar?"

"Nothing so childish, Jack. Is it okay I call you Jack? No, it isn't. I can tell. You sound awful, by the way. Problems at home?"

"What do you want?" I said.

"Evacuate the Capitol, Stone."

"Capital of where?" I asked after a moment's consideration. "A hundred and ninety seven countries to choose from, never mind all the states and provinces within–"

"No, no, Capi-*TOL*. Washington D.C., Congress. You know, big white building with a dome on top of it. Quite iconic. Lots of politics involved."

I snorted. "We can't evacuate the Capitol Building! Are you joking?!"

"Suggesting that a chemical bomb will go off inside a Government building at midday is a rather poor joke, wouldn't you say? Therefore, if I were you I'd take this information seriously. Can you imagine if you took it light-heartedly? Down a bar with your friends, 'oh, have you heard this one?' and it turns out thousands of government employees and tourists died because you couldn't take a bomb threat seriously? Not good for the morale, Stone. Not good for the career either, I'd expect. Not that I *want* you to succeed-"

"OKAY!" I interrupted, happy to finally get a word in. He was playing the same tactic as me. We were both trying to rile each other to see who slipped up first. "I get the idea! Capitol, midday, chemical weapon. What is it? Ricin, anthrax, polonium dust?"

"No," Stringer answered simply. I waited for more but it was not forthcoming.

"Do you know what kind of chemical weapon it is?" I tried again, broader of scope this time.

"Yes," Stringer responded. The phone line went dead.

Just over one hour, I thought. That left just enough time to evacuate the entire building, ensure a safety perimeter was in place and conduct a basic search for the device. But I already had the feeling that the device would not be located in time. The increasing activity of the terrorists would produce another victory of unacceptable violence and fear.

I activated the phone and made the call to General Armstrong Miller.

"Stone! You have more questions about yesterday?"

"No, Sir," I answered. "Well, yes Sir, but that's not why I'm calling."

"Then what can I do for you?"

"Two things, Sir. Daniel Stringer's here. In New York."

"Really?" the General breathed. "That's very interesting."

"The other thing is that he's given us another tip-off."

"Where?"

"The Capitol Building. Midday. A chemical device."

The General's eyes widened in surprise. "The *Capitol?*"

"Yes, Sir. He was at pains to point it out as rudely as possible."

"It's a big target. Iconic. If they pull this off…"

"Yes, Sir," I answered. "I know."

The General studied my image for a moment. He looked quite ashen. "Good work, Stone," he said, and cut off the call.

Shortly after midday, the Capitol Building had been successfully evacuated of all staff. We had completely failed to discover the location of the chemical bomb.

It was a slow-acting device. It began with a small detonation. There was a low rumble in the ground and the building's windows flexed. A lot of people were expecting a huge fireball. They were disappointed.

The minor detonation merely served to spread chemicals throughout the building rather than cause structural damage itself. A thick, soupy pall of green-tinged smoke crept under doorframes and through open windows.

The gas released by the device was relatively harmless to humans unless ingested heavily. That would result in a heady feeling and wheezing throat for a few hours. But it was devastating upon the building itself.

A corrosive sour gas composite with over 500 parts-per-million of hydrogen sulfide, it generated calcium sulfide. That compound immediately attacked the cement and mortar binding the structure together. At over 125 times the required strength of sour gas needed, it cracked and weakened the very glue that held the Capitol together.

Within an hour all cement and mortar had crumbled to dust within the massive structure. The building wobbled uneasily like a mass of white, domed jelly – an unsupported Jenga set ready to fall.

All it took was a strong gust a further 35 minutes later to begin a chain reaction. This giant, iconic building wobbled too far and collapsed upon itself.

The South wing of the building crumbled first. As it fell and a billowing cloud of choking dust rose in its wake, the destruction spread towards the dome in the center. Amid a devastating roar, the dome fell backwards then in upon itself. Its impact with the ground blasted rubble and thick smoke throughout the remaining structure, pushing it all into collapsing as well.

Screaming crowds panicked and fled as a tsunami of thick dust flowed toward them like a volcano's pyroclastic cloud. A few brave, determined souls remained at the barriers with their video cameras recording, only to emerge a few minutes later the color of worn concrete. From the air, a sizeable portion of Washington D.C. was lost amid a low-lying cloud of beige and grey.

It was hours before the dust settled. When it did, all that was still recognizable from the Capitol was the Statue of

Freedom. Once proud atop the peak of the vast dome, it stood drunkenly amid the rubble, chipped but unbroken.

Thanks to the lengthy delay between attack and collapse the incident was seen live across the world, and the impact on the collective mind was devastating.

That evening, Andi Clayton was heading down a ramshackle New York street. For once she was about to turn up on time for an appointment with Daniel.

There was the hint of stormy weather troubling the skies over the city. Crimson blotches flowed through the stratosphere. The pregnant underbellies of dark, heavy clouds were painted by the sun's ochre orb as it melted on the horizon. The dark brick of high-rise tenements bathed in the soft, soothing light of dusk. Windows reflected swathes of orange fire into the lightly swaying canopies of limp, ill-maintained trees.

Andi reached Daniel's apartment door. It was a dulled slab of metal down a dark, diseased corridor in a ramshackle tenement building. Even the buzzer felt ill and sticky. She faintly heard a shout of "Enter!" and the door clicked open.

The smell of cooking immediately assaulted her senses. The apartment was a large open-plan studio. A bedroom and bathroom lay tucked away behind doors to the left. One corner of the open space was taken up with an old, ill-maintained grand piano. A small dining table and large shelf of tattered, dog-eared works of fiction lay across from it. The sunken living area was crowded with two couches and an armchair. They faced an archaic wall-mounted LCD TV at least an inch thick. Two huge, overgrown potted plants framed the screen. Across from this, Daniel occupied the kitchen. A breakfast bar and cupboards lined the rear wall. The hob and chef-prompter occupied an island facing the doorway.

He continued his cooking with an air of frazzled commitment. A small plate with an egg pancake lay to one side, next to another plate of fried onion slices and a bowl of fluffed rice. A wok sizzled with heated oil. The chef-prompter was an old design with the screen rolled down from the ceiling. It showed a frozen image of a stern, middle-aged woman over a stove. Daniel slid a green pepper into the auto dicer then a moment later removed the cut, de-seeded cubes.

"Green pepper," he said, almost to himself. "Couldn't find any chilies." He looked up and shrugged. "Shouldn't make too much difference, but it's the thought that in this day of international commerce it's so difficult to locate a simple foodstuff."

"What are you doing?" Andi asked, moving towards the living area.

"Nasi goreng," Daniel answered. The chef-prompter burst back into life.

"Good," the on-screen woman said. "Now add the garlic, ginger and chili pepper to the wok." She again froze.

Daniel added the ingredients to the wok and gave the pan a flick, mixing the spices.

"So," he began. He looked at her with disapproval. "Take a seat. Shed the coat. All that stuff. Get settled. Nice dress, by the way. Shame about the wine."

"This?" Andi asked, removing her coat and indicating her dress. It was sexy, but not overtly so. "It's old," she told him. "It's just... What wine?"

Daniel raised his eyebrows and sighed. "Exactly," he answered.

"I can't stay long," she told him.

"I know," Daniel responded. He was interrupted by the chef-prompter telling him to add tamarind, turmeric, shrimp paste, coconut, lime juice, salt and sugar. This list of ingredients sent Daniel into a panic, but he located everything and provided the wok with an extra sizzle.

"I have to get back," Andi mentioned.

"No, you don't. You just don't want to stay. Sit."

She perched on the edge of a sofa. "Still second-guessing me?" she asked.

"Inevitable, I'm afraid." Pork and prawns were added to the mix in the wok. Daniel switched on the automatic stirring machine and set it in the right position. It blew a raspberry at him. It reluctantly began to stir following a vicious punch to its outer casing.

"So," he said, sitting on the opposite sofa. "More questions? More talk? Or just wallow in my charms? How would you like this to progress?"

"I'm still not sure where it's started from, never mind progressing to," Andi admitted.

"Reluctant to believe, are you?"

"You tell me."

He grinned. "That wouldn't be fair. I could reel off the entire conversation we're going to have tonight, but I think you'd get bored with a lack of participation."

"Whenever you ask a question, you already know the answer, right?"

"I think *you* know the answer to *that* question."

"I just don't get you. If you have this ability, surely there's ways you could make money out of it. So why this place?"

Daniel looked surprised. "Did I mention I'm on the run? Hiding from the bad guys? If you think about it, this is a little less conspicuous than a 14-bedroom mansion in the Hamptons."

"Even so, your stirrer doesn't work properly, that piano is on its last legs, the TV is rigid..."

"Material things. Power does not come from material gain, it comes from influence. Many people mistake the two because usually the people with the most power are those with enough money to buy influence. They're also the people too stupid to realize you don't need to physically pay for power, you just need the right amount of intelligence and charisma."

A beep emanated from the auto-stirrer and Daniel moved over to it. The screen kicked into life again. It told him to add the rice, bean sprouts and peas and stir for 10 minutes. The ingredients added and the auto-stirrer thumped into submissive servitude again, Daniel returned his attention to Andi.

"What matters to you then?" she asked him. "It's not material things, and, forgive me for saying so, but you seem like a loner to me so it can't be love. Is it power, then? Is that your ultimate goal?"

"I have to admit it is a little tricky to hold down a relationship and keep things fresh when you know every word and every move your partner will make. So, you're right, it's not love. Power? Do I want power? Let me ask you this. What's the purpose of our existence?"

"The...?" Andi stopped short. Suddenly she really wished she *had* brought wine. She could handle the occasional philosophical discussion, but Daniel had just gone straight for the jugular. "That's a question we've been asking for twenty thousand years. You've worked it out, have you?"

"Legacy. That's our purpose. If there is a higher being out there, an Almighty Creator, a God...to Him we are insignificant and ignored, so forget any of this 'be good on Earth, live forever in Heaven' rubbish. This is it. This life. This one chance. Our individual purpose, if you can call it that, is a legacy. Someone once said 'You are never really dead until the last person that remembers you dies.' *That* is our Heaven, our living forever. Most people can only achieve it in a minor way by having children to carry on their memory, their family name. Some don't even manage that. But others aspire to greater things, and they succeed, be it Columbus discovering the Americas, Homer's tale of the siege of Troy or Hitler sanctioning the deaths of six million Jews. They did something monumental. Something for which they will be remembered for centuries. Therefore they will live on in our minds and our books. Even if you're talking about having a child or killing someone. The power to find a mate or take that life. Power equals legacy, legacy equals afterlife, and there is nothing else."

Andi let this sink in. After a few seconds, she spoke. "You're a pessimist, aren't you?"

"A realist."

"And all these people who *do* believe in an afterlife, they're just deluded and you're the only one who can see the truth?"

"Religion is for the weak. People who can't accept that they're in control of their own lives so need to seek out a higher being to ask for help."

"Hmmm, an *arrogant* pessimist."

Daniel sighed. "Look, I know what you're doing. I'm here to give you a story. You want to know the person behind the story. It isn't going to work like that. You want to sleep with me? Fine, I'm up for that. But I got in touch with you to tell you about a national crisis, not my personal philosophy."

"As far as I recall, *you* were the one on the philosophical rant, not me. And if you presume I want to sleep with you, then I guess you're not as good at reading people as you think." Andi felt a hot, reddened flush in her cheeks. It was brought on partly because of her anger, and partly because she knew that her last statement was not strictly true. She grabbed her coat defiantly. "I think we're done here."

"Fine," Daniel responded, leaning back on the sofa. "Don't want the story? Your prerogative. I'll just find someone else who *is* willing to leave their legacy on this world."

Andi kept her coat spread across her legs, ready for a quick exit, but remained seated.

"Okay," she finally said. "So tell me then. Tell me all about these grand conspiracies that no one else knows about. The Government blew up the Capitol itself, did it?"

"No, of course not. And other people know about these conspiracies. There are blogs and podcasts hidden on the internet, accessed via a special codex. There are DJs broadcasting the truth from mobile stations."

Andi shrugged. "Yet we never hear about any of them."

"Some do. Most don't. After all, why would the Government want people to know this is out there?"

"So come on then, give me the dirt. You've told me nothing yet, no concrete details."

Daniel sighed. "And where's the fun in that, giving you all the answers? To use an analogy, I'll give you the blueprints of the house, but you'll have to build it brick by brick."

"Up all night working on that one?"

He grinned. "Not *all* night. You staying or going? Meal's nearly ready."

"What is it?"

"Nasi goreng."

Andi glared at Daniel in frustration. "Stop saying that, and answer my question in English!"

"Indonesian fried rice dish. The properties of which pale in comparison to what we're discussing."

"Which topic? That you're an arrogant bastard, or that my country is shafting its citizens and we're all too stupid to notice?"

Daniel shrugged. "I always thought 'naïve' would be a better word than 'stupid'. But yes, that topic. Not the other one. Coming from someone who has the reputation of a ruthless man-eater and a predatory thirst to screw over anybody who gets in the way of a good story, I think 'arrogant bastard' is probably a compliment."

Andi stared at Daniel with a shocked, defiant glare. Again, she felt the hot flush of anger. But again it was also tempered by the knowledge that her reputation did have some grounding in the truth.

She put her coat on with more force than was strictly necessary. "It really seems like you're trying your best to insult me here," she spat.

"I know."

"And you're getting very irritating."

"I know."

"And I'm leaving."

"I know."

She stood and grabbed her purse from the couch. "Will you stop saying that?"

Andi shook her head in frustration. She headed towards the front door. Daniel moved back to his stove and, upon prompting, tipped the sliced egg and onion into the mix. The front door swished open.

"You know," Andi began. "If you're so good at predicting the future, why cook me dinner if you knew I was going to leave, eh? Explain that one!"

Daniel shrugged again. "Just give it seven seconds."

"What? What for?"

He paused, letting the seconds tick away. The auto-stirrer in the kitchen beeped and the chef-prompter sprang back into life. "Dinner," the screen said, "nasi goreng for one, now ready. Enjoy your meal."

Andi gave Daniel her best withering look. He didn't respond, only smirked. She stepped into the damp-smelling corridor and the door closed behind her.

This was a love-hate relationship, she thought. She wondered which of the two would win out. As she headed down the dank corridor, she removed her cell phone and dialed a cab. It was dark out there now, and dangerous. How apt.

"Stone," the General barked at me over the phone without just cause. Suddenly I wasn't sure about updating him on the current situation. "We got him yet?"

"The investigation is progressing well, Sir," I began, softening the blow. "But no, we haven't quite located him as yet."

The General harrumphed. I saw him glance wistfully at the lone, forever-unsmoked cigar to the side of his desk. "And what progress have we made, exactly? Can we expect a capture before Christmas?"

It was a harsh comment to direct at me. This man had eluded the best of us for years. With the progress I'd made in the past couple of weeks congratulations were in order, not vitriol.

"Sir, you are fully aware of how difficult this assignment is. I would appreciate less sarcasm."

"I...of course, Stone. Apologies. Just had my ass chewed off by the Permanent Defense Undersecretary. You got the ricochet. Now, give me good news."

"I'm afraid we've hit a bit of an impasse at this moment in time."

He sighed. "You can't find him."

"Not yet. He's managed to disable his RFID, or at least prevent it from being tracked. Aside from scouring through..." I checked my notes before continuing, "...six hundred and seventy two hours of footage each from three hundred and seventy two thousand networked CCTV cameras in the New York City area, we're fast running out of options. I've implemented a scan of all Government reports from the field to see if anyone has seen him and not known who he was, or if maybe he's been in contact with a person or group we're watching."

"Hmmm, good, good. Hopefully that will get some results."

"I was thinking of maybe putting out an APB now we have his photograph. We could instruct GovPol to report a sighting of him but do not approach or allow him to become suspicious of their presence."

"No, that wouldn't be a good idea, Stone. I think the fewer people involved in this the better."

I felt frustrated. All our resources for capturing this man were based on technology, and that was one area in which he seemed a dab hand at thwarting us. We needed manpower. Plain and simple bodies on the streets.

"Listen, Stone," the General told me. "I was about to give you a call anyway. The Undersecretary and I have been discussing this very situation."

"Sir?" I asked.

"She...*we* have come to a decision about the fate of Zeus Jackson."

"We call him Daniel Stringer around the office now, Sir. What decision is that?"

"Before, your remit was to capture the man by any means necessary. Even dead, as long as his brain was intact."

"Yes, Sir. But we haven't even seen-"

"Never mind that," the General interrupted. "The situation is becoming untenable. The threat he poses is becoming greater every day. The Capitol Building really shook everyone up. Stone, I am now authorizing you to bring...Stringer in dead or alive, even if this requires a headshot. Alive is still very much preferable, dead with an intact brain is desirable. But if there is nothing else you can do, if it looks like you are about to lose your quarry and are uncertain if you will be able to apprehend him again, then we will find it acceptable if he receives a bullet in the head. The details of his experiment is damned near essential to us to help protect this nation. But the threat posed by the man himself outweighs that. Do you understand me, Stone?"

I nodded. "I believe so, Sir. As a last resort – shoot to kill."

"Good. Now...how long before you have results?"

"Results, Sir?" I asked.

"You mentioned scouring the CCTV footage..."

"Well, there's so much of it, Sir. A good two hundred and fifty million hours of footage. Even if the character recognition software is going at the full 5000x speed and operating 24/7 it would take..."

There was a moment of silence while I consulted my notes. The General filled the gap. "What?" he asked.

"Five point seven years?"

The General sighed. "That is not acceptable, Stone."

"I am aware of that, Sir. That is why we are concentrating on people marked as potential dissidents, those who have been flagged up in the past month."

"And you think that will bring you the results you need?"

"It's our best option, Sir," I responded.

One day later, the results of our intensive search had trickled in. We had detected 1,321 potentials. Each of these people had been flagged up on suspicious activity in the previous month, specifically in an area that suggested they could become revolutionaries. Nearly two thirds of these were students, and I couldn't really see them being the group of people that Stringer would fraternize with if he wished to do the Government any major or lasting harm.

I had told my team to sift through the other 503 candidates first – investigate their background, check emails and telephone records, correlate RFID movements with CCTV and drone footage. I estimated this would take at least another 24 hours to complete, even working at full tilt. I decided to personally look into the 43 closely associated with politics and the media because I believed these stood the most chance of bringing up results.

I quickly flicked through the list, glancing at the reasons these people had been flagged. The Congressman was having an affair with a foreign national. Two senatorial aides had gambling habits that could make them easier to blackmail, as had a Congress aide. A fashion reporter seemed to be spending quite a bit of time in North Africa, particularly Morocco. Three journalists had been asking questions about the Mars finances. Two more journalists had been overheard discussing the Cuban war in their spare time, as had half a dozen Mayoral assistants. The Mayor's senior aide had been reported as seeming unfazed by the last New York terrorist bombing in a GovPol café. Three City Hall employees were half Chinese. It seemed quite an eclectic bunch, just from these 43. I wondered what the other 460 had been flagged up for.

I walked over to my office door and swung it open. "How are we doing, people?" I asked.

"There's a lot here," Al told me. "Yourself?"

"Tricky," I answered truthfully. "It's going to be a long haul, I understand that. So make sure you take regular breaks and keep that coffee pumping."

"Sir," Brent said from behind his screen. "What exactly are we looking for? I understand some of us don't have the clearance to know everything about this case, but what constitutes 'suspicious'? I've got a man here who's been heard whispering quotations from the Qu'ran in a Catholic church. Strange, yes. But that's not suspicious, is it?"

"Not in our context, no. Just use your judgment, and if there's anything you're not sure of, make a note of it and pass it on to me."

"Yes, Sir."

I returned to my desk.

I clicked open the first folder. Bob Silvers, District Assistant to the New York Congress Press Secretary. Problem: a $5,000-a-year roulette habit. How could a minor gambling habit be connected to Stringer? Not a good, strong start to my search, I thought. But very few of these had potential and I needed to work my way through all of them. I had past histories, friends and contacts, RFID tracing and CCTV to work through 43 times.

Maybe, with luck, I could get through all of this by the end of the day. With even more luck I or one of my colleagues would find what we were looking for sooner than that. Maybe this whole thing could be over by the onset of night and Stringer would be in custody. Dead or alive. And with him I was taking no chances and handcuffing him even if he was quite clearly dead. I'd seen enough movies to know the bad guy would rise again just when you thought you'd beaten him.

TEN

Andi was running late for her next appointment with Daniel. And this time, to make a change, he was due to call at *her* door.

He wished to progress both their business and personal relationships with something a little more relaxing. He'd decided it was about time they got to know each other a little better without all the secret discussions and clandestine rendezvous. So they were going to a bar for some drinks.

She'd barely stepped out of the shower when the front door bell buzzed.

"Damn," Andi muttered. "Yes?" she asked over the intercom.

"Well, I'm not early," Daniel said. "But clearly I could have done with taking another hour before coming over."

"It won't take *that* long. Come on up and make yourself comfortable."

She buzzed Daniel in and skipped to the confines of her bedroom.

"What are you wearing tonight?" Daniel asked as the front door closed behind him.

"A big chunky sweater," she called back. "All lumpy and stuff."

141

"Perfect for a night out, I must say," he answered distantly. "Maybe you should combine it with ripped fishnets to go for that truly classy heroin addict look."

"What are you doing in there?" Andi asked as she seated herself at her vanity cabinet.

"Laughing at your photographs, drinking all your booze and stealing your TV," was his response.

"No, really," she said.

"Really? I'm sitting on the couch, soaking in the ambience and wondering why you keep asking me inane questions instead of getting ready."

Andi sighed. It sounded as though Daniel was in a difficult mood again.

She decided to leave her nails to last and wafted a bit of blusher on her cheeks. Then she picked up the mascara box and set it to black for both eyeliner and shadow. She held the box to her closed eyes and activated it for two seconds. She set it back on the cabinet.

"So what's the plan?" she called. "Aside from a few drinks, of course."

"Erm..." came the forced reply. "How do you mean?"

"You know what I mean," she chided, "Mr. Future...See-er...Guy..." She closed her eyes in disgust at herself and whispered "Dammit!"

"Mr. Future See-er Guy! Now there's a clever nickname for me! But no, I don't know what you mean. My powers are occasionally fallible."

"How?"

There was a long pause. Andi took this break in the conversation to apply her lipstick. She applied two drops on the lower lip. The mnemonic red substance spread itself out.

It intelligently and precisely worked along the contours between the skin on her lips and that of her face.

"We'll discuss it later," Daniel finally offered. "So what do you mean about the plan aside from a few drinks?"

"Just checking you haven't booked dinner or a show or something."

"Ah...no," he said reluctantly. "Just a couple of bars. Cheap night."

"And what about tonight's discussion? What's the topic this time?" Andi applied her mnemonic nail polish next.

"Well, I wasn't really planning on any proper discussion tonight. I was going to give you a little demonstration of what I can do instead. But I guess you also have a story to write, so we can do the serious bit now if you want. What would you like to talk about?"

"The Evil Government of course," Andi answered, changing hands and continuing with the polish.

"Okay," Daniel responded. It was quickly followed by a clatter and a hushed "Shit!"

"What was that?" she asked.

"There may be a slight chip on the mantelpiece," he answered. "And one of the picture frames. Never mind. Neither of them are expensive."

"Put the photo back and sit down," Andi chided.

"Sorry. You start."

"What?"

"What what?"

"Start what?"

"Oh, that," he answered. "Start the conversation. Any particular areas you'd like to discuss?"

"Well…" Andi shrugged, then realized Daniel wasn't even in the room to see it. "You're the one who knows stuff. Just tell me what else they're doing that's so underhand."

"You mean apart from manipulating the media, performing illegal experiments and stealing money from the Mars project?"

Having finished her nails, Andi turned her attention to her hair. It would take a good two minutes to program the correct settings into the BrushDry StyleMax, so she was more than happy to continue the conversation without interruption. "Well…yes," she said.

"How about America influencing the break-down of the China-Korea ceasefire because we're selling munitions and supplies to both sides? We'll therefore have a stranglehold on their economies for several years."

"Erm…" Andi said. "Anything closer to home?"

"Ah, of course. Because of the Government's subtle manipulation of the press, no one cares about foreigners any more."

"That's not true," she said. "We're having great fun reading about the English Prince."

"Yes…well…"

"So, *is* there anything closer to home you can tell me? Oh, wait, hang on a minute."

Andi picked up the heavy, automatic brush and began combing. It dried, separated and styled her hair in a specified, programmed fashion. It smoothed the hair out into a fashionably layered wave. After two minutes the hair was dry and styled. She replaced the brush.

"So, go ahead," she called, standing up from the vanity cabinet.

"Erm…" Daniel started. "Yes. Schools."

"Schools? What about them?"

Andi stood in front of her full-length mirror and picked up the clothes handset. She was pretty sure which outfit she'd wear but she wanted to check it matched her make-up first.

"The Government has lowered funding for schooling," Daniel told her. "They claim it is because the grades are going up, so why invest more money when we're already doing fine? Guess they've never heard of 'going the extra mile'."

"Right. So what's really happening?"

Andi activated her mirror's handset and cycled past the 'evening wear' and 'club' options to 'casual: outdoors'. The first outfit was recreated in a high-quality 3-D image on the mirror. It mimicked her body shape and real-time movements. It was a short, A-line purple dress with baggy pants. The computer had selected an option that didn't even slightly work.

"Technically what they say is true, but only because the actual scoring of grades is being lowered. If before a pass grade was fifty percent and now it is forty percent more students will pass and they can say the grades are going up. Perfect excuse to cut funds, redirect it to the Mars Commission and siphon off even more for themselves."

Andi fiddled with the handset. She saved the purple dress option, located a long-sleeved black Tee-shirt to go underneath it, then continued flicking through the lower body selection until she came across a pair of 15-dernier black panty hose. A quick browse through the accessory options and the outfit was completed with a thick black belt and a pair of black knee boots. She shifted from side to side and strained to view herself in the reflection from all angles. The outfit suited her needs perfectly – sexy and feminine, yet casual. She wanted to look good, but she didn't want to be seen to be trying too hard.

She pressed the 'accept' button and the wardrobe spat out the selected items on rails.

"So they're rigging the stats, then?"

"Manipulating would be a better word. They're not lying. They're just lowering the bar."

"And whose accounts is all this money from Mars actually going into?"

"The Board of Executives on the Mars Commission. A few high-level NASA Directors. Government employees in the loop all the way up to, and especially including, the President himself. After all, he's been in power far longer than he should have. He's been manipulating the public to believe he is benign and free from corruption. Once the public finds out what he's really like it might be a good idea for him to have a quick exit planned and a little nest egg set aside for his enforced retirement. You ready yet?"

"Ask me that in two minutes," Andi replied.

She quickly slipped her clothes on, then pulled on her stiletto boots. She checked her slim silver watch that was masquerading as the middle of three bangles on her wrist. It was just under fifteen minutes since Daniel arrived. Grabbing the clutch containing all her essentials, she checked herself in the mirror one last time and walked into the living area.

Daniel was wearing fashionable attire. It consisted of an open, knee-length suit jacket with flared cuffs, drainpipe jeans and walking boots. They were all in the deepest, darkest black imaginable. He had combined it with a white shirt unbuttoned at the collar. He was also guiltily holding two pieces of a cheap, ornamental picture frame.

"I...pffft..." he began when he saw her. It was followed by an enthusiastic: "Foxy!"

"Can I take that to mean I meet with your approval?" Andi asked, smiling.

"I'll show you how much I approve later on."

"Well you look very nice too," she said, furrowing her brow at his last comment. "Hair brushed, stubble trimmed, clothes ironed. Very impressive." She nodded at the picture frame. "How did that happen?" she asked. "Weren't you able to predict the frame's demise like five days ago or something?"

"I told you, my ability is fallible under certain circumstances."

"And I said 'such as?' to which you refused to reply."

"Ah, yes, well, it's emotions that do it. They're not logical, so I can't accurately predict them."

"What emotions?" she asked, confused.

"I don't know," he answered, scratching his head behind one ear. "I mean, you look great and this is kind of a date and...well..."

"You mean that going on a date with me is messing up your superpower?" she asked.

He nodded.

"Well," she said, "I can see why you said relationships are awkward for you. Predicting stuff one moment, being completely useless the next. Must be tricky."

"Thanks for boosting my confidence during this difficult time," he chided. "I'll...ummm...pay for the picture frame. Probably not the chipped mantelpiece though."

"As long as you're paying for tonight, that will do."

"Ah, okay," he said, brightening up. "So, are we ready?"

"We are," Andi answered. She grabbed a simple black jacket from her coat rack and slung it over one arm. She sidled over to him and slipped her other arm through his. "Anywhere particular in mind for tonight?"

"I thought we'd see what life was like back in a time when bars were covered in neon and governments were only slightly corrupt. Ever been to the Retro Bar?"

"No," Andi answered.

"Well, don't worry. You're dressed for it."

A second bottle of beer in his hand, Daniel sat back down at the table. Andi frowned at his drink and glanced at her own empty glass. When he said he'd pay for the whole night, he lied.

"Better get *myself* another drink then," she said. Slouching and with a mouthful of beer, Daniel silently nodded and tipped his bottle toward her in acknowledgement.

Andi glanced around the bar before she stood. The floor was dark wood paneling. The chairs and tables were made of the same wood so in the ill-lit surroundings they almost became invisible. An open staircase at the far end led to the restrooms, and an outdoor patio was to its left. To the right, the chrome bar top gleamed under the glare of neon fittings. The neon surrounded a vast array of alcoholic beverages on the back wall.

There was a juke box in one corner. It was a 1990s wall-mounted design, but it was updated to use the latest RFID technology. It could access her favorite playlists if she approached it, or she could make a selection from a web-based back catalogue. The jukebox came with the option of a directional facility. It was able to record a person's RFID location and fire a tight beam frequency to them, meaning only they could hear the track they selected. Andi considered using this option. It would be better than letting it continue playing the random noise that passed for music 50 years ago. But she was here to talk, not listen to golden oldies from Nine Inch Nails and Shania Twain.

An RFID ping alerted the bar staff to Andi's favorite tipple as she moved to the chrome bar top. "The usual?" he asked. She nodded.

The barman mixed her vodka and lime. He pressed a button on his console, and her account was automatically debited via another RFID ping.

There were a couple of dozen patrons in the bar, and more filed in as the evening wore on. There was an eclectic mixture, from high school students to old timers who may even remember what a 1990s bar looked like. There were also businessmen and women, manual laborers, shop workers and intellectuals. The past seemed to cater to everyone.

Andi returned to the table with her drink and angrily put it on the table. Daniel immediately knew what was wrong.

"I bought you the first drink, didn't I?" he suggested.

"Yes," Andi answered. "Thank you," she continued insincerely.

"With the Government hunting me down it is actually quite tricky to hold onto a job. You're the rich one here."

"Okay," she agreed. "So, you're not being chivalrous. Therefore I can assume either we are not on a date or you're just *really* bad at them. You have nothing planned for us after we leave this bar. You don't want to talk about the conspiracies. So, tell me Daniel, why are we here?"

He grinned. "I want to show you something."

Andi looked around the bar. Nothing stood out. "Show me what?"

"That you can be just like me."

She thought about that for a moment. "A deluded, arrogant asshole?" she offered.

He grinned again. "All this predicting the future stuff. You keep saying you want to know how I do it. How about I get *you* to do it?"

Andi took a sip of her drink. "Slight flaw in that plan. I'm not a super-freak."

"It's all about reading people. Working things out. Want to give it a go?"

Andi nodded with a little reluctance. She wasn't sure if this experiment would be fun or disturbing. Either way, it wasn't what she had expected from this night out.

Daniel glanced around the bar, and picked out two people to study.

"See those two chatting over there?" he asked.

Andi glanced in their direction. There was a tall, wiry young man of maybe 21 years. He was very excited, energetic and gesticulating wildly despite being in danger of spilling his drink. He was talking to a pretty girl of a similar age. She was torn between paying attention to the man and ensuring none of his drink was spilled on her slim line dress. Andi returned her attention to Daniel and nodded.

"What can you tell me about them?" he asked.

"Erm…how do you mean?"

"Are they a couple, for example?"

"Well…" She glanced across again. "The boy seems over-eager to make an impression. Especially his hand gestures. Nothing more off-putting for her, and he wouldn't be trying so hard if they were a couple, so no."

"But…"

"But…" she began, and took a moment to think. Where was the 'but' in her analysis? What had she missed? "But," she said again with more surety, "she's trying to pay attention. She hasn't run away from him in disgust or what-have-you."

"Which means…"

"Which means it's not just a case of him trying to chat her up. She'd have blown him off and gone back to her friends by now."

"And his friends?"

"He's the kind of idiot who'd keep glancing across at them to garner their approval. But he's not doing that."

"Which–"

"Which means," Andi interrupted, "that they're alone…together…you know what I mean."

"No friendly back-up. Just the two of them."

"Right. So, that means they must be going out with each other…after all, the way they're both acting clearly shows they're not just friends out for a drink. But he's trying too hard to impress. She doesn't know whether to stick around or not. So I'd say tentative early dating rituals are in play. Maybe this is the…second date?"

"More likely the third, but very good all the same."

"Why, thank you. So, I've figured out that two people have just started dating. It's not exactly seeing into the future yet, is it?"

"Now let me direct your attention to the bar. What do you see, most prominently?"

"Drunk guy."

"Yes. Now fill in the blanks."

"Err...sorry, you've lost me."

"Okay," Daniel sighed. "I'll give you a helping hand as this is your first time peering into what is yet to come. We've established he's drunk."

"Very. He's a bit wobbly just trying to stand up."

"And he's at the bar."

"Ordering a drink, I'd expect."

"But the barman is doing what?"

"Err...sorry?"

"He's about to pour two."

"Right. One for a friend."

"Yes. And see that glance and brief wave he just did, behind him?"

"To his friend, I presume. To tell him he's being served."

"Good, this is getting better."

"I'm sorry." It was Andi's turn to sigh. "I'm really not following this."

"You've got the dots now. You just need to join them together."

"Please, at least join the first one before I get a headache."

"Okay. The friend is at the table over there. Directly between that table and the bar is..."

"The newly-dating couple. Ooh!" A sudden moment of inspiration hit Andi. "Does the drunk guy know the couple? No, wait, wildly-gesticulating guy is going to knock drunk guy!"

"Because drunk guy is, well, drunk, and he's carrying a drink in each hand, his balance isn't that good and some of the drink will be spilled as he walks past. That's good. However, you've got one vital part wrong."

"What? Which?"

"It is not wildly-gesticulating guy, as you call him, who is going to knock into drunk guy."

"Why do you think that?"

"Because he is becoming more animated, and the more animated he becomes the more he directs his gesticulations straight at the girl rather than to the side. I can understand their body language more than you can, and I can read lips too so I can tell where the boy is in his conversation. Therefore I know that at the spot-on perfect moment, the girl will step backwards out of the way of a particularly vigorous hand jiggle and collide with the drunk guy."

"So," Andi clarified, "just by glancing at the couple and the drunk guy, you know all that will happen?"

"And more besides. After all, what do the following have in common? A very drunk man who's just had some of his beer spilled, and a youth full of beans who is hoping to impress a very pretty girl on their third date."

"They're both up for a fight. So, the drunk guy's going to insult the girl and the boy will step into defend her honor. Ruckus ensues."

"Pretty much. You see, train your mind and it's easy. So, anyway, now *you* have two choices."

"What's that?" Andi asked. She rested her elbows on the table top and smiled. For some reason her fanciful mind had latched onto the idea that Daniel was about to present the following choice to her: "Your place or mine?" It was a proposition that had been touted before. But this time Daniel seemed less arrogant, and Andi was certainly less angry with him. She may indeed have chosen one of the two options the question would present to her.

Her fanciful mind was, however, wrong.

"Either stay here," Daniel offered, "wait and see if we're right, and become witness to a particularly vicious and bloody barroom brawl. Or we leave right now and you'll never know if we've just predicted the future."

"Are they really...?"

"The barman's just finished serving him. You have eighteen seconds to decide."

The smile vanished from Andi's face. She realized how dangerous and out-of-control a brawl could get. Maybe, she thought, it wasn't such a bad idea to leave now. They'd both finished their drinks.

She stood and plucked her coat from the back of the seat. Daniel motioned with one hand for her to head to the exit. She did so, but her head felt a bit foggy. She was torn between the options of a) confirming what may have been about to happen and b) personal safety. With a story, personal safety had always come second. But this was not a news-worthy event. This was not something that could benefit her in any way to witness.

As Andi reached the bar's door and swung it open, she shivered. It was more with the thrill of the evening than the sudden bite of night air whipping in from the street.

The street was busy. It was a heady concoction of human and vehicular traffic. The burning glow of street lights mixed with squares of white lancing out from shop and bar windows. A thick layer of cloud obscured the night sky. Andi breathed in deeply. The crisp, cool air went to her head in a way her vodka limes could have only dreamed. It was exhilarating: the feeling that she'd just witnessed, and partaken in, an ability to see into the future. Could it really be that easy, she wondered? Reading people and logically predicting the next step in their behavior was an ability most people did on a small scale every day. All it required was concentration and brain processing power to control Fate.

She looked across at Daniel. He offered his arm and she slipped hers into his. They began walking down the street.

"What now?" Andi asked.

"What would you like to do?" Daniel responded.

Andi smiled and hugged his arm. "I want to get better at that."

"Okay," Daniel grinned. "New bar, new people. No clues this time, Andi. Let's see what you're really made of."

"Don't you already know?" Andi asked, looking up at him. She stopped. "Come on," she said. "Tell me. What am I thinking right now?"

Daniel shook his head. "I've told you before, it doesn't work like that. I only know *events* that will happen."

"Okay," Andi grinned again. "So what am I going to *do* next, then?"

He considered this for a moment, then a wry grin started to form on his face. Partly because she wanted to curb his smile before it developed into smugness, and partly because she simply wanted to, Andi quickly leaned forward and kissed him on the lips.

ELEVEN

It was nearing 1.00 am. I'd managed to sift through twelve files, all to no avail. My eyes were starting to hurt as I worked through case number thirteen. I could see through my office window that my team were flagging too.

I began scouring the next batch of CCTV footage for this latest case, footage from two days ago. This case was one of three journalists who had been asking awkward questions about the Mars Commission. The footage hadn't highlighted anything particular as yet. Befitting the role of a journalist, this one had been back and forth across the city several times. She'd been captured occasionally on street cameras or networked department store footage. She'd disappeared into buildings. She'd traveled and stayed put. I was growing weary of watching people move around New York, going about their daily lives.

I opened up a new file on my computer and named it Andrea Clayton 3.29.56. Using the RFID tracks and CCTV footage I noted everything Miss Clayton did on Wednesday.

She woke at 06:45, left the house at 08:01. Caught the subway, grabbed a schmeer and lox at H&H Bagels. Arrived at work, the offices of the New York Times, at 08:42. Left at 10:11 and headed to City Hall. Interviewed aide Jacob Furtwinger. Arrived back at work 11:05. Lunched at 12:25 –

a home-made salad consumed in Madison Square Park. At 13:13, spent 37 minutes window-shopping. Caught a cab to Coney Island at 13:52. Entered the BattleKarts track at 14:07.

That didn't make much sense. Having devoured her profile, Miss Clayton didn't strike me as the kind of person to enjoy BattleKarts, and it wasn't a location to conduct a professional interview. It must have been a meeting for a work-in-progress report. Could hold potential.

I brought up the relevant CCTV footage. Around three hundred people were watching the races. I used the wide angle footage first to better locate a dark-haired woman wearing a smart cream pant suit. Nothing visible even remotely close to that attire. Then I spotted someone of similar build, similar hair, similar bag, but dressed like she was going to a heavy metal gig. I scrolled the footage backwards, followed her reverse progress. Sure enough, there was a woman going into the restrooms in a smart cream suit and coming out a few minutes later in a black top and denim shorts. A journalist would often need to blend in to their surroundings to avoid unwanted attention, so changing at the BattleKarts arena made a lot of sense.

Now determined I was onto the correct person, I turned to more focused, closer CCTV and followed her progress as she searched for someone. Then she found him. And sat next to him, absently scratching one leg. He was dressed in faded jeans, grey Tee-shirt and a black suit jacket. He was relaxing on the steps of the arena, his eyes masked behind black shades. But I felt in my gut that it was him.

"Sam," I called through the computer's phone connection. "Patch my desktop feed through to your system."

I entered the outer office just as Sam brought up the CCTV image on the large OLED screen.

"This could be our man," I stated to everyone. I walked over to the image. Without prompting, Sam dutifully zoomed in so the image showed just the man and Miss Clayton.

The Erinyes left their desks and studied the image closely. "Has potential," Al responded.

"Sam, run it through facial recognition," I ordered. Sam patched into the relevant software and waited.

"I've got a strong feeling that this is him," I said, pointing at the image. "I think we've found him."

"Eighty one percent," Sam told me. "Facial recognition is at eighty one percent."

"That wouldn't be enough to stand up in a court," I pointed out. "But it's a grainy image when zoomed in and he's wearing sunglasses. If we factor in those variables, what do we get?"

"I'd say a plus or minus ten percent error threshold," Sam informed me. "Could potentially be a ninety one percent match. Courts accept ninety percent accuracy."

I nodded. "So we could be wrong. But let's play the numbers. Let's say this is our man. If he turns out not to be, we go back to searching the files. But right now, let's assume this is Stringer."

I turned my back to the screen and addressed my staff.

"This was taken two days ago at the BattleKarts track in Coney Island. At 2.10 pm. Stringer is meeting with Miss Andrea Marie Clayton. She's twenty nine, single, originally from Fremont and is a reporter for the New York Times."

I turned to Sam. "Can we get audio on this file?"

Surveillance shook his head. "Sorry."

"This isn't just a casual meeting. They're discussing something important. *This...*" I pointed to Miss Clayton's face. "*This* is our lead. But she's a journalist. We can't just storm in and interrogate her. Too many questions would be asked, too many loose ends to tie up. I want you to collate every scrap of information you can about her, and don't forget to back everything up on the archive mainframe. Sam, show me where she is right now."

Sam brought up a real-time map of New York City and entered Miss Clayton's personal details. The map zoomed in on her RFID chip. The map focused on a residential street.

"She's at home" Sam told me. "In bed. Remember those things? The places where people who aren't us go to sleep sometimes?"

"I know it's been a long night. But this is our job, and it isn't over yet. Sam, keep monitoring the RFID. Al, with me. The rest of you start collating that data."

I headed back to my inner office. Al followed.

"What are we going to do, Stone?" he asked.

"Stakeout," I answered. I shut down my desktop and removed my sidearm from a drawer.

"Lieutenant, it's past one am. She's asleep. Tomorrow's Saturday. Technically, *today* is Saturday. She'll probably lie in."

"And if she doesn't, we'll be there to follow her."

"Sir," Al said. "Can I be frank?"

"Yes. Say what you have to."

"I'm sorry your house is empty right now, but my wife is going to kill me as it is, and if I'm still not home by the time she wakes up—"

159

"Duly noted," I interrupted. "Doesn't change a thing. Your job causes problems at home? I'll write you a note. But we still need to go and stake out Miss Clayton's apartment."

"She may not see him again for days," Al pointed out. "She may *never* see him again."

"Or she may meet him for breakfast. You coming?"

"Yes, Lieutenant. Of course. I just want you to understand why I may not be the best company tonight."

"Again, duly noted. If it helps, I'll take first watch. But I also get the passenger seat."

Dawn had come and gone when I stirred. Through blurry eyes my mind barely registered the HUD time display. It was 6.42am. I could hear the broadcast news, soft but apparent. I grunted and did my best to stretch my aching limbs, constrained by the car seat.

"Morning," Al greeted.

"Wh…?" I began. "God…" I continued, stretching some more and stifling a yawn. "This is the most comfortable car I've ever slept in, and it still feels like the damn seat has paralyzed me. Any coffee?"

"Some," he said, resting casually in the driver's seat. "But it's cold."

I stuck out a hand. Al reached behind him and grabbed an insulated cup with the biodegradable lid firmly attached. I took a few sips of the liquid. It was tepid but not quite cold thanks to the insulation. However, tepid coffee was worse than cold. Especially when I could feel a thick layer of skin veering dangerously close to my lips with each sip through the small hole in the lid. I shook my head free of the nasty taste. I felt a little more awake now, and glanced past Al towards the lifeless Brooklyn brownstone building.

"No movement, I presume," I asked.

"Bit of wildlife, couple of joggers on early morning runs, etcetera, etcetera. But, no, not of the kind we're after."

I cleared my throat and smoothed down my suit as best I could. "Okay. Anything on the news?"

"Not really. Bit about the exchange of prisoners with Havana, but still nothing confirmed on that front."

"Anything *at all* happened while I was asleep?"

"I considered shaving your eyebrows," he told me.

I looked at him slightly annoyed. "That had better be a joke."

"Of course it is. I am ever the professional. To the extent in fact that I really, *really* need to urinate but I didn't even consider using that coffee cup you're holding."

I glanced at the coffee cup. The mere thought was enough and I set it on the dashboard in disgust.

"I think at some point we're going to have to take turns leaving the car," Al said. "We can't even be guaranteed she'll leave the house. I for one will require a visit to the restroom, something to drink, something to eat and the chance to move about a little before my muscles shrivel and my bones fuse together in this position."

I sighed. "Okay," I said. "Go, do your thing, bring back supplies. Just make sure no one's staring out the window at us before you leave. I'll be very annoyed if our cover is blown because you have no bladder control."

Al picked up a pair of sights and checked out the apartment windows for signs of life. "Want me to bring you anything from the shops?" he asked, one hand on the car door.

"Coffee, pastry-based products, the usual. Go!"

Al opened the door and was half-way out when I grabbed his arm.

"Toothpaste. Mouthwash. Something like that."

Al nodded at me, stepped out and quietly closed the door with a soft thunk. He stepped quickly and professionally down the sidewalk, looking for all the world like a businessman heading for an early meeting. I slid over to the driver's seat and kept watch on the apartment.

After a dozen minutes I plucked my cell phone from my pocket, dialed Sam at Surveillance and activated my earpiece.

"Surveillance," he said.

"It's Stone," I told him. "What's your status over there?"

"All is fine. Most of the data has been collated and archived. Clayton's blip still shows her in bed. Her RFID has hardly moved these last few hours, and it's consistent with body movements during REM."

I sighed. "And Al?" I asked. "Where's he?"

"Hold on…looks like a 7-Eleven. At a guess based on the latest layout data of the store I'd say he's buying Twinkies."

"Thanks," I told him. I cut off the signal and dialed Al.

"Hello?" he called, looking a little taken aback when he saw my face on the screen.

"Leave the sugar products alone and get pastries," I told him. I cut off that signal too and pocketed the cell phone. It was going to be a long day and I was already feeling irritable.

8.44 am. All the breakfast pastries had been consumed. Copious quantities of coffee had been imbibed. Al's pathetic bladder had let him down a second time.

Sam reported in through my earpiece.

"Movement," he told us. "Looks like she's stirring and...hallelujah, she's off to make friends with the porcelain throne!"

"We're only really interested in her *outdoor* movements," I answered back. "Keep a track of her meantime, but please don't report to us until she's leaving the front door."

"Okay Boss," he answered. "Just thought...you know...keep track of *all* movements. Bowels included."

"I admire your commitment to the job, but don't be a pedant."

I glanced across at Miss Clayton's apartment just to make sure Sam was right. Sure enough a light shone through the hastily-closed curtains. A cyclist whooshed past us in a garish and rather funny uniform. Suddenly the light was off in the apartment. The ground floor hallway lit up.

"Why's the light off?" I asked. "Is she on the move?"

"No, Boss, gone back to bed," was the response.

I felt tension dissipate from my muscles and breathed a sigh of relief. A man opened the apartment block's front door.

"So, who's the guy?" I asked. "If he's a neighbor maybe we can slip into his apartment to monitor–"

"What guy?" Sam interrupted.

"Front door guy."

"Come again?"

I sighed with exasperation. "Whose RFID is pinging at the front door to the apartment block? Come on, Sam, be on the ball here!"

The man had stepped outside and was slowly, quietly closing the front door now. I could see him clearer. Definitely male, definitely human.

"There's no RFID at the front door," Sam told me.

"I can see him right…" I paused. He was there for sure, but there was no RFID ping. "It's him!" I hissed.

"What?" both Al and Sam uttered at the same time.

"It's him!" I repeated. "He spent the night. Son of a bitch was in there the whole time!"

"How are we going to play this?" Al asked. "If he can predict the future, doesn't that mean he knows we're here?"

"I'm not sure how it works," I responded. I cut off Sam's signal – he was not authorized for this conversation. I kept a close eye on Stringer as he happily, slowly skipped down the steps. "I'd say he doesn't know we're here. He's spoken to me, he knows me. That's how he works. But he doesn't know you. I'll get the MPF out of the trunk. As a precaution. You just go up to him right now and shoot him in the leg."

I quietly opened the passenger door and slid out of the car, keeping low to avoid detection. Al was more confident in his movements, knowing that Stringer would see him straight away no matter what. He stepped out of the vehicle, took two paces and raised his firearm.

"Daniel Stringer!" he shouted.

Stringer stopped mid-skip. He looked up at Al with exaggerated surprise.

"Hello!" he called.

"Lay down on the floor with your hands on your head," Al called.

"It's not very clean down there," Stringer pointed out.

I was astonished. It took me a moment to react. "Dammit, Al! Shoot!"

Al discharged five rounds into the sidewalk next to Stringer's feet. "I will not warn you again!" he called.

"For fuck's sake!" I shouted in return. I grabbed the MPF from the trunk and rushed to Al's side with my own sidearm drawn in my free hand. "Don't warn him the *first* time!"

Stringer waved one hand at me and smiled. "You must be Jack," he said.

I brought my sidearm to bear and fired at him, but I was too late. He was effortlessly able to dive to his right behind the cover of a parked vehicle. My shots drilled harmlessly into the apartment complex steps.

I immediately dropped my sidearm and transferred the MPF to my right hand. I brought the heavy, Uzi-shaped machine gun up to bear and sprayed an entire clip into the vehicle and the two adjoining it to my left. The roar of the MPF filled the air. Holes punched the vehicles. Toughened glass spidered and shattered inwards. Tires punctured and slumped. The sound dissipated in an echo. The last empty casing clattered with a tinkle on the floor. Curtains began to twitch along the street.

I released the magazine. I quickly snapped another off the top of the MPF, in front of the carrying handle and above the muzzle. I slid the new magazine in, automatically loading a fresh round into the chamber. The MPF's servos whined as it adjusted itself to the new weight distribution.

I was ready to navigate the broken cars and with luck discover the punctured but alive body of Daniel Stringer on the sidewalk. Before I could move there was the sound of a car engine whirring into action further down the road. The vehicle, a silver Chrysler, pulled out quickly and shot off in a straight line. It headed towards the perpendicular main street, which was already showing signs of the Saturday rush.

Walking quickly down the center of the road, I emptied the second clip into the rear of the Chrysler. It reduced the trunk, rear windshield and back fender to a mass of twisted carnage. I must have hit something important – engine, computer systems, Stringer himself – because the car slowed of its own accord. It rolled to a halt just past the end of the street.

I broke into a jog. I removed the expended second magazine and pulled the final clip from its position behind the carrying handle. "Al!" I shouted. He picked up my disposed sidearm and followed.

I heard a distressed blast of horn before the bus came into view. Its tires squealing in an attempt to halt its progress, the bus slammed into the left side of Stringer's car. The impact flung the car back and to the right. Lifted off the ground, the car cleared the curb and wrapped itself around a streetlight. The pole quickly gave in to the impact and crashed to the ground. The bus shuddered to a halt past the edge of the road, already half out of view down the busy street.

I slowed to a halt, shocked. The fallen streetlight fizzed as Stringer's shattered car groaned to a rest.

"Too easy," I whispered to myself. "Too easy."

Al came to a stop alongside me, looking surprised himself.

"Where's the foam?" he asked. "The safety foam. Why didn't it deploy?"

He was right. It was a very valid point. Safety foam would always deploy within a car to protect its passengers if the impact registered strongly enough by the on-board systems. There was no chance my auto-fire could have knocked all of the systems out. The only reason why the foam would not have deployed is if no one was in the vehicle.

"It's a decoy!" I called. I spun and started to run back to my original position. Stringer must have pre-programmed that car to speed off, driverless, and divert our attention while he made his escape. A second car further down the road pulled out and headed off in the opposite direction.

"Al!" I shouted. "That's him!" My call was unnecessary as Al, unencumbered by the MPF, was sprinting past me to our car. I knew already that Stringer's vehicle was too far from my position for a third burst with the firearm to be of much use.

Al had the driver's door open and was sliding into the seat when I got to the car. Stringer's vehicle was turning to the right, down a side street. Then he was gone. Pressing a button on the side of the gun, I activated the MPF's secondary sniper mode. Now with an extended butt, a silencer and a telescopic sight, the MPF would provide me with more accuracy in a pursuit environment. I rushed past the car's trunk to the passenger door.

The car was moving before I'd closed the door. With a squeal of tires, Al set off in pursuit. I called Sam up, pocketed my cell phone and activated the in-car speaker. I then lowered the passenger window and poked the rifle out, ready for aiming.

"Surveillance," the phone said.

"Track that car," I shouted. "The one that's just left the apartment, heading South East. We are in pursuit but the vehicle is currently out of sight."

Al slammed the car to the right, sliding it expertly round the corner. I braced myself against the door. When we were moving in a straight line again I took a look through the sights.

"He's up ahead," Sam told us. "About one and a half blocks from you."

"Got him," I called. I could see the car in my sights, but traffic was thickening and there were several other vehicles between us and our quarry. "Where's Meg and Tisi?"

"They've just left," Sam answered. "They should be able to cut across his position in five minutes."

Stringer's car weaved to the left. Sam informed us of this instantly, but I'd already seen Stringer's movements. "Come on, Al," I said. "Catch him, will you?"

"I'm trying my best here," Al said, straining with the wheel as he flung our car into a left-hand turn at reckless speeds. We narrowly missed a vehicle waiting dutifully at the lights.

I had another look through my sights. I spied a very brief clear line of sight and snapped off two silenced, high-velocity rounds. Stringer's car weaved out of sight. I was not even sure if the shots hit his vehicle.

I waited patiently for the next opportunity as Al threw the car left and right in accordance with Sam's guidance. He was going to escape, I felt. The net may have been closing on him, with Meg and Tisi about to come into play too. But I had this dreadful feeling that Stringer was going to slip through. Using the decoy car was an act of genius.

"Do we have a clear idea where he's heading yet?" I asked Sam.

"He's weaving pretty randomly at the moment, but if I had to hazard a guess he seems to be heading in the general direction of the freeway."

"Christ," I muttered. Traffic was already quite thick on these streets. When we hit the Manhattan-Trump freeway, the Saturday rush hour would be in full swing. I just needed one clear shot. I just needed the traffic to part for one second so I could fire a bullet through the rear windshield, through the driver's seat, through his chest.

I fired off a couple more snapshots, but civilian traffic was just too dense for them to be of much use. Then the car had turned and he was out of sight again.

"Redirect Meg and Tisi to the freeway," I told Sam. "If they can't cut him off, maybe they can build up a head of steam and catch up to him once he's off the slip road."

We were now dangerously close to the bustle of the freeway and the bridge out of Manhattan. Sam should have no problem tracking Stringer. But for us it would be a nightmare trying to fight past the commuters, the juggernauts and vans and buses. Stringer, I realized, knew this. He was planning for it, just to extend his freedom that little bit longer. He was planning to create chaos on New York's streets.

I tried a couple more shots at Stringer's car to no avail. Al punished the tires several times. We hit the slip road leading onto the freeway. The traffic was moving orderly and at a steady speed, crossing over the Hudson to New Jersey, but it was quite congested and offered us little opportunity to overtake. The freeway itself, bathed in the morning sun, was no different. For someone whose duty it was to protect ordinary citizens, this chase could not have ended up at a worse location.

"Meg and Tisi are six cars behind you," Sam informed me. "Five…four…ah, damn, a semi's in the way, they've lost the speed advantage."

"And Stringer?"

"Seven cars up, one lane to the left, looks like he's pretty hemmed in as well."

I seated myself on the window frame and aimed across the roof of our car. I could see his vehicle, nestled next to a large car transporter. A shot would be risky. It would need to pass through two other cars. The trajectory seemed clear though. Only windows barred its way. I gave it a try.

The bullet punctured clean holes in the cars' windows, through the rear and front of the first vehicle, the side and front of the second. I briefly saw a puff of fabric as the shot slammed harmlessly into Stringer's headrest.

The two vehicles I hit panicked and swerved. It was only a brief swerve by each car, a moment of terror before they realized that the damage was not yet life-threatening. But it was enough to disrupt the flow of traffic. The cars slid out of the way and the gap between myself and Stringer closed. I slid myself back into the car.

"Get into his lane," I told Al. "Worry the cars in front, make them move."

Al careened into the left lane, enticing more angry horns and more swerving. He started tailgating the car in front, leaving a gap of just a few inches. Suitably worried, the car moved to the side. Just five cars between us now. But Sam had spotted a big problem.

"He's doing something," he informed us.

"Like what?"

"I don't know but...wait, there's something coming out of the driver's side window."

"Something like...?"

"A...a pole, maybe? He's pointing it at the car transporter."

"A pole?" I asked confused. Then a light switched on in my head. I turned to Al and shouted: "EVASIVE ACTION!"

Poking and prodding, Stringer managed to dislodge the rear car's couplings on the transporter's upper tier. Now free from the burden of shackles, the brand new car rolled backwards off its perch. It fell to the road, its rear end slamming into the surface and spilling debris. Carried by momentum, the front of the car was thrown into the asphalt and it cart wheeled forward. It lifted off the ground, shedding more debris. Vehicles skidded out of the way of the impact zone, smashing into each other in the panic.

Still in mid air and rapidly slowing its trajectory, the broken vehicle flipped by us. Its hood passed close over our roof. I checked behind me to witness the carnage it caused. More vehicles screeched to the side. Some successfully avoided the wreck. A couple slammed into it and spun the broken car even faster. I saw their foam protection deploy. It was a burst of white covering the cars' interiors that hardened to absorb the impact before collapsing and dissipating into the air. It left the occupants shaken but unhurt.

Meg and Tisi's car flashed past the debris, closely followed by the 18-wheeler that had held them up for so long during our pursuit. Several other vehicles skirted round the carnage and continued on their way, having decided that reaching their appointment on time was of greater importance.

There were far fewer cars between us and Stringer now. Utilizing this new freedom, I took aim out the passenger window again and began firing round after round at him. A few shots punctured the chromed bodywork, but his erratic weaving succeeded in avoiding several more.

The dynamics of the traffic altered once more as the final turnpike passed before we hit the bridge. Several vehicles slid off the freeway and others joined it.

"Stone!" Sam called to me.

"Go," I told him. I cracked off one more round then concentrated on the speakerphone.

"That was a bad crash, man," he told me. "You'd be best to take Stringer out soon too. There's a Charge Grid in less than a mile."

"Damn," I muttered, then added: "Maybe that's not a problem. Gives us a chance to rethink our tactics."

I changed speaker on the phone to talk to the car behind. "Who's driving there?" I asked.

"Tisi," Meg said, slightly grumpy. I guessed he wanted to be in control for the big chase.

"Okay. Tisi, draw off to the left and try to catch up. Give Meg a chance for a side-on shot. We've got a Charge Grid coming up, so let's see if we can take him out before then."

I could see the Charge Grid now at the far end of the bridge. On the horizon it looked like nothing more than a simple tunnel. The Heads-Up Display flashed on the windshield in front of Al.

"Warning," an electronic voice informed us. "Charge Grid imminent. Please ensure all persons are inside the vehicle and windows shut. Please do not deviate from your current lane. Control will become automatic in ten seconds."

"Shit," I exclaimed. Time was running out faster than I thought. I put all my effort into firing off another two rounds at Stringer's car. He was now just two cars ahead of us, but as we were in the same lane my bullets ricocheted harmlessly off the side panel. Meg and Tisi were still too far behind. They'd moved into the outside lane but were trailing by a good ten seconds.

I pulled back into the car, deactivated the MPF's secondary mode and closed the passenger window. The Charge Grid loomed large now. It was a tunnel of latticed wire smothered in solar panels. It was fronted by a large interactive sign informing people of the impending danger. The road under the tunnel was a bronzed copper bristling with static charge.

"Automatic control initiated," the computer voice told us. Al let go of the steering wheel. We felt the car slow to a steady 55mph. To my right, a slower car we were about to overtake quickened pace so we all trundled along at the same speed. We were fixed to our lanes by computer control.

I sighed heavily as we rolled under the lip of the Charge Grid tunnel. The sound of motion altered, becoming deeper and more resonant with a hint of echo. The tunnel was dark, lit from above by yellow lamps and dances of bronzed reflection. To the rear of our car a small prong lowered to just above the floor. It fed the electricity generated by rooftop solar panels directly into our recharging battery. Every so often signs flashed past ensuring we all knew to stay inside our vehicle or risk being electrocuted.

"Any ideas on new tactics?" Al asked. He cautiously handed my sidearm back to me. I holstered it.

"Doing what I say would be a help," I told him. "We are going to have a serious talk about what happened earlier."

"How do you mean?" Al asked.

"I told you to shoot him!" I answered angrily. "Wound him, cripple him. One shot as soon as you got out of the car...*bang*...and all this would be over."

"I...he was unarmed."

"I gave you an order, Al. That's the thing to remember here. Order given, order followed: no problem. Order given, order *not* followed: car chase and freeway pile-up. Get the idea?"

I could see there was movement in Stringer's car. He was too distant and enveloped by other traffic for anything to be clear. "What's he up to?" I said. I removed the sights from the top of the MPF and looked through them at his vehicle.

"What is it?" Al asked.

"It looks...I don't know. Is he putting on a coat? He's got something else in there. I really can't tell."

The image was confusing. Stringer was a silhouette, blurred in my sights by the half-dozen car windows that separated the two of us. He was moving, that I could tell. His arms were flapping and he was juggling with a large rectangular thing. Then I spied something else, something very surprising. He was opening his car door.

"What the...? He's opened the door. He's going to fry himself! Sam! Can you see more clearly?"

"I've got nothing," Surveillance told me. "The tunnel doesn't allow normal vision and the heat and static from the Charge Grid makes everything else useless. All I've got are RFIDs and we know they don't help."

"Well...wait," I paused. The car looked vacant. "He's gone."

"Must be lying down on the seats so you can't see him," Al informed me. But I had a gut feeling that wasn't the case.

I caught a blur of black out the corner of my eye. I turned just in time to see a large smudge weaving its way through traffic as it slowed, sparks dancing around its base. It had gone from sight in an instant. It took my brain a few seconds to properly process what I'd just seen. When my brain pinged that metaphorical light bulb above my head, I was left with a vision of a man dressed in black and lying down on a street luge board. He was dodging what was effectively overtaking traffic as friction slowed the board's momentum. Clever, very clever.

"Did you see that?" I shouted. I turned in my seat and peered backwards through the sights. Al joined me, wishing he had his own binoculars.

"Whoa...!" Meg called. "Was that him on a luge board? He just shot past us!"

"God damn it!" I said. "He's gone where we can't follow. Man's far too smart for his own good. Meg, can you see what he's doing?"

"Searching now...looks like...yes, he's heading down the maintenance slip road."

"Bingo!" Sam called through. "I can see him. He's out of the tunnel, going down the slip road."

"Where does it head?" I asked.

"Maintenance section under the Charge Grid. Miles of pipes, tunnels and circuit boards."

"Any other route in or out?"

"The slip road continues out the other side as a track."

"Right," I said. I was distracted by the sound of squealing tires and a computer voice muttering away, but I filtered it out. "Monitor the exits, let me know if he comes out either..."

As I was speaking, I turned to face forwards. Sunlight flooded over me as we left the cover of the Charge Grid tunnel back onto the open freeway. I realized in an instant what the muttering computer voice was saying and why I could hear the sound of screeching tires.

"Al…" I said in panic. I already knew it was too late.

Having left the tunnel, the vehicles' automatic controls had been replaced again by human control. Thanks to him wedging something on the brake, Stringer's car had come to a quick stop. The two drivers between his vehicle and ours had managed to regain control of their cars. They were just in time to swerve out of the way of Stringer's now almost stationary vehicle. Distracted, neither Al nor I had noticed this until we were almost upon it. There was no time to brake, no time to swerve, only enough time to say the aforementioned "Al…"

The safety foam deployed the instant we hit the rear of Stringer's car. The hood crumpled and the windshield shattered. I was kept rigid by what amounted to little more than hardened polystyrene. I felt the foam flex a little, dissipating the pressure put on my body by our sudden halt. Then it reacted with the air and began to crumble and collapse into separate molecules, its job done.

I coughed twice, shook my head. Behind and to the side cars were squealing out of the way into already full lanes. They began sideswiping other road users. An impressive pile-up began to form to our left.

Al and I quickly exited the crumpled car, preferring our chances on foot.

Tisi's vehicle came out of the tunnel to our left. She threw it into a skid to avoid the pile-up. She only succeeded in flipping the car over the central reservation and into oncoming traffic. It slid into the middle of the other freeway on its roof, the safety foam deployed. The oncoming traffic swerved maniacally and a refrigerated trailer jackknifed in panic. Meg and Tisi reacted immediately to this danger and scrambled out of the car. They cleared the vehicle and flattened themselves on the road moments before the jackknifing trailer slid overhead, taking what remained of their vehicle with it.

The 18-wheeler that previously held Tisi up was moments too late to be saved by the Charge Grid's automated Accident Emergency Systems. It had no chance of braking or swerving like the smaller civilian vehicles. It shunted what remained of mine and Stringer's cars further down the freeway. Fortunately neither Al nor I were close enough to be affected by the impact, but now we were stuck on foot and Stringer was already slipping out of our net.

I had no time to take in the carnage wrought on the freeway. Alongside frequent whoops of warning from klaxons, the automated Accident Emergency Systems activated. They halted all the traffic on the Charge Grid and warned drivers further back down the road of the dangers ahead. But the Charge Grid was not fully switched off.

"Sam!" I called, ensuring my earpiece was still active. I ripped my cell phone from my pocket and activated the screen.

"You okay?" he asked, both on the screen and in my ear. He looked a little pale.

"Turn off the Charge Grid!"

"What?"

"Turn it off! Turn off the power now!"

Before Sam told me he'd accomplished his task I could feel the static charge of the Grid disappear. The klaxon failed in a plaintive wail. I pulled my gun from its holster and started sprinting back into the tunnel.

"Still monitoring the exits?" I asked. Al was not far behind me as we dodged parked cars. I did not have time to look around, but I presumed Meg and Tisi were following too.

"The signal's been very weak due to the Charge Grid's interference," Sam told me, "but I haven't seen anything. Patching the live feed through to you now."

The live image of the slip road and its dirt-track exit on the other side of the tunnel came through on my screen. The image was clear now. The Charge Grid's interference was removed when it was powered down.

We reached the top of the slip road and swiveled 180 degrees back into the light. We headed down the road as fast as we could. I abandoned all pretence of surprise and barreled into the maintenance section of the tunnel with my sidearm raised. If Stringer was waiting for us down there, I'd rather have charged him and risk being shot than waste precious seconds on stealth.

The tunnel was barely lit by the sunlight flooding in from both entrances. Three corridors ran in both directions under the freeway, following its route. Thick maintenance pipes were strapped to the ceilings. An electrical hum vied for pride of place with the stench of damp on the concrete floor. There was a pile of black belongings on the floor in the centre of the maintenance underpass. It looked harmless enough and I ignored it to concentrate on the search for Stringer. The corridors were checked, but there was no sight. If he'd gone down one of those he could be lost in a subterranean labyrinth by now. We'd have no way of tracking him down here. I quickly checked the dirt track but the only sign of life was the real-time, top-down image of myself on my cell phone. Daniel Stringer had melted into New Jersey.

I screamed in anger. So close. We were so close.

I looked across at Al. He was checking through the black pile. A three-wheeled Pyronics All-Terrain Engineered Recreational Module was his transport. The PATERM looked customized, retrofitted for use on the hardiest of surfaces. The other object on the floor was an ankle-length rubber cloak from a fetish emporium.

He insulated himself. Retrofitting the PATERM and wearing the rubber cloak allowed him to be insulated from the deadly static of the Charge Grid. There was now no doubt in my mind about his abilities. From the decoy vehicle to the car transporter to the escape on the Charge Grid, this whole chase had to have been planned in advance.

I moved my attention to Sam at Surveillance. "Get a clean-up crew out here," I told him. "We can't let anything in our vehicles get into public hands. And I want his car going over with tweezers."

I gathered the Erinyes around me and sighed heavily. "Okay, let's pack this up. Gather all the evidence and ship out."

"What next, boss?" Al asked. "We've run out of options."

"No," I shook my head. "We haven't. We just go back to what we were doing before we caused the biggest freeway pile-up in two decades."

"And that was?"

"Andrea Clayton. I need to have a talk with her. She could be all we've got left."

TWELVE

I rang the door buzzer three times before I was let into the apartment complex.

Andi opened her apartment's door to me still dressed in her night-clothes. She wore a white Tee-shirt and striped boxer shorts. Her hair had only been brushed to a serviceable level. The last vestiges of the previous night's make-up still adorned her face. Her bare feet slapped on the apartment's laminate flooring with every step.

"Yes?" she asked suspiciously when she saw me. People rarely expect a be-suited stranger to appear on their doorstep on a Saturday morning.

"Miss Clayton," I began. I reached into a pocket and withdrew a highly-convincing fake ID. "Agent Tom Harriman, FBI. We need to have a word."

She slowly looked me up and down with a mixture of distrust and suspicion. "What about?" she eventually asked.

"May I come in?" I asked back. I didn't wait for a response and slid through the gap in the doorway.

"Well…" Andi began, but realized that any protestation was already too late. She sighed heavily. "Take a seat," she offered in a way that suggested she really didn't want me to sit.

The apartment was open plan. A TV adorned one wall, above a fireless mantelpiece. Two burnished leather couches faced each other with a large coffee table in the centre. Across another wall was a breakfast nook and dining table. To one side of that a door led through to the bedroom and en suite.

Andi padded to the breakfast nook. She picked up a mug and poured some steaming black coffee from a pot.

"I wouldn't mind one if you're offering," I said with a smile, trying to put her at ease.

Andi stared at me for a few moments. She was trying to figure out exactly what she would gain by refusing my request. Her conclusion was 'nothing' so she poured me a mug and brought them both over to the coffee table.

I sat on a couch with my back to the TV and mantelpiece so I could observe the entire apartment. It was a move imbued upon me by my training. Keep as much as possible within your field of vision.

Andi sat cross-legged on the couch opposite, blew on her coffee and sipped it.

"What's this all about, Agent...?"

"Harriman."

"Harriman," she reiterated.

"Did you hear an incident outside your apartment this morning?" I asked.

Andi took another slow sip of her coffee. I recognized it as a professional stalling technique while she gathered her thoughts.

"Yes," she answered. "There were gunshots. I saw a bit of it from my bedroom window."

I nodded slowly. "What did you see?"

She sipped the coffee again. "As I said. Gunshots. Cars speeding off. It was all a bit confusing. I couldn't see much. What was it all about, Agent Harriman?"

"We're tracking a man we suspect was involved in the incident this morning." I told her. I reached into an outside pocket and withdrew two photographs. I kept one close to me and handed the other over to Andi. It was the photograph of Daniel Stringer we collected from the ID forger's files.

"Do you know this man?" I asked. I kept my eyes on her as she studied the image. She masked the recognition well, but I could see her working through her options. She had the choice of telling me everything and ruining all she had worked for, or lying to a Government Agent.

I took a sip of my own coffee. "Mmmm," I said. "That's a good cup of Joe." Her eyes momentarily flicked up to mine. I had distracted her train of thought and put her very much on the back foot. Just where I wanted her.

"So?" I pressed, refusing to give her any more time to mull over her decision.

She looked up at me. "No," she answered. She leaned forward and placed the photograph on the coffee table. I picked it up and held it out in front of her.

"You sure?" I asked. "Have another look."

"I don't know him, Agent," she said firmly. "Sorry, I can't help."

I nodded again and pocketed the photograph. I took another sip of the coffee, studying her. She didn't like the scrutiny.

"Is that it?" she asked.

I handed the second photograph to her. It was a close-up of her meeting with Stringer at the Coney Island BattleKarts track.

"Can you tell me who that is, please?" I asked.

She stared at the image. I could see the panic rising deep inside her. "It's me," she said quietly. She stared at me, annoyed. "Have you been spying on me?" she demanded.

"Who's next to you, Miss Clayton?" I insisted.

She uncrossed her legs and perched on the edge of the couch. She stared intently at the photograph, fingering the edges of it. Her mind was working overtime.

"My brother," she eventually answered. That took me by surprise. She was smart enough to know we could easily check on the validity of her statement. Within seconds we could check if her brother looked like that, or even if she had a brother at all.

"Brother?" I asked.

"Yes," Andi answered. "My brother." She handed the photograph back to me. "John."

I took the first photograph back out of my pocket and held them up to her side-by-side.

"This is the same person," I told her.

She shrugged. "I can see the similarity."

"You're saying they're not the same person?"

"No, they're not. I can see the similarity, Agent Harriman, but that doesn't mean anything. There's a court case in Los Angeles at the moment. The film star Max Cane is suing seven people for breach of identity because they used plastic surgery to look exactly like him. Even without plastic surgery, people can look the same."

"So where is this brother of yours?" I asked.

Andi drained the last of her coffee. "I don't know. He was staying with me for a few days, but now he's gone."

"Is he in any kind of trouble?" I asked, picking away at her story to find the thread that would unravel it.

"No."

"Then why did he run from Federal Agents this morning?"

Andi stared at me again before answering. "Assuming that was my brother this morning–" she began.

"He came out of your apartment block," I interrupted. "And he looked exactly like this." I showed her the Coney Island photograph again.

Andi sighed. "Why did he run? Think about it. A man…a good, law-abiding man, visits his sister for a few days. One morning he leaves her apartment, maybe to buy a newspaper. Suddenly two complete strangers are screaming and pointing guns at him. Most ordinary people will do one of two things in that situation. Some will freeze and hope that this is all a big mistake and they won't get shot. Others will, fearing for their lives, flee. My brother is not used to having guns pointed at him, Agent. He would flee."

I nodded, then glanced behind me at the mantelpiece. "What does he think about you not having any photographs of him on display? Why is that? Are you ashamed of him for some reason?"

"I've never seen a photograph of him that does him justice," Andi answered. This woman was very smart, very good at thinking on her feet. While I didn't believe a word of it, her story thus far was technically plausible. I needed that one moment where her story would fall apart. Once I had that I could wheedle my way into her psyche and prove to her that protecting Stringer was the worst thing she could do. But first I needed to get past her stubborn defenses.

I picked up my coffee mug and realized the contents were tepid. I placed it back on the table.

"Do you know how RFID chips work, Miss Clayton?" I asked.

"More or less," she responded. I could see that the initial panic she had felt when she saw the second photograph had now disappeared and been replaced by a growing confidence. She thought she was winning this battle. But I was about to deliver the kill shot.

"They transmit all the time, Miss Clayton. With sophisticated enough equipment you can actually track someone all day long. It was what they were originally designed for back at the start of the century, so people could track parcel deliveries online. Our tracking system shows that when you were at the BattleKarts track on Coney Island a few days ago – the day this photograph was taken – your RFID signal was strong, but there was no signal next to you. No signal coming from your so-called brother. Would you care to explain that?"

Andi wrung her hands together. "If you insist," she answered. She stood and picked up her mug. "More coffee?"

I shook my head. She padded out to the breakfast nook to replenish her mug from the steaming pot.

"Would you mind answering the question, please?" I called to shorten her stalling tactic.

"I know full well that we live in a Big Brother surveillance state, Agent Harriman. But not everywhere does."

She returned to her couch, tucking one leg under her and confidently blowing steam off the top of her mug. I realized she was about to dodge my metaphorical kill shot.

"My brother, Agent Harriman, doesn't live in the US. My parents separated when I was young. I stayed with my mother. John went to live with my father in Marseille. In France, RFID implants are recommended but not compulsory. My brother had his US implant removed and didn't get another installed. Instead he has a card. But that doesn't transmit a signal all the time. It only transmits when he presses his thumb to a sensor to activate it. So, no, Agent, he wouldn't have been transmitting a signal that day."

"You have an answer for everything, don't you Miss Clayton?"

She smiled. "The truth always provides an answer, Agent Harriman."

"And I suppose if I check the records for details of you and your brother, I will find everything is in order?"

"No, you won't. We grew up in Fremont, Nebraska. As I'm sure you recall, Agent, ten years ago a computer virus hit the city and wiped every bit of electronic data."

"I remember," I answered. "Christmas. The Santa Virus. An upgraded version of the Stuxnet malware. Targeted every scrap of online data about Fremont and destroyed it. Presumably it was a show of force, an indication what could be done to a city, a country, the world. But we never found out who did it, and they never followed it up with another attack."

"We were given new chips," Andi explained. "But all the data had been lost. For days people couldn't get back in their homes because the locks had frozen. We couldn't start our cars. We couldn't pay for groceries. So the Government decided that on the new chips they would just install the basics for us to get by on and leave it at that. Family connections, school grades, criminal records…everything had just gone. I hear a few people even decided on a whim to change their name and create a completely new identity. In a paperless society, our memories were all that was left as proof."

"I know the stories," I told her. "The point you're making, in such a long-winded way, is that there's no record of you ever having a brother. Is that right?"

"That is right," she confirmed.

I perched on the edge of the couch and stared deep into her sparkling green eyes.

"Miss Clayton," I began. "You weave a good yarn. But you are playing a very dangerous game with a very dangerous man. If you side with Stringer in this, you will get burned."

She studied me for a moment. She knew what I said was true. But I could see in her eyes that she already considered herself to be in too deep to back out now.

"I don't know who you're talking about," she answered quietly, looking down at her coffee mug.

"I know you've been lying to me," I told her.

She looked up at me, a bit of that fear and panic starting to creep back into her. "And I know you're not really an FBI Agent," she answered.

Our facades had fallen. We'd exposed each other within this web of falsehoods. Nobody had won here. Nobody was going to win.

"Where is he?" I tried one last time.

She opened her mouth to speak, but couldn't find the words. She half shrugged, half shook her head. She didn't know. She had no idea if she'd ever see him again. I was finished here.

"Back away from this right now," I told her as I stood. I crossed to the apartment door and opened it. I looked back at her. "I can't guarantee your safety," I finished, before closing the door behind me.

Andi had been worried the rest of the day. She'd been in a near state of panic on several occasions. The gunshots and screeching cars had initially shook her up. She had begun to fret that some serious injury had befallen Daniel. Then there was the visit from the fake FBI Agent. That had really shaken her, made her realize she was getting in very deep and there was little chance she could swim back out. The visit initially helped ease her mind about Daniel's safety, though. She knew that if he was still being hunted, he must have escaped from his pursuers that morning. But the doubts grew again as the afternoon wore on. Daniel had not been answering her calls all day. Why? Had he since been cornered? Was he grievously injured?

She had remained in her apartment, pacing ragged paths on the floor and mowing the edges of her nails with her teeth. But there had been no response, no communication, no sign that he was okay. She'd been unable to relax, to eat.

Giving in to a need to know the truth no matter the consequence, Andi dressed in casual attire – jeans, grey Tee-shirt, sneakers. There was a bit of a chill in the wind so she donned her mac and wrapped a light scarf around her neck.

As evening loomed and darkness fell, she left the apartment and made speed for Daniel's own abode.

She felt uneasy on her trek across the city. She felt sure her every move would be monitored. She'd be observed all the way. There was no clear indication of this, no confirmation of her suspicions. But there was a gurgling in her gut that told her she was being watched.

She was.

The apartment complex unsettled Andi more than the last time she was there. Before it seemed like a rough and decrepit area. Now it felt more dangerous. The shadows were more foreboding. Every sound conjured up an image of an armed government officer watching her, her chest squarely within the sights of their semi-automatic. She wished she had something more than a digital voice recorder and a taser in her pockets. The archaic recorder would be utterly useless, and in this neighborhood the taser probably wouldn't slow anyone.

On edge, Andi's senses were heightened. Before she reached Daniel's apartment door she felt he was not there. There was no need to knock. The door's RFID scanner detected her. The vidscreen to the right activated.

Daniel's face appeared on-screen. He told her he was fine. He informed her that the transmission would only play when she was detected at his door, and it would delete itself after playing once. He insisted she paid attention. He briefly explained the occurrence in the morning. He asked to meet her after dark in the alley system of a very rundown and aggressive area of the city. He promised she would have safe passage. He told her to hurry and be wary of anyone whom she thought might be following her.

The message ended and the vidscreen confirmed the message had been erased. It switched off.

Andi's anxiety over Daniel's wellbeing had now been replaced by another form of mild panic. Surely Daniel was taking a great risk in asking to meet her. Surely his enemies would be trailing her. Surely he didn't expect her to be able to shake off highly-trained Government agents.

But more than that, she was perturbed by the concept of walking through a known drug and crime haven to meet him in a darkened alley. She was acutely aware of the dangers for a woman by herself at night in a place where no one should ever tread alone. She silently wished she could convert the low-powered taser into a switchblade. Or a gun.

She left the apartment complex. She decided to check her route on her cell phone map, but realized that in her rush she had left everything behind. All she had with her were the items she forgot to remove from her pockets the last time she wore that coat. She located a breath mint, slipped it in her mouth and realized this was the only food she'd had all day.

She headed off down the road, confident that she knew New York well enough to reach her destination without GPS aid.

With real-time, top-down video streaming, Cyclops followed her.

The network of alley systems was complex. It was confusing and so dark that Andi wasn't completely sure she was actually treading on the alley's concrete floor. The occasional squelch emanated from under her sneakers, and she was convinced that sometimes the squelch moved.

Sounds rang down the alleyway. Some were muffled and ghostly. Others were sharp and frightening. Gunshots? Breaking glass? Sobbing? Or merely distorted voices and slamming doors? She quickened her pace. She could feel her heart teasing the scarf with its insistent thuds. Her quickened breathing was starting to drown out the dissipating sounds of the streets beyond the alley system.

She turned the corner. And there he was. Daniel. He was waiting patiently with his back against the wall. He seemed unaware of, or at least unfazed by, his surroundings. He was absently rotating a length of metal piping in his hands, like he was the baton-twirling State champion. He glanced across at her as she breathed a heavy sigh of relief. He rested the piping against the wall and beckoned her over.

"Hello," he greeted. He briefly glanced up beyond the high-rise buildings to the star-specked night sky, and smiled. Andi ran into him, relieved to finally be with another person in this disconcerting locale.

"Are you okay?" Andi enquired, still slightly breathless. "After this morning, I…"

He nodded in return. "Course I am. They're not as incompetent as usual, but still no match for me."

Andi couldn't keep still. The adrenaline rush of fear was keeping her twitching. She gestured about her with a mix of fear and disgust. "Why meet here?" she asked.

Daniel merely tapped one forefinger to his temple knowingly.

"So what…what happened this morning?" she continued. "Was it the Government?"

"In a way," he responded. "They're kind of freelance in that respect. Like the Men in Black. Nothing to worry about."

"Nothing...?" she began. "When people are shooting machine guns down my street, I worry."

Daniel shrugged. He opened his trench coat. "No holes," he said. "I'm fine."

"One of them visited me," she told him.

"I know," he answered.

"I didn't tell him anything. I lied."

"I know," he repeated.

Andi stopped pacing. She briefly put one hand on his chest. She was not sure why. It could have been because she wanted to confirm he wasn't injured. It could have been because she wanted to feel the beating of his heart. Suddenly, there were butterflies in her stomach. She stifled a gasp of surprise. The danger, the sexual tension – she'd never felt so alive.

"Do you trust me yet?" Daniel asked after a short pause. She nervously glanced up and down the alley.

"What? Yes. I think...yes, yes I do."

"Then you will need to do exactly...*exactly*...what I say, and *nothing else*. Okay?" His face was stern, insistent. Daniel was in serious mode.

"How do you mean?" Andi said.

"They will have followed you here. It's inevitable. That's why we're meeting here. We need to escape and ensure they can never follow you again."

"H...how?"

"The escape part is why I need you to do only what I tell you to. Nothing else. Just follow my instructions to the letter no matter how strange they sound. Otherwise you may wind up dead, and that would be…annoying for me. As for ensuring they cannot track you again…I need your right hand, your trust and your ability to endure pain without crying out. We need to do this now. So if you're not up for it, then just turn around. Go home. Forget this whole situation ever happened."

Andi slowly offered her hand. She was letting her heart trust this man although her brain seemed stuck on the word 'pain'. She slowly nodded consent. "What are you going to do?"

"Use a device to short out a part of your RFID. It uses an algorithm that multiplies Pi by itself again and again until it simply can't cope with the calculations involved. You'll still be able to open doors, pay for things and the like, but they won't be able to constantly track you through the signal it gives off."

"And…you do this by…?"

Daniel took her wrist in one hand. With the other hand he withdrew a small, sleek black object like an obese pen from his jacket pocket. "Using this," he answered. "A homemade device I've called Cobra because it's got one hell of a bite."

"It bites?!" Andi asked. She felt that her question was quite ludicrous.

"No," Daniel chided. It seemed like he agreed that her question was ludicrous. He spoke like he was addressing an idiot. "Of course it doesn't bite. But it's going to burn like a bitch."

Andi had hoped for a warning, maybe a countdown or just the question "Are you ready?" But without further ado

Daniel pressed one end of the object against the soft flesh on the top of her hand.

A high, barely audible whine increased in pitch. She started to feel what seemed like a match being lit within the skin of her hand. She gritted her teeth, but the feeling got worse. She hissed, but the match became a roaring hearth. She let out small, quiet gasps, but the hearth became a blowtorch. All her best efforts to remain quiet despite the charring occurring within her body looked like they may be for naught. She involuntarily took in a deep breath ready to fire it back out her mouth in a scream. Just in time, the pain abruptly stopped and Daniel removed the offending object.

"Good," he said, pocketing the device. "No screaming." He kissed her on the forehead. She slumped her back against the wall and took in deep breaths. She looked at her hand. She was not surprised to see a fleshy reddened lump.

It looked like Daniel had displayed all the affection he was going to with that one quick kiss on the forehead. Now he stood with his back to her. He cleaned the nib of the device and pocketed it. He turned to her, sniffed once. "Ready?"

"For what?" Andi responded.

That was when part of her RFID exploded in a puff of acrid black smoke, puncturing and charring the top of her hand. There was the sudden, unexpected stab of vicious pain. Despite all her promises, despite all her self-control, Andi emitted a short, sharp yelp.

Andi clutched her hand, trembling. Daniel grabbed the hand and checked the wound. Annoyed, he angrily let go. He looked at her with a disappointed expression.

"And now they know where we are," he chided.

"What?" Andi asked.

"The bad guys. They'd have heard your yelp. They know where we are."

"Weren't they tracking us by my RFID anyway? They'd already know where we are!"

"That's not the point. I told you to keep quiet."

"Quiet?!" Andi exclaimed. "That really hurt! Why didn't you warn me, you arrogant asshole?"

Daniel sighed and glanced down the alley. "Sure you want to do this? Have an argument now? Here?"

"Fine! You're right. I just would have preferred a bit more of a warning. But this isn't the time or place. Let's go."

"Wait," Daniel said. He seemed completely calm. He thought for a moment. He glanced down at Andi's hand again. "Is it bleeding?"

Andi froze for a moment. She was sure she'd just heard something. Distant and unintelligible. A radio, maybe. Blaring out of a car passing hundreds of feet away. But it had put her on edge.

"No," she said absently. "It's fine." She listened intently to her surroundings. She put one finger to her lips, indicating to Daniel to remain quiet.

He ignored her advice. "Are you sure it's not bleeding?" he asked.

And that was when Andi realized he *wanted* to be found.

THIRTEEN

"Err…Boss?"

"This had better be important, Sam!" I whispered. "I asked for radio silence, and it wasn't supposed to be a request."

"Yeah," Surveillance responded through the tiny earpiece. "She's gone."

I stopped in my tracks. If it wasn't for a plan view of the alley system on my cell phone and Sam's directions I would have been lost in this place by now. It was one of the few places in the country where being a Government agent *decreased* your life expectancy. "Gone?" I asked in disbelief.

"Signal just…disappeared, Boss," Sam answered. "Switching to heat vision and…oh, we have *two* people!"

I switched to a general frequency. "Okay everyone, we have our quarry pinned down. I want you all to keep the perimeter tight and start closing in on my location. If you see the suspect, shoot first and ask questions later. Do you all understand?"

I received positive signals from everyone involved. In addition to my three Erinyes, I had commandeered 15 SWAT ground troops, an equipment truck and a medic. The General's orders were that no regular forces were to be involved in this operation. But I had found this restriction to be unacceptable. I couldn't afford to play by his rules. All I had given the SWAT to go on was a face. But I was sure there would be consequences later on with the General. In this vast maze it was ridiculous to think just four of us could corner Stringer by ourselves.

"Meg's coming up behind you," Sam told me. "He'll be with you in one minute. I suggest you wait for the back-up."

"No. I need to move now. Where are they?"

Armed with Sam's guidance, I slid up to an intersection. If Sam was correct, Stringer was just a few feet round the corner. I could hear voices. Keeping tight to the corner, I pressed up against the wall to hear better.

The first sentence was unclear as I positioned myself better and held my breath. The voice sounded female. She said something like "It's time" or "It's fine."

"Are you sure it's not bleeding?" came a male voice in response.

"It's fine!" the frustrated female answered. "What are we waiting for? What the hell are you up to?"

"You seem to have some anger issues. I told you it would hurt. But no, you just presume you can take it, then go shouting your mouth off…"

"I'm sorry I was vocal when my hand exploded! But why aren't we heading somewhere else? Why are we waiting here? Aren't they right behind us?"

That seemed like my cue. If Stringer was as good as he seemed, he must have known I was right around the corner. I found it suspicious that he wasn't running yet. Maybe he didn't know me well enough. Maybe he thought I'd try to talk him down or arrest him.

I drew my sidearm, brought it up to bear and strode into the alley. I fired three shots. They all hit Stringer in the chest and he was thrown to the floor.

Andi jumped with the shock then looked in horror at his body. She wasn't expecting the shoot first policy either. But this man needed to be stopped.

I stopped opposite Andi. Stringer's body was in front of me. I looked at the journalist. She was holding a length of metal pipe in her left hand but she looked too shocked and weak to even consider using it.

I aimed my weapon at her temple. I had a moment of indecision. She'd seen what I'd done. She'd seen my face. She probably knew all about Stringer, about NASRU, about what we did to him. The General would have no hesitation. He would authorize the kill order immediately. But this woman was still an innocent civilian. A respected journalist. If something were to happen, she would be missed. I should shoot her right now. I knew that. But I hesitated. And that was enough to lose me the advantage.

Stringer was still alive. Sprawled on the floor, he kicked out with his legs. His first kick hit Andi viciously in the shin.

In surprise I depressed the trigger and my gun retorted loudly down the alley. Shorn of one leg, Andi had already been thrown off balance. As she fell to the ground, her head had already slipped below the firing line of my weapon. A brick shattered in a puff of dust and shrapnel as the high velocity bullet drilled into it. Andi landed harshly on her hands and knees. Stringer followed his first kick with another, this time at my legs. It caught me in the shin and I stumbled.

Having been literally kick-started into action, Andi quickly got to her feet and swung the pipe at my head. It caught me on the nape of the neck. It was a soft blow, but it was enough to knock me to the ground, dazed. A harder blow could have snapped my neck. As I hit the ground, my gun skidded away from me.

I struggled to get to my feet, but Stringer was already on his. He plucked my sidearm from the floor and stood over me with it aimed at my head.

"April Fool!" he said. He tapped his chest with his free hand. "Kevlar, Stone! How stupid do you think I am?"

I grunted, still on my hands and knees, and rolled my sore neck. There was no point moving, trying to disarm him. He'd drill a bullet through my brain before I could flex my muscles.

"Andi," Stringer said. "Meet Lieutenant Jack Stone of the North American Security Response Unit. Now, say goodbye to him."

Stringer slid back the firing pin. Andi dropped the metal bar and it clattered noisily on the concrete.

"Wait!" Andi called. She put one hand on his arm. "Daniel...no!"

He looked at her, confused. His aim faltered a little. It was still too risky to make my move – the gun was on a hair trigger and it was still too close to my face. Maybe if I waited this out a little longer, Andi could persuade him not to execute me.

"He shot me–" Stringer began, hurt. He looked back at me and corrected his aim.

"Do. Not. Kill. Him!" Andi demanded.

Stringer looked back at her, even more confused.

"Why?"

I heard the pounding of steps before either Stringer or Andi did. Meg came barreling round the corner of the alley, his gun already drawn.

Stringer's reactions were quick and he was able to adjust his aim as Meg opened fire. In the chaos and the noise they shot each other three or four times.

Both men were put on their backs with the power of the impacts, their guns skidding from their grasp.

I looked across at Stringer. He seemed dazed. Andi had been taken by surprise again.

"Shit!" she whispered. She ran across to Stringer. "Come on!" she screamed. Grabbing him by one arm, she dragged him to his feet and together they stumbled down the alley away from me.

I dived at my gun. I was able to fire one shot down the alley, but they'd already turned the corner out of sight.

I glanced back the other way.

"Meg?" I called. "Megaera!"

He was lying prone on the floor. I could see blood seeping into his white shirt around the abdomen. It was dark, almost black. Proper blood, not a flesh wound.

One of my men was down. He could be fatally injured. He could already be dead. I should be at his side, trying to stem the flow of blood. But Stringer was getting away, and our only lead had just gone off the grid as well. If I didn't catch him now, it was likely I never would. I knew which option the General would go for. He'd go for the pursuit. Last time, in not shooting Andi when I had the chance, I went against what I thought the General would do. It cost me dearly. This time, the mission took priority.

"Man down!" I shouted to Sam. "Get a med team down here stat!"

I broke into a run from a crouch. I set off in pursuit of Stringer, but he had enough distance to give me the slip. I was entirely reliant on Sam's directions. I could feel I was going to lose my quarry again.

"They're out of the alley," Sam told me.

Stringer and Andi were still a significant distance ahead of me. If anything went wrong with the Cyclops system, Stringer would slip through the net again.

"They've gone into a courtyard," Sam continued. "Heading for the building in front of them. They've gone inside."

I entered the courtyard moments later. It was framed by alleyways and narrow, empty roads. Across the courtyard in front of me was an old, worn and derelict 4-storey tenement building.

"Is it the one in front of me?" I asked Sam.

"Yes."

"Bring up the plans for it. Floor layouts. Exit routes. Tenants. I want to know everything about it. Where's everyone else?"

"A few seconds away for the most part."

I waited for Sam to bring up details on the property in front of me. "The building's abandoned," he said. "It hasn't been used for years. Judging by the last survey half the walls and floors are missing, and the stairwell is set to collapse at any time. There's one other exit out the back, and that's it. Cover that and you've got them cornered."

"Keep tabs on that exit," I told him, "and switch Cyclops to heat vision. Let's see where they are in there."

I heard the pounding of footsteps. The reinforcements were arriving, filing down every alley and road to this location.

"No activity at the rear exit," Sam continued. "Heat signatures...none. At this distance from orbit maybe the brickwork of the roof is too thick to penetrate."

"Yeah, I know. They don't make them like they used to. Just see what you can do. Boost the signal or whatever."

"This isn't the movies, Boss," Sam pointed out. "I can't rewire it to make it better. The satellite does what it does, and no more."

My people were starting to gather in the courtyard now. "Fan out," I told the SWAT. "Keep your distance but surround the building and post four at the rear exit."

The team began to move. They were all clad in bulletproof vests and riot headgear. Each one held a snub-nosed machine gun.

Al and Tisi had arrived. "Where's the van?" I asked. I had a plan to end this quickly and non-fatally.

"Looking for a road big enough to squeeze down," Tisi told me. "Should be here in less than a minute. What's happened with Meg?"

"Medic's en route," Sam answered over the comms. "I'll keep you posted."

"Are we moving in?" Al asked.

"No," I responded. "Just keep them cornered. Son of a bitch shot him. I'm not taking any more chances."

I got a call through that all the SWAT team was in place. Sam informed me there had still been no noticeable movement within the building or at the rear exit.

The equipment truck arrived in the courtyard. The black, boxy van pulled up to the rear. The driver got out and flung the rolling rear door open.

"Set the screen on that wall." I motioned towards the blank brick wall of another building to my left. "Al, bring out the VF10 Firebomb. Tisi, grab the guidance controls and set it up."

"The Firebomb, Sir?" Al said. "Isn't that a little excessive?"

"Ask Megaera if it is. We're ending this *now*."

The van's driver removed a large tube from the rear of the vehicle. He opened it and removed the 84" OLED screen. He stuck one end of the roll onto the brickwork of the wall. He carefully unfurled it across the side of the rundown tenement building, ensuring it stuck in place throughout. The screen was activated but remained blank.

"Sam," I said. "Patch your signal through to the screen down here."

The screen winked into life. It showed a slightly blurred plan view of the building and its surroundings. Several red heat signals surrounding it denoted the SWAT team, the Erinyes and myself. A smaller box to the top right of the screen showed another real-time image of the building's rear exit, this time in normal vision.

Al and Tisi had almost finished setting up the VF10. It was a crude tube standing on a tripod with a wireless control box nestled three feet to one side of it. The missile within the tube aimed directly at the building we were surrounding.

"Ready?" I asked.

Tisi nodded and switched on the power to the box.

"Front door," I told her.

She used the controls to aim the missile at the front door and servos whined as it moved into place.

"Stone," Al said. "Sir. Are we going to give them an ultimatum?"

I considered this. It was a tricky situation I was facing. Not because of Stringer, but because of Andi. I was faced with another dilemma.

Sending men into the building could allow Stringer to slip away. The decrepit nature of the place could even cause injury or fatality. Half the building looked set to collapse and people charging around firing weapons would only exacerbate the situation. On the other hand, I could use the VF10. No one would die, that was almost guaranteed. But the result would see my quarry detained in a hospital for weeks. And, unfortunately, Andi as well.

On the other hand, Stringer had shown quite clearly that he wouldn't think twice about taking the lives of any of us. Why should I show him the respect of an ultimatum? I didn't before, and that was before I felt the rush of anger when he shot Meg.

Negotiation was a swear word. It was time for action.

"He's given up his rights as far as I'm concerned," I responded. I turned to Tisi. "Fire."

Tisi fired the missile.

With a whisper more than a whoosh and the barest of vapor trails, the missile pelted out of its holding tube and rushed into the building. It splintered the closed wooden door in the entrance. I did not know what it impacted with, only that it did. It exploded, releasing a broil of superheated oxygen that instantly turned to flame. The burning air rushed through the building, climbing up floors and flowing across walls. It leapt with ferocious relish out of every window, every exit and every vent in a bright, loud, orangey-yellow fireball. The heat signal on the OLED screen briefly whited out.

It was done, I thought. An explosion so fast and powerful it barely burned anything. If there were curtains in the windows of the building, they would still be barely aflame and flowing in the breeze. If all had gone well, the flash fire should have hit Stringer and Andi then blown itself out with its own power a moment later. It would leave the first few layers of their skin blackened and their bodies in a state of comatose shock. It would take a few weeks to recover from the burns, but otherwise there would be nothing physically wrong with either of them. Quicker than gassing, more humane than shooting, less devastating than a Scud.

"Move in," I said to the SWAT. "Check every nook and cranny. And be careful in there."

The SWAT team moved in. The Erinyes stayed with me. I checked the large screen to view their progress. It took me a moment to realize what was wrong.

"Al, could the VF10 have significantly weakened the building's structure?"

"It would have blown away a few cobwebs, but barely marked the surface of brick and wood. So no, not at all. Why?"

"Because," I said with dawning horror, "we can see the SWAT teams' heat signatures." I took a few paces towards the screen. "Sam, you copying this?"

"They didn't show up before," Sam answered in astonishment. "Stringer and Clayton didn't show up. Did they mask their signatures somehow?"

I shook my head then realized Sam couldn't see that. "They couldn't have had anything on them that could mask their own body heat," I pointed out. "They're not in there."

"I…I…" Sam stuttered. "Cyclops saw them go in."

"A trick. Sleight of hand. However he did it, Stringer foxed us and they're still out here somewhere. Okay, change of tactics. Call the SWAT back." I turned to Al. "Now!"

I moved closer to the screen again, studying it. "Sam, bring up two images, side-by-side. One RFID, one heat signature. I want to see the area around us in a half-mile radius."

Sam did as I'd instructed. One image showed constantly moving red dots over a wire frame image of the neighborhood. The other image displayed a satellite feed showing heat escaping from vents, vehicle engines, humans and the odd stray animal.

The SWAT team was filing outside now. They were not sure what was going on.

"Okay, now correlate the data and flag up any heat signatures that don't have corresponding RFIDs. Also check for any buildings where there's no signatures – the roofs could be thick enough to mask heat."

The screens removed all the people who had working RFID chips. Most vehicles were removed as well, as all modern models came with built-in RFID ignition and locking devices. Flashing red boxes highlighted the rest. At quick glance we could confirm that all the non-RFID heat signatures were benign. We could easily identify steam from vents, a bin fire keeping the homeless warm and a smattering of starved, potentially rabid dogs. Nothing highlighted could be human.

Three buildings were also highlighted as they contained no RFID and no heat signatures within their walls.

"Three teams, check out those buildings! Sam, rewind the footage back by five minutes and see if you can spot any vehicles speeding off. They can't have covered more than half a mile on foot."

"Knowing Stringer," Al said, "he might have had a push bike hidden in one of these alleys."

He was slipping my net again, I knew that. Once again, I had Daniel Stringer in my sights and now he was getting away. There was the added danger of Andi having seen me as well. She knew what this was all about. She could spread the word to the unassuming and unknowing public. She could compromise us.

It would take a few minutes for the SWAT team to get in position and begin checking the buildings. I sent Al and Tisi on an errand to check out the rundown building we'd just firebombed. I demanded a status report on Meg.

"Medic's with him," Sam told me. "He's stabilizing him. Lost a lot of blood, but the bullets hit his shoulder and stomach. As long as he gets immediate surgery there's a good chance he'll pull through. Ambulance is two minutes away."

"Good." I breathed a heavy sigh of relief. I'd lost people in my command before. It wasn't something I wanted to experience again.

"Tisi," I said, concentrating on the current task. "What's the status in the building?"

"This place is wrecked," came the report from inside. "We can't get past the second floor. The ground floor's collapsed into the cellar and beyond. Pillars have crumbled into our path. This is useless. We can never search every part."

"Come back out then," I sighed. The SWAT teams had more or less completed their search and come up with no results. The three buildings were devoid of all life.

I kept glancing around my surroundings, in a semi-daze. I was wondering what the hell just happened. How did they both flee from me? How did he escape again?

"Nothing," I whispered when Al and Tisi returned. The van driver was busy packing up the VF10 and the OLED. He'd realized before me that this particular operation was at an end. It was a complete failure.

"What now?" I asked, a rhetorical question. "We've lost him, we've lost *her*. All we can do is go trash his apartment and just hope he's been sloppy and left a clue in there." I sighed, exasperated. "How the hell did he do it?"

"You always said he's a genius," Al said. "Maybe he's invented a teleporter."

I gave him a disparaging glance and looked away in annoyance. Something caught my eye, something circular, metal, around three feet wide and imbedded into the floor. My memory quickly recalled Tisi's report from within the building: "…the ground floor's collapsed into the cellar and beyond…"

I let out an exasperated groan and threw my gun at the manhole cover.

They were in the sewers.

FOURTEEN

8.45pm. Things were rushing along out of control. I had returned to my office to grab some equipment. The elevator was still broken, the statue still stuck in the stairwell. I now had no way to track Stringer or Andi. The only lead I had was now off the grid. I could only hope she slipped up and tried to purchase something. Even then it would help little. By the time we'd reacted the purchase would be complete and she would once more be lost in the crowds.

I'd left Tisi to monitor Stringer's apartment. Al and I had returned to the office. We needed evidence bags, medical gloves and an RFID lock pick. With nothing else to go on, we would spend the night searching through Stringer's apartment in the hope of finding clues. We'd flick through every book, shred every furniture covering, check inside food. If there was a clue in the apartment that we could use, we would find it.

But before we had gathered everything we needed, the large screen in the outer office fuzzed over in a wash of static. The other screens in the office did the same, including my own. It looked like we were being hacked.

"What's happening?" I demanded. "Is someone compromising our systems?"

"I…" Sam began, but he was clueless about this new development. His ultra-sophisticated monitor was the only one still working. "No. That's impossible. A supercomputer would take years to get through our firewalls. It looks like this is a nationwide comms hack."

Then my cell phone rang. And Sam's. And Al's. And all the phone lines, land and cell, in the office. Warily I activated it and the screen showed the same fuzzy static. The static was replaced by the image of an Indian girl. She was small, frail and deeply upset. A voiceover started up.

"This is Samera," it began in a digitally distorted voice. "She is an orphan. Four months ago her parents peaceably campaigned against their Government's failing human rights policies. They were arrested and she never saw them again. Samera's father was beaten to death with bats, her mother repeatedly raped before being strangled. This gross injustice went unreported and unnoticed by the worldwide community, just like thousands of other similarly illegal murders by the authorities. The Government officials themselves have stolen funds from education, redevelopment, health care, the environment. All to line their own pockets. The ruling body has repeatedly pushed back supposedly democratic elections by years and stifled the media while ruthlessly murdering their own citizens with a campaign of destruction and terror.

"You may be thinking 'that is terrible, but what can we do, as individuals and as a nation?' Far more than you realize. For this is not some third world country struggling under the yoke of dictatorship. This is not a country in Africa, Asia or even Europe. This is here. This is America."

The image altered from Samera's haunted face to that of the Stars And Stripes. It fluttered gently in the wind. The Star-Spangled Banner overlaid the image, patriotic and proud.

"The country is stirring. The country is ready to rise. Ready to take back the freedom that is our constitutional right! No longer will we be silenced! No longer will we be pushed around! No longer will we sit back and let the despots rule our lives!

"Tomorrow we will rise. Tomorrow we will show this corrupt, murderous Government of ours that we will not lie down and die. Across the country, we ask you all, all those with families to protect, all those with lives to live, to join as one in a *peaceful* but mighty protest. We will put on a show of strength, a vindication of the power of the people.

"Visit the website www.freedom4america.com to see where your nearest protest will be held. Do not fear, the government will not be able to track you if you visit this site. Do *not* bring weaponry, do *not* bring a violent temperament, but rise up, be heard and show there is strength in numbers.

"America. Let's make it the land of the free once more."

All the screens turned back to static. They slowly rebooted to their usual image. I switched off my cell phone and looked around to gauge the reactions in the office. Surprise was the most persistent facial expression.

"Was that...?" I began. "Did they just hack into the *entire* communications net?"

"Looked like it," Sam told me. "It's been rumored that it might be possible. Gaining access to every TV, monitor, phone, everything with video capability. And at this time of night…I'd estimate eighty percent of the country just witnessed that broadcast."

"Who did it?" I asked. "Is there any way to track the source?" I was vaguely aware that my landline was ringing in my office. I presumed it was the General.

"Track it?" Sam exclaimed. "According to computer records there wasn't even a signal in the first place. Technically, that broadcast never happened."

"Damn terrorists," I muttered. "Who do they think they are? Illegal murders? Media manipulation? This is America, damn it! We don't do that kind of shit!"

I looked around the office, at each person individually. No one was backing me up. We all knew there had been some shady, underhand dealings going on. But that was par for the course with a large, developed country. Unlike the developing world, we kept it behind closed doors and did it in moderation. But this broadcast… The allegations went far beyond what we knew. *Thousands* killed? Peaceful protestors at that? And funds being siphoned off education for personal gain?

"We don't," I repeated confidently. I didn't want my team to be doubting the validity of their jobs under the current government. I didn't want to doubt it myself. But the evidence was mounting.

Andi Clayton was one of the 80% of the population who caught the broadcast. Following her flight down the sewers, Daniel and herself had wandered the streets. He'd bought her a slice of pizza and a bottle of water. He'd reassured her that neither of them were being followed. He'd explained that her RFID would still work but could only be tracked when she purchased goods.

It was too risky to return to her apartment right now, he'd told her. Her cell phone would have to be abandoned there. In a couple of days it would be safe enough to purchase a change of clothing. But for now Andi was homeless, owned only what she was wearing, and needed to search for a cheap hotel to stay the night.

She'd asked Daniel how it was that he, unlike her, could buy goods without being detected. The resulting techno babble speech would have foxed an MIT professor. She'd enquired as to how long she would need to stay on the run. How long could she be absent from work without justification? How long before she was able to return to the home she sank all her savings into? Daniel said there may be some fall-out: GovPol interviews, FBI investigations and the like. But he estimated that in a few weeks she would no longer pose a threat to the Government. Or at least no more than millions of others would. Then she would be able to return to her old life again.

A few weeks on the run seemed like a depressingly long time, she thought. But at least it was finite. At least the tunnel was showing a glimmer of light. Resting for the moment in a bar, she asked why she would only be as much of a threat as millions of others?

"Something is about to happen," he told her. "Something terrible and something wonderful. Change on this scale always begins with pain. Thomas Jefferson said 'The tree of liberty must be refreshed from time to time with the blood of patriots and tyrants.' This country is about to discover exactly what that means."

"How?" she asked. "The terrorists?"

"There are no terrorists, Andi," he answered. "Unless you count those running the country. What is about to happen is that the people of this nation will show the world what they are made of. The Government will show the world what it's made of too. The epic struggle begins."

Daniel breathed in deeply, then indicated the old, solid, unbendable screen hanging above the bar. Its color and picture quality looked horribly dull when compared to the latest OLED. The image turned to snow, a wash of static. Someone seated at the bar grumbled to the barman. He tried flicking through channels to no avail. Cell phones began to ring shrilly throughout the building. Then the image of Samera appeared and all the patrons of the bar became part of the 80% of the nation who witnessed this peaceful 'call to arms'.

Once the broadcast was over and baseball highlights resumed on the screen Andi turned to Daniel with surprise.

"The audacity!" she exclaimed. "You knew about this?!"

He placed his arms on the table and leaned closer to her. "Andi, I can predict the future, remember?"

"Will anyone believe that?"

"Why not?" he asked.

"Maybe because we've all been indoctrinated to believe they are terrorists. They're the enemy of the people. Suddenly they're firing off all these allegations against our own ruling power. I can't see anyone believing that. So what's going to happen tomorrow? A small gathering of a dozen conspiracy theory nuts, or what?"

Daniel took a swig of his drink. "A more appropriate term would be 'civil uprising'. An even more appropriate term would be 'revolution'."

"So you think a lot of people are going to turn up?"

He nodded.

"Are you?"

He shook his head this time. He was being frustratingly uncommunicative. His lack of response was making her even more weary than she already felt.

"Why? I thought…you believed in this stuff."

Daniel finished off his drink. "Come on, it's been a long day and you look tired. Let's find you somewhere to stay."

"Find *me* somewhere? What about you? You can't go back to your apartment…"

"There are some things I need to sort out," he answered. He collected his coat. She did the same. "I'll be fine. And I'll see you tomorrow morning."

"But…I thought…you know…after last night…"

He grinned with that. "Not tonight. Tonight you need to sleep."

It had been a long and tiring day for me. The last time I slept I had just a few hours in a car. Since then I'd shot up a street. I'd headed a car chase. I'd indirectly caused two pile-ups. There had been a foot-chase through alleyways. One of my team had been critically injured. A building had been blown up. I'd witnessed a call to arms by the very terrorists I should be hunting down if Miller had kept me on the case.

It had just turned 9pm. My back ached. My feet were weary. My neck throbbed from where Andi hit me with the pipe. But the work continued.

Al and I had made a spectacular mess of Stringer's apartment. The couches were no longer stuffed. The bed was short one mattress. Piano wires were broken and curled into submission. Books had been removed, ripped apart and discarded on the floor. The bathroom contained a broken bath and empty toilet cistern. We were nothing if not thorough.

Tisi was keeping watch in the car downstairs. It was a precaution in case Stringer was stupid enough to return here. I didn't hold out much hope of that.

We'd tagged and bagged a few items of minor interest. But so far we hadn't uncovered any earth-shattering evidence.

"Kitchen?" Al asked me, having finished carefully shredding all the clothes in the bedroom. I nodded back. I was still working my way through the living area. Al moved across to the kitchen. He removed a cutlery drawer and spilled the contents on the floor.

"Check the food," I told him. "Cans. Cereal boxes. Everything. This is one crafty son of a bitch. I wouldn't put it past him to hide something important inside a can of soup."

I sighed and rested on one arm of the armchair. I made a mental note to start shredding that next. I removed my phone and called General Miller. I'd tried three times already but thus far I'd been unable to get through.

Finally, I made it through to him.

"Stone!" he said when the call was answered. "You have news for me?"

I sighed heavily. "We had him, Sir. Twice"

"Had?"

"He slipped through. Both times. Using immense skill and foresight."

The General tutted. "I told you he'd be tricky, Stone. You should have been more careful."

"Sir," I said. "We couldn't have done any more. One of my team was shot. He's in surgery right now."

"What were the situations?"

"A chase through rush hour traffic this morning and a confrontation in an alley a couple of hours ago. Both times there was no way he could escape. But he knew *exactly* what to do to pull off the impossible. This seeing the future thing is a pain in the ass.

Miller took a few moments to gather his thoughts. "What are you doing now?"

"Ransacking his apartment. Looking for clues."

Miller nodded and steepled his fingers. "Very well. Your Erinyes can deal with that side of things. I want to be briefed on the situation in person. Get the next flight to D.C. We'll talk when you arrive. I expect to see you in my office in two hours."

I glanced around the room. Two people checking every bit of this apartment was a long job. With one it might not even be finished by the morning. I'd have to pull Tisi off stakeout duty.

"Maybe I should finish up here first, Sir. This could take all night."

"Then let your team take all night, but I want you-"

There was a strong knock on the apartment door. Miller stopped abruptly. I caught my breath and listened intently. Al had also frozen. I couldn't hear anything.

"Who's that?" Miller whispered over the phone.

I made the telephone symbol with one hand and silently mouthed "I'll call you back." The General's brow furrowed in frustration. It looked like he might be about to get angry, so I switched the phone off.

There was a second knock on the door.

"Hey, girl," a deep male voice boomed from the other side. "Open up. I'm frosty and you're my hearth."

I stared quizzically at the door. I glanced at Al in the kitchen. He looked just as confused as I did.

There was a third knock. "What? I say it wrong? Come on! I know you're in there. I need help!"

It fell into place. He was using a code phrase. There was no girl. He was not frosty. He wanted in.

I quickly withdrew my sidearm and readied myself. I activated the vidscreen.

The man on the other side was tall, strong, black and had a mass of dreadlocks on his head. I recognized him immediately. It was The Duke from the Everglades mission. He'd recognized me too over the vidscreen.

He grinned broadly. "Shit, man," he laughed. "Wrong apartment." He immediately broke into a run. He was heading for the stairwell.

I slammed the door back. I leapt into the corridor and fired two shots. It was too late. He'd turned the corner and was building up speed. I remembered he was shot in the leg in the Everglades, but the injury didn't seem to be slowing him at all.

I activated my earpiece to speak to Tisiphone, the only other person with a chance of stopping The Duke if she could cut him off in time.

"Tisi! We've got a man on the run! Coming your way! Get him! Alive!"

I'd reached the stairwell. I rushed down it so fast I nearly tripped. The Duke was already on the next level down and heading for the ground.

I fired off a few more shots to no avail. He was keeping to the walls, allowing the stairs above him to act as cover.

I charged down the rest of the stairs. I was aware he'd got enough of a lead on me. I skidded into the lobby and glanced around. He was nowhere to be seen.

Tisi crashed in through the front doors. She was out of breath. Just like me. She shrugged and shook her head. If he didn't go out the front...

He was heading out the back.

I broke into a run again. I negotiated two corridors. Then the rear fire door was in front of me. I smashed through it. It took me into a dingy, littered alley.

The Duke was waiting for me. He brandished a metal dustbin lid in one hand. He rammed it into my face. I had just enough reaction time to lower my head. My crown took the brunt of the impact. It knocked me off my feet. My gun buried itself in the litter.

The Duke dropped the bin lid with a clatter. He broke into a run away from me. At the far end of the alley was a street. It was on the opposite side of the building to Tisi. If he reached it, we'd lose him.

I stood quickly. I picked up the bin lid and tested its weight. I threw it down the alley like a Frisbee. It hit The Duke on the nape of his neck and knocked him out cold.

I brushed down my suit and collected my sidearm. I walked up to him. I checked in my right jacket pocket for a plastic wrist tie. Nothing. I tried the left and found half a dozen. I secured his hands behind his back just in case he regained consciousness.

"Got him," I told the Erinyes through their earpieces. "Stand down."

I let out a big sigh. Finally, the break-through I needed in the terrorism case. I felt elated.

I removed my phone and called the General again.

"Who was it?" he asked before I could say a word.

"The Duke, Sir. From the Everglades. I've got him."

Miller looked surprised. "Excellent work, Stone. Well done."

"Thank you, Sir. He just came knocking on the door."

"Quite a coincidence, isn't it?" he said.

"Maybe not, Sir. I think this answers why Stringer knew where the terrorists would strike. He's infiltrated them. Acting as their fixer when things go wrong. I'll know more once The Duke's regained consciousness."

"Bring him with you," the General said.

"Where?" I asked.

"To D.C. I'm still expecting you here in two hours."

"I..." I paused to regain my faculties. "I was about to take the suspect to our New York offices. He needs to be questioned, Sir. Interrogated."

"He will be."

"By whom?"

"Someone else, Stone. Bring him with you. We'll handle it from there."

My elation had drained away. It was being replaced with frustration. "Someone else? Sir, I've been working on the terrorism case. I've made the collar. I–"

"You are no longer on that case, Jack," Miller interrupted. "I understand your frustration, but you have a different remit. You concentrate on Stringer. We'll handle this."

"*This* connects to Stringer. The suspect came to his apartment!"

The General sighed. "Very well. You can lead the initial interrogation. But I still want it done here in D.C."

"I…" I began. I looked up and down the alley in annoyance and puffed out my cheeks. "Yes, Sir."

"I'll see you in two hours," Miller told me. The line went dead.

I pocketed my cell phone. In anger, I kicked The Duke's leg.

FIFTEEN

The Duke woke halfway through our flight. I questioned him several times. I didn't even get his real name. All he did was squirm in silence.

Two minor-league custodial agents were waiting to escort The Duke to the interrogation facilities as soon as I arrived at the NASRU HQ. Having John Hancocked the man into their care, I headed up to Miller's office.

The General offered me a seat as soon as I entered.

"Tell me all," he said. "About how you let Stringer slip through your fingers."

"We didn't exactly let him…" I stopped. It was best not to argue with my superior. Not until I had a strong, valid reason anyway. "We were tracking a presumed associate of his and we happened across Stringer himself. He foxed us by using a decoy vehicle and when we gave chase he knew exactly where to go and what tools to use so he could give us the slip. Even a suit to insulate himself from the electricity in a Charge Grid. He could exit the car when we couldn't. He knew what he'd need."

"The second encounter?"

"Alley system. He had the same associate with him. A New York Times journalist called Andrea Clayton. I shot him but he was wearing a bullet-proof vest. When he shot back my operative Megaera was wounded. Shoulder and abdomen. I've just heard the surgery was successful, but he'll be out of action for a few weeks."

"And Stringer escaped again," the General filled in for me.

"Yes, Sir. Using the sewer system this time. Even when you have the man directly in your sights he still proves to be a slippery bastard."

"That he does," Miller agreed. "That's why he's eluded us for three years. Still, you've made far more progress than anyone else. For that you should be commended."

"Thank you, Sir."

"What's your next plan of action, Stone?"

I puffed out my cheeks. "That is a tricky one, Sir. With his RFID disabled we can't track him. It would take ten minutes for character recognition software to spot him on a live video feed, by which time he's likely to have moved on. We need to put out an APB."

"No." The General shook his head. "Certainly not. It's enough of a security breach that you involved some SWAT in the last operation."

"You heard about that?" I said.

"I did. I can see your reasoning, but we need to be careful who knows about all this. So no APB. How close is Stringer to this woman?"

"From what we can tell he spent the night with her. Biblically. And I'm not talking a prayer meet."

Miller slapped his hands together. "Then there you go. Go through her again."

"Unfortunately she's off the grid too. Stringer disabled Miss Clayton's RFID as well. Her apartment and office are being monitored, but it's highly unlikely she'll return to either of them."

"Friends?" he asked. "Family?"

"No family. Background history's a bit hazy. She was in Fremont during the Santa Virus outbreak a decade ago. We're looking into her contact list on the cell phone from her apartment right now. But if she's with Stringer, she'll be playing by his rules. And that means no contact with people she knows, no visiting favorite haunts. She'll have abandoned her old life as a precaution."

Miller sighed. "So there's nothing to go on. What about Stringer's apartment?"

"So far: zip. Again he won't be going back there any time soon. We haven't found anything of particular interest yet either."

The General sighed. "We seem to be at a bit of an impasse, Stone. The chase has ground to a halt."

I silently nodded in agreement.

"What about this Duke?" The General asked. "Think you can get something out of him?"

"About Stringer? Maybe. But he's far more valuable in the hunt for the terrorists. Where the bombs come from, who buys them. We've cut out the middleman, but that isn't enough to stop them."

"Indeed. It is still a very real threat. Do what you have to, Stone. We can't afford to abide by Amnesty International's wishes here."

I entered the interrogation monitor room. It was long and thin, dark and covered with an array of monitoring, recording and control equipment. One man was stationed at the control panel. Another provided security.

A large two-way mirror spanned across most of the wall. The door into the interrogation room was to the left.

"Ready?" I asked the man at the control panel. He nodded.

I walked through the door and closed it softly behind me. The interrogation room was stark white and brightly lit. There was a grilled metal desk in the center. To one side of the desk were two small metal-grilled chairs. On the other side was The Duke.

He sat in a high-backed iron chair. Heavy metal cuffs around his wrists, ankles and neck were tethered to the chair with short loops of chain. It allowed some freedom of movement but kept him restricted to his seat. His bare feet rested on a shiny metal panel. It was spring-loaded underneath to ensure he couldn't lift his feet off it.

The Duke had already undergone the embarrassment of having a thorough enema. We didn't want him emptying his bowels during the interrogation. It wouldn't be pleasant for any of us.

He looked up at me silently and defiantly. The chain attached to his collar clanked against the chair's headrest.

I'd already ruled out the possibility of using the Melp device. This man was made of harder stuff. The threat of the device wouldn't faze him, and actually using it would only be effective for a few minutes. This way was cruder but it always delivered results.

"I'll explain the situation you're in first," I told him. I pulled up a chair and sat in it. I rested my arms on the desk.

"Let *me* explain the situation to *you*," The Duke responded. "I know my rights, so you'd better let me go now!"

"You don't have any rights here. Your friends aren't going to come bursting in the door and rescue you. The United Nations will know nothing of the human rights violations that will occur here today. You have one way out of this, and that is to talk."

"I ain't telling you shit."

I nodded. "You will. The panel your feet are resting on is electrified. We can turn it on, we can turn it off. The current is a moderate one. It will hurt. A lot. But there'll be no brain damage, no convulsions, nothing to show for it but reddened skin on the soles of your feet for a few days.

"If you're interested, we've attached the current to the soles of your feet rather than your genitals or teeth because it is actually a more intense experience. Most times when you feel pain, the transmission is degraded as it travels along increasing clusters of nerves to the brain's pain receptor. It's almost like Chinese Whispers. Some of it gets lost en route. But the soles of the feet have a direct line to the brain. Faster, sharper, no degradation. Compare standing on a drawing pin to having one stuck in the palm of your hand. Standing on it hurts a lot more, despite the thickness of the sole.

"We're not going to play good cop, bad cop here. I'm not going to play hardball. I will lay it out for you simply. I ask a question. Once. If you don't answer, we switch on the machine and it will electrocute you for fifteen seconds every minute until we turn it off. Got it?"

I leaned forward on the desk.

"What is your real name?" I asked.

The Duke stared back at me with defiance. "You don't scare me," he said.

I stood and carefully placed my chair under the desk. "I'm going to grab a bite to eat. Keep me going through the night. I'll be back in…let's say one hour. See if you've softened up a bit."

I turned to the mirrored wall and nodded. "Turn it on," I instructed.

I headed out of the room as the machine powered up. Surprised that I hadn't even tried asking him any more questions, The Duke didn't shout after me until I was halfway out the door. I ignored him. He needed to learn some manners.

"Keep an eye on him," I instructed the security. "Make sure he doesn't swallow his tongue or anything."

I headed out into the corridor and rubbed my weary eyes. I was not too familiar with the set-up of the Washington HQ but I knew there was a canteen around here somewhere. I headed for the elevators to see if there was a floor plan on display.

As I neared the elevators I saw another member of the Everglades mission patiently waiting for an elevator. It was Hera. Her arm was in a thinner sling than before, her shoulder nearly healed. She was wearing professional attire – a smart black suit, white blouse, heeled ankle boots and black hair tied back in a bun. She was dressed just like the Erinyes when I first met them.

I jogged to meet her so we could catch up but I was too late. Her elevator arrived and she stepped inside. I pressed the button just too late to get the doors reopened. It was a pity. I would have liked to see how she was getting on, if she was back on active duty yet. I absently wonder if she was going to the canteen herself, so I watched her elevator's progress.

The elevator headed down, past Ground, past the underground parking lot, past Basement Level One and Basement Level Two. She must have been going to Basement Level Three, I thought. But the elevator didn't stop. The Basement Level Three light winked on then off while the elevator was still moving. Where had that elevator gone? There was nothing lower than Basement Level Three. At least as far as I knew.

I called the elevator back up, determined to discover where Hera had gone and what was below Basement Level Three. It was empty. I stepped inside and checked the button panel. Basement Level Three was the lowest button I could press. But there was something below the Basement Level Three button. On the blank metal of the panel was a fading fingerprint, a smudge of condensation. I touched it and felt a hidden button under the panel. I pressed it and the doors closed.

What was going on down there? Why did I not know about an entire level of this building? What were we hiding?

The elevator stopped. The doors opened. I peered out into a corridor that looked vaguely like a brightly lit dungeon. It was stark white. The fluorescent bulbs were exposed. The walls were made of painted concrete. Heavy steel doors lined either side in both directions.

I could see Hera far down the corridor to the left. She was talking to someone in a room. She entered the room and I heard the door close behind her. The corridor was now empty.

I left the confines of the elevator and headed down the corridor to my right, away from Hera. The steel doors were windowless. They had name tags in the center. The first one read "Benjamin Dyson."

I slowly, quietly opened the door. The room was dark and empty. It was small, like a cell. One wire sprung bed lay in a corner with a disused mattress folded on it. A wash basin and toilet occupied another corner. The room smelt musty. It hadn't been used for a long while.

I quietly closed the door and checked the second room, labeled "Mark Headley." The room was larger but also vacant. I checked a third room. Same as the first.

I was aware we had cells on Basement Level Three, but why were there more cells down here? More importantly, why were they buried on a lost floor, accessed by a hidden button in the elevator?

I continued down the corridor, glancing at the names on each door and checking the cracks for any sign of light being emitted from within. Robert Mitchell. Samantha Rogers. Ayesha Murphy. Jordan McIntire. Zeus Jackson.

I stopped. Zeus Jackson? Stringer's original name? I tried the door but it was locked. Was this where he was held? Was this the facility he broke out of? Who were all these other people? *Where* were they?

I tried the door more forcibly. It wouldn't move. There were three more doors to go, one on each side and a final one facing down the corridor. Paolo Garcia. Shim Kan-hui. Laura Fox.

The final door – Laura Fox – had an energy about it. It didn't feel like it was empty.

I carefully opened the door. I could feel the presence of many objects in the dark. I quietly closed the door behind me. I found a light switch and flicked on the lights.

It was a far larger room than the previous ones I had looked in. It was also very homey. Light brown carpet lined the floor. There was a large bed with a pink quilt on it. A vanity cabinet cluttered with cosmetics. A walk-in wardrobe in the far corner. An en suite bathroom. A computer terminal on a desk, shelves of books above it. To one side an ornament cabinet cluttered with stuffed, wood and pottery alligators. A large OLED facing an armchair, and even a small breakfast table nestled in another corner.

I picked up one of the stuffed alligators and stared at it. This wasn't a cell. It wasn't a holding pen. Someone lived here. Happily and comfortably. And I knew who. There weren't many people who like alligators.

I heard the door open behind me. I replaced the alligator and turned around. I already knew who was going to walk in.

Hera was a little startled when she saw me. She nodded. "Lieutenant," she said.

She walked over to the breakfast table. She removed her sling, placed it on the table and rubbed her shoulder.

"Can I help you?" she asked, turning to me. She looked different to how I remembered. Taller, slimmer, prettier, more confident and less stern without her camo. She unclasped her bun and let her hair spill down to her shoulders. "Were you looking for something in particular, or do you usually browse through other people's belongings without permission?"

"You live here," I stated.

"Well done," she answered. "Very deductive."

"You're like Stringer..." I said out loud, realizing the implications.

"Who?"

"Zeus Jackson."

Hera glanced at the door, then back at me. "Not really," she responded. "How much do you know about him?"

"Project Omicron," I said. "The Oracle Design. You're a part of it as well."

Hera sighed. She nodded in a noncommittal way.

"Comms," she addressed the OLED screen. "Armstrong Miller."

The communications system patched her directly through to the General. He appeared on-screen looking tired.

"Laura," he said. "Something wrong?"

Hera glanced at me. "Lieutenant Stone is here with me, Sir."

The General's eyebrows raised in surprise. It was a few seconds before he spoke. "Right," he said. "I guess the two of you had better come to my office, then."

The line went dead. Hera crossed the room to me. She slipped her arm in mine and patted me on the shoulder. "Come on, then," she said, and smiled. "I think it's time you learned the truth."

"Project Omicron ended with Zeus Jackson," General Miller said.

"Daniel Stringer, Sir," I corrected. I was seated in his office. Miller was across the desk from me. Hera took up a seat to my left, facing us both. We formed a perfect equilateral triangle.

"Stringer, yes," he agreed. "With him, we had succeeded. But before then there were dozens of other test subjects."

I glanced across at Hera. She was sitting very still. Legs crossed, hands on the arm rests, looking faintly embarrassed that we were talking about her.

"Some went mad," Miller continued. "Most we had to put down."

"Put down, Sir? You make it sounds like they were dogs in kennels."

"If you had seen these people, Stone, what they were like... You'd have done the same. Four survived, and still do."

The General clicked open a folder on his computer and briefly consulted the notes.

"Captain Todd Driscoll of the 3rd Infantry. Age 32, from Pensacola. He has lost all motor functions. Can't even control his own blinking. We think that in all other respects the experiment worked. We can't see anything wrong with the way we hot-wired his brain, and there seems to be quite an intense intelligence behind those eyes. But he's trapped, completely, in a body that doesn't work."

"That's quite disturbing, Sir," I said.

The General shrugged. "I know, but that's what happens. The second survivor is Able Seaman Roger Blakely, on secondment from the British Royal Navy. Naturally we've told them he suffered a fatal injury in a training exercise. He started off well. Very intelligent, very coherent. Then his mind got stuck in a loop attempting to solve an age-old problem. Now he spends every moment of his waking life reciting Pi to as many decimal places as he can. He's managed roughly forty eight thousand, but the next day he resets and starts again. He's constantly on a saline drip and his vocal chords gave out a long time ago. But he still attempts to recite the number all day every day. We can't snap him out of it. Still, calculating Pi to forty eight thousand decimal places has rather excited the boffins."

"The third and fourth survivors, Sir? Hera and Stringer, I presume."

"Yes. Stringer was the last. Hera...Laura was the penultimate test subject in Project Omicron."

I looked across at Hera again. She smiled weakly at me and clasped her hands together.

"We decided to take a fresh approach with Laura. She graduated with a double-degree from MIT at the age of nineteen. We recruited her straight away. One year later, she was selected for Project Omicron. We decided to start small this time and enhance the brain functions of someone who was already very intelligent."

Hera shrugged nervously, a little shy about the compliment.

"She seems fine," I said. "There's nothing wrong with her."

"There's always something wrong," Hera answered. "With everybody."

"I don't mean in a philosophical sense. Did it not affect you at all?"

"It did," she said.

"Three ways," the General said. "Three side-effects to the experiment. She occasionally gets...a feeling about what to do. Always spot on."

"A feeling?" I asked. "You mean like in the Everglades? When I jumped out of the window, dragging The Duke with me, I expected to hit water. But she'd parked the dinghy exactly where it was needed so we landed on it."

Hera nodded. "I just...felt it was the right place to be."

"Maybe she has similar powers to Stringer," Miller continued. "If she does, it is buried deep in her subconscious. It has no practical long-term application. It just works in the here and now. An infallible gut instinct, if you will."

I studied Hera for a moment. Again, she attempted a smile back, uncomfortable with the scrutiny. I turned my attention back to the General.

"You said there were three side-effects, Sir."

"The second side-effect completely foxed us. We still have absolutely no idea how or why this occurred. The first voice Laura heard when she woke up after the experiment is a voice she feels compelled to obey no matter what."

"I presume not Stringer," I clarify.

"Good Lord no! You think we'd keep her around if that was the case? No, it was me."

"You?" I began. Suddenly it made sense. "You were in charge of Project Omicron."

"For my sins, yes. The road to Hell is paved with good intentions, Stone. Oppenheimer wanted an end to the Second World War. He couldn't envisage that his A-bomb would radically alter the world, give birth to a 50-year Cold War and end up destroying so many lives. He just wanted the war to stop."

"So…" I began. I looked across at Hera again. "Hera has to do anything you say?"

"I don't exploit it, Stone. It is an unfortunate side-effect. Not a tool. Not a weapon. Laura is no puppet."

"But," I shrugged. "You keep her here."

"She is free to come and go as she pleases."

"That's right," Hera interjected. "The General just thought it best if I actually live at the facility for a while to acclimatize. I...have a curfew. But I can go out if I want."

"It's just the illusion of freedom," I said.

"Well, it is about to change anyway," the General said. He turned to Hera. "We said three years, didn't we? You've made fantastic progress. Those three years are nearly up. Maybe we should start looking for an apartment for you."

"Wait, wait," I said. "Three years to acclimatize? Fantastic progress? Is there something else I'm missing here? What was the third side-effect?"

The General sighed. "This is the rather sensitive one. Laura, would you prefer to wait outside?"

"No, no," she answered. "As you say, I've made progress. It is something I've accepted."

"What?" I asked. My mind was swirling with possibilities. She was missing something, I decided. That was why she was occasionally naïve or childish. Something had been lost in the rewiring.

"I have no memory," Hera told me. "From before Project Omicron," she clarified.

"Anterograde amnesia, effectively," Miller said.

"Retrograde," Hera corrected. "I can make fresh memories, and I still have all the skill sets I learned when I was young. But events, people...there's nothing."

"So you've been wiped clean," I said. "Blank slate. Everything that shaped your personality just disappeared overnight."

She shrugged slowly, then nodded.

"That explains a lot," I decided.

"Apparently I have an older sister out there, somewhere," she told me. "We can't find her. But...even if we could, she'd be a complete stranger to me."

"So you see why we had to keep her here. She could solve very complex equations. She could still cook a fantastic Eggs Benedict. But she had no social skills, didn't have a clue how to interact. She was as naïve as a toddler. Still is in some respects." He turned to her. "Sorry, Laura."

She looked down at her hands and fidgeted. "I know," she answered quietly.

It was difficult to believe this had happened to her. She was strong-willed, she was feisty, she was beautiful, but in many ways she was so vulnerable. She was effectively three years old, starting life all over again. Taking those first nervous steps in the world when she should be at her prime. And her surrogate father through all this was the man who did it to her in the first place.

"Considering past results," I said, "I guess it's no surprise that Stringer turned out psychotic and wanted to exact revenge on us."

"Quite," Miller answered. "But the last few days have shown you the danger he poses to us. You can see why he must be stopped at all costs."

"Yes, Sir. I can."

The General sighed, then slapped his hands on his desk. "I'm sure you have many more questions, Stone. But I have a wife to get home to. Thank you for your patience. Hera will escort you back to The Duke and assist with the interrogation."

"Yes, Sir," I answered.

Hera and I both stood. She opened the office door for me and we stepped through. We walked to the elevators in silence. She pressed the 'down' button.

"It's strange," she said, smiling at her feet.

"What is?" I asked.

She looked at the elevator doors, her hands clasped behind her back. "You know everything about me now, and I hardly know anything about you. That will have to be rectified."

She looked up at me with a warm, friendly smile. "How about a coffee before we get started?"

SIXTEEN

The Duke had softened up nicely. Drenched in sweat, his eyes were rolling and he was panting when we returned to the interrogation room. It had been 37 minutes, of which he had endured over nine minutes with electricity running through his body.

I informed the control room operator to switch off the electricity panel. We heard the hum dissipate.

I opened the door for Hera and she stepped inside. As The Duke lolled in his restraints, we each took a seat opposite him. The room stank of his sweat. It was a sweet, salty odor. A trickle of dark blood ran down the chair from The Duke's leg. It seemed the electricity had re-opened his gunshot wound.

I offered no platitudes, no introductions. I got straight back to the interrogation with my control question.

"What is your real name?" I asked him.

The Duke breathed in deeply for a moment, his eyes closed. He was physically drained.

"Elkington," he breathed.

"First name?"

"Rufus."

"Middle name?"

"No middle name," he told me.

"Lies," I pointed out. "We know who you are. It was easy to bring up your data from your DNA profile. You have a middle name."

I nodded at the control room operator behind the mirror. He gave The Duke another 15 second jolt. It wasn't powerful enough to make all his muscles stiffen so he writhed in his restraints. He grunted several times before finally he couldn't hold it in and shouted out in pain. Hera looked away, uncomfortable with the sight. I wondered if this was the first interrogation she'd been a part of.

"Middle name," I demanded when The Duke's excessive panting had calmed down.

"Levi," he whispered.

"Good. When people lie their eyes dilate, their sphincter muscles contract and their body temperature raises slightly. We can tell when you're lying, and that will prompt another burst of electricity. Do you understand?"

"No," The Duke answered. I listened to the verdict from the control room operator in my earpiece.

"You're telling the truth about that," I said, surprised. "You lie, you get hurt. Do you understand *that*?"

The Duke nodded. "Yes," he told us.

Hera took up the interrogation. "Where do you get the bombs from?" she asked. "Who makes them?"

"No names," he told us. "No contact number. We put a marker on a buoy with the order details and payment. A week later the package is left on the sea bed. A diver goes down, inflates the balloon and brings the order to the surface."

"Where's the buoy?" I asked.

"Off the West coast of Africa."

"Where exactly?"

"I'm no good with geography. Somewhere in between mainland Africa and Cape Verde I think."

"You ever spoken to them? Seen them?"

The Duke shook his head. "My predecessor made the initial contact. He's dead now."

"So you get the bombs from Africa. Then what? Who do you deliver to?"

"Same kind of system," he said. "We drop them off in a remote location. We've already been paid. It's based on trust."

"So again, no contact, no meeting?"

"No."

"Then how do you get payment?" Hera asked. "How do you know what they want to order?"

"There's a website. I don't know which one. It's all in code anyway. The order is put on there, then translated and downloaded to my email. I tried tracing the source once. Didn't work. I don't know who orders the devices, and I don't know who makes them. I just distribute the product. I'm a middleman. Or I was. They won't be using me anymore. They'll know I've been compromised."

"So sorry to hear we've made you redundant," I said sarcastically.

"What about the money?" Hera asked. "How do you get that?"

"Transferred into an off-shore account. Hundred thousand dollars per oil drum. I take twenty percent commission."

"What's in the drums?" I asked.

"Don't know. Don't ask. The contents are still in code. The buyers are only known by initials. I get instructions to deliver five oil drums to a specified farmhouse barn in Kentucky by the sixteenth. So that's what I do. We take them by boat part of the way, then transfer to an unmarked truck."

"How many oil drums on average?" Hera asked.

"Varies. Recently the orders have gone up. A lot. This terrorist activity we've been seeing? That's nothing. Something is coming. Something big. Someone wants to raze this country to the ground."

Hera and I looked at each other. Something big was coming and we were the last line of defense. It would fall to us to stop it. But we didn't even know what it was.

"What about Stringer?" I asked.

"Who?"

"Daniel Stringer. The man whose apartment you visited."

The Duke shook his head. "I don't know his name. I didn't even know he was male. We were all told that if something went badly wrong to go to that apartment for assistance. We were given a code phrase to use."

I nodded. "I noticed. So you don't know anything about the person who lived there?"

The Duke shook his head. The control room operator confirmed in my earpiece that he was telling the truth. He held no information relevant to my current assignment. I was wasting my time here.

"I think that's covered the basics," I said. "Someone else will have more questions for you later. Meantime you'll be transferred to a cell."

I nodded in the direction of the control room operator. He activated the electrified panel and The Duke convulsed for another fifteen seconds.

"What the fuck...?" he breathed when it was over.

241

"That's for getting my colleague here shot," I informed him, nodding at Hera.

"But you shot her!" he complained.

I shrugged. "Details." I stood and Hera followed suit. "We're done here."

We left the interrogation room. I slowly rubbed my eyes. "Send me a copy of the transcript," I told the control room operator. He nodded silently in response.

I opened the door for Hera and she walked through into the outer corridor. I followed and accidentally banged my arm against the door. Hera put one hand to my arm, concerned.

"Stone," she said. "When was the last time you slept?"

"Feels like weeks," I sighed.

"I'm sure we can find you a bed round here somewhere." She smiled coyly before saying: "I can make you my Eggs Benedict in the morning."

I shook my head. "I can sleep on the flight," I informed her. "My quarry is in New York. That's where I should be."

She nodded. "Maybe another time, then. I'll find someone to drive you to the airport. Head down to the parking lot, and they'll meet you there."

She trotted off down the corridor, away from the elevators. I watched her go for a moment. She turned and flashed me a warm smile. "It was good seeing you again, Lieutenant," she called.

I wished I could say the same. No matter her friendliness and perkiness, Hera unwittingly represented the dark, seedy underbelly that I had spent all my life fighting against. And it was an underbelly I worked for.

That night, Andi Clayton slept like a baby. She failed to realize just how tired she was until she was presented with a bed. Daniel had accompanied her to the check-in desk of a minimal two-star hotel. He paid for her room and left her to it. Once in the room, seeing that mattress, all the adrenaline drained from her. She fell into a deep slumber that lasted ten hours.

Andi woke reluctantly ready for another day on the run. She wondered when she would next see Daniel. His instructions were uncommonly vague. The only thing he said was that he would catch up with her later that morning.

She showered and dressed in the same faded denims, grey Tee-shirt and long overcoat she wore the previous day. She had no other clothing. She even had to wear the same panties.

By the time she was ready to check out, she had convinced herself that she *must* attend the protest rally that morning. She approached the check-in desk with a grim determination.

"Hi, I'd like to check out," she began. The middle-aged, lank-haired clerk silently updated his computer system.

"Thank you," he said.

"Erm..." She scratched the back of her head. "Do you have net access?"

"Of course," the man answered.

"Could I...maybe...look something up?"

"Sure, what would you like to look up?" He waited poised over the keyboard. Slight spanner in the works, she thought. She was hoping he'd give her access herself. She'd rather not let anyone else know she was attending the protest, even if she was going under the guise of a journalist.

"Erm…" Andi began again. She rapped her fingernails on the desk in thought. It was too risky, she realized. It wasn't worth it. Not when she was on the run. "It doesn't matter. I'll look it up somewhere else."

"You sure? I can–"

"No," she cut him off. "It…I'll be okay."

She started to walk away, across the threadbare carpet of the lobby to the old wooden front door.

"It's at Sheep Meadow, eleven am," the man called after her.

She stopped, turned. "Sorry?"

The man faltered a little. He had the same insecurities as Andi. "I…I heard something was going on today in Central Park. I thought maybe I might…you know…go and see what it's all about. Maybe."

Andi nodded noncommittally and left the hotel. Sheep Meadow, she thought. Eleven am. She decided to head straight there. At a slow walk, it would be timed just right.

The closer she got to Central Park the thicker the human traffic seemed. At first people were milling in a seemingly random manner. Then traffic in the opposite direction started to thin out and she found herself being swept along with an increasing tide of bodies washing towards the Park. She'd never seen the city so busy on a Sunday. If 50% of these people were heading in her direction, and this represented just one corner of one city in one State, the thought of the sheer size of the gatherings countrywide overwhelmed her.

She headed onto Central Park West Drive, turning south towards the vast expanse of lawn that was Sheep Meadow.

Daniel caught up to Andi amid the crowds.

"What are you doing?" he asked. He grabbed her arm and pulled her to a halt.

"Hi." She smiled back at him. Something about his worried expression deflated her greeting. "I'm...going to the protest."

"No," Daniel stated simply. He refused to release her arm. His grip was starting to bruise. Andi tried to shake him off.

"What do you mean 'no'? This is something I have to see. This is what it's all been about, all our meetings, all the secrets. This is what it's been building towards."

"True," he shrugged. "Even so...no."

"Why? You think Stone will find me in *this* crowd? Look around you. Look at the number of people..."

"That's why you can't go. Too many people."

Her annoyance and frustration at Daniel's persistence faded. It was replaced by a growing concern. "What's going to happen?"

"It's not that exactly, it's—"

"You know," Andi interrupted quietly. "Something's going to happen. What will happen to me?"

Daniel shrugged slowly. He looked a little lost and confused. "I don't know."

"Bullshit, Daniel! You know everything! You've forced your damn precognitions on me so much, I'm not going to buy that! What is going to happen?!"

"Honestly," he said quietly. "I don't know. I *do* know the Government will not sit idly by and let this happen." He took her other arm and held her fast. He willed her to concentrate on his next words. "Andi...people will die today." He released her and looked away. "More than that, I cannot say. Too many people, too many variables. My powers can only process so many moving and free-thinking objects at once." He looked at her again. "I honestly don't know who, or how, or when...I just know people will die."

"Oh my God," she heard herself respond. She involuntarily took one step away. It was as though her whole body had separated from her consciousness and was acting independently. "But I...I..."

"I cannot guarantee your safety, Andi. I cannot predict what will happen to you."

She looked at the throng of New Yorkers all around her. They looked so fresh, so eager. Some were carrying placards, others their own infant children. Some touted megaphones, some sported music players. Some even carried hampers, hoping to turn the event into a family picnic. All seemed reinvigorated by the possibility of being part of something huge, something that could change the country. None could imagine that soon they may be dead.

"I have to go, Daniel," Andi said. There were so many reasons to attend this protest and only one reason not to. If Daniel was to be believed, she knew she could die. But she needed to be there, to witness what would happen. She had to go.

Daniel looked shocked and confused at her decision. She suspected he'd always known what she'd say. He had warned her, that was all he could do. But he'd always known she would join the protest no matter what he said. "Andi," he said quietly, stepping forward and taking her hand in his. "Don't..."

She smiled sadly, gripped his hand momentarily, then let it slide from his weakening grip. Turning, she walked with the tide. She headed past the trees, down the road, and hung a left onto the vast grassy plain. Bordering the western road to her right stood a large, hastily erected stage. She gathered into the crowds to the north of the Sheep Meadow. She was close to the stage. She strained her neck to look around. Trees lined the lawn area two hundred and forty yards to the east and two hundred and eighty five yards to the south. In between, in an area the size of twelve football fields, not a blade of grass could be seen beneath the mass of protesters.

That afternoon the Government released a press statement:

> At 11am EST today, several cities across our nation including Washington D.C., New York City, Chicago, Boston and San Francisco were witness to an illegal mass gathering of unpatriotic citizens. They colluded to incite violence within our own borders and against our own governing body. This was perpetrated by the terrorists who have murdered innocent citizens and destroyed government property in a series of cowardly bombing attacks over the last three years. These protests sought to undermine the freedom and values of our proud nation.
>
> In response to the illegality of these protests and the increasing threat of violence, GovPol officers were deployed to maintain order and disperse the gatherings peaceably. The first incident of violence occurred in Washington D.C.

on the steps of the Lincoln Memorial. The second occurred in New York City in Central Park. More cities followed suit. GovPol officers tried to calm the situation, but these gatherings descended into riots. The protestors cared little for their cause and the welfare of others. All they were interested in was mindless destruction and attacking the figures of authority we have all come to respect and rely upon. We had no choice but to invoke the Riot Control subsection of the Patriot Act in these cities. Armored mobile units were deployed before these riots spread further.

As the situation became increasingly desperate, tear gas, water cannons and rubber bullets were called into action. Finally we had no choice but to authorize the use of lethal force. This was in order to protect the majority of our citizens, who wisely did not engage in seditious acts.

We are happy to report that very few GovPol officers were injured or killed thanks to their excellent training. Several arrests were made. In the pursuit of their duties, some GovPol officers had to implement the use of lethal force.

Investigations will be conducted into these incidents. If any officers are found

> to have acted unlawfully, they will be brought to justice.
>
> We'd like to thank the GovPol officers involved in these operations for the courage and resolve they displayed under such extreme conditions. Our thoughts go out to the families of those fatally wounded in this tragedy.

In the evening, the Government released an update to their first statement. It was designed to combat the public outcry on the internet:

> We would like to make you aware that some of the dissident parties in today's tragic events have swamped the internet with fake news. They include supposed eye-witness testimonies of what occurred in the cities hit by insurrection.
>
> We can now confirm that there were one or two isolated incidents whereby lethal force was used before all other options were explored. Following a thorough investigation and using testimony from the GovPol officers involved, we do not consider this a serious breach of the code of conduct. Events were already spiraling out of control and authorized lethal force was inevitable in these situations.
>
> The parties involved will be disciplined, but there will be no further investigation

into these allegations. Those who claimed they were fired upon without provocation or that lethal force was used before non-lethal options were deployed are simply fanning the flames of discontent for their own seditious agenda.

There have also been reports that a media blackout was enforced during these riots. To an extent this is true: it is policy that when the Riot Control subsection of the Patriot Act is enforced, we prevent the ringleaders from engaging in further electronic communication. This is to ensure they are unable to request further forces or weaponry from their terrorist allies. This is a standard policy. It is one that has served us well in the past, and served us well during the events today. We welcome the media to report on all activities that occur within this country with complete impartiality. The suggestion that we would actively seek to exclude the media from these operations is inflammatory and slanderous.

There have been reports of indiscriminate firing into crowds, of infants among the dead, of executions. All of these reports are completely false. This was a challenging operation undertaken across several cities where the wellbeing of innocent citizens was paramount. In every sense this operation was a success. While fatalities were inevitable, casualties were kept to the minimum possible.

As an eye witness in the thick of events, Andi Clayton saw a very different story.

SEVENTEEN

It had been ten minutes, and the crowd was growing restless. They were starting to feel like they had been duped. Finally the organizers took to the stage armed with a powerful megaphone. The sound was easily captured on Andi's old voice recorder without her needing the narrow-band receiver beam.

The organizers began their speech well and received rapturous applause with every sentence. They talked about a diverse range of topics. There was little of substance for Andi beyond what Daniel had already revealed. The Government massaging the figures of both education and healthcare to reduce the budgets. Their relinquishing all responsibility for deprived inner-city areas. Using the Mars terraforming project as an excuse to line their own pockets. How the war in Cuba was just as illegal as previous invasions this century including Iraq, Iran, Saudi Arabia and Panama. How the Government went behind the backs of the UN to influence the China-Korea war. The media control. The lengthy term of office. The disappearing activists.

The crowds lapped it up. All of it. Some were in the know and cheered with every anti-Government statement. Others were previously blinded to all this but saw the light with aghast clarity. They were unable to fathom how they hadn't noticed it before. Daniel was right all along, Andi realized. Not just because of the crowds, but the enthusiasm being built here: this could well become revolution.

It was inevitable that the Government would try to prevent this, to halt the speeches and the mass gatherings. A GovPol presence was soon felt. It began on the outskirts, a ring slowly forming around the crowd. They loosely surrounded the protesters without malevolence. Their machine guns lay lazily across their armored chests. There were murmurs of surprise and one or two anti-Government slogans were called out but the crowd stood fast. They were calmly defiant against this potential threat.

The head of GovPol took to the stage. He was closely followed by several officers. They chased the three protest ringleaders off. The ringleaders disappeared into the crowds. Andi trained the recorder's narrow band receiver beam at the Lieutenant in center stage. She would now be able to pick up not just what he said through the megaphone, but also any asides he delivered to his colleagues.

The Lieutenant was greeted with derision and booing. He waved his hands, calling for quiet. He didn't receive it.

"This..." he began. He stopped. He turned the megaphone up to full volume in the hope of reaching the rear quarters. "This is an illegal gathering. Disperse at once."

The crowd took little notice and the boos increased.

"I repeat: this is an illegal gathering. Disperse immediately or you could face criminal charges. We have been authorized to use non-lethal force to break up this illegal protest. Leave now before we have to take action."

No one moved. Despite the warning, the protesters stood fast. It was mostly out of curiosity than a real desire to rally against the system.

Frustrated, the Lieutenant tried again. "I will warn you one more time to disperse now. We are authorized to use water cannons, tear gas and rubber bullets to ensure this protest stops now. People will be hurt. Arrests will be made. Turn away now before it is too late."

The Lieutenant listened to chatter on his top-of-the-line, magna-cased radio set. This immediately sparked Andi's suspicion. Why would a GovPol officer be equipped with military-grade equipment?

Her narrow band receiver beam broadcasted the Lieutenant's private conversation through the earpiece connected to the voice recorder.

"Nothing," he said to his colleagues on the stage. "No one's moving." He turned his attention to his radio's mouthpiece. "One zero zero nine six to Sigma Control. One zero zero nine six to Sigma Control. They're not shifting. Send in the ROTECs. All other units stand ready."

It was five minutes before the ROTECs arrived. During this time the Lieutenant tried again to disperse the crowd. Half way through, the Lieutenant's words were drowned out by chants. The crowd only quietened down when the whispering rush of helicopter rotors became apparent.

Two black and foreboding transport helicopters swung into view over the Manhattan skyline. Each one was laden with a large cube of disjointed metal. They swooped down low over Central Park and positioned themselves above the stage at either end. The cables holding the metal cubes were released and the six-foot blocks dropped. Pressure balloons burst into life under the cubes, cushioning their fall. The balloons deflated and disappeared back inside the dulled silver blocks.

The crowd was quiet and expectant. Only the blaring of music players and rotor whispers of several personal, video-recording drones punctured a silence even the birds were adhering to.

The Lieutenant went back to his radio. "One zero zero nine six to Sigma Control. One zero zero nine six to Sigma Control. Activate ROTECs."

With a whir of servos and hiss of pistons, the metal cubes began to unfurl. Clanking and whining, they moved into their activated position. By the time they had finished they represented huge, bastardized humans. They stood on three splayed toes, with thin legs connecting to a rotund, heavily armored torso. On top was a sensor-strewn head that looked like little more than a steel bucket with a 360 degree red LED. Two large, highly maneuverable, multi-barreled Gatling guns stood in for arms. Ten feet tall, the mere sight of the Remote-Operated Tactical Engagement Cybernetic units instilled fear in the crowd.

This shouldn't be, Andi thought. These were top of the line, brand new military front-line devices, drones designed specifically for hot-zone urban warfare. Why would the GovPol be allowed to use such technology for urban pacification? Why would they *need* to?

The mere sight of the ROTECs was enough for some people. A few protesters realized that their safety and civil liberties were at risk. There were murmurings among the crowd. Several hundred left, heading back into other areas of Central Park. Their way was not barred and they left freely.

The brunt of the gathering, some quarter of a million people, still remained.

The Lieutenant made a show of preparing the ROTEC units by issuing orders through his radio and the megaphone at the same time.

"ROTEC operators, arm with non-lethal ammunition."

The beastly, military-grade units altered the feed lines to their guns. Live round-filled tubes retracted from the rear of the Gatlings and were replaced by feed lines of rubber bullets. Although they were not moving, the ROTECs were scanning the crowds for targets, relaying the information to their distant pilots and optimizing their firing capabilities for maximum dispersal.

"One final warning," the GovPol Lieutenant announced to the masses. "Go home now, while you still can! If you do not disperse, we will use non-lethal force. If any incident of violence occurs against my officers, lethal force *will* be authorized. Don't let it come to this, don't believe the lies of a few dissidents. Go home!"

His plea fell on deaf ears. But if the crowd knew what was to happen next there would be no doubt they would have headed home straight away.

The Lieutenant dropped the megaphone. He had no more use for it.

"Bring the TEMPer," he said to a colleague. His order was picked up by Andi's recorder. "Let's get this done."

Two of the officers on the stage brought forth the Temporary Electromagnetic Pulser. It was a 3-ft high pole with fold-up legs. They set it in front of the Lieutenant. The top of the pole, a large semi-sphere like a mushroom head, was extended up another foot. The Lieutenant checked around, ensuring his officers were in place. He pressed the top of the pole, ramming the upper half into its housing. The crowd felt a static charge wash over them.

Andi's recorder crackled then fell silent. Music from the players faded into nothingness. Protesters using cameras, video recorders and cell phones looked confused as their equipment switched off. Dozens of little drones fell from the sky into the gathered masses. Consternation grew among the crowd. Andi quickly checked her watch. It had frozen. There was an eerie silence from the roads surrounding Central Park. Every car had halted as one. She realized now why the officers were using military radios. Aside from the magnetically-shielded GovPol radios and ROTECs, every electrical system for several blocks had ceased working.

Concerned, she concentrated on the stage. The Lieutenant looked harried. He reluctantly raised his comms radio to his lips and quietly gave an order he felt may haunt him for the rest of his life. Andi saw the two robots switch their ammunition feeds back to live rounds and suddenly everything made sense. They'd blacked out all media: all video and audio, both professional and amateur. There were no longer any recording devices to provide proof of what was about to happen. Non-lethal force was an option they'd decided to skip.

"Oh my God," Andi whispered in horror. She raised her voice to warn the people around her. "They're going to kill us! Run!"

In the thick of the protesters, Andi's warning was lost. No one in the near vicinity seemed to believe her enough to take her advice. Several others in the vast crowd had come to the same conclusion as her. They started pushing their way through the throng, hoping vainly to leave the protest before the terrifyingly inevitable happened. Andi followed suit. She was pushing back towards Terrace Drive. She was barely halfway through the crowds.

It began.

The ROTECs started it off. Their rapid-fire Gatling guns spewed out hot lead. It ripped through the closest protesters indiscriminately. The ROTECs were able to spread their fire across a wide area, biting into the heart of the crowd. Panic spread like a wave. Those closest to the carnage screamed and stampeded. Details of what was happening gradually filtered through to the outer rim of the crowd. Shocked and disbelieving, the fringes took a few moments to react. It was a few moments too long.

Following orders, the GovPol officers ringing the Sheep Meadow brought their machine guns to bear. They began to pump bullets into the outer rim. It didn't take long for the protesters to realize these weren't mere rubber bullets. Screaming erupted from the exterior of the crowd, mixing in with those centre stage. A second stampede began. Protesters fled back from the GovPol officers on the extremities. Slowly, the panic-stricken people herded themselves into a tighter ball. They were crushing those in the center of the field. Like dolphins attacking a bait ball of herring, the GovPol officers and ROTECs picked out people on the edges. The rest swirled in the centre, trapped, crushed, and struggling to move.

The ROTECs advanced. Their triple-toed feet retracted to a single stiletto point as they negotiated the steps down the stage. Their Gatling guns swung in wide arcs. Entire families were cut down, left in bloody ruins on the reddened grass.

Andi was swept along with the crowds. They were jostling each other in blind panic. Their minds were not yet tuned in to the fact that all they were doing was bunching up and presenting easier targets.

"Rush them!" a man called to her right. He was also attempting to squeeze through the masses towards the outer edges. Another took up his call. More followed suit. Soon there was a gathering of hundreds shouting the call to rush the lines. But for now there was no action. It was understandable. The first to rush the GovPol officers on the edges would almost certainly be cut down. It may allow others to escape, overwhelming the officers with sheer panicked numbers. But no one wanted to be the sacrificial first wave.

Finally desperation got the better of the outer edges. They realized they were about to be shot anyway. They'd prefer to die attempting to escape than being hit in the back whilst huddling in fear.

The ranks were broken. The northwest corner of the desperate protesters pushed through the blockade, crushing any GovPol in their way. Andi joined the exodus. She was pushed this way and that, always moving forward with a blind faith. More officers joined in the turkey shoot from the sides and the ROTECs thinned the crowds behind her.

People were being felled all around her. But she was through the barrier, heading into the tree line. Ahead to Andi's right, a GovPol officer was cursing in horror as he witnessed the carnage his colleagues were delivering. His weapon was by his side. The crowds didn't see this. They only saw the uniform. They tore into him with the kind of brutality reserved for the desperate.

Andi's fellow escapees still numbered in the thousands. They all made a mad dash through the trees. The trees offered cover, but more were picked off. The sound of shooting was dulled now, distant and echoing. But Andi could still feel the whiz of bullets through the air. She could hear the crack of them impacting on tree trunks. Her ears were filled with the screams of the wounded as they fell.

Through the trees, and over Terrace Drive, she kept running. The escapees had thinned out now. Everyone was branching off in different directions. She headed to The Lake. She circumnavigated part of it. Finally, she slowed. Wearily, she walked over to an empty bench and collapsed onto it. She was out of breath. Her mind reeled. She leaned forward, clutching her stomach. She stared blankly across the water. None of this registered. It couldn't. Not yet.

All was quiet around her, peaceful. A few birds were alive in the trees. Wildlife made itself known in The Lake. There was little human traffic here so close to Sheep Meadow. Only the occasional thunder of footsteps as another distressed protester dashed past.

One man stopped. He was gasping for breath. The limp body of his daughter was clutched to his chest. His body was soaked in blood. He could tell by Andi's expression where she'd just been.

"Miss, please," he said. He constantly glanced at the tree line. "Keep moving."

He lingered a moment. Only when she registered his presence by looking at him did he move on. She wanted to call out to him. She wanted to tell him that his child was already dead. She wanted to chase after him. She wanted to ease his pain.

But Andi did not follow. She knew it would do no good.

She'd traveled far enough. The GovPol wouldn't follow people this far. It was at a point where protesters and the general public could easily mingle. They wouldn't want to start another bloodbath in a place where the media could see.

She was safe here, from the massacre. From the Government itself, she was not sure if anywhere in America was safe anymore.

I was back in my office when the news reports of the so-called rioting came through. I didn't take them on face value. I was in a better position than the media to learn the truth. The sanction for what occurred went all the way to the top. The President himself advised the use of lethal force before all non-lethal methods were deployed. I was not in a position to discover if the civilian reports were true. I did not know if innocents were fired upon indiscriminately. I did not know if non-lethal options were ignored. Maybe it was a slaughter. Maybe the rubber bullets and tear gas were left to one side in favor of hot lead. What I *did* know was that the public was being lied to. The reports I had seen could destroy the Government if they fell into the wrong hands. They'd certainly tarnished my faith in them.

I never considered going to Central Park to witness what would happen. The previous day had taken its toll on me. So much had happened.

What I learned during my trip to D.C. had shocked me. I always thought evil Government experiments were the stuff of fiction. To discover they were real was disheartening. Worse still was that it was my own organization conducting these experiments. And at a time when I was a rising star in their ranks. What I had learned was that NASRU couldn't be trusted even by its own employees.

The visit would help little in my search for Stringer. It merely confirmed my fears. The experiment *must* have altered his personality. He was intelligent, that was beyond doubt. But I'd heard what very similar experiments had done to the others. He'd be unpredictable. He'd be delusional. Probably psychotic and an anarchist. All this spelled one thing for me. I was in agreement with General Miller: Stringer had to be stopped at all costs. Next time it would be a headshot, no hesitation.

The riots had made me realize just what a dangerous country this was becoming. It was part of my job to face mortal danger. But for the accountants, the gardeners, the store workers and stay-at-home parents, their own mortality was something they would have seldom considered.

It had made me think about the people I truly cared about. Any of them could have been victims of this massacre. I felt the need to call them and make sure they were safe.

When I had run through my phone list there was still one person. A person I cared about greatly but whose new number I did not have. Nat. I needed to call her. I needed to make sure she was okay. That meant I needed to do something that was morally questionable. I needed to use top secret and technically illegal Government surveillance equipment for a personal quest.

"Sam," I called over the intercom link. It was a few moments before I spoke again. "Locate someone for me, will you? Name: Natalya Czernokovsky. Date of birth: 18th March 2028."

"What's it in relation to?" he asked.

"Sam, just find her for me. I need her location and latest cell phone number."

"Ah, doing a bit of stalking in our spare time? Here we go, got her."

I sighed. "Where is she? Roughly?"

"Erm…Boston. Is that 'roughly' enough for you?"

Boston, I thought. She was staying with her mother. "Do we have reports of protest casualties for that area?"

"Not yet," Sam responded. "You want the cell phone number then?"

"Yeah."

"I'll patch it through to you. Checking up on an old friend?"

"Mind you own business," I told Sam. "Just put the call through."

I switched Sam off and waited for the phone to light up with Nat's new number. As soon as it did I grabbed the handset and dialed.

It was a tense, terribly long wait before the other end was answered. I presumed Nat still had my work number listed on her new cell phone. It must have taken an immense amount of thought to decide if the call was worth answering.

"Бог дает мне прочность! How did you get this number?" she asked wearily. She frowned at the camera.

"Hi," I began.

"Don't call me again," she told me.

"Wait," I said before she hung up. "Are you okay?"

She sighed. "What do you want, Jack?"

"Just to know you're okay. Bad things happened today and I just wanted to make sure…you know."

"I'm fine. I was nowhere near it."

"Good," I said. "It's good to see you again."

"Jack," she warned quietly. "Don't do this."

"I understand why you left," I began.

"Jack…" She looked into the camera in frustration.

"I know I wasn't there for you. But it was always like that. It was what we agreed upon. If you'd changed your mind, decided you wanted more from me, we could have at least talked about it first."

"How, when you were never there? I can't…I just can't."

There was a protracted silence. I stared at her beautiful face on the vidscreen. I realized perhaps for the first time that I had truly lost her. She was waiting patiently for me to respond. But I didn't know how.

"Jack, I have to go," she finally broke the silence.

"When do you think you'll be back in New York?" I asked. "So we can, you know, meet up and maybe discuss things." I stopped. I already knew it was no use.

"Goodbye, Jack," she said quietly and the line went dead.

"Goodbye," I whispered into the handset. I slowly replaced it in the cradle. I could try again, I thought. Call her back. Try one last time to reason with her. To explain. But even if she did answer, what would I say that would make any difference? I was still in the thick of this assignment. I still didn't have the time that I would need to give her. Nothing had truly changed. The reason why she left would remain a reason why we stayed apart. I needed to come to terms with what had happened. She wanted to change the rules of the game, and they were rules I could not accept.

Everything around me was disintegrating. I was stalled at work. I had lost Nat forever. My beloved country was under attack. Maybe justifiably so.

There was one thing I needed to know. One thing that could well determine my future. Was America under attack from terrorists and civilian dissidents? Or was it under attack from the very Government I had placed all my faith into?

"Sam?" I asked over the interlink.

"Yep?" he responded.

"Have you stored any Cyclops footage from today?"

"Some," he answered. "Relevant bits and general important stuff with the country at large. Why?"

"Did you manage to get footage of any of the riots?"

"Of course," he nodded. "All of them. They'll be going to Archives later. You want me to patch one through to your computer?"

"Yeah," I said. "Send the Central Park one through. Thanks."

I cut Sam off and sat back in my chair. I rubbed my chin in thought. I couldn't trust the Government report. I couldn't believe what they told even the most authorized of personnel. I needed to see the footage myself. Check if the reports were true. Did they shoot innocent men, women and children without provocation? I needed to know.

Because I worked for the Government, did that mean *I* was the bad guy?

EIGHTEEN

Andi was not sure how long she'd been waiting in the hotel reception. She'd been sitting shell-shocked on one of the two threadbare armchairs. It must have been hours. Darkness was falling outside. The clerk wasn't there. She hadn't seen him since the morning. She hadn't seen anyone. The hotel was deserted.

Andi had sat on the bench in Central Park long after the last echo of a gunshot seeped through the trees. There was little human traffic around her. One by one more birds began to chorus again until the chirps and rustle of wind in the canopy soothed her shaking mind. She felt the mechanical need to move. She walked slowly out of the park and headed blindly back to the hotel. There was nowhere else to go, she realized. No one else to contact. Just head back to the hotel. Wait for Daniel and hope he showed up.

As she traversed the streets, Andi heard the distant wail of sirens as emergency service crews rushed to clear up the carnage they had created. A few minutes later, her digital recorder sparked back into life. She slipped it back in her pocket without reviewing the contents.

The roads were quiet. There was far less traffic than usual. The news of the so-called 'riots' had seeped through to the public. Cities across the country ground to a halt. Everyone was intently listening to or watching the reports. It affected the country in the same way as the JFK assassination, 9/11 or the sinking of the USS Nimitz. Life had come to a standstill.

The door to the hotel's reception was wide open when she arrived. She timidly stepped inside. She walked to the desk and called out to the clerk. She received no response.

She wrapped her coat around her. She was shaking with chill despite the warmth of the heated reception area. Feeling lost, she sat in the old armchair. And waited. All alone. Completely undisturbed. No one entered the hotel. No one left. Darkness slowly dulled the day into cold, bitter shadows.

She was still feeling the shell-shock when Daniel arrived. When he saw her he breathed out a heavy sigh of relief.

"You're here," he said unnecessarily. He took hold of the other threadbare armchair. He dragged it in front of her and sat. He lightly took one of her hands in his. She continued staring at the floor. "You okay?" he asked.

Andi looked at him at last with wide, wet eyes. She slowly shook her head.

He sighed again. "I told you not to go," he insisted

She removed her hand from his. "They…" she began. Then stopped. "Did you know?"

"I…" he hesitated. "Know what?"

"Did you know?" Andi asked more forcefully. "That they would open fire without… We did nothing. Not one person showed signs of violence. And they…just…"

"It must have been terrible," Daniel answered. He was avoiding her question.

"Terrible?" she whispered. She became angry. "You knew they would do that. You could have stopped it. Warned them all to stay away."

"How?" he asked. "I...I couldn't."

"Why? Because you might expose yourself?! Thousands died today. Maybe *hundreds* of thousands."

"You don't understand what it's like for me," Daniel said calmly. "You never can. Knowing what will happen. All those people were...calling out to me like Sirens. They'd lead me astray. They'd lure me onto the rocks. I have to blank it out. I have to drown out their cries for help and focus on the bigger picture. For the greater good some will have to be sacrificed."

"Sacrificed?!" Andi exclaimed. "I saw a six-year-old girl, alone on the field, screaming for her mother..." She began to cry. "And then her head exploded! That's *sacrifice*?!"

She buried her face in her hands. The emotion and horror of the day was finally released. Daniel tried to take a hand again, but she shrugged him off.

"How could this happen?" she asked. She wiped away her tears. "How could America come to be like this?"

"It's not over yet," he answered. "Not by a long stretch."

"More massacre? More innocents dead? And will you warn people the next time? Or just let them blindly go to their deaths?"

"There is something else in store for me," Daniel said.

"What does that mean?"

He didn't answer.

"Tell me!" Andi demanded. He remained tight-lipped. A car's headlights illuminated the reception as it sped past.

"Look," he said eventually. "What will happen has to happen. It may seem horrible now. But when it is all over, you'll look back on it and realize...it was all worth it."

"A child shot dead can never be worth *anything*," she responded bitterly. "Short term, long term...how can that ever be justified?"

He sighed. "You're tired. It's been an emotional day for you..." He paused when he saw the expression of disgusted amazement she threw at him. "*Very* emotional... Look, perhaps you should rest. Go to bed. Doesn't look like the clerk's coming back so it'll be a free night. Every cloud and all that."

"The clerk isn't coming back because he probably died on that field. There's no silver lining here, Daniel."

He shrugged. "Maybe. Maybe not. Look at when we fought for independence against the English. Or when India fought for independence against...well...the English again. This isn't supposed to be an anti-English rant. It's just...well...ordinary people got killed, massacred. But in the long run, they died for a purpose. They finally managed to remove British rule and become free."

"That does not make it okay!" Andi shouted.

"Depends on your viewpoint. It gives their deaths a purpose, a reason. Those people out there have not died in vain. Their lives were not lost senselessly."

"Listen to you! Maybe I am really tired because right now it sounds as though you don't care one bit about all of those people. How can you remain so clinically removed from all this? Have you no heart in there?"

Daniel sighed again. He was a little annoyed at the comment. "Just get some sleep," he told her. He started to leave.

Andi lunged for one of his hands and grabbed it tightly. "Wait!" she exclaimed. Eventually he looked at her. "Don't leave me," she whispered. "I don't want to be alone tonight."

"There's things I need to–" he began.

"Please," Andi begged.

Daniel glanced around the hotel reception. He mulled over his options. "How about a compromise? I'll stay with you until you fall asleep."

"Don't you want to stay with me?" Andi asked timidly. She was like a frightened child who'd just learned her father was leaving home.

"This has nothing to do with what I want," Daniel responded. "But that's academic at the moment." He sighed again. "Come on, let's get you upstairs."

He led her up the stairs. He found an open, empty room. He laid her down on the bed. He lay next to her. He cradled her in his arms. And he shushed her into a deep sleep.

I ordered another shot of Wild Turkey. As soon as it arrived I threw it down my throat. It was harsh and burned. But it was cheaply effective. Besides, I'd had so many already that the bitter aftertaste barely registered. I took another clumsy sip of my beer to temper the taste. I gently, carefully and drunkenly laid it back on the bar.

My head was wobbling slightly and my vision was in a dream-like fug. I looked at the hazy image of an attractive woman to my right. Black dress, blonde hair, red lips, pink nose.

She was staring at me. Smiling. Hoping I'd be charming and buy her a drink. I was in no mood to be picked up in a bar by a stranger.

"Hey good looking," she said. "I'm Jo."

I nodded at her. "I'm not interested," I told her. I turned my full attention back to my beer.

"Asshole," the woman muttered. She headed away with her drink, back to her group of friends. Two more of them had already tried it on with me. I absently wondered what the fourth and final woman's opening gambit would be.

I took another sip of the beer. I gave another non-verbal indication to the barman to top up my shot glass. Then I realized that for the last minute or so there had been a male presence on the barstool to my left.

"Bud," he told the barman. Before I was able to recognize his face my subconscious informed me the voice belonged to Al. "Fighting off the ladies are we?" he asked.

"Hey Al!" I called out, slapping him on the back. I indicated his beer. "I'll get that for you."

"What are you doing here?" Al asked me.

"Drinking. What are *you* doing here?"

"My boss has decided to get wasted. None of us know why. So I thought I'd come find out."

"Ah," I responded. "Sounds like your boss has got the right idea." I threw the next Wild Turkey down my throat. It still didn't taste any better.

"Any particular reason why you've drunk so much you're barely able to stand?"

"I'm standing just fine, thank you very much."

"Stone...you're sat on a stool."

I glanced down. "Oh yeah," I said with mock surprise. "That's handy."

Al sighed. He took a swig of his beer. "Stop messing about, Stone. You're not *that* drunk."

"Maybe not. But it's what I'm aiming for."

"Why?" Al asked simply.

"Why?" I repeated. "Let me tell you a secret, Al." I leaned in close and placed one hand on his shoulder. "We're the bad guys," I whispered. I leaned back, nodded sagely and took another sip of my beer.

"You don't really believe that."

I nodded again. "The Government," I continued quietly, "is screwing everyone."

"I think that's what governments are supposed to do," Al joked.

"I watched the footage of the riot, you know. The one here. They didn't do anything, those people. And we just shot them all."

"*We* didn't, Stone," Al insisted. "*We're* not the bad guys. We don't answer to those monkeys in the White House. Barely a dozen of them know we even exist. This is not *us*."

"But don't we technically work for the Government?"

"You want to blame the massacre on school teachers as well?"

"Oh, come on," I chided. "It's not the same. We have the technology. We have the security clearances. We could have known about this. We *should* have! And we should have stopped it. Because we are here to protect *America*. Not the land. Not the Government. But the people. The ordinary citizens who never know what the hell's going on and who never know how close to death they've been. Because we've been there to save them. The men in black, protectors of the light." I signaled the barman again with a flourish.

"How poetic. Don't order another…"

I ordered another shot and one more beer.

"You know what *really* gets to me, Al? They've been doing this for years. And *I've* been doing this for years. All those times I've risked my life, risked everything for my country… How many of those times have I been doing their dirty work for them? How many times have I been unknowingly shafting the people? And what have I got for my troubles? Nothing. I've even lost…" My voice trailed off. I took the opportunity to down another shot of whiskey and finish off the dregs of my previous beer.

"That's what this is really about, isn't it," he told me. "Natalya."

"I called her today. She doesn't want to know me."

"Relationships break down, Stone. It's what happens. It's all part of the natural cycle of life."

"You're a real comfort," I told him. "Thanks."

"All I'm saying is, you're not alone. All across the world people are getting together. They're making love. They're arguing. They're splitting up. They're getting drunk and trying to drown their sorrows. But you know what? After a while, they meet someone else. And the cycle starts again."

"So what you're saying is it's pointless. Just an endless merry-go-round of heartache. There's no point ever falling in love in the first place."

"Well…" Al shrugged. "I…don't think that's the point I was trying to make. More that you will get over it and meet someone new some day."

I looked at him in annoyance. "I don't want to get over it, Al! I don't want to meet someone new. I want Nat. I want to show her that I *do* love her, I *do* appreciate her, I *do* want to spend my life with her."

"Getting drunk isn't going to make that goal a reality. Besides, isn't it her fault you've split up? She can't just suddenly demand more and expect you to instantly fall into place like a good little lapdog. Maybe it's for the best. Maybe you need to meet someone who isn't going to change their mind every five seconds. Maybe one of the legion of women over there who are swooning over you…"

"You know, I did meet someone else," I told him. "Nothing happened. But I think she wanted me. She was beautiful. And inviting. And…so fucked up."

"Sounds perfect for you."

"You have no idea what they've done to her." I shook my head in annoyance.

"O…kay," Al responded. He didn't have a clue what I was talking about. "Going to see her again?"

I shook my head again. "No."

"Why not?"

"She wasn't Nat," I pointed out quietly. "I called her, you know. Nat. To explain."

"Yeah, you said."

"No. After that. I called about half an hour ago. Left a message on her answer phone."

"Oooh, that's bad," Al pointed out.

"I asked her to forgive me."

"Were you by any chance drunk when you called her? What am I saying? You've been drunk for hours."

"That's bad, isn't it" I asked rhetorically.

"She's just acrimoniously split from her boyfriend of several years and he's leaving slurred answer phone messages declaring his love. Yeah, that's bad. You'll wake up tomorrow and the first thing you'll think is 'oh, I feel terrible'. And then you'll stumble about hung-over for a few minutes. And then it'll hit you. You'll remember the message. You'll remember what you said and how you sounded. You'll realize that you've just slammed that final nail in the coffin."

I frowned at him. "What can I do? It's too late now."

Al studied me for a moment. With a sigh he took his cell phone from his pocket and dialed a number. It took a few rings before the other end was answered.

"I need a big favor... Yeah, I know it's late, but I need you to head back into the office... I'll owe you big time, I know that... No, it's not work-related. It's...personal... For the boss."

He slid off the stool. He headed towards the restroom to find a quieter area for the conversation. I may have been drunk but I was acutely aware that Al's activities were illegal. The less people who heard him the better.

I took a few more sips of my beer. I considered ordering another Wild Turkey, but reluctantly decided I'd probably had enough to drink. Besides, the whiskey was repeating on me.

Al returned to his stool.

"As long as Nat doesn't check her cell in the next hour or so, the message situation has been resolved."

"How?" I asked.

Al shrugged. "We have the technology, we have the security clearances. We can access and delete anything."

"You're a good pal," I told him. I slapped him on his back. It was just at a moment when he was trying to drain the rest of his bottle. He spluttered a little. I ignored it. "Tomorrow, I'm going to promote you."

"Thanks," he told me. "Now, how about we call it a night so you can at least feel a *little* sensate tomorrow?"

"Alright," I nodded and gulped down my remaining beer. "Do you know where I parked my car?"

Al carefully pushed me off the stool and started escorting me out of the bar.

"As if you're driving," he told me. "Where do you live?"

"That's classified material, soldier," I answered.

Al sighed. "Okay, I guess you can crash on my couch."

Andi woke at six o'clock to an otherwise empty bed. The side where Daniel had lain the night before was now cold. He must have vacated the hotel hours ago.

Andi felt a sense of abject loss coursing through her. She was unable to analyze exactly why. Was it because Daniel wasn't there? Was it because of the horrific loss of lives yesterday? Was it because she could not locate a single thing in her current situation that connected her to her normal life? It seemed like her entire being was slipping away to be replaced by someone else. It was disconcerting, to leave everything behind and never know if you'd be able to reclaim any of it again. But there was hope, she felt. Hope and joy. For though he wasn't there at present, Daniel would be back. He would be with her again.

That caught Andi short. That thought... That brief rush of excitement amid the gloom of her lost life. It occurred when she thought of Daniel. Indeed, whenever she thought of him. He was arrogant, egocentric, rude and often callous. So how could anyone have these giddy feelings over him? More to the point: how could *she*? It was no secret that she did not love easily. She preferred to cut relationships short when it looked like they may get too serious. It had earned her several derogatory nicknames, of course. She didn't mind that. A name was a name. But she'd always been careful not to get too deep with anyone. Admittedly it was because she always seemed to go for the wrong kind of guy. But even on the occasion she'd found someone nice that defense mechanism had kicked in and he'd been kicked out. So why now? Why should she start feeling like a schoolgirl with a crush? He was bad for her. So bad. Was that it? The stronger the danger, the more intense the emotion? Or was it just that when she was at her most vulnerable and helpless he was there for her?

Andi checked herself. She needed to dismiss these silly thoughts. She needed to enforce some self-control to avoid falling for this man. She needed to retain her faculties.

She slipped back into the clothing she'd worn for the last few days. They were musty and slightly itchy, but she had nothing else to wear.

There was a note left on the hotel room's screen. She activated it and watched the brief message. Daniel said he had gone to complete some errands. He should be back with breakfast soon after she woke. He advised her not to wander off but stay within the hotel.

The hotel was still deserted. It was a large, open, desolate place devoid of life. There was nothing to occupy her there. She flicked through the latest news bulletins but found little of note. The 'riots' continued to be the headlining story. The

Government had effectively closed its borders to foreign news crews. Aside from this there was just a smattering of news. The initial hearing for the English Prince's trial would begin in a few days' time. A plea of insanity was expected. The hand off of POWs between the US and Cuba was to go ahead the next morning. Pop sensation K-Lee had been hospitalized with the same unidentified virus rumored to have caused the deaths of TV actors Grant Michaels and Storm Braddock plus several others. Someone had been tortured and murdered live on the internet with viewers able to vote on what happened.

Andi grew increasingly concerned during Daniel's absence. That strange feeling of abject loss had begun to abate, as had her foolish desires. But it was now one and a half hours since she woke. She was very aware of that being a long time to locate some breakfast.

Maybe something had happened to him.

NINETEEN

My eyes were gummed when I tried to open them. I could already feel I was in an alien environment before I could take in my surroundings. When my eyes cleared enough to focus I was presented with the image of a blonde, mop-haired four-year-old boy staring impassively at me.

I blinked several times, but the image remained. "Hello," I croaked. I began levering myself up on a worn fabric couch. The child's eyes remained fixated on my face. Aside from that tracking movement, he remained motionless.

I swallowed painfully with a dry throat and noted that I was in the living room of a traditional family home. Slightly chintzy furniture jarred with mod cons.

I heard a recognizable male voice drift through from a room behind me. "Linus," he called. "Come on. Breakfast."

I didn't have the headache I was expecting from a hangover. I didn't feel ill either. But my throat was parched and my brain felt like it was operating from a position six inches to the right of my body.

"Linus!" the voice came again, closer this time. Al rushed into view, scooped up the child and disappeared again.

I stood slowly, ensuring my balance was acceptable, and licked my lips.

"Becky!" a female voice hollered from the rear. The sudden increase in decibels made me pause. I blinked twice more just to ensure this was the correct reality.

I turned to witness a family home hard at work. An archway led from the living room to a large kitchen. The amenities were lost to view on the left. Dominating the view through the arch was an oval dining table. It had already been laden with breakfast foods and more were en route. Al, already dressed in his work suit, was wrestling the boy Linus into a chair. He succeeded in his task and slid a half-eaten bowl of cereal in the boy's vicinity. "Finish it," he ordered.

Al came into the living room. A thunder of footsteps preceded the appearance of his six-year-old daughter Becky from the stairwell.

"Who's that?" she called, staring at me.

"Get your breakfast, sweetie," Al answered. With one hand on the back of her ponytailed head, he softly pushed her in the direction of the kitchen. He turned his attention back to me.

"You good?" he asked.

I wasn't sure if I was up to nodding quite yet. "I'll live," I told him.

He nodded himself. "We all need a good blow-out from time to time," he said. "Want some breakfast?"

He led me into the kitchen area and sat me down at the table. He introduced the two children. Becky silently waved her spoon at me. Linus stopped eating and decided to stare again.

Al called his wife over. Her name was Sandra. She had been preparing the last vestiges of the breakfast buffet. She placed a plate of crispy bacon on the table. She was an attractive blonde woman. A girl-next-door type. Not someone who would make people stop and stare, but someone they would want to settle down with in that American Dream picket-fenced suburb.

"Nice to meet you, Mr Stone," she said with genuine warmth. I smiled and nodded back.

"Honey," Al said in a half-whisper. "He's a Lieutenant."

"Not in my house, dear," Sandra responded. She smiled at me. "Work doesn't enter this house, Mr Stone. Kevin even has to keep his gun in the car. Would you like some coffee?"

I nodded. "Thank you." She poured me a cup. Al sat opposite me.

"Daddy," Becky called. "I've finished. Can I watch cartoons for a bit?"

"Okay," Al responded. "Take your brother with you."

Becky slid off her seat and escorted her younger brother into the living area. I noticed that while Becky turned on the TV and sat on the couch watching it intently, Linus chose to stand motionless next to the couch staring back at me.

"I don't mean to be rude," I said, "but your child is staring at me."

"Ignore him," Sandra told me. "He's just curious. I guess you don't have kids yourself."

"No," I responded and blew on the coffee. "No, I don't."

"Help yourself to some breakfast," she told me as she returned the coffee pot to its base.

I selected three pancakes drizzled in honey and bacon on the side. Al offered me some scrambled eggs, which I refused. He overloaded his plate with food and sidelined a bowl of Lucky Charms for dessert.

"I apologize for the inconvenience of last night," I said, mainly to Sandra, before I tucked into my food.

"No need," she offered back. "I know what's going on out there. Someone in your line of work is going to have a hard time watching their country rip itself apart."

"My line of work?" I asked. I wondered exactly how much Al had told her.

"Well, I don't know what you do, exactly," Sandra responded. "But I'm aware it is top-secret, dangerous, save the world stuff."

"Not...saving the world exactly," Al muttered.

"Whatever it is," Sandra continued, "I know it's tough. That's why, Mr Stone, that as Kevin's superior, you have to look out for him."

"Sandra," Al warned quietly.

"All I'm saying is he's your responsibility, Mr Stone. It is up to you to make sure he returns home safely at the end of the day."

I swallowed a portion of pancake. "I can assure you, Mrs Jacobsen, that is my top priority as well."

"Honey, you're embarrassing me in front of the boss," Al complained.

"No animosity intended, Mr Stone. I just wanted to get things clear straight away."

"Of course," I answered. "I understand completely." I pushed another piece of pancake into my mouth and combined it with a swig of coffee.

"You're welcome to come round for dinner any time," Sandra said with a warm smile. "We don't want you eating on your own every night."

I looked up at Al. His cheeks went red. Sandra patted the table. "You boys finish up. I'll get the children ready."

When she left the kitchen, Al took a nervous swig of freshly-squeezed orange juice.

"You told her about Nat?" I asked.

He shrugged. "She wanted to know why my boss was drunk on the couch."

I looked past Al into the living area. Sandra was ushering Becky away from the TV and up the stairs. She dragged Linus by one arm to the foot of the steps. Only when he had to turn to ascend the stairs did he stop staring at me.

I envied Al. All the pressures we were under at work, and he could just shed them as soon as he entered this vibrant, warm, loving environment. It wasn't for me. Too cozy, too traditional. But it worked for him, and a successful work-life balance was something I coveted.

Al dropped me off at the bar and I picked up my own vehicle. The shadows of an overcast day dulled the streets. I refused to remove my sunglasses.

I parked in the underground lot and groaned at the still-broken elevator. I wearily climbed up the stairs. I paused en route to affectionately pat the marble statue in the stairwell. It seemed to have become a friend to all the employees.

I entered the outer office. I was struck by how deserted it looked.

"Where is everyone?" I asked Sam. He was the lone occupant. He looked very tired. He looked like he'd been up all night. I realized who Al called up to take care of my embarrassing answer phone problem.

"Brent's out getting coffee," he answered. He indicated my glorified PA's empty desk.

"And the rest? Where's Analysis?"

"Didn't you get the memo?" he asked. He cursed his stupidity. "Of course not, you've only just got here."

"Memo? What's going on?"

"Re-allocation. The department's overloaded since those riots. You've got me, Brent and Alecto left."

I blinked a few times, processing this new information. "They've taken my men?"

"Technically two were women, but yeah. We've been downsized. I guess the General isn't too happy with our progress so far."

"Shit," I muttered. When I thought about it, it made sense. We were getting nowhere. All our leads had gone. We were currently relying on blind luck or Stringer making a mistake. That didn't require two people to analyze data. It didn't need a couple of field assistants.

I entered my office. Al was sitting across the desk.

"They've gone, Stone," he told me as I settled into my chair.

"I know."

"What do we do now?"

I paused for a moment, hoping for a flash of inspiration. It was a false hope.

"I'll have to think about that one," I answered.

"I guess we don't really need seven people to help you do that, then."

"No, not really." I said. "Any news on Meg?"

"I visited him before rescuing you from the bar. He's…in pain. But he'll be back. Fighting fit and all that."

"Right. Yeah."

"Still feeling fuggy?" Al asked.

"Remind me never to touch cheap whiskey again."

"Next time you want to get drunk, I'll point you in the direction of a nice single malt Glenmorangie. You know, I've been thinking…"

Al had paused for dramatic effect. I was not in the mood for such things. "Yes?" I asked.

"Well, there's only one of me now. One of the Erinyes. It doesn't seem right. Maybe I should be allocated a new code name."

"You're not getting a new code name," I told him.

"Just think about it. I was thinking maybe Prometheus?"

I shook my head. "That was mine when I was a field agent. Not good. People call you Prom Queen."

"Ares?"

"Taken."

"Odysseus!"

"Taken."

"Athena?"

"*Female!*"

Al paused. "Oh, right. Of course. Pythagoras?"

I silently stared at him until he gave up on the idea of having a new code name.

"So," he said. I could tell he was embarrassed now. He wanted an excuse to leave my office. "What shall I do?"

"To be honest, right now I really can't think of a better option than cruising the streets and hoping to bump into our quarry. I'm going to get Sam to run a citywide RFID sweep and see if we can spot any people without a signal. Could take weeks, but it's something to do. Meanwhile I need some quiet time to formulate a cohesive strategy."

"I guess…" Al began. He was cut short by the telephone. I picked up the handset.

"Stone," I said.

"Stringer!" was the response I got from the familiar voice on the other end of the blank screen.

I paused for a moment to figure out what to say. I switched to speakerphone for Al's sake. Stringer took this opportunity to analyze my mental state.

"Stuck for words?" he asked. "So what do you choose? 'Where are you?' Or 'what do you want?' Or maybe 'please let me find you or I'll get fired!' Are you desperate enough to try tracing this call even though you know there's no chance of it succeeding? Tell me, Stone. What are you thinking right now?"

"I'm just wondering how to get you to shut up," I responded. I rubbed my temple. It felt sore.

"No you're not. You're wondering how you can possibly turn this conversation into a method of tracking me. I presume you have someone else listening in on the speakerphone? Kevin Jacobsen, I'll bet."

Al glanced at me with surprise but didn't respond. There was a moment of silence before Stringer spoke again.

"What? You only going to say something if I call you Alecto? So cheesy."

"*Was* there a point to this call, Stringer?" I asked.

"Yes. Of course. I guess you just want to get down to business, eh? No dwelling on the marital problems. No wondering if your beloved employers are trying to kill every human in the country."

I greeted that with a cold silence.

"Hmmm," Stringer continued. "Okay. Well, I'm calling because I have another hot tip for you."

"Terrorist attack," I said.

"If you call them that, yes. There is growing public concern over the state of the Government. One final push is needed to set things in motion. But it needs to be something big. Something spectacular. The general public needs to know that if they challenge this administration they have some seriously powerful back-up behind them."

"They're going to attack the White House?" I asked with sudden, and misguided, realization.

"No, that would be small fry. They're going to hit Fort Belvoir in Virginia tomorrow at midday."

"It's a big military base, Stringer. I need more info than that. Which part are they going to hit?"

"I don't think you quite understand," he told me. "They're not just hitting the base. They're hitting the whole lot. The HQ *and* the surrounding town."

"What?" I called. "They can't! The people, the innocent citizens there. The public won't rally behind *that*!"

"True, there are thousands of families in Belvoir. But they are military families. The entire city has been taken over by them. That makes it a viable target."

"But there are still women and children in the city," I pointed out.

"Who are you trying to persuade, Stone? I know that. But I also know that you have more than twenty four hours to evacuate. That shouldn't be too much trouble for a disciplined military city. Even a whole city of sixty thousand."

"And the fallout?" I asked.

"It will show the public that the people standing behind them have the power and weaponry to oppose any Government action."

"No," I said. "I mean the radioactive fallout."

"What...? There won't be any fallout. They're not nuking the place, Stone!"

"Then how? The military base *and* the town? What the hell are they going to do? Go into space and fire a meteor at it?"

"No, don't be silly," he chided. "They've got a fully functional gravity bomb."

"A what?"

"A gravity bomb."

"I repeat – a what?"

"Oh, poor Jack!" Stringer cried out. "How out of the loop do they keep you? The military's been trying to make one of these for ten years, and you've never heard of it?!"

"Make me feel worse. Thanks. So what is this gravity bomb then?"

"Maybe you should ask your boss, Stone," he answered.

"Maybe you should stop being so damned cryptic and properly tell me something for once!"

"And maybe you should give someone a call and start the evacuation procedure now, Stone. No one and no thing will survive in this bomb's vicinity. Evacuate thirty square miles, just to make sure. Because this thing, it's like a little black hole. It grows in mass until it sucks things into it. Then it collapses under its own weight."

"Think I dated one," Al pointed out.

Stringer ignored his comment. "Believe me, Stone, they *will* be able to get it within city limits before you can do anything about it."

"And how exactly do you know all this Stringer?" I asked. "How do you know about the gravity bomb? How do you know the terrorists are going to use it? Your abilities are based on observation, Stringer. That must mean you know the terrorists."

"Stone, don't insult me. I know very well you've figured out I have a connection with them. I heard I had a visitor recently. Came to my apartment, took a detour to your holding cells in D.C. You know what I was designed for. You know part of my remit was as an early warning system. You know that I can only do that if I am in regular contact with both sides. So stop wasting time. Fort Belvoir. Midday tomorrow. Evacuate thirty square miles."

The line went abruptly dead. I looked at a silent Al.

"Gravity bomb?" I asked.

He merely shrugged. "Never heard of it."

"Okay, go start scouting around the city for him. Sounded like a public phone amid heavy traffic."

"Right, boss," Al responded. He left the office. I waited until the door was fully closed behind him. I gave General Miller a call.

"Stone!" Miller barked as soon as he answered.

"Good morning, Sir," I offered. His facial expression dissuaded me from pursuing the pleasantries further.

"Good work with The Duke," he told me. "Sorry I can't spare you to work on the terrorism case, but you're our best hope for getting Stringer. Any news on that front?"

"News on both the Stringer *and* terrorism fronts, Sir. I've just received a call from him. Another bomb warning."

"Go on," the General said after a short pause.

"He wants us to evacuate Fort Belvoir, Sir. Thirty square miles of it. Apparently at midday tomorrow the terrorists will use something called a gravity bomb."

"What?" the General breathed. "They've perfected it?" he said to himself. "We've been working over a decade… We've got to get the evacuation underway."

"The bomb, Sir. What is it?"

"You don't need to know the details, Stone. It's like a black hole."

"That's what Stringer said, Sir. How exactly does it work?"

"Very good question, Stone. Otherwise we'd have perfected it ourselves by now. How did a two-bit terrorist operation manage something the top US military scientists could not? It defies belief."

"So this *is* a very real threat?" I asked.

"Very. I have to go, Stone. Good work."

Just as abruptly as Stringer did, Miller killed the call. I stared at the blank image for a moment. I cut the signal.

"I *am* being kept out of the loop," I said to myself.

Andi was waiting in the hotel room, perched on the bed and sitting on her hands. The panic had been slowly bubbling inside her. Daniel had been absent for two and a half hours now. It was too long, she thought. He'd been gone too long. What would she do if he never returned? How could she cope by herself, on the run and with no money? How could he have abandoned her so easily?

She heard Daniel's familiar footsteps traversing the corridor outside. She felt a flush of embarrassment that she ever doubted him. It quickly turned to anger. How dare he make her feel this way!

"Hey," he said casually. He breezed into the hotel room. He set a brown paper bag on the table and began to remove the goods within. He handed her an egg McMuffin and a large black coffee.

"Where have you been?" she breathed, controlling her anger.

"Breakfast," he responded. "Didn't you see the note?"

"I *did* see the note. Nearly three hours ago."

"Yes, well..." He took a seat from the table and pulled it up close to the bed. "I told you I had a few errands to do first. If you let me do them last night..." He shrugged.

"What things?" Andi asked. She didn't want to let him off the hook so easily.

"Well...you know...things."

She mimed a 'such as?' motion.

"Okay...err...I had a chat with Lieutenant Stone, for example."

"The bad guy?!"

"Yeah. Bad guy. Another bomb threat to warn him about. He's having a hard time, you know. Personal troubles and the like. Actually sounded rather hung-over-"

"Wait," Andi interrupted. "Where?"

"The bomb? Just don't go near Fort Belvoir for a while. Actually," he laughed, "if you really want to, we could go there today. It won't really be around for much longer."

"And how long did that chat take?"

"Hmmm, I can see you're more concerned as to my whereabouts than for the safety of the citizens of Fort Belvoir."

"Well?" Andi demanded.

He took a long sip of his coffee. He indicated her muffin. "Going to eat that?"

She glanced at the muffin herself. She looked back at Daniel, demanding answers.

"I had a few things to take care of," he said. "As preparation."

"Preparation for what?"

"You really should eat up before we begin this discussion, you know. Breakfast is important after all."

Defiant, Andi grabbed the egg McMuffin and stuffed it all in her mouth in one go. "Well?" she grunted through the food as she struggled to chew the mass.

"Errr..." Daniel started. He was momentarily surprised. It was a seemingly genuine look that meant she had, for the first time, actually done something he wasn't expecting. "Preparation for...me going away."

She swallowed a portion of the muffin. "Where?" she managed.

"That's...not something you need to know."

"Why?"

"Because...well, because I don't *want* you to know."

She swallowed some more of the food while composing her thoughts. "Why?" she asked again.

"Because..." he sighed. "I'm going away. For good."

Andi paused. In that pause she polished off the muffin. "So, you buy me breakfast and then dump me?"

"Don't look at it as me dumping you. Look at it as me saving you."

"Saving me…yeah I've heard that one before. You're not good for me, right? It's not me, it's you. Don't worry, I'm a nice person. I'll find someone else in no time."

"Fine," he shrugged. "Look at it as me dumping you if you want. And you know what? It *is* you. It is what *I* have done to you. I don't want you to go through any more. You're living in a hotel and you're on the run from the Government, for Christ's sake! Unless I leave soon, things are going to get so much worse."

"Fate has a plan, is that it?"

"Yes," he nodded. "Yes it does. It has a plan for me and a separate plan for you. The two no longer intertwine."

"I don't believe that," she said. "I genuinely don't believe that."

"I…I can't really answer back to that. I *do* believe. That means I'm leaving and you're not. This *has to* happen, and that's that."

"Just go then," she said. "Go. What was the point of all this, then? Telling me what a state our country is in. Telling me all about your amazing abilities. And then you just wander off and leave me homeless, on the run and without a job to go back to. You wanted me to tell everyone the story? How can I do that when I become so desperate to live I'm whoring myself out to fund my crack habit?"

"I think that's taking things a bit too far. You don't need a job in the media to be able to tell your story. You'll find another way. And don't worry about the homeless, no money, crack-whore thing. You'll be okay. Besides, I don't have to leave *right* now." He began rummaging in his pocket.

"But it's just delaying the inevitable, though, isn't it."

"Here, take this." He offered her a small plastic rectangle.

"What is it?" Andi asked.

"A cell phone flash card."

"No, I know what it is. What's on it?"

"Account details," he said. He was not more forthcoming.

"Of?"

"Remember Seraph?" he asked. Andi shook her head. It rang a bell but the details were fuzzy. "A private company sent a probe to the Europa moon to search for signs of life. Then they floated themselves on the stock market."

"Yeah," she answered. "It…failed, right?"

"Four years into the journey, the probe stopped transmitting. The stocks fell through the floor."

"Right, I remember."

"Well I hacked into the Very Large Array in New Mexico," he told her. "Into their communications station. Yesterday, the probe started transmitting again. They're still collating data, but I heard enough. They've done it. Landed on Europa. Drilled through the ice sheet. Found life. Microscopic. But life."

"I…haven't heard…"

"No, you won't have," he shook his head. "They haven't released anything yet. But they will. In a few days. On this card are details of an account I set up for you with some stockbrokers. I bought you ten thousand shares at eighty three cents each. Sell them when they hit a hundred and forty seven dollars."

"That's…"

"Around one and a half million. It's not *that* much, I know. But it will be enough. Use some of the money to stay in a different hotel each night for the next three weeks. As soon as media outlets start speaking out against the Government they'll be swamped with problems. You'll be able to go home and go back to your job without much trouble. See? Problem solved."

"But...," Andi began. "Won't you need the money for wherever you're going?"

"I've been slicing funds off the military black ops budget for three years. I'm fine."

"How?" Andi asked.

"Details are irrelevant," he shrugged.

"Fine," she said. She took the card. "But at least give me the respect of answering this. Where are you going?"

"I told you it is best if you don't know."

"Rubbish," she insisted. "Tell me. If you have any feelings for me at all..."

"Emotional blackmail?" He sighed. "I'm not telling you where I'm going. I'll be heading to Seattle to catch a connecting flight tomorrow evening. But where to...? Not saying. After that I'll be out of the country and out of touch."

"Just like that," she shrugged.

"Yeah."

"Just catch a flight to Seattle, then...whoosh gone, vapor trail. All that remains is a memory."

"Pretty much," he nodded. "Believe me, I don't want to. But we all have to play our little part. We all have to sacrifice."

"And why can't I go with you?" she asked.

"You'll understand later. I can't explain now. But in a few days, maybe you'll understand. Now, drink your coffee and get ready. At the very least we can spend today and some of tomorrow together before everything changes."

"What are we going to do?" Andi asked quietly.

"Whatever you want. Have a nice meal. Watch a movie. Go shopping."

"We might get caught," she pointed out.

"Very good," he told her. "You catch on. We can't do any of those things. So, I recommend a combination of two things. I can teach you a bit more on how to read people. And we can have sex. Sex first?"

"Read my thoughts on *that* one," Andi told him.

"I'll teach you the finer tricks of my trade, then. By the way, you didn't actually want to go to Fort Belvoir, did you?"

Andi shook her head and delicately sipped the coffee.

April 4th 2056. Fort Belvoir had been successfully evacuated. It was a clear sign of the precision of the country's military. We had set up closed borders in a thirty square mile area and were on high alert. We were ready to destroy any vehicle, plane or missile that may come our way.

I was with several high-ranking officials. We were in an elevated area with a clear view of the evacuated town. We awaited the midday chime.

We didn't hear the approach of the bomb-laden drone flying in from the south. For one it was traveling at an estimated mach 3. For another, it was cruising at an altitude of 50,000-ft. It was an automated, radio-controlled craft with a polished sphere slung under it.

Fighters were already on standby and in the air. They were scrambled to intercept the target. The enemy drone decelerated. Our fighters whizzed past it. The drone slowed down so fast it started to break up in mid-air. Chunks of the fuselage and wing spilled off. Just before the drone shattered under the strain and fell in a crumbling wreck, the bomb was released. It began its descent through the cloud tops.

Fins on the bomb's casing spun the device faster and faster. It established a level equilibrium for the components inside. At 900 feet the casing disappeared. It collapsed in upon itself as the components were activated. The destructive potential of the bomb was unleashed.

The device began its chain reaction insubstantially. There was the merest blip of energy as deuterium was created, split and converted to helium. This released more energy and more matter. The reaction occurred again and again. More matter and energy was produced. The device's zero point began to take shape. It was a sphere of quietly growing energy and matter 900 feet in the air. It became denser and heavier with every nano second.

The reaction was building. The device started to exert its power. It collapsed under its own weight. It now resembled for all intents and purposes a tiny black hole. It slowly expanded, sucking up everything within its building circumference. Clouds were pulled mercilessly towards it. They spun and broke up like soap suds down a plughole.

As the sphere increased in size, it began to claw at the tops of the larger buildings. It tore at brick, mortar and steel. The debris was drawn into the center of the hole, fuelling it even more. Smaller buildings started being attacked. They emptied their contents along with their outer shell in a display of gravity gone awry. The sphere tickled treetops. It ripped leaf from twig, twig from branch, branch from trunk and trunk from ground.

But it didn't stop there.

The ground itself was assaulted. Asphalt, concrete, grass, soil, cabling, sewer systems and rock were ripped up. Lakes, streams, the river, Accotink Bay and the shores of Gunston Cove flew up in a curtain of vapor. The water mixed muddily with the torn rock and soil. The concoction headed to its apex in the sky.

Finally the matter within the heart of the device was squashed into energy. It exploded in a shower of blinding light, electromagnetic microwaves and barely-heard static. Air rushed into the vacuum with a thunderous clap that bowled me over and shattered glass two hundred miles away. Reverting back to gravity, the sliced waters gushed into the bowl of the perfectly smooth crater that was once Fort Belvoir.

TWENTY

I picked up my car at JFK and headed back to the office. I was still a little shocked by what I'd seen.

We had always thought a nuclear device was the ultimate weapon we could feasibly construct: something so powerful it could reduce an entire city to rubble. But there'd be rubble. There'd be survivors. There'd be radioactive fallout. This new weapon left nothing. Not a speck of dust or residual trace of its usage. All it left was a massive, smooth crater. Stringer told me the terrorists would show they had the power to topple the government. From what I'd seen, they could topple the world.

Things had changed in New York since I'd been gone. I'd been away for just a few hours, but the literal bombshell of Fort Belvoir had huge repercussions. Stringer was right. All the public needed was impetus and one show of strength. The streets were thronged with chanting protesters carrying banners. As I came closer to my office the crowds increased. I was only able to negotiate the rabble at a crawl, weaving between incensed citizens baying for the blood of any government worker. I removed my tie and tried to look more casual as a precautionary measure. I parked a little way down from the office block.

I felt my way through the throng. The sense of bitterness, of anger and disappointment and resentment towards the Government was a palpable feeling. Even if the banners were gone, the chants muted, the talk subdued, I could have known exactly what the crowds were feeling because it was a physical presence in the air. A few loyal citizens still attempted to make their way through the protesting masses, too terrified of losing their paycheck to vent their frustration at the world. The protests were unorganized. There was no megaphone-wielding leader, there was no march, no destination. Thousands and thousands of people had crowded the streets each on individual whims, not knowing what to do or where to go but insistent that their outrage be heard.

The mutual bonding in the streets was intoxicating. It was overwhelming. It would be a struggle for people to fight against this tide, to stay in their homes, their shops, their workplaces. And when they broke and joined the swell, the wave of justice would grow larger until it engulfed the city. I had to get out of the crowds. Knowing what I knew, knowing that the disease of corruption had spread further than even the internet bloggers realized, I would be a prime target if caught out.

As advised earlier in the day, I sneaked in through the high-security rear entrance with several other employees. It was a precaution. No one actually knew this building housed Government workers. It looked innocuous, set up as a generic equity firm. But all it would take was for someone to question the high security in the lobby. If the crowds were to find out, we'd be ripped apart.

The elevator was repaired. I breathed a sigh of relief as it took me up the floors. The streets were chaotic and dangerous. It felt good to be encased in this fortified building, away from the potent threat of public violence.

I could still hear the chanting as I walked into the outer office. The height of our building and the reinforced glass could only do so much to lessen the sheer noise of the protesting masses.

"Bit hairy out there, Sir," Brent told me. "Al's still out in the thick of it as well."

"Don't worry," I told him. "He's well trained. Al can handle himself. But you two be careful, okay?"

I glanced from Brent to Sam and noticed he was studying a map of central Manhattan.

"Will do," he said lazily. He didn't turn to acknowledge me.

"Still scanning the city for people without RFIDs?" I asked.

"Erm...ahem...well, the system runs that by itself. We don't have anything else assigned to do right now, so...Brent and I are using Google Maps to play real-time Monopoly. I wrote some software. It uses current housing prices then adapts it to allow for fluctuations in the market as we buy up more property. Not *really* buying property, you understand."

"Yes, I got that," I said. "I'm presuming that doing this doesn't slow down the scan."

"No, the system's processing speed isn't affected at all, Sir."

"And you really don't have anything else to do?"

"No, Sir. Unless you have a new project for us?"

"I'll think of something," I told him. "I guess I can overlook the blatant misuse of office equipment for now. Just as long as you're ready to react if need be."

Sam mock saluted me. Brent looked faintly embarrassed about being caught out.

"Sam," I said. "Get me access to some records while you're messing about."

"What kind?"

"Protest casualty lists from Central Park. All GovPol reports from that day onwards. And guest lists for all cheap and mid-range hotels in the area."

Sam swiveled his chair to face me. "You think maybe the Clayton woman was injured or arrested in the protests then?"

"Highly unlikely, but she's a journalist. She must have been there in some capacity. And if she was, chances are she's staying in a hotel nearby."

"Need us to help search through it all?" Brent asked.

"It won't take long to go through. One man job really. You two deserve a break, so I can handle this. I'll be in my office if anything even remotely interesting occurs. But I won't hold my breath."

I entered my office and flopped into my seat. I booted up the computer. Something had caught my eye. Something unusual. It took a moment to register the difference in the office. I stormed back into the outer office.

"What the hell is that statue doing there?" I demanded.

"Statue?" Sam asked. "Oh, yeah, the Venus De Milo thing. It's nice. Very classical."

"I did not ask for Art Appreciation 101. I asked what it is doing there."

"Didn't you...?" Brent began. "They said you'd ordered it. I mean, I thought it was a little extravagant, and it barely fits in the corner of the room. But they had the documentation and everything."

"Call them back," I snapped. "Get rid of it."

"Errr...right, okay."

I headed back into my office. A genuine admin cock-up, I presumed. I'd witnessed that statue being hauled step by step up the stairwell these past few weeks. All that effort for it to be delivered to the wrong office. Why would anyone think I'd ordered *that*?

The PC had booted up. I flicked onto the news channel to see how the state-controlled media was handling the protests. Either they were growing in confidence or they had suddenly been let off the leash. The reports were making occasional fair judgments. They were citing the protests as rallies by the general public. I'd usually expect them to describe it as something more along the lines of seditious riots.

Washington D.C. was particularly badly hit by these protests. Traffic was gridlocked as citizens covered the streets. Some of the more important Government departments were struggling to cope. Many sit down protests clogged entranceways into buildings. There had been reports of minor clashes between GovPol and the public in Austin, Los Angeles and Philadelphia. Certainly nothing on the scale of what occurred a few days ago. It was almost as though the Government realized it could no longer subjugate the public or media as before. They were slowly but surely giving up their hold on the people.

Despite all the protests and the increased terrorist threat, the President had announced he would not cancel his appointments. Did the President really think people would warm to him because he was hosting a party in the penthouse of a skyscraper? He was urging the country to get behind him in celebrating the grand re-opening of the Willis Tower in Chicago that night. It had been closed since it received all that structural damage the previous year. Most of which I was responsible for during another highly classified operation.

Something that was likely to incense the public even more once they got wind of it was the Cuban war. It had ended in a dirty and underhand way. The exchange of POWs went ahead that morning. Video footage showed a stream of shiny new, specially-commissioned Ford Colt army trucks ferrying Cuban POWs into Havana through heavily-guarded gates. A smaller line of battered Jeep Cherokees were bringing US POWs out.

Then the image changed to shaky camera footage a few hours later. Explosions ripped Cuba's capital apart. Great fiery rents were torn in the defensive walls. The laser-assisted gun batteries that had kept this city safe from aerial bombardment were shattered. It was not clear at first what had happened. The newsreader was quick to explain.

The US didn't exactly release Cuban POWs back to their own side. The so-called POWs were actually disguised US Army soldiers. They were surgically altered to look Cuban. Each soldier carried an explosive charge within their bellies. Still bearing the seeping wounds of operation scars, the soldiers infiltrated key positions within Havana. They acted as suicide bombers, destroying the facilities along with themselves. It left Havana defenseless. Scattered reports suggested the Cubans immediately surrendered. This failed to prevent aerial bombardment followed by a ground invasion. It had been suggested that these reports all came from international news agencies. They were merely propaganda. Seeking to undermine the success of victory by painting the US Army as a brutal regime who refused to recognize the white flag.

I was in two minds about this. On the one hand, we finally had victory in Cuba. But on the other hand I could readily believe that my own government would use such underhand tactics. I did not know if the reports were true. But I did know that as soon as some of the protesting masses caught wind of today's news, the Government's position in this country would become even more difficult to maintain.

I was consumed by mixed feelings. I may have been a Government employee, and that in itself was starting to taste sour. But I still loved my country and wanted to do everything possible to protect it. I began to seriously consider if now might be a good time to quit. The job had already ruined my love life. The stress of trying to locate Stringer was taking its toll. Now, it was starting to become clear that the old adage of 'first up against the wall when the revolution comes' could be said very much with me in mind. I'd have preferred to be in the firing squad, not their target. I felt extremely wary of my own employers and the Government as a whole. I decided to find out exactly how brutal they could be. I needed to find out how far this corruption had seeped into the different branches of the organization.

A few minutes later, Sam ported through the records I requested. Protest casualties, GovPol reports and hotel guest lists. Before I started poring through them, I had to report in and give my daily update to General Miller. Besides, I needed to broach my concerns to him.

I dialed him up. It rang several times before it was answered. I was in no doubt that he was a busy man.

"Stone!" he barked unnecessarily. "It's getting bad out there. How are you holding up?"

"Still no breaks on the Stringer case, Sir. But we haven't had any trouble from the public yet."

"I have every confidence you'll find Stringer soon. I know we had to reallocate some of your team, but you can see what's happening to this country."

I sat back in my chair. "About that, Sir. About what's happening. Did we know about this?"

"What? The protests? Or what they're saying?"

"What they are saying, Sir," I answered. "The mass, rotten corruption in the government."

"Stone, this is none of your concern."

"I believe it is, Sir."

He sighed. "You have your own assignment. Don't go butting into the work of others."

"I'm not talking about assignments or investigations. I'm talking about the allegations that the country we work hard to protect has been shafting its citizens all along."

"Why do you need to know all this right now?"

I leaned forward. "*I* am a citizen, Sir."

Miller sighed. "You're a good man, Stone. You're dedicated. Loyal. You care about this country and its people. You want what is right. So do we."

"Who's we, Sir? NASRU? The Government? POTUS?"

"NASRU, Jack," he confirmed. "We're a splinter group. We're beyond the remit of the White House. We're separate from the armed forces. We're totally independent. We may be financed by different branches of the Government, but we don't answer to them. As for POTUS, he doesn't know we exist."

"And judging by the word of the masses," I said, "we didn't know how corrupt he was. How can the President get away with all that right under our noses?"

"Quite simple, really. We never thought to look. We've been looking at threats both foreign and domestic, but we don't know something is wrong if we haven't been looking in that direction. We never considered checking *inside* the White House."

I nodded angrily at the video image. I was fully aware I was committing career suicide, but I couldn't let this rest. "Convince me," I demanded.

"Jack?" Miller asked for clarification, surprised.

"Project Omicron, Sir. You kept me in the dark until I discovered the truth myself. You hid from me the fact that we conducted highly illegal and morally reprehensible experiments on volunteers who were told lies about what they were getting into. That smells of corruption to me. How many more secrets are we hiding?"

The General rested back in his chair. He steepled his fingers and considered his response.

"I understand, Stone. Your faith has been shaken, and now you don't know who to trust. As your superior I have kept things from you. Things that I thought you didn't need to know, that you weren't ready to know. But I have mentored you all these years, Jack. I've given you plenty of leeway. You've continued operating in the field when you should now be desk-bound. I have you report to me, not your regional director. Whether you realize it or not, I've taken care of you. You have great potential. You're like a favorite student. If you believe one thing, believe this. I will *not* lie to you. Ever."

"Then tell me we did not know about this," I demanded. "Tell me we're going to do something about it."

The General nodded. "Okay. We did not know about this level of corruption. We did not know POTUS was involved. As for whether we're going to do something about this or not… We do not take sides. We do not fight for causes. We neutralize potential threats to American lives wherever they may be and whomever they may be perpetrated by. We do it indiscriminately. Do you understand what I'm saying?"

"Yes," I responded. "We're not with the people. And we're not with the Government. We're just sitting back and abstaining from what is gearing up to be another civil war."

"If you want to see it that way. But we are still operating within our remit here. We're looking for and neutralizing any terrorist threats from the citizens. But now we're doing the same within the Government as well. If they're considering unleashing their own Fort Belvoir on a town of protestors, we'll be there to stop them.

"I understand your sense of frustration, Stone. I feel it too. Like we've been used. But we have to get on with the job, because there's no one else who can. We have to do the best we can, and learn from our mistakes."

"What about Hera, Sir?" I asked. "She was part of the mistake. And now we're keeping her prisoner. Have we truly learned anything?"

"She lost her memory, Stone. You can't just leave someone like that to fend for themselves. Not until you feel they're ready. Sometimes we have to do things that are wrong. If it is the only way to stay on top of the game, the only way to ensure we are better than the enemy. Yes, we did that. And yes we've learned from it. Laura is no prisoner if she's there for her own good. You can't say a coma victim is imprisoned in a hospital when you know if they're taken home they'll die without life support."

"So what you're saying is we're doing the right thing, even if it seems wrong."

The General leaned forward. "I guess you can say that. We're not the bad guys, Stone. Sometimes we're not the good guys. We're the grey area. The moral ambiguity."

I nodded grudgingly. "It was a shock to me, Sir. Both the footage from the protests and what we did to Hera."

"I know, Jack," Miller responded. "I know. She was quite taken with you, by the way. Laura. Thought you were very strong-willed, very professional. Thought you kept yourself grounded more than anyone else she's met at NASRU. I think you'd make a good team."

"Sir?" I questioned.

"She's ready for independence. I was going to wait until you'd finished the Stringer case before telling you. I've decided she should be operating under your command. Alecto too. They will be your permanent field agents in New York, Stone. I'd trust no one more than yourself to look out for her."

"I can't think about that kind of thing now, Sir." I shook my head. "That's in the future. I don't even know if there will be a future."

"The country will right itself, Stone. It always does. It may take years, but the President will be removed. Assassination, public force, a military coup. It will happen eventually."

"I know it will, Sir. But until then we're right in the firing line. The public won't give a damn about grey areas."

Miller leaned in close to the screen. "That is why I need you to take care of Stringer as soon as you can. He can expose us. Now more so than ever, he is a threat to us and a threat to the stability of this country."

"Yes, Sir." I nodded. "I know."

"Good man, Stone. Chin up. Things will pan out in the end. By the way, make sure you check the news later. They're putting out a statement about what happened in Fort Belvoir. I think you'll find it interesting. Classic example of Government spin and half-truths."

"Yes, Sir," I answered.

"Thank you, Jack," he told me. "For standing up to me and having the courage to voice your concerns. You've justified my faith in you all these years. You're not a 'yes' man, you're a 'why?' man." He smiled. "I can see you running this place one day."

He cut off the line. I stared at the blank screen for a few moments. I had been reassured by the knowledge that NASRU wasn't mired in all this. We didn't know about any of it, and now we did we'd do something about it. Technically we weren't the bad guys. But I was also acutely aware that this wouldn't make the slightest difference to an incensed public if they found out we were here. Besides, nothing could cure the ache I felt as I watched my country rip itself apart.

Andi felt like a different person. Daniel had coached her in the art of reading people. She was a novice, that much was clear. But she saw the world in a different way now.

The day before, he taught her to concentrate. He taught her to focus, and to think. It sounded simple enough. But she didn't realize how much her mind drifted until she started controlling it.

Observation was the key. Study someone, and you could build up a picture of who they were.

"Do they speak too quickly?" he told her. "They could be nervous. Too slow, and they may be mentally challenged. In turn that means they could be easily manipulated. Does their use of language denote intelligence? Are they erudite? Arrogant?

"What are their mannerisms? Random gestures or controlled confidence? What hair style do they have? What clothing? How do they walk? Do you hold their attention or do their eyes wander?

"Can you tell anything about objects they have with them? The brand of beer a man is drinking? The number of sugars in a coffee? Carrying an umbrella when the sky is clear?"

It was a lengthy list. But Andi could see why. Observation. Build up a picture. Notice the band of paler skin around someone's ring finger, and you know they're divorced. Observe how pale the skin is, and you may be able to pinpoint how long ago the divorce was. Every element builds up. By doing this, you could get to know a person without ever speaking to them.

That was the first task, Daniel told her. The one she had to perfect. Mastery allowed you to read someone at a glance. When you could do that, you could progress to complex combinations. Maybe read two people talking to each other. Build up both their profiles. Understand their common ground. Then you can work out how close they are, how they react to each other, what they may be talking about. Start factoring in inanimate objects in the proximity.

At that point, Andi promptly announced a headache and went to bed.

The next day, Andi discovered that she could make a better judgment call. She watched out of the hotel room window. She noticed the gait of businessmen. She observed the interplay between friends. She calculated the shopping a woman had purchased based on the size, shape and brand of the bag.

But she found it hard to fully concentrate on any of them.

Daniel was leaving her.

The feeling of elation she had experienced over the last day was starting to dissipate. Her conscious mind had finally wrestled back control of her burgeoning desire. It was far more adept at quashing such silly notions than her subconscious. She had found it immensely frustrating to be falling for Daniel despite the fact that she kept telling herself not to. He was like a drug. She knew how much harm he would do, and she dearly wanted to kick the habit. Just one last hit to take the edge off and maybe this time she could do it. But now she was craving another hit, and it was taking control of her rational self.

The impact of Daniel leaving for good was now hitting home. She was facing the prospect of going cold turkey. She had just said goodbye. He had left the hotel. The full force of the situation had battered her senseless. This was it. He had gone. She'd never see him again.

After everything the two of them had been through those last few weeks, it seemed like a terrible anti-climax. She had grown so fond of Daniel. She'd convinced herself that she'd actually begun to fall in love with him. And now he'd left. Just as the world was crumbling all around her he did the same to her inner sanctum.

Andi had tried to rationalize his reason for leaving. It didn't make sense. He'd avoided detection for three years. He was always one step ahead of his pursuers. He had the foresight and intelligence to do anything. Why couldn't he stay here or take her with him? She knew her rational mind was now losing the battle. She was about to enter that paranoid delusion whereby his actions encompassed her whole world.

Maybe it was a test. It seemed far-fetched, but perhaps Daniel was trying to find out how committed she was. Maybe he just didn't feel the same way about her. Maybe he was a commitment-phobe. Maybe, maybe…

Maybe there was just one way to find out. One way to make sure. She cared about him a lot, and she was willing to fight for him. That was something he needed to know.

I caught the news and the statement the Government released about Fort Belvoir. Having witnessed it myself, I found it quite hilarious. But I could see the reasoning behind it. The official line was that we did it ourselves.

Apparently, terrorists released a chemical weapon in the center of the city. Fort Belvoir was evacuated without incident. But we discovered that the chemical was a highly contagious airborne virus. Left to its own devices, it would spread across the country. It needed containing and annihilating. We had no option but to use a prototype new weapon on the city.

I was not sure how many people would be taken in by this. But it created an element of doubt. If we'd told the truth, we would have looked weak and powerless. Instead, we had told the world that the weapons at our disposal were far more advanced than anything they possessed. It also showed the international community that we were strong and determined to do whatever it took. Even if it meant destroying one of our own cities. We came out of it as bullish and arrogant. But also as a country not to be messed with.

It was now late afternoon. Al had managed to battle his way through the mass of protesters. He arrived back at the office as the sun was starting to ebb and hide behind skyscrapers. It was pointless driving around trying to spot Stringer in this situation.

While I had been poring over the casualty lists and GovPol reports, Al had brought his laptop into my office and joined in a new game of real-time Monopoly with Sam and Brent. There had been accusations that Sam was manipulating the gaming code to cheat. There had been exclamations over how much hotels cost in affluent areas these days. There had been copious swearing when sent to jail.

I had been scanning the reports, and had found nothing of relevance thus far. I passed some reports, such as bar fights, over to Al. It was highly unlikely Andi Clayton would have been involved in such things, so he could quickly check over them. I concentrated on more relevant fare such as reports of breaking and entering. Even then a cursory glance over the first two lines of the report were enough to establish they had no connection to Stringer.

The latest one I was scanning through linked to all three subsets of reports – a hotel owner killed at the protest was name-checked in a GovPol report. I glanced away from it to Al, having realized I had some news to convey.

"Al," I said to my lone assistant as Sam took his last $2m and put him out of the game.

"I've lost," he responded despondently.

"I know. Shut up. I've got some good news for you."

"Good news?" he asked.

Sam superimposed the words 'you suck' on the image of the Monopoly board. Al closed his laptop.

"Define 'good news'," I ordered.

"Something that won't have me weeping into my bowl of Lucky Charms every morning," he suggested.

"Al. I have some news for you."

"Hmmm," he responded. He was wondering where the word 'good' had gone to.

"You're stuck with me for a while."

"How long is a while?"

"Indefinite."

Al nodded. "So some top brass has seen that we make a great team, then."

"Maybe they just can't figure out how to get rid of you," I responded. I scanned the last few details of the report in front of me. "Let's see how good a team we make. I think we may have a bite here."

I patched a comms line through to Sam.

"Is Al crying because he lost?" he asked.

"Don't get smug," I answered. "I need you to check something out for me."

"Okay, go ahead."

"You said we can get proper RFID tracking going back the last five days, yes?"

Sam nodded. "Wire frame maps, no images. But yes, five days."

"Check out the Lucky Break Hotel on West 169th Street over the last few days. I want to know all RFID signals in and out of there."

"What have you got?" Al asked me.

I shrugged. "Probably nothing. Hotel owner killed during the protests. Since then neighbors have seen a couple entering and leaving the hotel several times. They reported it as suspicious because they're wondering who'd spend time in an empty hotel with no staff."

"Squatters?" Al offered. "Bums? Addicts?"

I nodded. "That's why it's a long shot."

I minimized the report on my desktop screen. "Anyway, to reiterate: you're stuck with me. Once we've closed the Stringer case we'll get a new field agent on the team. Code name's Hera. I worked with her a few weeks ago. Everglades. Can be scatty. Sarcastic. Too happy for her own good most of the time. But very smart, very confident."

"So Tisiphone isn't coming back then? What about Megaera when he's recovered?"

I shook my head. "You, me and Hera. That's the new team."

"Surely that's even more reason for me to have a new code name."

"Not going to happen," I told him.

Sam patched back through to me.

"Anything?" I asked.

"Last person in the hotel was the owner/manager, a Gerry Butler age 52. He left the building Sunday just before eleven am. Went to Central Park for the protests. Didn't return."

I turned my attention to Al. "So how come neighbors have seen people in the building since when there's been no RFID traces? Could be foreign nationals using cards, no RFID implants. Still, sounds like it's worth checking out."

"Then let's go," Al told me.

"My car's parked down the block," I said back. "Yours?"

"Basement," he answered.

I stood, took my sidearm from a drawer and holstered it.

"I guess you're on chauffeur duty again. Let's go."

TWENTY ONE

Having weaved through the evening traffic in record speed, Al slowed as we approached the dark hotel. There were few things that gave away your presence more than screeching to a stop outside the place you were about to raid.

He pulled up gently and we exited the car.

When we entered the hotel, I silently directed Al to the reception so he could check the computer's registry. I closed the front doors and secured the handles together with a plastic tie. If someone tried to slip past us and flee, this would delay them long enough for us to catch up.

"Third floor," Al whispered. "Room 32. Registered to a Mr. and Mrs. Keene. No other rooms taken."

"Can you shut down the elevators from there?" I asked. Al nodded and tapped a code into the computer system.

We took the stairs. We moved silently but swiftly. Our guns were drawn.

Keeping our weapons raised, we moved quietly to room 32. We were both listening intently. Any sound of movement from anywhere within the building and we'd be ready to react instantly.

Al crouched and peered at the door frame next to the handle. He could see through the gap that the tumbler lock was open. He carefully took the door handle in his hand.

I nodded.

Al threw the door open. I rushed in first with my weapon primed. Al followed quickly behind me. One room and an en suite. There was no space to hide under the bed. They were not there.

I checked the en suite. Al searched for clues in the main room.

"Bed's sloppily made," he told me. "Empty wrappers in the bin. Subway, McDonald's, Starbucks. They've been living on junk food."

"Towel's damp," I said back. "Water residue in the shower cubicle. It's been recently used."

Al holstered his weapon. "Is it them, though? Stringer and Clayton?"

I checked every detail of the en suite. A small, half-used bottle of shampoo would provide fingerprints, the towel would give us a DNA sample. But these things would take hours to get results and we needed to know now. The only other evidence of habitation was a smudged mirror.

Whoever it was, they'd cleared out. "Have you checked the TV?" I asked Al.

He activated it. "One message," he told me. "From yesterday. Already viewed." He played the message.

Stringer appeared on the screen. It was a brief message, telling Andi he had gone to locate breakfast and would be back shortly. It ended and the screen faded to black.

"I think it might be them," Al told me.

"He's been sloppy," I said. "Left clues behind."

Something clicked in the back of my mind. I headed back into the en suite and inspected the mirror closer. "Something's been written on here," I said.

319

I turned on the hot tap and switched the shower on. "Start a quick sweep of the rest of the hotel," I told Al. "Ground floor, work your way up. Just in case they switched rooms."

He nodded and headed back for the stairwell. I remained in the en suite as hot water started steaming the room up. Gradually an image became clear on the mirror. Written by hand when the shower had previously steamed the room up, the mirror displayed the numbers '8:13'.

I turned off the water and headed back into the bedroom. I quickly checked all the drawers in the room. No Bible. I didn't expect one, but I could at least dismiss the number as a reference to a Bible passage. It was a time reference.

8:13 was too accurate a time for another meeting between Andi and Stringer. It had to relate to a specific event occurring. Again, 8:13 was too obtuse to be a reference to a dinner reservation, a play, a movie. It related to travel. I couldn't see them meeting another person. Not in the situation they were in. It wasn't an arrival time. Something was leaving New York at 8:13, and they would be on board. But did it refer to morning or evening? And which day?

I had to make a supposition. Look into the possibility that it referred to 8:13pm this very night. If I turned out to be wrong, we would still have time to research other possibilities.

I patched through to Surveillance. "Sam," I said. "Give me a list of public transportation that departs at 8:13 this evening."

"Okay," he told me. "There are subways running from 7th Avenue, Franklin Street, Union Square, Bleeker Street–"

"No," I said, cutting him off. "Leaving New York itself." Subway trains were too frequent to demand a specific time to be noted down. It was definitely departing the city.

"Well, there's a Greyhound to Camden, Maine. One to Marietta, Ohio. And one going all the way to Thornfield, Missouri. There's a flight from JFK to Seattle and one to Moscow. A train leaves Grand Central Station for Atlanta at 8:12. And the New Jersey ferry departs at 8:14."

I could dismiss both the train and the ferry – the times may have been only one minute out, but they were still out.

Greyhound coaches didn't seem to fit Stringer. They provided long, slow journeys. If he was on the move, he'd want to move quickly. Besides, what would he be doing heading to Camden, Marietta or Thornfield? He needed bigger cities to hide in.

That left the flights. Which one was still open to debate, but at 8:13pm either Stringer or Miss Clayton would be at JFK airport. We had our break.

I checked my watch. 7:17pm. We were running out of time.

I switched comms frequencies. "Al," I called. "Meet me in the lobby."

I rushed down the stairwell and into the lobby area. I slid past the reception desk into a small dining area, and through that into a kitchen. I grabbed a chef's knife. Al joined me in the lobby. I ran up to the front door and hastily sliced the plastic tie off the handles.

Sam queried his role as we rushed to Al's car.

"What do I do?" he asked. "Any of those any good?"

"Yes," I answered. "Wait."

I clambered into the passenger seat.

321

"Airport," I told Al once we were both inside the vehicle. "JFK."

He spun the car around and barreled off down the road.

"Sam, check the flight manifests for the Seattle and Moscow planes. See if there's anything strange. Odd names. Last minute bookings. Paying without using an RFID. Things like that."

"Nothing," Sam said absently. "Nothing." He was talking to himself with the comms line open.

"Sam!" I called. "Come on! I need that info now!"

"Wait..." He paused dramatically. "Nope. Nothing."

"Why Moscow?" I asked Al.

"Sorry?" he responded. I quickly filled him in on the details.

"Well...he wants to flee," Al answered when he had all the facts.

"But why Moscow? It doesn't feel right. Russia doesn't care about the U.S. any more, so it wouldn't be to sell information to them. We have extradition treaties with them so he still won't feel safe. Seattle on the other hand is still internal so he remains a threat. He wants to be a threat. He has that arrogance. But it is a big enough city for him to disappear in. It makes far more sense."

"So we're going for Seattle, then?" Sam asked over the link. "I'm still not finding anything untoward."

"Question," Al said. "If Stringer is going to Seattle, where's Clayton?"

"We have to assume she's going with him."

"Could it be just Clayton catching the flight? Stringer's remaining in New York?"

"No," I answered. "Stringer knows we're getting too close. He'll be looking to bail. Besides, why would Andi be taking off to Seattle by herself?"

"Holiday?" Sam suggested.

"To Seattle?!" Al exclaimed.

"I think we can rule that one out," I confirmed. "Andi wouldn't be fleeing by herself. She's intelligent. She'll know that if she's no longer in contact with Stringer she becomes far less of a threat to us and fleeing to another city would be overkill. She'd only leave if she was with him. Besides, Stringer may be able to bypass security with a false ID, but Andi can't. If she were traveling alone, she'd have been flagged up buying a ticket by now."

"Could this be a trap, then?" Al suggested. "To lure us away from him?"

"Why would he set a trap?" I said. "What possible use could he have for that? He knows we have absolutely no other leads. We have no way to track him down. So why go to the expense of setting something up when leaving things well alone will obviously benefit him more? The same goes for trying to throw us off the scent. If they're catching a flight somewhere else, at a different time or to a different place, why do this when there'd be no way of us knowing he was catching a flight in the first place?"

"But equally so," Al said, "Stringer isn't the kind of person to slip up at all." He flung the car harshly round a corner. I grabbed onto the dashboard to steady myself.

"Exactly," I answered. "Which means that Stringer is going to be on that flight, and Andi is going with him. *She* left the hotel room after *him* and she forgot to cover her tracks. They're going to meet up there. Or at the very least, Andi

323

thinks they'll be meeting up so she will be present. That will allow us to re-establish a trace on her movements. She may still lead us to Stringer at some point."

"There's a lot of variables in there, Stone," Al pointed out.

"I can't predict the future, Al. But we've got a break and we have to take it. I've got a good feeling about this. I think *he's* going to be on that plane as well."

Al nodded slowly. He was coming round to my way of thinking. "Agreed," he eventually concurred.

"Sam," I called. "Book me a ticket on that flight under a pseudonym. And tell them I will be armed and boarding the plane early to run a security check."

"And me?" Al asked.

I shook my head. "If Andi's there, she doesn't know what you look like. Therefore you're in a far better position to keep an eye on her. I'll keep track of people on the flight. You keep track at the airport."

"Think I've got some casual attire in the trunk. Should help me blend in."

"Good," I said. Things were finally starting to fall into place. "I'll have to call the General," I pointed out. "Discuss tactics. We can't afford to fail this time. I've got a back-up plan."

Andi arrived early and sat down in the airport to surprise Daniel. She hoped he took her unscheduled appearance well. He warned her off several times. But she still couldn't work out any viable reason why he wouldn't want her to come along with him. Even so, she had held off purchasing a ticket until she had reasoned with him.

Passengers trickled into the departure terminal, faceless and pre-occupied.

When Andi started feeling she may become lost amid the crowd, Daniel arrived. He spied Andi immediately and walked straight over.

Andi smiled nervously at Daniel as he approached. She removed her folded coat from the chair next to her. He took the seat. He looked more weary than annoyed or elated.

"You're really damaging my calm, you know that?" he said. He looked at her. "What did I say about not coming along?"

"Well, I…" she began.

"What did I say?" he asked again.

"Erm…not to come along. But I thought that was just…I don't know."

"Me being afraid of commitment? A test for you to pass?" Daniel sighed. "Look, I know what you were thinking. I know why you're here. This *really* can't happen."

"Why?" she hissed. "Give me one good reason, damn it! Don't just leave me hanging here!"

"I can't give you the reason you are seeking. But I can help you along the path-"

"Stop talking riddles, Daniel. Just…at least give me the decency of knowing why. If you ever cared for me…"

"I'll tell you what you're going to do. You're going to go back to the hotel, spend the night there. Tomorrow, move somewhere new…"

"Like Seattle?"

"No," Daniel answered, annoyed. "Not like Seattle. Besides, I'll be gone by then."

"Then no deal. You don't want me to go along with you? Fine. I'll just get a ticket and sit somewhere else on the plane. But I'm still going to get on it."

He sighed. "You just don't understand."

"Only because you won't allow me to," she answered.

"And maybe there's a good reason for that. Maybe you *can't* understand. Maybe you're too damn stupid to realize..."

Andi looked at Daniel with hurt in her eyes. "To realize what, Daniel? I'm smart enough to know you're just saying that to make me leave. But I won't leave. Because...I think I love you."

Daniel studied Andi's face for a moment. He watched a single tear slide down her cheek. "Then you really *are* stupid," he said finally. He looked away from her. "Because I don't love you."

"That's not true. I don't believe you."

He turned to her. He drew her face close to his. For one moment she thought his defenses had crumbled and he was about to passionately kiss her. She couldn't have been more wrong.

"When are you going to realize? I gave you the best story of your career, and in return you gave me your body. I'd say that was a fair deal. But the deal's finished. You don't need me, I don't need you."

Andi shook her head. She refused to acknowledge it. Fresh tears welled up in her eyes. "No," she whispered. "Not true..."

"No? You still think I'm saying all this to protect you?"

Andi nodded jerkily, hopefully. Daniel sat back and thought for a moment.

"Yeah," he agreed finally. "I guess that's the one thing that *is* true here. I *do* want to protect you. After all, who else is going to tell my story?"

"Then protect me," Andi responded desperately. "Let me go with you. You can—"

"No. Stop degrading yourself."

"But I want to be with you."

"No."

Andi paused for a moment to fight back fresh tears. "Why?" she whispered.

"Because I don't want you." He turned to her, an air of finality about him. "Now, you know they can track your purchases, so don't be a silly bitch. Promise me you won't buy a ticket."

Andi stared at him, disbelieving. "No," she whispered. "I…"

Daniel leaned in close. His face turned angry and threatening.

"Don't. You. Dare. Buy. A. Fucking. Ticket! You got it?"

Not knowing what else to do, Andi slowly nodded. "I…I won't," she whispered.

"Good," he said calmly. He exhaled deeply. "We're starting to board. You can either stay here to wave me off, or you can leave. I suggest leaving."

"Why are you doing this?" Andi asked in a voice breaking with emotion.

"Because it needs to be done. Because it is such a chore tolerating those who are beneath me. And simply because I can."

Andi grabbed her coat in a flush of anger. "You're an evil bastard," she said as she readied to leave. Daniel simply

327

nodded in agreement and didn't look at her once. Andi rushed, confused and emotional, out of the terminal. In her panic she dropped her bag and the contents spilled over the floor. Embarrassed and disgusted with herself, she shoved most of the contents back into the bag and rushed off.

Her heart was burning. Her head was pounding. She'd thrown herself at his feet, only to discover she was just being used.

Half an hour beforehand I had boarded the flight as part of a security exercise. I had completed a full sweep of the plane: There were two economy cabins, the first class lounge at the fore and the bulging transparency of the nose-cone viewing gallery. I had also checked the baggage hold and the stewards' cabin in the tail. Lastly I checked the cockpit, the spacious bulge where the fuselage met the tailfin.

Having completed my checks, I had settled in a seat at the rear of the plane where I was least likely to be spotted. I was supposed to leave the plane immediately following my inspection. Those were the General's orders. But that would allow Stringer to slip through, to board the plane unnoticed. I had decided to wait it out on the plane itself. Tactically it was the smarter choice.

I had kept an open channel with Al. He was seated in the departure terminal wearing a plain Tee-shirt under his suit jacket and a pair of denims. He was pretending to flick through an eMag.

He had quietly informed me of Andi Clayton's presence. He had informed me of Daniel Stringer's arrival too. Al hadn't been in a position to clarify what had been said between the two of them, but quick sideways glances confirmed that they were both getting upset.

I considered trying to grab him now, but there were too many civilians and too many variables. Stringer's best chance of escape would be in amongst an airport-wide panic. I wouldn't allow him to do that.

My best chance, I realized, was to wait for him to board the plane. Wait for the flight to take off. Wait until we were at the point of no return. Civilians would still be a factor. But I couldn't see Stringer being so ruthless as to endanger all of them. One or two maybe, but they would have to be considered as collateral damage. When he'd got nowhere to run, Stringer wouldn't be able to escape me.

"Uh, boss?" Al said in my ear mic. There was a brief wash of static. I waited until it had passed.

"What is it?" I responded.

"We have a slight problem here," he told me. "Clayton's just left."

The words rolled around my ear before sinking into my brain as an echo. "Restroom?" I asked.

"She's just run out of here. Deeply upset by the look of things. Think they had an argument. Primary's just sitting there. Looks a bit angry but otherwise calm. What's the plan?"

"Lock on to the primary until I see him on this plane, Al. He's the prize, she's a consolation."

"Don't we…need her?" he asked.

"I'll take care of it," I answered.

I took out my cell phone. I quickly glanced at the slow trickle of passengers starting to arrive and discussing the best way to locate their seats. "Make sure you let me know when he's boarding," I added to Al before concentrating on the phone.

"Sam," I said. I didn't give the other end of the line a chance to speak. "Tell airport security to detain Miss Clayton. She's heading out the exit so shouldn't be too hard to spot."

"She doing a runner?" Sam asked.

"That's what we need to find out. Just tell them to hold her and Al will be along soon to pick her up. Is what we discussed ready yet?"

"The rocket?" Sam asked.

I sighed. "Code words! Please!"

"Ahem, the HF1 has been thoroughly checked for any systems damage. Computer modeling is confident that its high-energy detonation system will leave no tangible debris to present a threat on the ground. A launch vector is being prepped as we speak."

"You could just say 'no'," I pointed out.

"It'll be ready. Soon. Within, say, half an hour. Look, Sir, are you sure about this?"

"If all else fails…" I said.

"General Miller wants to launch as soon as it's ready. Whether we've had the go-ahead from you or not."

"I thought he would. But the General doesn't have his finger on the trigger, Sam. You do. This has to be the last resort. Believe me. I can see families boarding the plane. Children."

"But the General…" Sam said. "I have no authority over him, boss. He wants you off the plane. It's an order. I…I'm sorry, but he told me if you called I was to patch you through to him straight away."

"Okay, Sam," I told him reassuringly. "Put him through."

The phone connected through to General Miller straight away.

"Stone!" he barked. "What is going on? I want you off that plane immediately."

"Sir, I know how you'd prefer this to end. It isn't in a ball of fire."

The General sighed. "Don't presume to tell me what I want, Jack. When that flight is in the air, when Stringer has nowhere to escape to, we are going to fire such a payload up its ass there won't be anything left but cinders blowing in the breeze."

"And the innocent citizens, Sir?" I demanded.

"Collateral damage."

"That is not acceptable, Sir."

There was a pause from the other end. The General's face slowly turned the color of a ripe tomato. "Are you questioning a direct order Lieutenant?" he eventually asked. "Again? I haven't forgotten the use of SWAT in the alley, Stone. Tread carefully."

This could have been the end of my career. But I knew it was the right thing to do. "Give me a chance to save these people," I told him. "Once we're in flight, Stringer is going nowhere for a good few hours. I can take him down quickly and quietly. Give me that time. And if you don't hear from me by the time the flight's due to land, then do what you have to."

The General contemplated this for a moment. "Stone," he said quietly and firmly. "One last time. Get off the plane."

I sucked in a deep breath. "I'm sorry, Sir." I answered. "I can't do that."

I pocketed the cell phone. I needed to do this. I couldn't just allow all these innocent people to be sacrificed when there was a clear way to avoid it. I had defied the General's orders. But my defiance would be justified.

I continued observing the passengers. A hefty man sporting a baseball cap and faded jeans headed my way. He took the seat next to me and we briefly exchanged nods.

"Boss," Al crackled through my ear mic. "He's heading to the gate."

"Okay," I responded. I realized this had garnered a confused look from my neighbor.

"Okay," the man responded, a little perturbed. He tried to focus his attention elsewhere to show he didn't want to engage in pleasantries.

"He's through boss," Al informed me. "He's heading your way."

"Okay," I answered back. My neighbor glanced in my direction again. He was a little annoyed this time.

"Yeah, okay bud," he said in a tone of voice that indicated he'd pop my head open between his bear-like hands if he heard another sound from me.

"I'm not talking to *you*!" I told him harshly. I didn't have time to defuse an irate passenger so I'd put him in his place now.

I turned my focus to the boarding passengers. I saw Stringer enter the aircraft. I moved down in my seat a little more to ensure he didn't spot me. I never shifted my eyes off my quarry.

"Boss?" Al came through the earpiece. "You see him yet? Is he there?"

"Got him," I responded. "I'll know if he moves. Go pick up Clayton."

I turned down the volume on my earpiece and concentrated more fully on Stringer. He'd found his seat now. I could still see the top of his head from my vantage point.

I waited patiently for the other passengers to file in and find seats. I always watched the back of Stringer's head. I was confident he was here for the duration. I'd wait until halfway through the flight before accosting him. He'd have nowhere to go and would be settled by then. He'd presume he was out of danger. He'd be easier to take down.

TWENTY TWO

We were cruising high above the clouds. We were halfway through the three-hour flight. Night was all around us. The deep blue of a faraway dawn tickled the far horizon behind us. A darker, star-specked black was in front. Passengers were, for the most part, quiet. They were engaged in an in-flight movie or reading literature. The occasional raucous child punctured the calm.

I had studied the situation at length. I had weighed the pros and cons. I had come to the conclusion that now Stringer was stuck on this flight with me, I should be able to arrest him with ease. Standing up and shooting him would not be a wise move. Firstly, there was little he could do to disarm or flee from me this time. Secondly, there were too many innocent civilians on the flight and I couldn't guarantee their safety if I opened fire. The third problem was the rising tension across the general public. They were already incensed with their own Government. If I opened with a shoot first, ask questions later policy it was likely I'd be lynched. I would shoot if necessary, but this time an arrest seemed the most palatable option.

I checked Stringer's whereabouts again. Center aisle. Right-hand seat. Twelve rows in front. I saw him stretch. He stood and moved towards the front of the plane. He headed into the forward passenger cabin. I couldn't let him out of my sight. Not for one moment. If he was heading to the restroom I needed to stop him now. No matter how desperate the man was to relieve his bladder.

I stood as well. I kept my right hand poised near my holster. I negotiated my neighbor. I began following Stringer. I waited until he was halfway down the forward passenger cabin before I made my move.

"Daniel Stringer!" I shouted. I drew my gun from its holster. I aimed it at his back. There were gasps of surprise. He halted. "Turn around!" I told him.

He did so, slowly. He was showing a lack of emotion on his face. He didn't raise his hands in the customary fashion. I could tell by the flow of his coat that he was unarmed.

"Don't worry, folks," I said to the crowd. They were muttering in consternation. "Official business. It's all in hand."

The muttering grew in intensity. The passengers found this an ideal time to voice their concerns about the current political situation.

"Stone," Stringer said calmly. "What are you doing?"

"I'm arresting you, Stringer. There's nowhere to run this time. I've finally got you."

"Things have a way of panning out in unexpectedly ways, Stone. You haven't won yet."

"Sir..." someone said. He was seated next to my position. I quickly glanced down. He was a heavily-built man. He looked at me with consternation. A twelve-year-old girl next to him seemed ready to cry. I returned my attention to Stringer.

335

"Everybody stay seated!" I called. "This man is a dangerous criminal. If necessary, I will shoot. So everybody stay out of the way."

I slowly moved down the aisle, keeping Stringer firmly in my sights. "There is nowhere to go. There's no way to escape. There are two ways off this plane. One is in my custody. The other is as a corpse. You choose."

"You're going to kill everyone, Stone," Stringer said. "I can see it. You're just like all the other Government agents. You don't care about the public. You're just in it for yourself."

He was trying to rally the public to his side. He wanted to make me out to be the bad guy. I had to defuse this now. I cocked back the firing pin.

"Were you involved in the protests, Stone?" Stringer said. He was hamming it up quite badly, but the plane passengers couldn't see through his lies. "Did *you* give the order to open fire?"

As one, the civilians in the cabin gasped with this revelation. They'd believe anything if it sounded convincing enough. In this plane, I may win the battle, but I knew I was going to lose the war. It was a sacrifice I was willing to make.

I aimed squarely at Stringer's forehead and pressed the trigger. I was a fraction of a second too late.

Convinced by Stringer's rant, the passenger with the girl grabbed me from behind. My shot was knocked off-aim and it hit Stringer in the shoulder. He was thrown back, pirouetting to the floor. The bang was deafening in the enclosed space. It was followed by a second of silence. Then the screaming started.

With a flick back of my head I smashed the passenger's nose. As his grip began to release I thrust one elbow into his solar plexus. But he was a big man, and very determined.

He lunged for my weapon. In the ensuing struggle, five rounds discharged into the fuselage in quick succession.

They created a neat little cluster of holes. Air began to whistle out of the cabin. It ripped the holes into larger, ragged punctures. The changing air pressure toyed with all our eardrums. The mnemonic gel in between the twin hulls hadn't had enough time to react yet. The holes were getting larger.

Then the widening holes met and a large chunk of the aircraft's double hull careened off into the depths of the cold night air.

Letting go of my gun, I grabbed onto the closest arm-rest and clung as tightly as I could. My assailant was not so lucky. In the explosive decompression he was torn from his position. He was thrust out of the hole, arms flailing wildly. His body took out an engine and the plane jerked, then began to drop like a stone.

Air and hand luggage flashed out of the hole with a deafening roar. So too did my pistol. It was a final visitor to the stratosphere before the emergency systems kicked in.

The mnemonic plastic gel was secreted between the twin hulls of the fuselage. It began to flow out over the hole. It flexed, buffeted by the wind. It retained its composition as it slowly did its job as a temporary patch. It began to seal the gap. Encumbered by less and less space in which to flee, the rush of air evacuating the cabin began to peter out.

The gel secured the hole. Pressure returned to normal. The cacophony of screams from terrified passengers came to the fore.

The screaming intensified as more emergency systems kicked in. Red lights winked on and off. A klaxon blared people into silence. This was followed by an automated announcement.

"Return to your seats and fasten your seatbelts. This is an emergency. Life pods will jettison in eighty five seconds. Ensure you are in your seat in eighty seconds. Life pods will eject in seventy five seconds…"

I looked around. Most of the passengers were secure in their seats. One or two stragglers were grabbing the nearest free space. Stringer was on his feet and backing away down the aisle.

I charged at him as he rushed through the corridor towards the first class cabin. I leapt onto his back, knocking him to the ground. I attempted to secure a headlock. Stringer pushed out with his hands and legs, twisting his body to one side. He slammed my back into the low hand rail that ran the length of the short corridor. My grip around his neck faltered.

I grabbed the toilet cubicle door and wrenched it open. It pinned Stringer at the waist, squashing him against the opposite wall. He kicked out at me with a mistimed shot. His boot scraped itself down my chest. It was enough to make me retreat for a moment. It gave Stringer enough room to squeeze past the door and begin crawling towards first class.

I slammed the door shut and jumped on Stringer's back again. This time I led with an elbow to his injured shoulder. He screamed and twisted onto his back away from me.

I reared over him. I brought my fist back for a knockout blow to his face. Stringer didn't try to defend himself. Instead he reached up with his good arm and wrapped it around the hand rail.

I paused a moment before dealing the final blow. I had suddenly realized what Stringer was doing.

I quickly looked into the first class lounge. Each seat had now been vacuum-sealed in a transparent cocoon and set back upon a horizontal rail. It would be the same with the two sections of economy seating behind me and the stewards' cabin.

The emergency systems countdown had reached zero.

Explosive hatch bolts next to each row of seats fired great rounded chunks of the fuselage up and away. They cleared the rest of the plane before pitching towards the ground. The wind whipped up again, far more than before. It ripped me away from Stringer. I flew down the corridor, heading back into economy class. I stretched as much as I could and my right hand secured a tenuous grip on the last few inches of hand rail. I was being thrashed about in the gale-force decompression. My eyes were streaming. My lungs were breathing liquid ice. My hand was a popsicle, freezing into a deathly grip.

The seat-pods rolled towards the gaping holes. They started at the back and worked forwards. One by one they were fired out of the plane like a World War II bomber shedding its parachutists. When the first row on either side was complete, the second row moved into place and sent its hapless occupants out into the freezing night sky. Ten seconds after clearing the plane, a parachute on the pod's roof deployed and homing beacons activated.

339

Slowly but deliberately, the mnemonic plastic gel felt its way over the gaps. It crept over the holes until the plane was once more sealed from the extreme temperatures outside. The atmospheric equilibrium was restored with brief bursts of oxygen. Stringer and I lay exhausted on the floor.

I coughed and groaned. The gale of wind, the freezing temperature and the lack of oxygen had taken its toll on my body. Slowly my aching limbs started to work. I rubbed my eyes, willing them to work again. I carefully stood using the very hand rail that just saved my life. Stringer was doing the same.

"You're...under...arrest..." I wheezed at him.

"I...don't...think...so," he returned. He caught his breath. "You've lost your gun."

"I don't need the gun," I told him. "I'm skilled in muay thai, jeet kune do and nagasu do. I've trained with Delta Force."

Stringer pointed at himself. "No formal training," he told me. "But I can control my mind to block out pain. Even this." He pointed to his wounded shoulder. He grinned. "Oh, and I can predict every move you're going to make."

"Really?" I asked. Good fighting skills are all about knowing when to block and when to punch. I was genuinely unsure if he could do this or not. I pointed at the gel-filled holes in the fuselage. "Did you predict that?"

He glanced at the holes. He seemed unsure. Then he moved back a bit until he was standing opposite the toilet cubicle door. "That's irrelevant," he told me. "I always come prepared."

He reached above the door. He unlocked a panel above it that I never knew existed on any plane. He threw the panel to one side. He reached inside the space. He withdrew a shiny new six-shooter pistol. He trained it on me.

"How did you get that in there?" I asked, surprised.

"Just need to charm the right stewardess," he responded. "I guess I'm in charge now. Let's go visit the cockpit."

I raised my hands in the traditional manner. I moved from the mid passenger cabin to the rear. They were both barren. They were stripped bare. Only the low-key glint of life pod tracks scoured the floor. Stringer followed me at a safe distance. His pistol was aimed between my shoulder blades.

"We're in an abandoned passenger jet," I said. "Cruising at thirty thousand feet. How can this be part of your grand plan?"

"You're an unwelcome addition, I'll admit that. Otherwise, everything is just perfect."

I turned around to look him in the eye, to see if I could gauge any reaction. Maybe work out what he might be up to. I failed.

"So, this is it," I said. "This is how you escape. You hijack a passenger jet. You eject all the passengers. You fly to a non-extradition country. A bit cowardly, don't you think? And clichéd?"

Stringer tutted. "Your problem, Stone, is that you always think too small. Keep moving."

I headed down the rear passenger cabin. I went through the side aisle. We entered the stewards' cabin. All the cabin crew's seats had gone. They'd ejected like the others. Cabinets had been torn open. The contents had been rent from their moorings.

In front of us were three manually-operated life pod tubes. Only the center one still sported a chair and life pod. The other two had spirited away the co-pilots. It left just the pilot behind to courageously bring the plane in alone. Or at least keep an eye on the automated systems as they did it.

To the right of the pods was a set of stairs leading down into the hold. Nestled just behind it was a spiral staircase heading up to the tail-mounted cockpit.

"Up to the cockpit then," Stringer told me.

I turned to face him. I lowered my arms. "Why?" I asked.

"What?!" he looked at me. He was amazed at my question.

"You're going to kill me anyway. Why not just do it now?"

He shrugged noncommittally. "Well, for one it will be easier to get into the cockpit if you're with me. Besides, for the moment at least you have sentimental value to me. You've gone through a lot to get to me, Stone. I think it only fair you spend a bit of time in my presence."

"I'd rather make life difficult for you," I said. "Why should I help you gain access to the cockpit? You may as well just pull that trigger now."

Stringer sighed. "Okay, I don't know who you're trying to kid, but it isn't working on me. I'll give you two very good reasons why you don't want me to actually kill you right now. Two reasons why you'll help me gain access to the cockpit.

"One, you *really* want to know what this is all about. You can't ask me if you're dead. Two, no matter how desperate the situation, you know that the longer you survive, the better the chance you have of foiling me. Unfortunately, that one is a delusion and you aren't going to stop me. But still, you cling onto that vanishing hope all the same."

He was right. I didn't want to die yet. Not for some sense of preservation but because I wanted to know what was going on. And I needed time to put my back-up plan into motion.

Stringer waved his gun at me and indicated the cockpit stairwell again.

We headed up the steps. They led into a narrow corridor. We headed down it. The cockpit door was at the end, flush with the right-hand wall. It was locked. Stringer was directly behind me. He was pressing the gun into the small of my back. I knocked on the door. I was fully aware the space was too confined to attempt any form of disarming procedure. I had to go along with Stringer's instructions.

"Who is it?" came a shocked, muffled voice from the cockpit, battling its way through the thick metal and air-tight locking mechanisms of the door.

"Lieutenant Jack Stone of the North American Security Response Unit."

"Never heard of them!"

"No," I answered. "You won't have. Tell whichever ground control you're in contact with to call up the White House switchboard and quote the Nu Kappa Psi clearance codes. That will patch them directly through to the Permanent Undersecretary of State. She can confirm my validity."

The wait felt like an eternity. I grew restless.

There was activity at the door. One lock, then the second, third and fourth were opened. The door swung wide. The pilot was a portly man. He was quite red-faced and sporting a pair of reading glasses. His belly folded gelatinously over the top of his pants. His voice was quiet and gruff. He said: "Lieutenant! What's going on?"

Stringer stepped from out of my shadow. He fired one shot point blank at the poor, unfortunate man. The pilot's face took on a surprised look. His forehead sported a deep red hole. His brains leapt carelessly out the back of his head. The gun discharged close to the right side of my face. The muzzle flash singed my temple. My right eye whited out in a glare of blindness. My eardrum perforated with a sharp, stabbing pain.

Stringer pushed me aside. I collapsed into the cabin. I banged my shoulder against the open door. He stepped through, over the pilot's body. He strode across to the controls. "Sorry," he called back to me. "Didn't realize you were there."

I blinked a few times, trying to restore the sight in my right eye. Shapes were blurred. Depth perception was absent. It would take a few minutes to recover my faculties. But it seemed like there was some permanent damage with my ear drum. All I could hear in my right ear was a high-pitched whine.

"You've deafened me!" I shouted.

"Oh, stop whining," he told me. He turned to me and guffawed. "Get it? I bet a whine's all you can hear right now."

I sat myself up. I rested my back against the door. I checked my temple to see if it was bleeding. There was some thick gloop there. It seemed to have mostly cauterized with the muzzle flash.

Stringer turned back to his consoles. He was slowly resetting the autopilot's destination with one hand. His aim, however, remained true. Even with his back to me, I was square within his gun's sights.

"So where are you escaping to?" I asked. "Going for the really big cliché and heading for Rio?"

"Stone," Stringer turned to me again. "I'm not trying to escape. There'd be far easier ways of fleeing the country. Even with your lowly intellect, surely you've figured that out by now."

"Then what are you doing?" I struggled to stand.

"Ah," he grinned. "The big reveal. Before I tell you, you have to do something for me first."

"What?" I asked wearily.

"Muster up some enthusiasm, will you? If you don't want to do it, I can just shoot you now and do it myself."

"What do you want me to do?" I asked impatiently.

"See those panels to your left? Get the fire axe off the wall and smash them. Why does this plane have a fire axe anyway?"

I moved towards the panels. There was a slight problem. "The axe is chained to the wall," I pointed out. I showed Stringer the three foot length of thick steel chain attached to the bottom of the axe. The other end was bolted to the wall and padlocked.

"Then unchain it," Stringer told me. "There's probably a key in the pilot's pocket or something."

I glanced at the pilot's body, then at the axe and its mooring. The plan suddenly took shape. It was a way to end this once and for all. I gripped the axe at the base of its shaft. I began to hack at the bolts.

"Or," Stringer shouted, struggling to make himself heard through the metallic clanks of my pounding. "Or you could ignore the intelligent option and use brute force. Well done you," he added. I finally ripped the mooring from the wall. I ripped off a hefty chunk of wall in the process.

Stringer watched me closely. He paid particular attention to keeping his gun trained on me now I had a weapon of my own. "Smash the panels please," he instructed me. "Pay particular attention to the panel in the middle and that little black box to the left."

"You want me to smash the Black Box?"

"Well, it's not *the* Black Box. Wherever that is, it's actually orange. Easier to spot in a crash. Anyway, whatever, doesn't matter. Get smashing."

"Are you feeling okay?" I asked, hoping to undermine Stringer's confidence. "You look terrible."

"Actually I feel rather giddy. Lost a lot of blood during the depressurization. Doesn't matter. It can be fixed. Get smashing."

I swung the axe into the control panel again and again. It sent showers of metal, plastic and electrical sparks in all directions. I was still a little disorientated and off-balance because of my eardrum. Some of the shots were wildly off the mark. Soon I had reduced the entire panel and the little black box to ruins.

"So?" I said. The axe dangled lazily from my hand. I was a little out of breath. "Tell me."

"Axe first," Stringer warned. "Throw it down the corridor. Down the stairs."

I stood in the doorway and did as he said. I heard the axe clatter part of the way down the spiral staircase. I returned back into the cockpit. I was starting to feel a little dizzy.

"Hands up," Stringer instructed. I obeyed.

"Thanks for your work over there," he told me. He indicated the destroyed panel. "You've just disabled the comms system, the auto-destruct settings and the tracking beacon. Now we cannot be found. Not by ground control, not by your guys with their swanky spy satellites, not by any city's surface-to-air defense systems. We are off the radar and cannot be stopped."

"Why are you doing all this?" I asked. It felt like a pointless question. Feeling drunk with blood loss, Stringer was on such a roll he'd tell me everything I wanted to know anyway. There was absolutely no need for any more prompting.

He clicked his fingers. "Forgot one thing," he told me. He aimed his gun at the dead pilot. He fired one shot. It blew the corpse's left hand apart.

I was too surprised to react. He pointed his gun back at me. He took careful aim. Then he fired another shot.

The force of the bullet knocked me back and to one side.

I was not sure what had just happened. Blood had spattered my face. My legs had decided to buckle. I slumped to the floor. I felt that the fingers on my left hand were involuntarily clawing up. I checked on them. I now had a sizeable hole through the middle of my hand.

My brain was oblivious to the wound before. Now it realized that I should be feeling pain. It opened the floodgates. I breathed quickly and shallowly. It felt as though my arm had turned to ice and was slowly splintering into shards from the wrist up. I used my right hand to grab the left wrist and strangle it. It was an involuntary reaction. My subconscious presumed that if the blood couldn't flow to the hand, pain couldn't flow from it. The presumption was woefully incorrect.

Stringer squatted beside me. He said: "We don't want anyone to track our RFID signatures, now do we?" He moved over to the pilot's swivel chair and sat in it.

"Bet you wish you knew how I control pain," Stringer called. He snapped his fingers to gain my attention. "Concentrate, now. It's big reveal time.

"I've seen enough movies where someone tells their hostage the big plan, then the hostage escapes and uses it against them. So really I shouldn't tell you anything, right? But, let's face it, I am obviously in control here. I have a gun in my hand. You have a hole in yours. You can't stop me now. And I *so* want to tell someone…*anyone*…about my grand scheme. After all, it's one of the greatest problems with being as intelligent as myself. You come up with all these great ideas. But you can't tell anyone about them because they just don't have the intellect to understand what you're saying. However, I think you're smart enough to appreciate this one, Stone. I've dumbed it down for you anyway.

"This public of ours: I don't trust them. *Now* they see red, *now* they know how corrupt the Government is. But are they actually going to do anything about it? I'm sure they will…*eventually*. But it is doubtful in the short term. And I just can't wait for them to get their asses in gear. They need another push."

"And you're just the man to push," I said. "Again."

"Again?" Stringer asked. "What do you mean by that?"

"You're the terrorist leader," I said. My head lolled back against the door. I needed to conserve my energy. I needed to make Stringer think I was worse off than I really was. If I could lure him into a false sense of security, I'd still have a chance. "That's how you always knew where they'd strike. Everyone thought you'd infiltrated them somehow. But that's not true. You're their leader."

"Leader? Yes, that's..." He hesitated. "Well...no. Not *leader*, Stone. It's just me. All my idea. A leader of one. Sure, there were other people. People I consulted. People I hired. The protest organizers. Weapons manufacturers. I believe you yourself took out the Everglades distribution contingent. That altered a few plans, I have to say. I'm very impressed with you, Stone. When did you figure all this out?"

I recalled the initials on some of the devices in the Everglades. D.S. It was right there all along. "I had an idea for a while," I said. "Then came Fort Belvoir. They just so happened to get their hands on a perfected weapon the military has been working on for a decade? Not possible. You designed it. And that means you had a vested interest. After that, everything else made sense."

"Very good, Stone. But you still thought it was a large network. Most of the people involved know nothing. They have no idea what they're doing, or why. There is no cell, no grand organization. There's just me. And I'm not a terrorist. I'm a patriot and a freedom fighter."

"You blow shit up. You're a terrorist in my book."

"Well then, you must have a very disparaging view on American foreign policy. Speaking of which... It's time the policy changed. And I'm just the man to do it."

"How?" I asked. I laughed. "By becoming President yourself?"

Stringer's joviality faded. I saw his expression, and everything started to become clear.

"That's what you're planning," I said with surprise. "Bombing places, exposing corruption. It was all to undermine the current President. And then what? When he's out of the way, you stand for election? More electronic tampering? More plastic surgery? Reinvent yourself as the Great American Hope?"

"Well, we're not going to want his patsy the VP to take over, are we?" Stringer answered. "So, yes, within a few months there would be an election. And a bright new hope would emerge in the running. Someone who would know the kind of policies that the public is really crying out for. The kind of man the public would really get behind and support. JFK reincarnate."

"You'd never get away with it. We'd know you. We'd hunt you down."

"How, Stone?" he demanded. "How would you know which candidate I am until it is too late and I become President? Even DNA tests can be fooled."

I grinned. "All this time I thought you were special. But you're just a megalomaniac with delusions of grandeur."

Stringer snorted. "Delusions," he repeated. "I knew you wouldn't understand, Stone. You just don't have the intellect to comprehend this. All the work I've put in. All the contingencies I've accounted for. All the power I would hold once I become Leader of the Free World. The changes I could force upon the human race. The legacy I will leave…"

"Yeah, I get it," I told him. "I just think it's pathetic. What I don't get is how you can believe you'll suddenly become a political mastermind. Three years ago you were a grunt with poor exam results and a Daddy complex. I don't care what I.Q. you've got. Some things need years of study. Some things need experience."

"Some things need to shut up!" he shouted back, obviously riled. "I can do this. I *will* do this. Under my leadership, this country will be reinvented."

"And the plane? Where does a hijacked plane fit into your immaculate reinvention? It's Willis Tower, isn't it. The President's holding a party in the penthouse, and you are going to crash the party in the most spectacular way possible."

"Got me all figured out, haven't you Stone."

"I have," I answered. "You're a child. You think you're the center of the world. And when you want something you just don't have the patience to wait. You could have left it to the public to oust the President. Then they'd really appreciate a new candidate. But you just can't wait, so you're going to assassinate him. All this effort, and all you'll end up with is the chance that you may actually martyr the man you want vilified."

"Let the history books write of him what they will," Stringer said. "Soon, he will be dead. You will be dead. I'll be safely aboard that final life pod and no one will know that the man they elect to lead them is the man who killed their previous leader. The Oval Office is all that matters in the end, Stone. The path to it cannot be altered now. The plane can't be tracked. It can't be stopped. The flight path has been reprogrammed."

"And how long until the plane reaches its destination?" I asked. "How much longer will I have to listen to this drivel?"

"I'll be leaving soon, Stone. Don't worry about that. And you will be leaving…leaving this mortal coil…" Stringer kept his gun expertly trained on me. He leaned back and inspected the consoles behind him. "…in eleven minutes."

"Or less," I told him. I'd put my plan into action while Stringer had been distracted. I'd rummaged in my pocket with my right hand. I'd withdrawn my cell phone. I'd

351

activated it. It had already been answered when Stringer returned his attention to me.

"Lock onto this signal," I said quickly into the phone. "Send the HF1 now."

I left the phone activated. I posted it like a letter through the hole in the wall where the axe chain used to reside. It fought its way down through the innards of the plane. It slithered through wires. It slid over pipes. It clanged past brackets and supporting pillars. Stringer let his gun follow the sound of the phone all the way down the wall. It became firmly lodged somewhere far below the floor level, broadcasting a signal that could be easily tracked.

"What?" Stringer shouted, confused. He was still staring at the hole where I'd just posted my active cell phone. "What...what was that? What's a HF1? I've never heard of that. What is it?"

"Your powers of precognition suddenly seem to have escaped you there," I said to him. "In fact they've been failing quite a lot on this flight. So much so, that it almost seems as though you don't actually have any predictive powers at all."

"What? No. Extreme emotion does it. When–"

"When what, Stringer?" I interrupted. "When you were all blasé and happy getting on the plane, not realizing I was here as well? Where was the extreme emotion then?"

Stringer finally grinned. "Have I mentioned I'm rather intelligent? Yes? Have I also mentioned how easy it is to manipulate people? To make them believe what you want them to?"

352

"Huh," I said. "After all that, you're just a player. You can't see the future. You coerce, you manipulate and you hope for the best. But you're just a con-artist."

"No," he responded, still grinning. "I'm the next President of the United States. Now, tell me, Stone..." He pointed the gun at my head again. Behind my back, I slowly closed my grip on the cockpit door handle. "What's a HF1?"

"Let's say it stands for Hit the Flight. Or you can switch 'Flight' for an obscenity if you want. The General prefers it that way."

Stringer shrugged. It was his non-verbal way of telling me he didn't care.

"It's a rocket," I told him. "And it's heading straight for my cell phone."

For the first time during this whole ordeal, Stringer looked genuinely panicked. "But...if it hits us, you'll die as well."

"Maybe," I told him. "It's a sacrifice I'm willing to make. How about you?"

The truth of the situation dawned on Stringer. In shock, he slowly lowered his gun. It was the moment I had been waiting for.

I dove out of the cockpit exit. In the same motion I swung the door shut as I went. Stringer fired his last three shots. They impacted against the heavy security steel of the door's inner casing.

I ignored the pain shooting up my left arm and the throb in my head. Fighting against disorientation, I charged down the corridor. I half-ran, half-fell down the spiral staircase. I knew Stringer was only moments behind me.

I reached the floor and stumbled towards the single remaining life pod. Stringer leapt over the staircase railing. In mid-air, he hit me in my back with both feet. I was flung forward. I crashed into the life pod door. I landed on my wounded left hand. I screamed in pain.

Stringer regained his footing. I wheeled myself back with my heels. I found the wall behind me and slowly levered myself up. Seething with rage, Stringer raised his pistol and aimed directly at my heart.

The chamber clicked on empty. The surprise etched on Stringer's face was priceless. It only took him a moment to recover. I used that moment. As he dropped his gun and looked around for another weapon, I edged to the life pod door. I felt behind me for the button to open both the inner and outer pod doors.

Stringer spied the fire axe. It was hanging limply by its chain from the lower echelons of the spiral staircase. He rushed to it. He grabbed it and brandished it menacingly. He dashed back to me with a roar. The chain caught against the stair railing. It yanked Stringer back to the floor. Frustrated, he got back up. He untangled the chain and came at me again. I had used this opportunity to open the life pod door and slip inside.

Stringer was a fraction of a second too late. His fingertips slid desperately over the closing door. The outer door closed with a quiet, rubbery sound. The inner door shut moments later. The airlock was sealed. I immediately pressed the button that locked the seal from the inside.

I struggled to fasten my seat harness with one hand. I became more and more frustrated with myself. Outside the life pod's window, Stringer roared at me. He tried pressing the button to open the door. I'd ensured it was fully locked. The outer button refused to activate.

He swung back the axe and brought it crashing into the toughened glass of the outer door. The glass shook but barely registered a dent. He swung again, and again, and again.

"No!" he shouted between blows. "This isn't supposed to happen! It's not the plan! This isn't the fucking plan!!!"

A small chip started to form in the glass. He would get through eventually. Right then it was a race against time. What would happen first? Would Stringer break in? Would I get my harness on and blast out of there? Would the rocket reach its final destination?

I decided I'd suffered so many injuries already that a few more wouldn't matter. Screw the harness. I hit the launch button.

The life pod settled itself and readied to eject. Stringer realized his attempts at breaking in had been for naught. He dropped the axe and placed one hand on the chipped glass.

"I'm supposed to be in there," he said quietly, sadly. "I was promised."

The life pod ejected.

Small booster rockets blasted me backwards out the rear of the aircraft. I was thrown from my seat into the pod's transparent door. I felt something snap down below. The escape pod was thrown about by the wind shear, the speed of the ejection and the plane's turbulence. Also thrown about, I struggled to stay in one piece. I was aware of the computerized systems issuing me a warning. My altitude was too low and the parachute would only be 50% effective in reducing my velocity.

When the parachute deployed, the pod at least stabilized itself a little. It allowed me to view my surroundings. I could still clearly see the plane. It was heading into the bright, studded lights that represented the skyscrapers of central Chicago. A more pressing concern for myself was the rapidly approaching suburb below me.

Still traveling at a dangerous speed, the life pod slammed into a tiled roof. It slid unceremoniously along the roof. It fell, leaden, into a front garden. It bounced once before coming to a rest on its side. The pod's door had already buckled open in the landing. Blood entered my eyes from a gash on my forehead. I crawled out of the pod onto soft, cool grass. I was dragging a broken ankle behind me. I forced myself into a position whereby I could rest my back against the pod.

I checked the sky for the airplane. It was still visible by the running lights winking on and off.

There was a quiet whoosh. A flicker of red energy and a smudge of dark grey smoke signaled the arrival of the rocket. It was a device designed specifically to neutralize aerial terrorist threats. It slid gracefully up to the passenger jet. It burrowed deep into the aircraft's belly before exploding.

The explosion was powerful enough to disintegrate the jet. The citizens of Chicago would be spared being showered with deadly debris. The fireball was a cloud of yellow fringed with red. It cast a false daylight over the area. It snuffed itself out in a sparkle of burning, floating particles. I felt the resulting shockwave wash over me. I saw it bend trees. I heard it rattle window panes. It set car alarms screeching down the length of the suburban road.

Slowly the day turned back to night. The breeze re-established its dominance. The local wildlife relinquished their vow of silence. One by one the car alarms were switched off by neighbors wondering what on earth just happened. I waved, trying to beckon one over to garner assistance.

Behind me, the man whose house I'd just smashed stared in catatonic shock at the hole in his roof.

TWENTY THREE

Al opened the door to the interrogation room for me. He walked in first, a box of paperwork and trinkets in his arms. I followed him awkwardly, limping on one crutch.

This was the first day I'd been back at work. The last week I'd been under observation in NASRU's sophisticated hospital unit in D.C.

My right ankle was in a cast. There was a permanent hole in my left hand. It was currently bandaged up. There was a very visible scar on my forehead. A big lump on the top of my right hand showed where my new RFID chip was slowly integrating itself into my flesh. They were all healing quickly.

The damage to my ear proved to be trickier. Despite my misgivings, I'd been augmented. My eardrum had been replaced with a top-of-the-line electronic version. It could pick out more detail. But the sound was tinny and scratchy. To cap it all off, it had been integrated with my cell phone. I now had a wireless connection between them that allowed me to download sound from my own head. It was difficult to describe how I felt about all this. 'Disconcerting' seemed like a very weak word to use. I was now part robot. The idea terrified me.

I hobbled over to the dark metal desk in the center of the interrogation room. I seated myself on the opposite side to

Andi Clayton. She was looking tired. She was disheveled. She was still wearing the same clothes she'd been in for nearly a fortnight. But her expression was defiant.

"Good morning, Andi," I said. I settled my broken leg and placed the crutch up against the table. She stared silently at me, her arms crossed on the table. We hadn't secured her to her chair. There was no need. "How have you been?" I asked.

"I've been here for a week now without the merest hint of any charges leveled at me. That's unconstitutional."

"Yeah. We tend to work outside the constitution. But you've been looked after, haven't you? TV access, three squares a day, fresh clothing...although you seem to have refused that one."

She snorted in derision. "Thanks for keeping me locked up."

"Well..." I began. I leaned a bit further back in my seat. I glanced around the drab room nestled in the basement of NASRU's New York offices. It wasn't as clean and shiny as the one in Washington. "What would you have done on the outside? Associating with Stringer has caused you all kinds of problems. You've lost your job. Your apartment is under quarantine by the FBI. Your savings have been seized."

"I'd have struggled by," Andi responded bitterly.

"Oh, right," I began. I rummaged through the box to my right. I removed the electronic paperwork folder first and put it to one side. I one-handedly poked around the box until I located what I was looking for. I held a cell phone flash card up in front of her. "With this?"

Andi blinked at it for a few moments. "I don't know what that is," she finally told me.

"Yes, you do. Or at least you *think* you know what it is, Miss Clayton. You think it's a card containing details of shares. Around one point five million dollars worth of shares."

"I..." She stopped. There was no point playing games. Over the past week, she had given us a very detailed account of everything that happened between herself and Stringer. An account that filled in many blanks.

"You've already told us about it in your statement, Andi," I said. "You think by feigning ignorance now we'll just let you walk out with it?"

She shrugged. "A girl's got to live on something."

I sighed. I tossed the flash card onto the table. It slid across to her. She followed its progress. Her arms remained crossed on the tabletop.

"Take it then," I told her. "Live a long and fruitful life with it. Here..." I took her digital voice recorder out of the box. I slid it across to her. "Take that as well. Stick it in a museum. All it's good for."

"Wh...?" she began, confused. Her fingers crawled across the table to the objects. She stopped herself before she touched them. "What's wrong with them?"

"They're blank."

"You've wiped them?!"

"No. They were always blank. Both of them. The flash card was absolutely brand new, from what we can tell. It never, ever had any data on it."

Slowly she picked up the recorder. "Blank?" she asked, aghast. "This too? The...the recordings I did...of the protests..."

"Nothing on there either. I'm surprised it still works. Maybe he was worried you'd recorded him too. Switched the SD card with a new one."

She dropped the recorder with a clatter. She prodded the cell phone card with one finger. "This too?"

"That too. Completely blank. No share details on it. And there was no transmission from the Europa probe. It was just another way to appease you, Andi. To make you feel financially secure. To allow you to trust him more. A way, I guess, to persuade you not to catch a flight to Seattle."

"But..." she began. "Didn't he know that wouldn't work? In the end?"

"With his predictive abilities, you mean? We've been able to retrace his steps, backwards, by using CCTV footage over the last few weeks. We knew where he was. He was at the airport a week ago, although the CCTV there kept shorting out. Useless stuff. But we knew when he spent the night in your apartment. When you met at the BattleKarts track. And, thanks to the laudably comprehensive statement you've given us, your first meeting at the Memorial Pool. Together with what we found secreted around his apartment, it paints a very interesting picture of Daniel Stringer."

"What are you driving at, Mr. Stone?"

I smiled. "You want a drink?"

"No."

"I fancy a coffee. Al?"

Alecto nodded silently. He left the room and locked the door behind him.

"What is it?" Andi asked, a little worried. "What is it you want to tell me that even *he* isn't allowed to hear?"

"What? Oh, no. I haven't sent him away. He knows all this stuff already. I just genuinely want a cup of coffee."

"Fine," she stated. "What did you find?"

"You remember the first time we met? In your apartment? I pretended to be FBI, you pretended to have a brother? I chased him that morning. Big long car chase. And he eluded me. He had the right tools for the job. Exactly the right tools at the right time to escape from not just myself but a *very* sophisticated satellite surveillance system. He even had a decoy vehicle set up and pre-programmed outside your apartment to fox us. Even though my superior had explained to me about Stringer's predictive abilities, I was flummoxed by that. Then we did some retrospective research, and do you know what we found?"

Andi shrugged. She was really confused as to where the conversation was going. She had no idea of the point I was about to make.

"In the mashed-up ruins of his car," I told her, "we found many more tools. Many more parlor tricks, if you will. An object for nearly every occasion. Took us a while to find them. His vehicle really was badly crushed. But no matter what happened, no matter where we went, he had something in that car that would have allowed him to escape our clutches 95% of the time. CCTV footage showed us that he always, *always*, had a remote-controlled second car follow him wherever he drove. It was a vehicle pre-programmed to act as a decoy any time, anywhere."

"Meaning?" Andi asked. She still wanted me to join the dots for her.

"Meaning he didn't know we were coming for him that morning. He just knew we'd catch up to him eventually. So he planned ahead. Planning ahead and predicting the future are completely different things, Miss Clayton. He couldn't predict the future. He was just smart enough to plan for every eventuality."

Andi snorted again and shook her head. She was not yet ready to accept this truth. "Sometimes I thought that he was just planning ahead too, Mr. Stone. But some of the things I saw, some of the things I witnessed...he couldn't plan those without predicting the future."

"Unfortunately, Miss Clayton, he could. And he did. I have to admit, from your testimony and the few conversations I had with Stringer, some times his words sounded scripted. It was like he really did know what was about to be said. But, in hindsight, I guess that was just him being prepared."

Al returned with my coffee. I took a sip and smacked my lips. "Mmmm, sure you wouldn't...?" I asked Andi. I offered her the cup.

"I presume you have proof?" she asked.

"Mmm-hmm," I responded through another mouthful of coffee. I set the cup to one side. I delved into the box again. "Let's start at the beginning, shall we? Your first conversation with Mr. Stringer."

I removed an A4 sheet of card from the box. Next I brought out a cell phone-sized electronic device. It was sprouting wires. Finally came a small, discreet microphone. All of them were connected to each other with fine filaments. I held the card up in front of Andi and spoke into the microphone.

"This is not card," I said. In a messy, marker-pen scrawl, my words appeared on the card itself. "It is the latest electronic screen technology. It is in the latter stages of

363

development. It is coupled with a font in a hand-written style."

I put the 'card' down. "Your first presumption," I told her, "was that it was a voice-activated screen. You were correct. It is made out to look like handwriting on paper."

"Did you already know about that?" Andi asked, astonished.

"Oh, no. We didn't even know it was being researched until we contacted Sony after the fact. We discovered they'd been working on it for nearly five years now. We found this one in Stringer's apartment. Hidden inside a piano leg."

"That son of a…" she muttered.

"Shall we continue? Let's see. The conversation in the Memorial Pool. Remember that one? Think about what was said, about exactly what happened. Did he prove to you that he could predict what you were thinking, what you were going to say? He just manipulated you and made you believe.

"He was good, I'll give him that. Very observant. Very good at creating a coherent story on the spot. But if you talk the talk, you can convince people about any old bullshit. If you think about it, did he ever at any point actually predict the future? Or did he just say things that made you think he did? 'I knew you'd be late'. 'I know exactly what you're going to say'. Just words and subtle mind manipulation, Miss Clayton."

"Then what about the BattleKarts track? How could he have predicted who'd win? Random guessing and a massive amount of luck?"

"Exactly, Miss Clayton," I nodded. "You've got it spot on."

"Too convenient."

"Oh, no, not really. It's all my fault, to be honest. We found Stringer through you. The way we did that was by trawling through the files of thousands of people marked as potential dissidents. When I came across the CCTV footage of you and Stringer at the BattleKarts track, we leapt into action. We never thought about all those other people we didn't get round to investigating."

"Meaning?" she asked.

"Meaning that when we were retracing Stringer's steps, we discovered something rather interesting at the BattleKarts track. Something that tallied up with more information we later unearthed."

"You're sounding as cryptic as he did," Andi insisted. "Mind getting to the point?"

"Not at all. But this one's rather a doozy, so brace yourself. You weren't special. You weren't unique. He contacted twenty journalists in all, including you. Eighteen agreed to meet him initially. Twelve were intrigued enough to attend a second meeting at the BattleKarts track. From there, he just randomly guessed who would win each race. He knew full well that most of the time he'd be wrong. Twelve chances. Ten racers a time. Technically the odds were in his favor that he'd get one right.

"He successfully guessed three of the race outcomes. Three journalists still on-board. Three journalists now convinced he had predictive powers. One fell by the wayside when he was nearly run over, having failed to 'predict' the traffic. A second was forcibly removed from the equation when she refused to go to those all-important story-shaping protests. And that left just you, a victim of random chance."

Andi sat back in her chair, blinking but silent. Her mind was racing. She was confused, angry and shocked.

"We were all fooled by him," I told her. "He was a genius, and a master manipulator. But the future was just as unknown to him as it is to us."

She looked at me finally. She was crestfallen and a little lost. She sniffed back a tear. "What time is it?" she asked.

"Nearly one thirty pm. Why? Somewhere you need to be?"

"I just want to go home," she answered in a quiet, timid voice.

"Okay," I told her. "You can go. We have your statement. I'm convinced you were as fooled by Stringer as I was. We have no more need for you. But what home?"

She shrugged. "I don't know."

I felt a rumble in the tabletop first. A slight tremor. I felt it through the chair legs. Finally, I detected a build-up of pressure in the air. I looked around the room, trying to gauge what just happened. Al was listening intently to his earpiece.

"What?" I asked, concerned. "What is it?"

"I don't know," he told me. "I'll find out."

He rushed out through the door, leaving it ajar. With my enhanced hearing, I could hear the faint sounds of a commotion further down the corridor. I hurriedly packed everything back into the box.

"Why did he do it?" Andi asked me. She'd either failed to notice or decided to ignore the new development.

"Something about being President in the end," I told her.

"No. Me. Why do you think he brought me into all of this? What was the point?"

"I guess when someone has the intellect he did, it's tricky to keep your ego in check. He wanted someone to tell his story. Someone to show the world what a genius he was. I guess, in the end, it backfired a little."

Al returned looking flushed. "There's been an explosion somewhere in the building," he told us. "We're being evacuated."

"The box," I told Al, indicating the evidence I'd just shown Andi. I carefully levered myself out of my seat. "We can't leave it here."

"I'll take care of it," Al responded. He quickly grabbed the box and left the room.

"Miss Clayton," I said. I picked up my crutch and shoved it under my right armpit. "I guess now's as good a time as any. You're free to go."

I led her out of the room. She was still dazed. We headed down the corridor, and into the stairwell. She kept pace with me as I awkwardly hopped up the stairwell. We headed across the lobby to the bright summer's day outside.

There was a large, organized crowd filtering out the doors. Everyone was heading across the road. It was an evacuation more professional than the GovPol could ever have hoped to conduct.

I limped across the road with Andi. We stopped on the far sidewalk. The other evacuees were filing into the adjacent park. I stared up the length of the tall glass-paneled building. There was a smudge of smoke drifting lazily from a shattered window. Debris littered the street below. I counted the storeys and mentally recalled the layout.

"That's my office!" I exclaimed "For fuck's sake! What the hell happened up there?"

"Daniel's dead," Andi told me. "The terrorists are no more. But with an earthquake there's always aftershocks."

"What? Shit!" I uttered. "Maybe it was someone else. But who else would know where I am? It must have been an electrical fault or something. Don't you think?"

Andi shook her head. "No, I don't."

I blinked a few times. My mind was processing information, and it was coming up with a complex answer. "The statue," I breathed.

"The what?" Andi asked.

I looked around, shifting on my crutch. I didn't know what I expected to find. It was Stringer, I was sure of it. Stringer blew up my office.

"You knew it was him," I said angrily. "Didn't you? You knew it was Stringer."

"I...I guessed," Andi responded. "Daniel taught me a few of his tricks. Having an eye for detail. Working things out in the here and now. But you can also see plans developing. Spot the signs. You can...feel...his handiwork."

"You can do all that?" I asked.

She looked at me with a smile in her eyes. "You're not going to try and recruit me, are you?"

"No," I told her. "Try the FBI."

"Maybe I will." She snorted. "If they'll give me my apartment back."

"I'll have a word," I told her. "But I've got more important things to sort out right now." I looked back up at the ruins of my office. "Stringer's dead. The terrorist organization died with him. I know that. I saw to it myself. Yet he's still managed to blow up my office from beyond the grave?"

Andi shrugged. "Maybe," she told me. "Maybe it's all been planned right from the start. Maybe you still don't understand what was going on. Or maybe I don't know anything." She turned to me and smiled. "Maybe you're just the victim of random chance as well."

She turned from the view and headed into the park. She joined the throng of suits still pouring out of the upper echelons of the building. She blended in with a band of anti-Government protestors chanting away on the grass. Soon she was out of sight. I didn't know where she would go. But wherever it was, that was where she would start rebuilding her life.

Al trotted over to me. He was still carrying the box under one arm.

"It's my office," I told him. "It's my fucking office!"

"I know," he answered. "I've just seen Sam. He was heading towards the elevators when it happened."

"He okay?" I asked.

"Will be. Bit of shellshock. Ambulance is on its way as a precaution. Any idea what happened?"

"Yes," I answered. "Stringer."

"Wh...?" Al began. "Stone, he's dead."

"He is. But three weeks ago when he decided to send me a bomb with a time-lapse trigger he was very much alive."

"What bomb?" Al questioned.

"That stupid marble statue, Al. The one they spent so long hauling up the stairwell. Stringer timed it to take me out after he'd completed his plan. After he'd crashed the plane and disappeared forever."

"But why go to all that effort?" he asked.

"Maybe he thought I would know too much by then. Maybe he thought I would be a threat. Maybe he knew he'd get pissed with me. Or maybe he just wanted to wipe the slate clean." I pointed at the box Al was carrying. "We've got

Clayton's statement. We've got some archived CCTV footage. But otherwise, we've just lost every scrap of data we had on Stringer."

I looked back up at the rolls of smoke billowing from my office's window. The final part of Stringer's failed plan had come to pass. He wanted to wipe the past and start a new life. He wanted Daniel Stringer to disappear completely. Now it looked as though he quite literally had.

I quickly checked the park again to see if I could spot Andi. She was right. She could tell at a glance that it was Stringer's final terrorist activity, before I'd had a chance to analyze the evidence. Maybe some of his tricks *had* rubbed off on her. Maybe Andi was supposed to become his protégé of sorts. I felt that I wanted to know more.

But she'd gone. No home. No job. No cell phone. No RFID. No way to track her. I thought it was for the best. As I closed the book on Daniel Stringer, I closed the book on Andi Clayton as well.

TWENTY FOUR

Al pulled the car up to the curb. He slotted it into neutral and switched off the engine.

"Nice place," he said. He looked out at the quiet, immaculately-presented suburb. "Peaceful."

The day was overcast. Drab smudges of grey sky nestled behind the wind-rustled elms lining the street. On the horizon heavily-pregnant clouds were ready to give birth to a downpour.

"Thanks for doing this," I told him. "You didn't need to."

"Ah," Al dismissed me with a wave of his hand. "I didn't have anything planned anyway. Was just going to kick back with a few beers and watch the baseball. A little road trip's as good as anything."

I patted him on the arm in thanks. He grinned at me.

"Of course," he continued. "Next time you have a day off and that foot's well enough to press the gas, I'll expect *you* to ferry *me* around."

I nodded in appreciation. I opened the car's door and levered myself out. Al handed me the walking stick. "Good luck," he told me.

I closed the door. I stuck my bandaged left hand in the pocket of my sports jacket. I took a long, studied look at the house in front of me. A worried smile was etched onto my face. I limped up the narrow concrete path towards the front door. It opened when I was only half way there.

"Jack?" came an astonished female voice with a hint of a Russian accent. It was the most beautiful voice I'd ever heard.

Nat slowly walked down the path towards me. She was wearing fluffy slippers, black wet-look leggings and a big sloppy brown jumper. Her arms were folded across her chest. Her straw-colored hair drifted across her face in the storm-front wind.

"Hi," I answered back. I was not sure how to break the ice.

"What happened to you?" she asked, glancing at my cane.

"Shot. Threatened with an axe. Thrown out of a plane."

She looked behind me at Al's sky blue Ford. "Were you in a car crash?"

I shook my head. "Shot. Threatened with an axe. Thrown out of a plane," I repeated. "It's what I do, Nat. It's my job."

She snorted in disbelief. "What do you want, Jack?"

"To tell you everything. To let you know I've changed. I work for the Government, Nat. Neutralizing threats. Saving the world. But if that keeps us apart, I can quit. Give it up. Become a pencil pusher in an office somewhere. Nine to five."

"Why?" she asked.

"For you."

An older, thickly-accented voice drifted over from the front door. "Natalya?"

"Hello, Mrs. Czernokovsky," I called.

Nat turned her attention back to the house. "It's okay, mum. Go back inside." Mrs. Czernokovsky peered out of the doorway suspiciously. "Пойдите назад внутрь!" Nat repeated in her native tongue. The door closed.

"She's looking well," I told her.

"Jack..." she began. She took a moment to compose her thoughts. "You think it was just about you working late? You don't get it. You can't quit your job. You can make promises, but I know you'll be unable to keep them. The job is who you are."

"*You* are who I am."

"No. I fell in love with *you*. With the man you are now. I take away your job and I take away your drive. I take away your commitment and ambition. Your passion. I take away a part of who you are. Who's to say I will love the part that is left?"

"Then what do I do?" I asked. I felt the first droplets of rain on my head. It didn't matter. It was only water.

"Nothing, Jack. Don't you get it? I want more than you can give. I want to spend time with you, I want the grand loving gestures, but I also want you to be who you are. I don't know, Jack. It doesn't make sense right now. Maybe you just have to lead your own life for now. Without me."

"Would you be willing to try again?" I asked. "Somewhere down the line? I still love you."

"And I still love you. I just don't know if it's enough anymore."

I nodded slowly. "Where do we go from here?" I asked.

She sniffed once. I couldn't tell if she was crying or if it was rain on her face. "We mend our broken hearts," she said quietly. "Get on with our lives."

"Okay," I answered. I felt a sense of great loss about to overcome me. I nodded once and smiled sadly at her. "Okay. I still have some of your stuff."

She nodded slowly, smiled. "I know. Keep it."

I stared at her for a few moments, to soak in her beauty one last time. She was right, though. No matter what I said, no matter what I promised, I couldn't quit. I was the job, the job was me. It was what I was born to do. And for that I would have to make terrible sacrifices.

I turned and headed back towards the car. My gait was even slower than usual. My ankle already throbbed with a pain that would soon consume my heart. I understood what she was saying. I genuinely did. But it didn't make any of it any easier.

"Jack!" she called out as I opened the car door. "Я всегда буду любить вас." I looked back at her, trying to determine what she'd just told me. She attempted a sad, pained smile and quietly said: "Помогите мне возвратиться Вам."

She was saying one final goodbye to me. She must have been. I stared at her, hoping for a translation so I may at least return the sentiment. But Nat turned from me, her arms still folded into her thick jumper. She slowly walked back up the path.

I suddenly felt weary. I was physically and emotionally drained. Once I'd negotiated my leg into the foot well, I slumped into the car's seat. I heavily drew the door to a close. I could feel Al looking at me, unsure what step to take next. I didn't return his gaze.

"Go," I whispered.

Without a word, he started the car and ferried me away from the love of my life.

The journey home was one taken in silence. I felt bad for Al. He'd wasted his day off to transport me to Boston and back. What miserable company I was. Otherwise my mind was a blank. I was unable to concentrate on the conversation I'd just had, on the implications of it. I was even unable to picture Nat's face right then. I knew that at that time it was all too emotionally raw for me to contend with.

I took my cell phone from my pocket. I wirelessly connected it to my auditory enhancements. I downloaded the audio file from my micro chipped head into the phone's memory. This way I could keep a part of Nat with me at all times. Playing the sound back, hearing her voice: it may ease the pain on lonely nights. It may help me to understand.

The in-car comms beeped halfway through our return to New York. I activated it.

"Secure transmission from Omega," an electronic voice informed us. "Please verify ID."

"Damn," I muttered to Al. "It's Miller."

He activated the screen on the dashboard. "ID: Jacobsen. Two nine zero eight nine seven."

"ID and voice recognition confirmed."

"Hello, Alecto," General Armstrong Miller said when he appeared on-screen. Al looked a little annoyed that he was still lumbered with what he felt to be an inappropriate code name. "Is Stone with you?"

"Yes, Sir," I answered.

"Good. How are you doing?"

"I'm getting there, Sir," I responded. "Ready to return to my desk. Another week and I'll be out there with the field agents."

"We may need to discuss that situation later, Stone," Miller told me. "Maybe have a chat about respecting authority and following orders.

"However, I'm sure you'll be glad to hear that I've officially closed the case on Jackson. Or Stringer, or whatever you want to call him. You did your job and you did it well. Thank you for tying up the loose ends with Clayton during your recovery period, and Hera would like to thank you for finding the apartment. She says it's perfect."

"Not a problem, Sir," I answered warily. He'd issued a threat followed by a compliment. It was supposed to make me subconsciously put the threat at the back of my mind, to effectively forget that I was in trouble for breaking his orders twice until he officially reminded me of it. His psychological trick wasn't going to work. I was too highly trained. But I could see there was something else bothering the General. Something more pressing. Disciplinary proceedings were on the back burner.

"I'm sorry to interrupt the last day of your vacation like this, boys," Miller said. "But we've got a situation developing. We need you both to come in ASAP. Hera will meet you at the office and brief you there."

I looked across at Al. He shrugged. "There goes the baseball."

I considered the situation for a moment. I still had injuries. I was in emotional turmoil. Less than two hours previous I suggested, albeit half-heartedly, I may even quit the job for good. But this kept me alive. You took away my job and you'd take away a part of me. I may not like what's left.

I turned my attention back to the screen.

"We're on our way."

Printed in Great Britain
by Amazon